The Trophy Wife

a&b

The Trophy Wife

PETER TURNBULL

First published in Great Britain in 2005 by
Allison & Busby Limited
Bon Marché Centre
241-251 Ferndale Road
London SW9 8BJ

http://www.allisonandbusby.com

A catalogue record for this book is available from
the British Library.

10 9 8 7 6 5 4 3 2 1

ISBN 0 7490 8257 7

Printed and bound in Wales by
Creative Print and Design, Ebbw Vale

PETER TURNBULL is the author of over twenty previous novels and numerous works of short fiction. He worked for many years as a social worker in Glasgow before returning to his native Yorkshire, where he is now a full-time writer of fiction.

Prologue

There is a game played by children in Greece, the woman had once discovered, of which the object is not so much to win as to make the other person, the opponent, lose. The spirit of the game appealed to her. Though she had never played the game as such, being an adult when she had first observed it being played, she had, on many occasions in her life, won by the simple, calculating expedient of letting the other party believe they had achieved victory. Challenging a friend to a meal-preparing contest, for example, had worked to her advantage on more than one occasion with the agreement that the person who prepares the meal should also clear away afterwards. She would cook the first meal, a simple casserole that required little preparation and little clearing away. The meal, once eaten, would be received with a, 'Well, I can do better than that,' and the following evening the friend would prepare a sumptuous three course dinner, upon the eating of which the friend would invariably say, 'I won'. 'Perhaps you did,' the woman would reply, 'but I had enjoyed the better meal without doing anything for it, and you've got a mountain of washing up to do.' The revelation of the true outcome of the "game" was often met with howls of protest and the straining, and indeed termination, of many friendships, but the woman would simply shrug off the complaints. 'Oldest trick in the book,' she would say, and, 'You fell for it. Didn't you ever read of the Wooden Horse of Troy?' The game she played required a victim, it required meticulous planning and, above all, she believed, it required the ability to withstand suspicion. And that was the way of it when she murdered her husband.

She had read about the phenomenon of powerful, wealthy men finding therapy in humiliation or subservience, of the professional dominatrix whose regular clients included High Court judges, captains of industry,

senior civil servants and merchant bankers. Such men with-
stood the pressures of lofty office because once a week they
found release in being led around a room on all fours on a
lead held by a woman in very high heels who makes them
sit up and beg and eat and drink from a bowl. The woman's
husband was one such a man. Wealthy – certainly very
wealthy – though not, she understood, to be particularly
pressured. Nonetheless, every Sunday evening they would
play their own special sex game, which she sensed he
needed to play though she received little gratification from
it. Like many women in such unions, she did it to please
him. She would dress uncomfortably but elegantly in
clothes which thrilled him and would sit on the settee while
he, with his wrists restrained behind his back with a thin silver chain and two small brass padlocks, and wearing only a
male thong and blindfold, would lie at her feet. At mid-
evening, about eight o'clock, after he had lain there quiet
and still for over an hour, she would announce "walkies"
and he would stir excitedly. She would put the dog's lead
and collar round his neck and walk him around the house.
They would visit each room, he walking behind her being
tugged gently by the lead, and would finish their tour in the
master bedroom wherein they would enjoy mutual pleasure. It was a walk they had done many times and from day
one, when the plot was hatched in her mind, she never var-
ied the route. In the early days of their marriage her husband had been content to confine their sex life to their bedroom, but she had suggested using the whole house. 'We
live alone, there's just little us...why not?' He had readily
agreed and their Sunday evening walk had become a matter
of routine. She'd lead him into all the rooms downstairs and
then go up the wide, angled staircase to the upstairs rooms,
telling him he was a 'good boy' as they went. On the night
he died – on the night she became a very happy widow – she
had tugged him to his feet and begun their tour walking out
of the living room into the dining room. She took him

round the dining room table, down the hallway into the kitchen and from the kitchen into the scullery, where the man would endure walking on cold concrete, then into the conservatory where the pathway between the rows of cactus plants was gravel, thus causing him further discomfort, and requiring more tugging of the lead and more encouragement from the woman. From the conservatory they returned to the scullery and the kitchen, and thence down a further short corridor of tiled floor into the canopy containing the indoor swimming pool. The walk round the swimming pool was the last tour of any room before the stairs were ascended, and this seemed to excite her husband. On that evening she walked him down the length of the pool and, unusually, sensing his sudden wonder, she stopped and said, 'Stay!' From beside the wall of the room, where she had placed them earlier that day, she picked up two silk scarves. One she rapidly tied to both his ankles, and the other she deftly tied to both his wrists. The man strained against the scarves, uttered her name in a questioning tone. Having left the keys in the padlocks as was their agreed "safety" rule, she turned the keys in both the locks, allowing the chain to fall free. Only then did her husband allow a note of alarm into his voice. 'What's happening? What are you doing?'

She took the collar from his neck. 'This,' she said, as she pushed him into the water. 'I am doing this.'

She walked away from the pool, away from the gasps, the shouts for help…the desperate splashing. She returned to the living room and sat and waited. She had passed the point of no return. If her husband could free himself it would all be over. She was younger than he was, possibly even stronger; she didn't fear physical harm, but the marriage would be over and she would be back in poverty. But if the knots held…if her husband didn't appear in fifteen minutes, angry, furious, attacking her, she would know she was a widow and set to inherit a fortune. She had planned the nerve-wracking quarter of an hour wait, and she steeled herself for it. Then she stood, slowly walked to the kitchen and took a pair of scissors from a drawer. She walked down the tiled corridor to the swimming pool and saw the body of her husband floating face down in the water, and she smiled. 'Good boy,' she said softly. She removed her dress and kicked off her heels before diving into the pool with the scissors in her hand. She cut the silk scarves away from her husband's wrists and ankles, she turned the body over, and swam it to the shallow end. She climbed out of the pool, taking the scarves with her, and collected the padlocks and chain, and the dog lead and collar from where she had dropped them. She walked slowly back to the kitchen and placed all the items in the waste bin and then picked up the phone and dialled three nines. She asked for the police and said, 'Please help...please hurry, there's been a dreadful accident.' She replaced the phone and smiled again, saying, 'Yes! Yes! Yes! Yes, you are a good boy, a *very*, very, very good boy indeed.'

The man felt nervous. He was anxious to serve, anxious to do his civic duty, and had been surprised – yet delighted – to be summoned, despite his tender years. He peeled off his waterproof jacket and threaded the anti-theft wire through one of the sleeves, clipped the end piece of the wire into the socket and retrieved and pocketed the numbered key. He then entered the retiring room feeling self-conscious, and he was relieved to note that few, if anybody at all, took any notice of him. For want of something to do he joined the queue at the refectory counter and ordered a cup of tea and a round of toast. He gave his numbered card to the lady on the till, who swiped it through the machine, debiting the cost from his daily refreshment allowance. His allowance, according to the information pack he had received a few days earlier, was sufficient to sustain him throughout the day. If he wanted anything more than this, he was expected to purchase it for himself. He carried the tray of tea and toast over to a table by the window, which afforded a view of the city centre, five floors beneath. The adjacent tables were either wholly unoccupied or occupied by a man or woman sitting alone, immersed in a quality daily newspaper.

The man, a keen observer of society, but still thinking of himself as ill versed in the ways of the world and believing he had a paucity of life experience, studied the reception area as discreetly as he could. He saw it immediately as representative of Britain's class-divided society, for in the middle of the room adjacent to the queue for the refectory, the tables had a greater level of occupancy and the folk sitting at them talked softly as they read tabloid newspapers. Beyond those tables was an area where comfortable armchairs had been placed facing each other along a narrow corridor, and those chairs were hungrily occupied by men and women, but mainly women, who talked loudly and did not appear to be reading anything at all. This group, the man noticed, also had the benefit of a television, which was tuned in to what he thought of as the most empty-headed of daytime television. Like, it seemed to the man, had found like: the three groups were the professional middle class with which he sat, the upper working class, of the tabloids and soft conversation, and the lower working class of loud conversation and television at 8.50 a.m. A fourth area, a room partitioned by glass was labelled "Smoking Area". He noted a few people occupying it, sitting each by themselves, not entering into conversation with anyone, like lone drinkers in a pub, seemingly wrapped up in their own thoughts. He glanced at the door: people were arriving still and doing what he had done, joining the queue for a cup of tea or coffee and a little to eat before moving to whichever area of the room their particular sense of place in the scheme of things drew them to. Only in the United Kingdom, mused the man, only here would people behave in such a way. Finishing his tea and toast he carried the tray to the "self clear" tray rack at the far end of the room where sat those who occupied the armchairs and talked loudly. As he slid the tray onto a vacant shelf on the rack he glanced to his side. The young woman sitting next to the tray rack was amusing herself by joining up the dots on a page in a book of similar "drawings". The man felt a pang of despair as he pondered that that young woman who seemed to be younger even than he was, was soon to be sitting in judgement of a man or woman who could be facing a sentence of life imprisonment. It seemed to him that what he had been told by people who had previously done jury service was going to be true; that it won't at all be like the film *Twelve Angry Men* where each juror puts in his tuppence worth. Rather the jury, nominally of twelve, will actually consist of two or three who debate then reach a decision, while the remaining nine or ten say little or nothing and during the conclave will, in the case of a unanimous verdict, meekly concur with said decision. It also seemed to him that the foreperson of the jury, for his or her sins, would be drawn from one of the people sitting at the tables near the window reading *The Times* or the *Guardian*. He resumed his seat, having claimed it as his by leaving his sports jacket slung over the back of the chair. It was then that he saw the woman, and she saw him. Their eyes met. He began to look away but she smiled at him, warmly so, he thought. The woman, dressed in a scarlet suit, walked confidently over to him carrying a cup of tea and said, 'Do you mind if I join you?'

'No,' the young man spoke hesitantly but smiled at the woman, 'please do.'

The woman sat down with grace and elegance, so thought the young man. He thought her to be in her mid-thirties. He noted the expensive looking clothing, neatly kept short hair, he scented perfume, and thrilled at the scarlet suit and black shoes; so striking an image, he thought.

'Is this your first jury?' She spoke softly with what the young man believed to be called "Received Pronunciation".

'Yes...yes...' The young man spoke nervously, but was calmed by her smile.

'Mine too. It should be interesting.'

'Is this seat taken?' The owner of the voice was a petite looking young woman in a blue top and matching skirt. She carried a briefcase.

'No, please join us,' the woman in scarlet replied, and the younger woman in blue slid into the seat. The fourth seat round the circular table was then occupied by a man in his middle years who sat down with a 'Mind if I join you?'

So they were four, so the youth and the woman in scarlet would later recall; the two of them, the petite woman in blue and the man in his forties. Conversation came rapidly and easily to the four, the man in his forties revealed himself to be an accountant for a large supermarket chain and for him jury service was a welcome break from the office, "as good as a holiday"; the small young woman was studying for accountancy exams. Only the woman in scarlet and the young man didn't disclose their occupation; they were not asked and it didn't seem appropriate to say what it was as the conversation moved on to a mutual despair at their fellow jurors, as the young man told of the woman he had seen moments earlier amusing herself by joining up the dots on a page in a book.

'Jury service ought to be compulsory,' the accountant said. 'The people we need are the most adept at avoiding jury service.'

'An intelligence test too,' sniffed the petite woman in blue, who, by then, was leafing through pass notes she had clearly prepared to assist with her exam revision.

'At least a general knowledge test,' the young man offered, 'with a low pass threshold because some knowledge of the world seems to me to be more important than intelligence for jury members.'

'Perhaps,' the petite woman replied, 'but then you'd run into trouble with the civil liberties lobby as the general knowledge questions would doubtless favour European Christians and the majority of the population; religious and ethnic minorities would be discriminated against by a general knowledge test.'

The conversation was interrupted by an announcement over the loudspeaker system calling for the juries in Courts One, Two, Three and Four. The young man watched as all about him people rose in ones and twos and walked towards the door close to the armchairs and television. There were forty-eight people all told. They seemed to form themselves into their respective juries as they recognised each other and were met by their usher, whom they similarly recognised.

'That fraud trial is on here, isn't it?' The accountant mused. 'Been going on for three weeks now. With a trial like that, the jury must have got to know each other quite well, they'll form a group...lasting friendships might emerge...that never occurred to me.'

'Only with some juries,' the woman in scarlet observed. 'Some juries won't last long enough for that.'

The accountant threw her a pained look as if to say, "You don't say".

The four juries filed out of the reception area walking behind their usher. Calm and hushed conversation once again fell on the jurors who remained in the area by the window. Moments later the loudspeaker crackled again and a calm voice asked people to listen for their names being called, and if it was called, to please make their way to the usher's office.

'Where's that?' The accountant hissed.

'By the television,' the young man replied, 'far end of the room.'

'Ah...'

Names began to be called out, clearly so, with a distinct pause between each name.

'Christopher Elms.'

'Well, that's me.' The young man stood. 'May see you later.'

'Hope so, Christopher.' The woman in scarlet smiled at him. 'I do hope so.'

Christopher Elms made his way to the usher's office where he stood with a group of people whose names had also clearly been called, and who, being strangers, stood stiffly, silently and self-consciously together. As names continued to be called, more people joined the group. Suddenly Elms was aware of a gentle stream of air blowing on the nape of his neck. He turned. It was the woman in red.

'Guess who,' she smiled.

He smiled at her. 'At least I know someone.' He looked up at her as he spoke. He hadn't realised how tall she was, standing, it seemed, a full head and shoulders above him. 'What about the other two?'

'Not called,' she said. 'At least not by the time my name was called.'

The door by the usher's office opened and a female usher with a warm countenance asked the people whose names had been called to please follow her. The group walked in silence along corridors, down flights of stairs and eventually were led into a courtroom.

The courtroom seemed to Christopher Elms to be a dark and foreboding place. The wood panelling was deeply stained and a High Court judge in red robes with ermine lining, and who seemed to the youth to be quite young to hold such a post, sat at the bench in a solid looking chair. As the jury entered, the defendant in the dock, a young and smartly dressed man, stood in a gesture of deference which Christopher Elms thought was unusual and was touched by it. He instantly felt he did not want to serve on this jury. He felt he did not want to sit in judgement on that defendant.

'The defendant in this trial is a serving police officer.' The judge addressed the jurors, who stood in a group in front of the jury box. 'The trial commenced last week and had to be abandoned when a juror disclosed that she was married to a policeman. She did not know the defendant, but nonetheless felt uncomfortable being on the jury and she was correct to disclose that when she did. We want to avoid that happening again and it is necessary we have a jury composed of people who are not related to police officers. Are any of you related to a police officer?'

'My husband is a policeman.' The woman in scarlet spoke and raised her hand. Other people raised their hands and claimed to have relatives who were police officers; Christopher Elms seized the opportunity and claimed a cousin of his was a police officer. In all, five of the twelve people called for that jury were excused and were escorted back to the retirement area.

'So your husband is a police officer?' Christopher Elms asked as he and the woman in scarlet resumed their seats.

'Nope,' she smiled. 'Is your cousin?'

'Nope,' Christopher Elms laughed softly. 'I just didn't want to sit in judgement on a police officer.'

'We have that in common. I didn't want a young man to lose everything because of my decision, no matter what evidence is against him. I think the other three pulled the same ruse. I mean, the first jury had one member who was related to a police officer, then ours, we had five…I think not. I think the others thought as we did. And speaking of others, we have lost our friends.'

'Seems so,' Elms glanced at the two vacant chairs, 'they must have been called for another jury while we were down below.'

'Clearly.' She stood. 'Well, let me buy you a cup of tea and you can tell me about yourself, Christopher. Or do you prefer Chris?'

'Either, really.'

'Well, I like Chris, so Chris it is.'

'Yes…okay.' He felt excitement grow in him.

The queue at the refectory being at that moment composed of only four persons, the woman returned to where Christopher Elms sat within a few minutes.

'So,' she said, placing a cup of tea in front of him, 'what do you do for a living, Chris?'

'I'm self employed.'

'As?'

'A landscape architect.'

'You build gardens?'

'No,' he smiled, 'that's a landscape gardener. I design what they build.'

'Ah…of course, architect. So sorry.'

'It's a common mistake. People just seem to hear the word "landscape" and don't differentiate between "gardener" and "architect".'

'Busy?'

'No,' he shrugged, 'no work at all. In fact I have been claiming benefit. I have a massive student loan to pay off.'

'I am sorry.'

'Well, it was my decision. The degree was fascinating, learning about garden designs through the ages, from the ancient Egyptians to the work of Capability Brown in the eighteenth century and Gertrude Jekyll in the nineteenth century here in England. Then I got a job with the local authority that had me designing the shape of the flowerbeds outside the old peoples' home and in the middle of the traffic roundabout...so I went freelance after eighteen months so as to have the opportunity of designing gardens. Had one or two contracts, nothing major...just large houses in the suburbs that had changed hands and the incoming owner wanted "something done" about the garden in which his newly purchased house stood. But nothing for a few months now.'

'So, nearly two years after graduation. And you are now what...twenty-three?'

'Twenty-two still, twenty-three later this year, in the autumn. I was seventeen when I started university.'

'Bright boy.' She smiled at him, holding eye contact as she sipped her tea. 'Well I could do with being twenty-two again...add fifteen years to your age and you have me.'

'Well, you seem to have done alright. I mean, those are not inexpensive clothes.'

'My husband is a wealthy man, we live in a large house. I wonder if I could put some work your way? Our garden is a bit of a mess, could do with an overhaul...and the house in Cumbria.'

'You have two houses?'

'Three,' she smiled. 'The main house...not too far from here, the cottage in the Lake District and a villa on Gozo.'

'Gozo?'

'Small island off Malta. Belongs to Malta. Small enough

for people to say you're "on" Gozo. You're "in" Malta, but "on" Gozo. Like you're in England but "on" the Isle of Wight. Just the way people talk.'

The loudspeaker crackled.

'Oh, oh…' the woman said, 'here we go.'

'Please listen for your name being called. If it is called, please make your way to the usher's office…Christopher Elms…'

'Me again.' Elms stood, feeling a little sad that he was to be parted from this elegant lady who seemed, he dared hope, to have taken a shine to him.

'Virginia Woolley.'

'And me…'

To Christopher Elms' delight, the woman also stood.

'Virginia,' he said.

'Yes, Virginia Woolley, VW for short. My maiden name was Woostencroft…so I was VW and was called 'Beetle' at school. Thought marriage would rescue me, but what do I become but VW again.' She put her hand to her head and imitated firing a gun into her brain. 'But nobody calls me Beetle anymore.'

'Virginia,' he repeated, 'lovely name. Suits you. It has an elegance about it.'

She smiled and inclined her head in gratitude for the compliment. 'We'll be late,' she said. 'We'd better start moving.'

Christopher Elms and Virginia Woolley walked through the jury reception area, she leading him, and joined ten other jurors who had gathered by the usher's office. The usher revealed himself to be a soft-spoken, silver-haired man, quite short in stature but who seemed, to Christopher Elms, to be well nourished. He asked the twelve to follow him. Christopher Elms and Virginia Woolley remained close to each other, actually walking side by side as if in recognition of a bond that seemed to have established itself between them, and occasionally during the walk down narrow corridors and narrow staircases, their bodies brushed gently against each other. The jury eventually reached a smaller retiring area with comfortable red chairs lining the walls of a long, narrow room. A few prints of paintings in aluminium frames hung on the walls. The jury was led into the court and asked to wait at the entrance. Elms noticed that this courtroom was lighter than the previous one had seemed. The jury stood in silence as the court clerk stood and addressed the jury.

'This trial is in respect of a gentleman called Wiggington.' He spoke solemnly, clearly. 'I will now read out the names of the defendants and witnesses in this case. If any are known to you lease raise your hand.' He then proceeded to read a list of names, giving both Christian and surname. Christopher Elms kept his hand down, none of the names were known to him, but more, he wanted to remain with Virginia Woolley and he sensed that she wanted to remain with him. The clerk turned to the judge, who, like the judge in the previous courtroom, was cloaked in scarlet and ermine. 'None are known, my Lord.' The judge nodded. The clerk turned to the jury. 'If the jury would be kind enough to retire for a moment or two.' The jury turned. As they did so, Virginia Woolley allowed the back of her hand to brush against the back of Christopher Elms' hand. He glanced at her. She smiled at him. Excitement rose in his chest. He exited the courtroom in front of her and sat in one of the chairs in the jury waiting room. Somewhat to his disappointment she did not sit next to him but opposite him though her eye contact and brief smile spoke of her approval of him. Christopher Elms looked about the room. Again there was no natural light and he was grateful for the prints, sensitively chosen, he thought, because they depicted exteriors, not interiors. Prints of paintings showing interiors would not have allowed the sense of escape that was provided by the scene of a beach that seemed to say Mediterranean coast, or by the print of a modest

painting of a sun drenched, ivory white villa, which definitely said Spain or Greece.

Sitting opposite Christopher Elms, Virginia Woolley
studied the younger man. He was slim, seemed to be quite
muscular, though also seemed a little nervous, as indeed she
would have been, she conceded, if she had to sit on a High
Court jury at the age of twenty-two. Whoever was going to
be the foreperson of this jury, it would not be young Mr
Elms. Over and above his tender years, he had not, she
thought, the gravitas of one required to deliver the verdict.
It was eager-to-please young men of similar appearance to
Mr Elms who had cheerfully told her of the balance of her
account and asked if she was interested in opening a new
account of a type just introduced by the bank. He was of
that sort of appearance, as viewed by Mrs Virginia Woolley.
And as such, she thought, as such, he would be ideal. Their
eyes met and not only did she smile at him, she raised her
eyebrows and then winked and watched as he flushed with
excitement. The jury waited in silence for a further ten minutes before their usher joined them from the courtroom.

'You are now to be sworn in,' he said. 'My name is Trevor.
I'll be your usher for the trial except at the very close, when
another usher will lead you into the court to deliver your
verdict. This is Court Five. Each morning you will be called
from the jury retirement room, not by your individual
names, but as a group, namely, "Jury for Court Five". As
you file in you may sit in any seat, but whatever seat you sit
in, you must then occupy that self same seat for the dura-
tion of the trial. Please follow me.' The jury was then led
into the courtroom, Christopher Elms following Virginia
Woolley. He followed her as she walked to the second row
of seats. She occupied the fifth seat, and he the sixth. By the
narrowest of margins he had contrived to be able to sit next
to her. The remaining members of the jury filed into the six
seats that comprised the front row of the jury box.

The clerk stood. 'Will the jury please look at the counsel

in the well of court? If any is known to any of you, please indicate.'

The jury remained still. Silent.

'Very good. Thank you, Mr Usher.'

Trevor, the usher, approached the jury box holding a bible in one hand and a plastic card in the other. The card contained printing.

'Please take the bible in your right hand,' the clerk said, 'and read the juror's oath as printed on side A of the card. If you choose to affirm, please place the bible on the shelf in front of you and read the words of affirmation which are on side B of the card. Whether you choose to take the oath or affirm, will you please stand to do so.'

The card and the bible were passed along the second row of the jury. When they reached Virginia Woolley she stood very calmly and read the oath in a calm, faultless manner. 'I swear by Almighty God that I will faithfully try the defendant and give a true verdict according to the evidence.' Christopher Elms was impressed. He took the bible and the card as she handed it to him with a "you can do this" look. Standing, as she sat, he then, feeling the vote of confidence she had given him, managed to read the oath without fumbling the words. He sat gratefully and as he did so Virginia Woolley's hand once again brushed against the back of his in a gesture that said "well done". Again he thrilled to her touch. This time there was no mistake, this time the body contact was deliberate.

The jury swearing was soon completed, with only one juror choosing to affirm: 'I do solemnly, sincerely and truly declare and affirm that I will faithfully try the defendant and give a true verdict according to the evidence.' The accused was escorted into the courtroom and was asked to stand in the witness box.

'You are John Francis Wiggington, aged thirty-seven years, of Selby Road, Church Fenton. You are charged that on the 31st of October last year, you did murder Mrs

Dorothy Wiggington of that address. Do you plead guilty, or not guilty?'

'Not guilty.' Wigginton's voice was strong, yet not over-bearing, not a trace of aggression or pent up violence in it, as far as Christopher Elms could detect. Wiggington had a pleasantness of manner, glimpsed by Elms in those few seconds, but the impression was a strong one. He knew that this was going to be a difficult trial. He had avoided sitting on the jury of the trial of the serving police officer hoping to remain with Virginia Woolley and also hoping to sit on judgement on a career criminal who had only his liberty to fear losing. He had achieved the first aim, but not, it seemed, the second, for John Wiggington looked like a professional man, with much, much more than his liberty to lose should the jury find against him.

The clerk turned to the judge and said, 'Not guilty, my Lord.'

The judge nodded and, picking up his pen, wrote on his notepad.

'Thank you, Mr Bailiff.' A court bailiff escorted John Wiggington to a separate part of the court where he sat, encased in glass panelling. It was, thought Elms, a curious arrangement, one of the sort he had never seen before, and he could only assume that this particular court, Court Five, had been thus designed for the trial of persons who, because of the nature of their alleged crime(s), were at risk from attack from the public gallery, or who were considered an escape risk. John Wiggington did not appear to meet either category and so Christopher Elms could only deduce that it was pressure of court space that had dictated the use of Court Five for his trial.

The trial unfolded and an intriguing story was told. It was said that the accused drove his daughter from their house one Saturday afternoon, leaving his wife gardening in the rear garden of their suburban home. Later, the accused and his daughter returned to find his wife battered about the head, apparently with a spade, which lay nearby with blood upon the blade. Mrs Wiggington was still breathing and Mr Wiggington, having called an ambulance, tried to comfort her, but she died before the ambulance arrived. The police arrived and summoned the police surgeon who pronounced life extinct at 4.33 p.m. on the day in question. It was the Crown's case that the accused had murdered his wife and had driven away with his daughter of fourteen years intending to "discover" the body upon his return and pass the crime off as an opportunist murder committed by person or persons unknown who had intruded upon the property.

The trial evolved over four days. For the Crown there was the argument that the Wiggington marriage was strained; neighbours gave evidence of frequent rows emanating from the house; police records showed a number of occasions when officers had been summoned to the house by a terrified Mrs Wiggington who had managed, she claimed, to have reached the phone before her husband could murder her. There was the testimony of a Home Office scientist who argued that the pattern of blood on Mr Wiggington's clothing was consistent with blood splatter, which could have been caused by the blade of the spade striking the skull of the deceased. Fingerprints on the handle of the spade were those of Mr Wiggington. For the defence, there was the argument that the fingerprints on the handle of the spade were irrelevant; one would expect a man's fingerprints to be on the handle of his spade in his garden. The deceased's blood was on the clothing of the accused because he had tried to comfort her upon discovering her body when he and his daughter had returned from the shops. Whether the blood on the clothing amounted to "splatter" was but one man's opinion. Also, there was the argument that the man's daughter, sitting next to her father in the front seat of the car, did not notice any blood on her father's clothing, nor did she notice anything strange or unusual in his manner yet he had, allegedly, moments earlier, viciously attacked his wife.

The solemn proceedings of Regina v Wiggington were frequently interrupted when the jury was asked to leave the court whilst legal submissions were made. It was during these intervals, when the jury sat in the retiring lounge adjacent to the courtroom, that the jury became known to each other and began to form up as a group. There was the middle-aged lady, Christopher Elms would recall, who lived wholly on fruit and would bring a large bag of fruit with her each day, a little of which was to sustain her, but most to give to her fellow jury members. An apple each on the first day, a banana on the second, an orange on the third, a massive bunch of grapes which was passed round the jury when it was in the retiring lounge until all the grapes had been eaten. Donald was a retired coalminer with a ready wit and provided the jury with its much needed source of humour, causing them to laugh sufficiently loudly that Trevor, their usher, had to enter the room and say 'Sshh', but did so with a smile, probably, thought Christopher Elms, because he realised that a jury which had developed a group spirit, and which needed to laugh as a release of tension, was also a jury which would work hard when it came time to deliberate. Though all the jurors shared the fruit and all laughed at Donald's jokes and anecdotes, few actually contributed. Of the twelve, the same four or five would make conversation. On one or two occasions when in the retirement lounge, they were joined by a jury from another court who had also clearly been asked to retire whilst submissions were made. Interestingly, observed Elms, the two juries didn't talk to each other, the other jury's entry to the room was greeted with polite smiles and nods, but the two juries were two different groups and so didn't communicate. Elms also noticed that the accountant and the slender young woman in blue who had sat with him and Virginia Woolley in the retiring room on the first morning were members of the other jury. Yet that was clearly no reason to talk or even acknowledge each other. They were in different juries and a fence had been erected between them. Elms found it fascinating; the process of the law, the emerging personalities of the jury, all very interesting, but above all, Christopher Elms' mind turned on a greater fascination, a growing and daily difficult-to-resist attraction to the aloof and stylish – and monied – Virginia Woolley, who allowed subtle body contact, even in the jury box, and who would look at him with dilated pupils, just briefly, very discreetly, when the jury retired to the lounge.

At 4 p.m. on the fourth day the defence concluded its case. The judge concluded the proceedings for that day, telling the court that he would be summing up the following morning, after which the jury would be invited to retire and consider its verdict.

Shane Parsloe sat forward with his elbows resting on the arm of his chair. Like all the others in the group save one, who sat in chairs arranged in a circle, he wore a white shirt of blue stripes, blue jeans and soft-soled training shoes. The one person in the group who was not thus dressed was a young blonde haired man who wore the crisp white shirt and black trousers of a prison officer. 'Well, I've learned my lesson.' Parsloe spoke with a solid Yorkshire accent. 'Prison has worked for me...I won't be coming back here unless the filth fit me up, and that's a danger 'cos once you're known to the filth they never leave you alone.'

'That's true,' growled another man. 'I wouldn't be in here if the filth didn't know me. Recognised me and acted on suspicion. Searched me and I was carrying enough to be convicted of possession with intent to supply.'

'Be fair, Tony,' the police officer spoke gently. 'You were known to the police, that's not the same as being fitted up.'

'Aye...alright, Mr Preston, but the thing that got me is that the filth were corrupt. I was carrying twenty pounds of Lebanese Black...'

his detached house on the fashionable and expensive estate on the edge of Wetherby. He unlocked the front door and entered the house, followed by the two dogs. His wife smiled a warm welcome from the kitchen. He walked up to her and kissed her on the cheek.

'I swear those dogs know when you're on your way home,' she said, kneading dough. 'They begin to get excited about twenty minutes before you arrive, no matter what time of day it is.'

'Coincidence, I'd say. What's for supper?'

'Chicken curry.'

'Sounds lovely.' He turned and walked into the sitting room where a young man sat reading a thick book.

'Wotcha, dad.' The young man smiled.

'What's that you're reading?'

'Toxicology...I'll be doing it in the Christmas term. Essential reading if I want to do the pathology option.'

'Still intend to spend a working life cutting up bodies?' Clive Hirst sank thankfully into an armchair.

'So far that's still the plan. I can't understand why it isn't more popular. You know, pathologists are the only doctors whose patients never complain, whose patients are never in pain, never need to be attended to in an emergency and they are the only doctors who don't have to fret about waiting lists or an overcrowded surgery.'

Clive Hirst smiled. 'Well, whatever...I am very proud of you.'

Later that evening, after supper, which was cleared away by David Hirst upon his insistence, allowing his parents a little quality time together, father and son strolled out together, relishing each other's company. They walked from the estate towards the centre of the town and, upon reaching the Goose Inn, entered therein and found a vacant table in the snug by the dartboard. They sat at it and spent the evening conversing and gently quaffing pints of Black Sheep.

'Twenty!' Mr Preston gasped. 'But you only got two years.'

'That's because I pleaded guilty. What else could I do? They had me cold and the filth only produced five pounds in evidence, having charged me with being in possession of five pounds, so the drug squad sold fifteen pounds of high quality blow back to the dealers. It's how it works. I didn't complain...look at me, in the pre-release group. If I had been done for possession of twenty pounds, I wouldn't smell a pre-release group for another five years. But that's the issue, Shane: you're known. You'll be stopped on suss.'

'I'll keep my nose clean. I'm not a cot and three merchant. I've met a few like that...the category B boys, hotel class accommodation, choice of meals at feeding time...library, gym...smoke...I can see why they keep offending, I can see why they become...what's the word, Mr Preston...?'

'Recidivists?'

'Yes.'

'But think of the end, Shane.'

'Of my bird?'

'No, the end of your life. What have those recidivists got to look back on...a life in the slammer and they'll end their days in a Salvation Army hostel. No, no matter what they say, they keep bouncing back inside because they can't handle life on the outside, but you're not like that...did a stupid thing once, burgled a house, collected two years...served what? Fifteen months? Out in a few weeks' time. You're how old? Twenty-five...?'

'Four.' An observer would see him as strong, muscular, a scar on his cheek.

'So, plenty of time for you to push your life in a more positive direction.'

'You got somebody to meet you at the gate?' Jeff Duncan was a middle-aged prisoner, he growled as he spoke.

'Yes,' Shane Parsloe nodded. 'I have someone to meet me

at the gate.'

'Well, you might make it, then. This is my third sentence, my third pre-release group. I've seen it so often, the ones who have no one to meet them at the gate, they're the ones that come back inside. So you might be able to keep out. Is that why you kept in shape, because you've got someone? Never a boy for the library, but they couldn't keep you out of the gym.'

'Maybe,' Parsloe smiled. 'Maybe.'

Christopher Elms lay on his bed. It was by then 10 p.m. and the sounds of Headingley passed beneath his window: heavy traffic, and noisy but good natured university students, the latter much disliked by the 'locals' who feared the "landlordism" that was destroying their community and causing property values to plummet. The trial had been fascinating but his thoughts dwelt to the point of obsession upon the possibly not unattainable Virginia Woolley.

Clive Hirst carried the drinks back from the bar on a metal tray. He placed the gin and tonic in front of René Lucas, a pint of beer in front of Richard "Dickie" Pulleyne, placed a second pint of beer in front of his chair and returned the tray to the bar. He walked back to the table and took his seat. 'Well, here's to another one tucked up.'

'Cheers, boss.' The man and woman raised their glasses and drank.

'Bit silly, though, I thought.' René Lucas put her drink back on the table. She was a woman in her early thirties, short blonde hair and would be considered by many to be attractive. She had an educated accent with a trace of southern counties and had the poise and bearing which comes from being of a privileged background.

'What was, pet?' Richard Pulleyne turned to her. He was a man, also in his thirties, but pushing his forties. He would be seen as thick set, and had a solid Yorkshire accent.

'Going NG against the weight of all that evidence.'

'Yes, that was silly.' Hirst, the man who had bought the drinks, the man who was addressed as "boss" drank his beer. He was a well-built man in his fifties, bald head, bristlingly clean. 'He was utterly pigheaded. His brief must have advised him to go G, but at the end of the day they have to act on their client's instruction. So he's got at least ten years to think about it…that's if he keeps his nose clean.'

'Fifteen, out in ten if he's lucky. If he had gone G…what do you think? Half that?'

'I would have thought. Yes, about seven or eight…out in four. Easy case for us, though, the evidence just fell in our lap…the verdict was a foregone conclusion.' Hirst drank deeply and looked around him. The pub was quiet, a few afternoon drinkers, blessedly free of smoke and music, just as he liked a pub to be. 'It's those touch and go cases, they are the ones that keep me on edge.'

'Oh, yes,' Dickie Pulleyne sat forward, 'when a felon walks because of a technicality, that really gets under my skin…all our work for nothing, and there's no justice for the victim. Those cases, and cases where there isn't enough evidence to sway the jury…'

'Frustrating.' René Lucas sipped her gin. 'I've had one o two experiences like that.'

'Aye…' Pulleyne nodded. 'Aye, me too.'

'And you'll have a few more before you collect your per sion. Believe me…it's just the way of it…it's just the ma ner of the beast. Win some, lose some.' Hirst drained glass. 'Well, have to dash. I have a report to prepare an want to get home on time today…for once.'

Later Clive Hirst drove home. He turned his car into gravel-covered driveway of his house. The sound of the tyres crunching the gravel set two dogs, a Labrador an smaller mongrel, to barking excitedly. He got out of his and patted the two tail-wagging dogs and strode tow

René Lucas returned home. "Home? Hardly," she thought. Home is really a few hundred miles away. Her heart was heavy. She felt regret at giving in to the impulse to move north; then it had seemed sensible, now it seemed like running away, a flight instinct. The rented flat was small, cramped and barely suitable for a policewoman's lodging. The area in which it was situated nudged a suspect, 'undesirable' area, but it would have to do for the time being. She sat in the armchair in front of the small television set and plunged her hand into her handbag, extracted her mobile phone and held it, just held it in the palm of her hand, staring at it, wanting it to ring, wanting to dial that number.

Virginia Woolley steeled herself for the nightly ordeal. She put it off and put it off until the bath water had stopped being merely cold and was by then chilled, until her husband appeared at the bathroom door in his stupidly short dressing gown...those pale pins protruding beneath the hem...his almost plaintive, 'Aren't you coming to bed, my sweet?'

'Just coming.' She forced a smile. 'Go ahead, I'll be there.'

When he had "gone ahead" she levered herself out of the suds and smoothed herself dry with the largest towel she could find. She thought of Christopher Elms and how he seemed to be able to be cultivated. Then feeling unwell, she began the long and reluctant walk to the bedroom, naked, as was her husband's insistence.

It was on Friday morning that the judge summed up the case of Regina v Wiggington, taking the jury over the evidence and summarising the conflicting arguments. He then invited the jury to retire and consider its verdict. Christopher Elms, who led the jury from the box, the front row being slow to move, noticed that a different usher collected the jury, a short, dark-haired woman, with a schoolmistress's black gown but with the friendly, affable manner which Trevor, the jury's usher for the whole of the trial, also had exuded. It seemed to Elms that the ushers had been instructed to pursue a "be polite to the jurors for they perform a public duty" policy. Though, despite this, it had seemed that the majority of the jurors Elms had met and observed, were more keen to jump at the opportunity for a break in a humdrum existence or from a brain numbing job than they were keen to be public-spirited. He included himself in that number: his small flat had become prison-like and he despaired of anyone phoning him in response to his entry in the *Yellow Pages* or to the ad he had placed in the newsagent's window. The invitation to do jury service had, for him, been very unexpected and so, so welcome. The lady usher, who had not, unlike Trevor, introduced herself, led the jury to a retiring room.

The retiring room was light and airy having, in contrast to the courtroom, a plentiful supply of natural light by virtue of a large window that afforded a view into the inner courtyard of the building where police vehicles were parked. The interior of the room had a functional quality. A table with five chairs down each side and a chair at either end occupied the middle of the floor, leaving enough room for people to walk round the table and select a chair. Nothing softened the room, no prints or paintings on the wall, no potted plants. Prior to leaving the jury, the usher pointed to a bell on the wall and said that when they had completed their deliberation, they should summon her by pressing the bell. She also showed them an anteroom where any juror could smoke, but asked that no smoking be done in the jury room itself. It was by then 10.45, so Christopher Elms would later recall, and the usher said that if they had not reached their decision by midday she would knock on the door of the room and hand the jury a menu from which they could choose a sandwich for lunch. She then retired and the jury seated themselves randomly around the table. Christopher Elms found himself seated opposite Virginia Woolley.

'Well, who's going to do it?' The man who had chosen to affirm addressed the jury. 'The chair, who's going to be the foreman?'

Silence.

'I think you should do it.' The lady who lived on fruit spoke, addressing Virginia Woolley. 'You've got the speaking voice, the manner...'

'Well, if nobody else wants to do it,' Virginia Woolley said, somewhat reluctantly, thought Elms, and pleasingly so. He would have liked her less if she wanted to be the foreperson.

No one spoke.

'Well, alright,' Virginia Woolley leaned forward, 'I'll be the chairperson and foreperson. I'll deliver the verdict we reach.' Elms noticed she didn't seem to want to sit at either end of the table, but was content to chair from her present seat at the side. 'Before we start,' she paused and glanced at Donald, the retired miner, who seemed to Elms to have a pleading look in his eyes. 'Are you gasping?' she asked with a smile. Donald nodded desperately.

'Alright, off you go.' She continued to smile and her gesture for Donald's plight bought a murmur of approval from the jury, particularly from Elms.

Donald left the table and went hurriedly to the smoking

anteroom and, showing respect for the jury, didn't enjoy a leisurely cigarette, rather he returned within perhaps, Elms estimated, about ninety seconds, having evidently taken two or three deep inhalations, just sufficient to satisfy his craving for nicotine.

'How long can you go without a smoke, Donald?' Virginia Woolley asked when Donald had resumed his seat.

''Bout half an hour.'

'Okay. Well, look, if you want a smoke, just say so and we'll stop the conversation then resume when you re-join us, so don't panic about not getting a fag.'

'Thanks,' Donald smiled with clear appreciation.

'So…let's establish a few ground rules before we begin talking about the case.'

Elms found himself to thrill at her calm assuming of control…authoritative without being overbearing.

'In the first place we have had a good example of debate given to us these last few days. I would like us to continue that form of debate here, by which I mean that if you disagree with someone, say why, but do not let this descend into a personal attack. I mean, if you disagree with someone, don't tell them they are "thick" or "stupid" or "don't know what they are talking about", but say why you disagree with them.'

'I'd go along with that,' growled the man who had chosen to affirm.

'Alright.' Virginia Woolley asked, 'Do we all agree on that?'

A nodding of heads, a murmur of agreement.

'Good. Secondly…again continuing from what we have witnessed, I think we should agree that if someone is talking, then that person should be extended the courtesy of being allowed to speak without interruption. If anybody abuses that courtesy by needless repetition, I will use the gavel.' She tapped a pencil on the table. 'This is the gavel. I will use the gavel to stop that person…agreed?'

Again a nodding of heads, a murmur of agreement.

'Anybody else want to suggest a gag rule?'

'Gag rule?' The woman beside Elms repeated the phrase. He saw then how skilfully Virginia Woolley used language that they could understand, and by that means, was earning the loyalty of the jury. She was, he thought, very clever indeed.

No one suggested another "gag rule".

The jury then began to discuss the case and it was just as Christopher Elms had been promised it would be like. In this jury, three people led the conversation, one of whom was Virginia Woolley, who spoke the most frequently; two others added their views briefly. The majority remained silent, one of whom, to his own disappointment, was Christopher Elms. He found that the longer he remained silent, the more difficult it was to join the conversation. It was as if his tongue had frozen, though he followed the conversation closely. His mind remained focused as Virginia Woolley guided the jury over the issues the trial had raised, the evidence that had been presented, the history of violence towards the victim by her husband, the accused, the description of the "blood splatter" on the accused's clothing. She then argued that it seemed unlikely that such a volatile personality could remain so calm so after the murder that his daughter didn't notice anything unusual in his manner, nor did she seem to notice any blood on his clothing.

'No one witnessed the murder,' was another growling submission by the man who had chosen to affirm. Virginia Woolley nodded. 'They were away at the shops for an hour. Plenty of time for someone to call at the house, probe round the back...an opportunist burglar, for example.'

'I used to live in Scotland,' the woman who lived on fruit said. 'Up there they have a third verdict available to juries...it's "Not proven".'

'Neat,' Virginia Woolley nodded her head. 'You mean it's

not the same as saying Not Guilty, which implies innocence, but it's more in the manner of saying "we think the defendant did commit the offence, but the Crown has failed to prove their case"?'

'That's it,' said the woman, 'that's it exactly. Believe me, if this case was heard north of the border it would result in a Not Proven verdict.'

'But we don't have that halfway sort of luxury, for us in England and Wales, it's either Guilty or Not Guilty.'

'They also have juries of fifteen persons,' the woman added, a little irrelevantly, thought Elms, 'and will accept a majority of twelve. There you have twelve people agreeing, but if the criminals want to "nobble" the jury they've got to bribe or intimidate four persons, not just one as in England and Wales.'

'Yes…' Virginia Woolley added dryly, 'but to the matter in hand. I am sensing a reluctance to convict this case because the evidence is circumstantial and, as the gentlemen to my left has pointed out, no one actually witnessed the murder…and the blood on his clothing, well, if he went to give aid when he discovered her…well, of course he'd get blood on his clothing.' She paused. 'Is anyone of the opinion that we should convict?'

Silence. Not a hand was raised. Virginia Woolley let the silence last for fully fifteen seconds, which Christopher Elms found was a long time in such circumstances.

'That's it then,' she said. 'That's our decision. Not guilty. Not because we believe his innocence any more than we believe his guilt…the case against him is just too weak to enable us to convict but we can't say that. All I can say is "Not guilty".'

'How long did it take us to reach that decision?' Again the man who had chosen to affirm growled.

'Not long.' Virginia Woolley glanced at her watch. 'Less than half an hour once we started to debate.'

'We should delay going back,' the growling man growled.

'It makes a better impression and impressions are every-thing.'

'Well, I don't think I agree with that,' Virginia Woolley replied. 'Impressions are important but I wouldn't go so far as to say they are "everything". Nonetheless, the suggestion is made that we delay returning so as to give a better impression. Does anyone object?'

Again there was silence; again not a hand was raised. On this occasion Virginia Woolley broke the silence after just three or four seconds, quite long enough in Elms' view. 'So that's agreed,' she said, 'we'll return...when...after lunch? It has the added advantage of giving time for anyone to have a last minute change of mind because once I press the bell, that's the point of no return. Alright,' she tapped the pencil on the table, 'meeting adjourned.'

The jury relaxed, people began to talk freely. Virginia Woolley caught Christopher Elms' attention and smiled at him. He returned the smile. The female usher knocked on the door and brought the lunch menu. The jury decided to order as differently as they could so that sandwiches could be exchanged, as with Christopher Elms, who ordered chicken sandwiches and swapped one for one of the ham sandwiches which had been ordered by another juror.

At 2 p.m. Virginia Woolley called the jury to order and asked if anyone wished to change their mind about the decision they had reached prior to lunch. Again no one spoke; again no one raised a hand. 'Very well.' She stood and pressed the bell and resumed her seat.

The usher seemed to respond rapidly. No less than twenty seconds, it seemed to Elms, had elapsed between the pressing of the bell and her knocking on the door. 'Have you reached a decision?' she asked warmly after Virginia Woolley had said, 'Come in,' in response to her soft knock-ing.

'Yes.' Woolley spoke for the group.

'Very well, I will have to notify the court and then I will

come back and collect you.' She shut the door. Moments later, sooner than Elms had anticipated, she returned and, having knocked on the door and being invited to enter, asked if the jury would follow her. She led them down the familiar route to the jury lounge with prints of Mediterranean scenes on the walls and, inviting them to sit, asked who was the foreperson.

'I am,' Virginia Woolley said with a ready smile. 'For my sins.'

'For your sins,' the usher grinned. 'Well, madam, you must lead the jury in, you must sit in the front row in the furthest seat, that is the furthest seat from the door, the nearest seat to the judge.'

'Understood.'

'The remainder of the jury, you may sit anywhere. For the verdict you do not have to occupy your usual seat. If you'd wait a moment.' The usher opened the door and entered the court and returned within a matter of seconds and said, 'Please enter the court,' and stood outside, allowing Virginia Woolley to lead the jurors into the jury box.

Christopher Elms thought the tension palpable. None of the counsel looked at the jury. The accused, on the other hand, eyed them keenly as if searching for a harbinger of their verdict. All eyes in the public gallery seemed to be focused on Virginia Woolley. When the jury had seated, the clerk rose.

'Will the foreperson please stand. Please answer "yes" or "no".'

Virginia Woolley stood.

'Ladies and gentlemen of the jury,' the clerk asked, 'have you reached a verdict?'

'Yes.'

'Do you find the accused guilty or not guilty?'

'Not guilty.'

A cry of 'No!' came from the public gallery. The police officers shook their heads. The judge himself seemed, to

Elms, to show more than a trace of disappointment. The accused smirked and then grinned.

'Not guilty, my Lord.' The clerk turned to face the judge. Then he turned to Virginia Woolley and asked, 'Is that the verdict of you all?'

'Yes.'

'Unanimous, my Lord.' Again the clerk turned to the judge.

The accused, being allowed to walk from the court having been dismissed, and six members of the jury, including Christopher Elms, decided to go for a drink to unwind, to complete the proceedings. It seemed to be a psychological need. Virginia Woolley did much to placate them. 'Alright,' she said, 'he shouldn't have smirked. That smirk said "guilty", we all saw that, but we still returned the correct verdict. It isn't our fault that the police failed to make a case against him. I'll sleep tonight.'

'I feel cheated,' said the growling man. 'I feel I was taken for a fool. That woman deserved justice. She didn't get it.' He drained his glass and, without another word, stood and walked out of the pub without a backward glance.

'I know what he means,' the fruit-eating woman said, 'but like you said...the decision was right.' She, too, then left the pub. Two other jurors left with her, as if wanting to put a bad experience behind them. None glanced back as they walked out of the doorway.

'Then there were two,' Virginia Woolley said.

'Then there were two,' Christopher Elms echoed.

'So,' Virginia Woolley opened her handbag and took out her purse from which she deftly extracted a twenty-pound note. 'Why don't you go to the bar and buy us something more to drink.' She handed him the note. 'I'd better not have any alcohol, I have a car to drive home. What can I have?' She glanced towards the bar.

'They do coffee here,' Christopher Elms suggested.

'Excellent...a coffee for me and whatever you want for yourself.'

'I'll have coffee too. I don't like to drink in the daytime.'

Virginia Woolley smiled. 'Good for you.'

Christopher Elms returned with two coffees, milk in a small plastic cup and sugar in sachets. He placed the change on the table.

'So...' Virginia Woolley poured milk into her coffee and stirred it with a slender white plastic spoon, 'tell me about yourself.'

'Not much to tell,' Christopher Elms shrugged.

'Well, I know you are an educated young man,' she sipped her coffee, 'and are somewhat courageously setting out alone, turning your back on local authority employment, which is safe, secure, reasonably well paid for one of your standing and qualifications, and offers an inflation-proof pension at the end of it all.'

'Yes...that was probably a mistake, in hindsight, wonderful, wonderful, all-knowing hindsight; it probably was not a good idea to resign. Designing flowerbeds in front of old people's homes is better than designing nothing at all.'

'Go back.'

He shook his head. 'They wouldn't have me. Didn't leave on good terms and I couldn't go to another authority, not with the reference they'd give me. I'm really out on a limb.'

'Sorry...but you're a young man, plenty of time to establish yourself. I might be able to help you.'

'Really?' He glanced eagerly at her. Their eyes met. He saw how dilated were hers, his pulse quickened.

'Yes...possibly...very possibly, it depends on your situation.'

'My situation? I told you, I am out of work. My parents think I am doing well...I can't go home.'

'Where is home?'

'Batley.'

'Where is that? I am from the south of England.'

'Near here, in the Pennines...small town...if you don't escape, it holds you forever.'

'And you escaped.'

'Via university. First generation graduate. My father is a bus driver...so fond of telling his mates that I am an architect. You're only whatever if you are actually doing whatever. It would destroy him if he knew I was drawing dole money. It's horrible keeping them in the dark.'

'Well...again depending...you just need one good commission to start you off.'

'Yes.'

'So your situation...is there anyone special in your life?' She avoided eye contact as she asked the question.

'No...' Christopher Elms stammered. 'No one at all.'

'Well,' she smiled and slid her hand across the table and placed it on his. 'Perhaps you and I could get to know each other a little better...would you like that?'

'Yes...yes...but...you are married and I am so much younger than you. I mean, you are very attractive, but I am only twenty-two.'

'And I am thirty-seven...yes, I know. The age isn't a problem unless it's a problem for you.' She raised her eyebrows. 'Is it?'

'No.' He shook his head vigorously. 'Not at all.'

'Good. In fact, not only is the age gap not a problem, it's the opposite, for me anyway. You see a younger man is very good for a woman...having a younger man rejuvenates her. When you are middle-aged you will find that twenty-year-old women will rejuvenate you.'

'I...I...don't know what to say,' Elms found it difficult to contain his excitement. 'Things like this don't happen to me.'

'You mean you've never had a girlfriend?'

'No...there was a damsel at Newcastle, but we never...'

'Really?' She squeezed his hand. 'Now that, young master Christopher, that makes you even more attractive.'

Elms swallowed hard. He felt himself blush. 'But you are married.'

Virginia Woolley turned her head away and seemed to Elms to grimace at the mention of the word "married". 'Well, there are marriages and there are marriages, Chris.'

'Yes...'

'There are marriages made in heaven and marriages that are forged at Satan's anvil in Hell. Mine's the latter.'

'Sorry...you could get out?'

'I can't,' she squeezed his hand, 'I have no independent financial means. If I walked out...well, I'd be one of your lot, signing on the dole.'

'Divorce?'

'I have no grounds...no grounds that could enable me to force a generous settlement despite his wealth.'

'He'd give you enough, surely. Isn't he generous?'

'Why yes,' she wriggled her fingers, 'look at my rings...my watch...my clothes from Harvey Nichols. The car he bought me is a Mercedes Benz...one of the small ones, a 190, but it's a Mercedes. There's nothing to stop me walking out of the door except there's nowhere to walk to. It's like being in one of those Japanese prisoner of war camps in the Second World War...you know the ones where they said, "We have no need of wire to keep you in the camp. If you want to survive you must remain here, because here is your source of food and water. In the jungle there is neither." So...here I stay.'

'What does he do? I mean, to make him so wealthy?'

'Well, let's just say he's good with numbers. Good with figures.'

'Like an accountant?'

'Yes, like an accountant. But the problem is that he is a lot older than me.'

'Another age gap?'

'Yes,' she smiled and stroked his hand. 'As you say, Chris, another age gap, a massive age gap. You may as well know

now...he's thirty years older than me.'

'Thirty...?'

'Yes, he's sixty-seven years old, so a thirty-year age gap. I pick 'em young or I pick 'em old.' She continued to stroke the back of his hand. 'But there are compensations...no children...that makes things neater and I have a sister whom I visit. He allows me to visit my sister...they farm, my sister and her husband, in Dorset, near where we grew up.'

'You just have a sister?'

'Yes...just a sister...Daddy was a merchant banker. Daddy was devastated when I married Maurice...Mummy said it killed him and she hates me for it. Daddy so disapproved of Maurice that he cut me out of his will, and Mummy won't leave me a penny, all Daddy's money will go to Charlotte.'

'Your sister?'

'Yes...the perfect Charlotte who married an ex-army officer, and who farms nine-hundred acres of the richest soil in England, whose two perfect children already have their names down for Eton...Unlike me who married a man with no background, who was older than my own father, and who left the beautiful south to live in the Pennines where mammoths still roam. Of course I have been cut off. Makes me utterly dependent on Maurice. But I can visit my sister...Maurice allows me to visit my sister...sometimes for two weeks at a time, but usually I go for a week or just a weekend.'

'To Dorset?'

She smiled. 'Youth is one thing, Chris...but don't be naïve. My husband owns a house in the Lake District and the villa on Gozo...I go there...to one or the other. Heavens, I am to be shot on sight if I go to Dorset...so I go to the house in the lake District or I go to Gozo. Sometimes alone, sometimes with a friend, if that friend is special enough...and there exists a vacancy for a special friend right now. Interested?'

'Very,' Christopher Elms held Virginia Woolley's hand, 'very, very.'

'Good,' she smiled. 'You've got the job. Start this weekend. Today in fact. I have work for you.'

'Work?'

'Yes…I want you to look at the garden of the house in the Lake District. It's flat and dull. I am convinced I can get Maurice to commission you to re-design it but you will of course have to make a site inspection.'

'Shouldn't take too long.'

'This will take from this evening until Sunday evening.' She smiled again. 'It's that sort of site inspection. Where do you live?'

'Cardigan Road.'

'Well, we'll pick up my car from the multi-storey…you can give me directions. Come on. This place suddenly seems very crowded.'

Christopher Elms, sitting in the front passenger seat, found that Virginia Woolley handled the car in an almost masterful manner, with the seat back as far as she could manage, not up close against the wheel in the overbearing way his father drove their small family saloon. Her movements were smooth and graceful and well coordinated, yet she controlled the car, she wasn't frightened of it, and she didn't fight it. She allowed her body to mesh with the machine as if it was just another component. 'First time I've been in a Mercedes. It's really…really impressive.'

She turned and smiled, allowing her eyes to leave the road for a split second. 'Well, Chris, you know that people say that if your first experience of anything is…is pleasurable, then it conditions your attitude to that experience for the rest of your life.'

'They say that?'

'Yes…so I hope you'll have many more impressive rides

in this and other Mercedes.'

Virginia Woolley drove sedately up Cardigan Road and turned left when Christopher Elms said, 'If you could turn in here...'

'What do I need?' he asked.

'Clothing for the weekend. We'll be coming back on Sunday evening...and a sketch pad to rough out some designs I can show Maurice. I'd like to come up with you, make sure you come back.' She reached out and held his hand. 'I'm not going to lose you this early in the game.'

'Okay,' he smiled. 'It's not much and it's a mess.'

'You're right and you're right...' She glanced about her. 'It's not much and it's a mess.' She viewed a small kitchenette, a smaller shower room with toilet, a room with a bed pushed in the corner and a settee and an armchair in front of a small gas fire. A wardrobe stood at the foot of the bed. 'Who else lives here?'

'Just me...no room for anyone else.'

'No...I mean in the building. It must have been a magnificent house once...just for one family...and servants.'

'Yes...quite some place.' He opened a battered holdall and began to feed clothing into it. 'The other rooms are like this...single employed professional people...thirteen flats all told. If the landlord finds out I'm a "doley" he'll throw me out...being in employment is a condition of the tenancy.'

'You were employed when you took the tenancy?'

'Yes, I was.'

She stood and watched him. There was a sense of strength about him. He had rolled up his sleeves and she saw clearly muscular forearms. His shoulders, too, seemed strongly developed. He knelt down, keeping his spine perpendicular and reached under the settee for a pair of training shoes. He was strong in the loins. "He'll do", she thought. "He'll do very nicely."

'Well...' He stood and smiled as he slung the holdall over his shoulder. 'I'm coming back...you haven't lost me. If we leave now, we'll miss the worst of the rush hour.'

She drove out to Harrogate. From Harrogate she drove to Knaresborough. 'There's a working-class affectation that insists this town is pronounced with a hard "k" not a silent "k"...you know, as if it should be pronounced "k-naresbor-ough" rather than "Naresborough"...strange, I have heard it often.'

'So have I. In fact, when I was a lad in Batley that's how we pronounced it. School took us to K-naresbrough for a trip...when I got to Newcastle I had to re-educate myself.'

They drove on in silence, leaving Knaresborough behind them; she then slowed and stopped the car at the side of the road. 'That,' she said pointing to a house that stood in its own grounds a field's distance from where the Mercedes was parked, 'is our house...Maurice and I...that's where we live.'

'Wow' was all he could say. He looked at the house, white painted, solid-looking, proud-looking. 'Third Georgian,' he said. 'Seventeen hundreds.'

'Very good.' She placed a gentle hand on his knee. 'The date above the door is 1775.'

'Well, landscape architecture has a bit of an overlap with architecture itself. He'd have to be good with figures to afford that pile of bricks.'

'Yes, he is...self-made, didn't inherit anything...it's all through his own industry that he acquired the White House.'

'Is that its name?'

'Yes...original, don't you think?'

'No.' And they chuckled together.

'Well...' she stopped laughing, 'Now you have to be seri-ous...we have to be serious. You do know what's happen-ing, don't you?'

'We are going to the Lake District for a couple of nights.'

'Well, yes...' she sat back in the driver's seat and once again took his hand, moving her thumb over his flesh in a slow, circular movement. 'Well...what is happening, Chris, is that you are beginning an affair with a married woman.'

Elms' heart thumped in his chest as he realised that "it" was finally going to happen to him.

'And when two people are having an extra-marital affair, they have to be discreet.'

'You've done this before?'

'Oh yes, with a marriage like mine, it's the only way a woman can survive. Women have their needs, as well as men.' She paused. 'My husband...he is impotent.'

'Oh...'

'He...we have never...as a couple.'

'I'm sorry.'

'Well, hardly your fault, Chris, but you see my interest in you...it isn't wholly emotional. You are interesting and intelligent and educated, we might be able to become good friends on that level alone...but I need more...you do too. We both do.'

'Yes,' he nodded, 'yes...I need more than that too.'

'I'll say you do, if at your age...well, that bit will come to an end this weekend. If you left your flat as a boy, you'll return as a man. We could make each other so happy.'

'Yes, Virginia.'

'That's the first time you've called me by name.' She squeezed his hand. 'Thank you.'

Elms shrugged. He smiled. He felt excited and sheepish at the same time.

'But, listen, we must be discreet...we must let discretion be our watchword.'

'Yes, Virginia.'

'So we mustn't be seen together and you mustn't leave any marks on me...understood?'

'Yes, Virginia.'

'Maurice isn't very possessive, so I can carry on a liaison

without too much difficulty…he also has a much younger sister and so seems to understand my need to visit Charlotte…but I can't come back with stupid juvenile "love bites" on my neck.'

'I appreciate that.'

'Alright, I am going to drive past the house, drop you at The Rising Sun…it's a pub three villages from here. Can't drop you in the nearest village, might be seen, or seen when I collect you. Have to rendezvous with you where I am not known.'

'You want me to get down out of sight?'

'Yes,' she smiled, 'that would be a good idea.'

Christopher Elms unbuckled the seat belt and slid down towards the footwell until his head was below the window.

'It's fun, isn't it?' She smiled as she drove away from the parking place. 'Exciting. It's more fun than being open, I often feel, adds to the "frisson".'

'Feels like I used to feel when wagging school. Playing with my mates by the stream in the fields was always more fun when we should have been in double maths.'

'You have an adventurous spirit, I like that in people, but in my lovers I like it especially.' They drove on for another few minutes until Virginia Woolley said, 'Alright, my sweet…you can get up again.'

Elms wiggled back up into the seat and fastened the safety belt. He saw that they were driving through open country and approaching a village, which revealed itself to be called Drayton St George. Virginia Woolley slowed as she approached the village and drove at a sedate pace, finally halting outside a black and white half-timbered pub with a yellow and brown sign swinging over the entrance proclaiming it to be the Rising Sun Inn.

'I'll be as quick as I can.' She looked at Elms intently. 'But I could still be as long as an hour.'

'An hour?'

'Yes…I have to pack and, being a woman, I tend to pack

for a weekend as if I were emigrating to Australia. I also have to tell Maurice where I am going and I have to seek his permission.'

'His permission?'

'His approval then…you'll know what it's like when you get married. I can't go in saying, "I'm going to visit Charlotte…be back on Sunday." It's more in the manner of saying, "I'm very sorry but would you mind dreadfully if I visit Charlotte this weekend? I know it's short notice but I really do want to see her." There will be a bit of persuading to be done but if I am lucky, he'll have been swimming in the whisky bottle since about three o'clock. He's very affable when he's tight.'

'Okay.'

'Have you any money?'

'Not a lot.'

'Alright…' she took ten pounds from her purse and handed it to him. 'Look, Chris, don't disappoint me by drinking too much while I'm gone…You've got to play your part this evening.'

'Understood. I'll walk around the village…read the names on the war memorial, it's something I do as a gesture of…of something, humility…gratitude. It's a fine day, I can keep out of the pub.'

She leaned across and held his head and kissed him on the mouth. His arm slid round her shoulders.

'Shall we say one hour?' She broke the embrace. 'Outside the Rising Sun…just here…one hour.'

Virginia Woolley turned the Mercedes round in a skilfully executed three point turn and drove back to the White House, arriving twenty minutes after leaving Christopher Elms in Drayton St George. She pulled up outside the front door and strode up the steps and let herself into the house, and was refreshed by the cool interior. She called out, 'Hello,' and heard her own voice echo in the hallway and corridors. There was no answer and she said softly, 'Hello, welcome home…how was the trial?' She walked towards the drawing room and said, 'Thanks, it's good to be home. He was guilty but we felt we had to acquit…he smirked…shouldn't have done that…upset the jury he did. But it's better that one hundred guilty men go free than for one innocent man to be convicted.' She opened the drawing room door and entered. 'Ah, here you are, my sweet.' She approached her husband, who sat asleep in a deep armchair. She stopped to pick up a near empty bottle of Bells that lay in his lap. 'It's not even five o'clock yet…you'd sleep through the burglar alarm in this state. Well, I just called to grab a change of clothes, my sweet, because I am going to spend the weekend with my sister.' She smiled. 'Okay?' She paused, then added, 'You know, you are a very good boy, a very good boy indeed, this will make things easier. And being the loving, dutiful wife I am, I will make up a round of sandwiches for you. You'll be hungry when you wake up.' She turned on her heels and strode out of the drawing room and climbed the stairs to their bedroom. There she peeled off the uncomfortable clothes, which she had worn all that day, kicking off the equally uncomfortable heels as she did so. She then poured herself into a pair of jeans, a rugby shirt and a pair of trainers. She then packed a suitcase for the weekend, over-packing as was her wont on such occasions and carried the suitcase downstairs and left it in the hall. She walked from the hall to the kitchen and made up a plate of sandwiches for her husband, beside which she left a note reading, "Gone to my sisters – back Sunday, much love, Virginia". She sat at the table and thought. She talked aloud, 'Am I certain? Am I going to go through with this? Perhaps…perhaps I should settle for what I've got, it's more than enough. It's not going to do me much good if this goes wrong…all that in the bank and I'll still be eating porridge…if I start I can't stop…if I start, it goes the full road.' She drummed her fingers on the tabletop. 'But if I am careful…won't be so easy this time, but if I am careful…Alright,' she stood. 'Let's do it…let's go the full road.' She crossed the kitchen floor with, an observer might have noted, a forced deliberateness in her walk, and took the largest knife from the nest of knives and carried it knife back to where she had left her suitcase. She placed the knife in the suitcase, closed the suitcase, and carried it outside. She locked the door of the White House behind her and drove back to Drayton St George, and to an excited Christopher Elms, whom she found waiting patiently for her outside the Rising Sun.

They drove to Penrith and then followed the A592 down the side of Ullswater to Windermere. The last hour of the journey was undertaken in complete silence, and yet with increasing excitement and trepidation. The silence was only broken when Virginia Woolley turned the Mercedes into the driveway of a large, rambling Victorian house set in its own grounds and said, 'Well, this is it.'

Christopher Elms gasped. 'Your husband owns this as well?'

'Yes.' She glanced over at him. 'It's quite lavishly furnished inside as well, as you will see.'

'And the villa in Malta?'

'Gozo…but yes, a villa as well.'

In the house, Virginia Woolley invited Elms to "explore" whilst she turned the gas on at the main and ran the cold tap, allowing the water in the system to flush and replenish itself. Christopher Elms returned to the kitchen to find Virginia Woolley boiling a kettle. 'It's huge,' he shook his head in disbelief at his exploration and the discovery therein. 'My dad's council house in Batley, it would fit in the living room…and that includes the roof…and my flat in Leeds, well, it would fit into this kitchen…with space to spare.'

'It gets to seem small,' she poured boiling water into a teapot. 'After the White House, this seems cramped. It's a question of what you are used to. Take a seat. How do you like your tea?'

'Tea? Oh…just milk, please.' He slid onto a wooden chair at the table. He heard his own voice tremble.

'Nervous?'

'Yes…yes…a bit.'

'A lot, I'd say, young man, you're shaking. Well, it's natural…we are all nervous the first time. In fact, I don't think I'd like you if you weren't nervous…it's healthy to be nervous. Women are nervous about what it will feel like…men are nervous in case they can't "do" it.' She handed him a mug of tea.

'Yes…' Christopher gripped the mug of tea with both hands. 'Yes…that's what I'm frightened of.'

'Well, don't worry…I am a patient teacher. I will teach you what to do, teach you how to make love to me… It is, after all, in both our interests. Have you at least seen a naked woman before?' She sat in the chair adjacent to his.

He shook his head. 'Only in pictures…you know, magazines.'

'I put the immersion heater on when you were exploring. This is number 23 Collingham Bridge Road, by the way…haven't got a name for this house… There was one poor tiger that hadn't got a Christian.'

'Sorry?'

'Old joke…just came to mind. The water will be hot enough for a bath in about an hour's time…so…we'll drink the tea, go up and make the bed, the linen's in the airing cupboard, then, when the water's hot enough, we'll take a bath, together. You can soap my body all over and I can soap yours…all over. Then, when we are dry, we can creep softly into bed…together. Do you like the sound of that?' She reached across the table and held his hand.

'Yes,' he nodded. 'Yes, I do like the sound of that. I like the sound of that very much, very much indeed.'

Two hours later they lay side by side, folded in each other's arms as the mid-evening sun sank over Lake

Windermere.

'You were very good.' She kissed him. 'You gave rather than took...you seemed to want to please me more than yourself, that's quite unusual in a man so young.'

'It was great. I didn't know women could be like that.'

'Multiple? Not all can...I suppose I'm one of the lucky ones,' she kissed him on the forehead, 'but not all men can make me multiple like that,' she whispered. 'I'm very lucky to have found you, Chris, very lucky indeed. You see now, don't you...with a husband who is impotent...you see why you are so good for me.'

'And for me...you know this afternoon, you said that if your first experience at something is a good experience, then it conditions your attitude to whatever that thing is for the rest of your life?'

'Yes.'

'Well, I know what you mean...I know exactly what you mean.'

She kissed him again. 'Well, tiger in the sheets, I'm getting hungry...don't know about you.'

'Ravenous.'

'Okay. We'll claw our kit back on, walk into Windermere, find an eatery...in fact, I know just the place...then a quiet pub...then...'

'Back here?'

'Yes, then back here.'

Gwendoline Fay watched her children, both teenagers, playing badminton on the rear lawn of her property. She was filled with pride and a sense of fulfilment. Then she shuddered as the realisation attacked her, as it so often did, that she, and subsequently they, were only alive because of a small amount of liquid and a turn of fate. She didn't know how much a "tot" of rum was, but it wasn't a large amount, she thought, perhaps about the same as the amount of milk that is put in a mug of coffee to make it white. And it was because of that they were in the world, she established, and they, they about to enter university...all because of a tot of rum.

He would recall later, when subsequent events had soured what he then believed to be a wonderful experience, how brightly the sun shone into the bedroom on that Saturday morning. How they had begun the day with more moaning and screaming and thrashing about, how she had then rolled out of her side of the bed murmuring something about walking into Windermere to buy breakfast and saying that they should have stopped to purchase food on the way there. He watched as she glided naked across the floor round the foot of the bed and then stopped. She seemed to be stepping into something and then she said, 'Your shoes fit me.' She smiled at him. 'You've got small feet, or I've got big ones.' She stepped out of his shoes and knelt and picked them up and examined them. 'They're worn out.'

'A bit of life left in them yet.' He lay on his back with his hands behind his head, wondering at the perfection of her body, and noting how the sun caught isolated strands of her hair.

'Nonsense,' she turned to him and looked at him warmly, 'there's hardly any tread left.'

'They're all I've got really, apart from some heavier winter shoes.'

'Well, these are going in the bin.'

'What am I going to wear?' There was a hint of panic in his voice. 'I can't afford a new pair.'

'Well, you are not a doley anymore...you are a rich woman's plaything and you are going to win your first commission to design a garden.'

'I am?'

'Yes...and yes to both. You stay there, I am going to walk into the village, come back with some bacon and eggs...sausage...black pudding...we'll have a proper breakfast. I'll also get food for tomorrow. A joint of something.'

'I'll come with you.'

'No...you stay there, I like walking alone in the mornings. I like being a dutiful woman, buying the food, cooking the meal, doing the washing up. I'll be back shortly.' She left the room carrying his shoes with her. He lay there listening to her take a shower, gasping at the coldness of the water, then dressing in another room, going downstairs, unlocking the door and stepping out into the sunlight. He heard her feet on the gravel drive. He listened as they stopped. He heard the rattle of a bunch of keys, a click of a lock, the thud of the boot of her car being closed. Had he watched from the window, he would have seen Virginia Woolley carry a plastic bag from the house to the car, a bag that clearly contained something. He would have seen her open the boot and place the plastic bag therein. Had he been close enough to hear, he would have heard her say, 'good boy', as she closed the boot of the car on the plastic bag, and his shoes, which the bag contained.

She returned from the village in less than an hour and let herself into the house and climbed the stairs to their room. She had dressed, he saw, in a long denim skirt and a cheese-cloth blouse. She held a shoebox in her hand. 'It's lovely out,' she said. 'It's going to be easy to buy shoes for you, all I have to do is try them for size. Have a present...from me to you.' She handed him the shoebox. 'Not a great selection. We'll go into Penrith or even Carlisle, if you like...these are just to enable you to walk from the house.'

He opened the box. 'Oh! Virginia! Nikes. These are not just to walk from the house, they're fantastic.'

'Glad you like them.'

'Where are my old ones? I could still use them round the flat...like a pair of slippers.'

'They're in the rubbish already...forget them, they're history. Breakfast in thirty minutes. Up you get, young man. The water in the shower is ice cold…you'll love it.'

Christopher Elms found that day to be joyful. A walk by the lakeside after breakfast, then a drive to Penrith to purchase more clothes…another pair of shoes…two pairs of jeans, half a dozen shirts, a flat cap which she insisted would suit him. They lunched in Penrith and then returned to the house in Windermere. At his own insistence, Christopher Elms spent the afternoon in the garden of the house, making rough measurements and preliminary sketches.

'I think I can do something for your husband,' he said as he entered the kitchen, where she sat reading a copy of *The Times*.

'Good.' She glanced at him and smiled. 'How long will it take you to do the drawings?'

'The plans…about a week's work. You have one or two established trees, I'll work round them.'

'Is that what you do?'

'Yes…plan round established trees, if they're healthy, and yours seem to be. I'll start work on Monday.'

'Good. I'm sure I can convince him to accept your plans.' She folded the newspaper and laid it on the kitchen table. She stood and took his sketchpad and pen from him and laid those on the table also. 'Lock the door,' she said. He turned and locked the door, then turned back to her. She hooked a finger round his shirt collar and drew him to her, kissed him and said, 'Let's go up.'

They remained in the bedroom until the following morning.

It was, he recalled, a leisurely Sunday. They were both reluctant to leave the bed but hunger forced them up for breakfast, followed by a further devouring, this time of the Sunday papers. Again they walked by the lake, silently, arm in arm, stopping occasionally to kiss and embrace. They returned to the house in the mid-afternoon, whereupon Virginia Woolley retired to the kitchen to prepare the roast dinner and Christopher Elms sat in the living room, feeling deeply content and fulfilled, and spent the remainder of the day making sketches of his plan for the redesign of his lover's husband's garden.

Three hours later Virginia Woolley invited him to come to sit at the kitchen table. He washed his hands and complied eagerly, though he tried to muster a sense of calm about him. Once seated, Virginia Woolley laid out a feast before him; roast pork and vegetables.

'Oh...' he sighed, 'this is a rare treat. I haven't eaten like this since...'

'Well, I hope you enjoy it.' She sat in her chair, hands on her lap.

He too sat, hands on his lap.

She looked at him. 'Carve,' she said.

'Sorry?'

'Carve, Chris...man's job.'

'Oh...yes...' He stood and reached for the knife and carving fork that lay beside the joint and roughly and inexpertly began to slice through the meat. After the meal, after a brief rest, Christopher Elms said, 'Well, I'll do the washing up, it's only fair...you cooked, I'll wash.' He reached for his plate and the bowl that had contained the roast potatoes.

'No.' Her voice was soft, yet had a distinct firmness about it.

'No?'

'I told you earlier...woman's work is woman's work.'

He reclined back in his chair. 'Well, if you insist.'

'I insist.'

'No one will ever call you a "new age woman".'

She smiled. 'Off with you...go and lie down on the couch.' He stood and walked to the living room, closing the kitchen door behind him. Virginia Woolley watched him go and she then reached forward and picked up the carving knife by the tip of the blade, then moved her fingers to the hilt. She wiped the blade down with a cloth and washed it with warm soapy water, but took care not to wipe or wash the handle. Having wiped the blade of her own prints, she held it by a cloth and dropped it into a plastic bag, which she then carried outside and placed in the boot of her Mercedes beside the plastic containing Christopher Elms' training shoes.

Richard Pulleyne rolled out of bed, washed and groped around the room looking for suitable clothing to wear. With most of his clothing in the bulging laundry basket ready to be carried to the laundrette, he realised that this was clearly one of those days when less than suitable clothing was going to have to be worn. The suit he had worn yesterday could be worn again that day, but he had to settle for a thick, heavy shirt, more suited to winter than summer and a pair of heavy woollen socks, again, more suitable for the colder months. They would have to do. Still feeling bleary eyed, he made his way to the kitchen and tried to avoid looking at the mountain of washing up in the sink. He boiled some water, sufficient to make a single mug of tea, and smeared jam onto a slice of bread. It would have to suffice until he got to the station, and the canteen, which kept him alive these days.

There was a stony silence between the man and the woman. They sat in the drawing room of the White House avoiding eye contact with each other. The woman glanced round the room, looking at anything, anything or anybody except the man; the chintzy decorations, cheap and tacky, she thought, which did not go at all with the outside image of the house; the large, widescreen colour television, so, so gross, she thought, so tasteless, but at least the computer with all its silly games was in an upstairs room. She glanced out of the window at the expanse of lawn behind the house and the small wood beyond the lawn, and the two fields beyond the wood that had been left to grass over, all of which belonged to the estate of the White House.

'It's only because I am concerned for you, Maurice.' The woman broke the silence, suddenly appealing to the man.

'Weren't concerned for me before. I was an

embarrassment to you all you life...you didn't even want me at your wedding, then my life changes and you're round here everyday.'

'It's only...'

'Because you are concerned for me...yes, you said.'

'I don't want to see you being taken advantage of.'

'She is not taking advantage of me.'

'So where is Madam the Queen?'

'Prison visiting.'

'Ha! That's a new one.' The woman sneered with derision and then glared at a fly that buzzed in through one of the open windows and began to explore its strange, new surroundings. 'Usually she visits her "sister". Now I find out she's a lady bountiful who visits criminals. I bet she's even visiting the animal that burgled our house...that would be just too rich.'

'She's a good woman...and she has got a sister.'

'I dare say she has, but perhaps you don't understand what she means when she says she is "visiting her sister".'

'I think I do.' The man shrugged his left shoulder. 'But what can I do? There's never any proof...and she has needs I can't answer.'

'You don't mind!'

'No.' Maurice Woolley shook his head. 'She comes back and I need her. I need an attractive woman in the house...the house needs a woman's presence. If I tried to stop her going away, she'd leave for good.'

'Going away? You mean she's out overnight some times?'

'Yes.'

'More than one night?'

'Yes...weekends mostly...sometimes a couple of weeks.'

'A fortnight!'

'Yes...' He looked sheepish. 'I have an idea where she goes. But she comes back. That's the main thing.'

The woman sank back and rested her head in her hands. 'That's not a marriage, Maurice.'

'It's better than what I had before.'

'And you're drunk each day and not just with beer either.'

'No, I am not...not that bad. I drink a bottle then spend two days recovering...sometimes three, so I drink a bottle about twice a week.'

'You hardly ever used to drink at all.'

'No money before.' He forced a smile.

'I'm only trying to protect you, Maurice. Sometimes only a woman can understand another woman. Mother and father wouldn't have allowed her anywhere near you, mother especially, you know how shrewd she was.'

'Too bloody shrewd. One of the reasons I never got wed was her shrewdness...no girl was ever good enough for me in her eyes.'

'That, and the fact you could never hold down a job longer than a month.'

'Two,' he said after a pause. 'Held a job for two months...and I didn't leave it, I got laid off.'

'Washing dishes in a Chinese restaurant. I remember that one.'

'The owner got a couple of illegals who washed for a pound a day plus keep. He was paying me minimum wage...a few pounds an hour...he had real control over them, real control. Anyway, mother and father are not here anymore. Mother's not in a position to object about anyone and I don't need to work.'

'I don't know...sometimes I think it was better before, money was tight but we were rubbing along...if we hadn't got this...this mess...that gold digger wouldn't be in this family and you wouldn't have a drink problem.'

'I'm not an alcoholic.'

'That's what they all say. Anyway...' she reached for her handbag, 'she'll be back soon from her good works. I don't want to run into her...doubt if she wants to run into me.' She stood. 'You need protection, Maurice, as much from yourself as from other people.'

René Lucas stood on the bridge, leaning against the parapet. She wore cool summer clothing and had a relaxed posture. An observer would see a woman in her prime, taking a moment to enjoy the view of the river and the townscape and the hills beyond. But for her – feeling as though a house brick was inside her stomach, the sense of failure, the sense of betrayal – for her, it was not the view that was inviting, it was the drop of the fall, hundreds of feet into the water. It was that which she found inviting.

Some hours earlier than when her husband and sister-in-law had conversed, Virginia Woolley thought that they could not be very good; in fact, she thought that they were not any good, any good at all. She did, though, wonder who was hiring him, or them. She doubted that it was her husband. She didn't think he'd actually want to know the truth, but her catty sister-in-law, she'd be capable of doing it, she had the means, after all. Again it was the same van, the same white 5cwt Renault with the one-way mirrors in the rear doors. They looked black but wouldn't be street legal unless the driver could see out of them via his rearview mirror. A single male driver, she noticed, and so easy to lose when it suited her to do so, play the stupid female driver and go through the lights just as they changed to red, invite a few blasts on the horn from irate motorists, but Jack the Lad in the Renault is left standing. Alternatively, she would drive onto the motorway and she, in her Mercedes, had usually lost the small Renault by the time she had reached the next exit.

That morning she had picked up her escort, as she referred to the van, immediately upon leaving the White House and had allowed it to follow her as she drove towards Knaresborough. At Knaresborough she took the A59 and drove sedately through summer pastures, with the little white Renault van in dogged attendance. She turned onto the A1 and put the pedal to the metal. By the time she reached the Boroughbridge exit six miles further north she had lost her follower.

She drove south on Deere Street and then rejoined the A59, followed it to the Ring Road round York, which took her through Rawcliffe and Huntingdon, turned onto the A166 to Stamford Bridge and thence to Full Sutton and onto to H.M. Prison.

She waited in the car park with the window down, listening to the bird song, watching the other people all clearly waiting for that day's discharge. They seemed, she thought, to be a very hard-bitten crew in the main, with cold, soulless eyes, clearly unabashed at waiting at the gates of one of Her Majesty's guesthouses. One or two even looked proud that their son or husband had done his "bird", got his gaol time under his belt, the rite of passage being completed, then serious inroads into the underworld could be travelled, and serious money made. One young woman stood apart from the group, she was well dressed, she had clearly put a lot of effort into making herself look her best to meet her lover/husband, but yet looked awkward, arms folded, head lowered, as if having been pressed into service. As if, thought Virginia Woolley, she carried a sign, that read, "I do not want to be with this man, but how do I escape?" Virginia Woolley was not close enough to see if the young woman was wearing a wedding band, though she guessed that she would be, otherwise she probably wouldn't have been standing there looking as if she wanted to be many miles away and safely in the arms of another man. Also distancing themselves from the group was a middle-aged couple who sat in a clean and polished Volvo, both staring straight ahead, neither of them talking. Not for them pride in a loved one who had completed his rite of passage. For them, thought Virginia Woolley, there was the shame of a loved one who had strayed and who had brought dishonour to a good name. Yet they had arrived to whisk him away to safety. Good for them, she thought. Good for them.

A door within the gates of the prison opened and a stream of men, mostly in their twenties, emerged in single file. They paused, blinking against the sun, then turned inward and briefly shook hands before the group fragmented, with each man, save two, walking towards those who had come to meet him. They were met with handshakes and embraces in the main. One man with his head hung low walked at a rapid pace to the Volvo, got in the rear seat, at which the car was driven speedily and angrily away. Another man approached the isolated young woman and enthusiastically threw his arms round her; her response was, thought Virginia Woolley, perfunctory, if anything and she said aloud, 'Oh, get out, pet. Get out while you can, get out while you still have your youth!' Two men who were not met walked together, yet separately, to the bus stop at the edge of the car park and sat at either end of the bench from each other. One fair-haired young man remained at the gates. Virginia Woolley flashed the headlights of the Mercedes Benz and the young man walked confidently towards her.

He opened the passenger door and slid into the seat levering a small holdall onto the rear seat as he did so.

'Hi,' she smiled and turned the ignition key.

'Thanks for coming.' Shane Parsloe breathed deeply. 'Fresh air...you don't know how good it feels! Blue sky...green...'

'I said I'd come.' She drove away. 'Let's get out of here, too much CCTV for my liking. Do you know how long they keep the tapes?'

'No. Can't see them keeping them at all unless something happens. You ought to have hired a car.'

'I thought of it but realised it wouldn't have made any difference, they could still trace me through the number plate.'

'Aye...suppose.'

She handed him an envelope. 'Here's the money.'

He took the envelope and counted it as Virginia Woolley turned onto the public highway. 'What's this? A hundred? You said three thousand...a thousand for every year I was sentenced to.'

'And I will keep my promise. Do you fancy a beer?'

'Do I? But a hundred...I could get angry with you. That's not a clever thing to do, to get me angered...you know what I'm saying?'

'Hush,' she glanced at him, 'you'll get your money.'

'I'd better, I know where you live.'

'I know you do, that's why you'll get your money. Just be patient.' She drove into Stamford Bridge and turned into the car park of a pub. 'We could probably get lunch here, it's time you learned again to choose what you want to eat.'

Shane Parsloe remained silent. Virginia Woolley could sense that he was flushed with anger.

She halted the car and switched off the engine. 'This is too public to do anything stupid.' She spoke with a menacing tone. 'So don't.'

In the pub Parsloe gulped down the first beer with speed and desperation, which drew a look of disapproval from the publican. Virginia Woolley saw that he was clearly used to released lags from Full Sutton stopping off at his pub for their first beer in many years. She could also see that he didn't like it. Parsloe had two more, both drunk with equal speed. Only on the fourth did he slow and seem to want to savour the drink.

'Can we buy a meal here?' Virginia Woolley asked the publican.

'If you'd choose a table,' came the snarling reply, 'I'll send a waitress over.'

'Thank you.' She carried her soda water and lime to a table by a window. Parsloe followed with the remnants of his fourth beer. 'I see you've proved my point,' she said as he sat opposite her.

'Oh yes?' He eyed her with rage. 'I did three years and

you give me a lousy hundred.'

'Listen...keep your voice down. I see this pub has CCTV...just can't escape it...so don't do anything that will make them call the busies, alright? Keep...calm...'

Parsloe gripped the beer glass with whitening knuckles. 'I...am...calm...'

'Okay. You'll get your three thousand. You just won't get it in a oner, that's all.'

'You said...'

'No...' she raised an admonishing finger, 'I said nothing but promising you three thousand, a thousand for every year of your sentence. I could have said a thousand for every year you served, or a hundred quid for every week – you would be coming out to eighteen hundred pounds – but you were sentenced to three, so you'll get three thousand. But I never said you'd get it in one go. You are going to get one hundred pounds in cash each week from now on, until you have received three thousand pounds.'

'But...I can't live on that!' He spluttered the words.

'It's not intended that you live on it. There's the dole...there's employment...and, in your case, there's crime. You are already a skilled housebreaker; a good break-in can net you hundreds, thousands, for a few moments' work. You'll survive.' She sipped her drink then sat back as the waitress coldly approached them. She seemed, to Virginia Woolley, to be under orders from the publican to be cold and distant. He clearly didn't want the Odd Fellows Arms to become a blaggers' pub. As if unable to make a decision Parsloe meekly asked for what Virginia Woolley had ordered: gammon steak with chips. 'You see,' Virginia Woolley continued when the waitress had withdrawn, 'if I were to give you three thousand all at once, you'd flash and splash it around and you'd draw attention to yourself and the busies would want to know where it came from. This way you get your three K, but it will trickle in.'

'It'll take years!'

'Not that long...one hundred pounds a week, thirty weeks, it will only take about seven months.'

Parsloe remained silent.

'It's in your interest...and in mine. It went pear-shaped, nobody's fault...Look at it this way, if you had done it and then it had gone pear-shaped, you'd be doing a life stretch. You've been stung but you didn't get burned. You're in your twenties, plenty of time ahead for you. Learn to keep your mouth shut...let your beer money trickle in over the next few months. I'll post it to your parents' address on the "Dial".'

'I might not be living there soon, I'm moving on as soon as.'

'Well, it'll make you visit them once a week, like the good son you are. I'll post it so that it arrives on Friday or Saturday.'

'Friday or Saturday?'

'Well, sometimes the post is delayed. So if I post it mid-day each Thursday by first class, just a plain envelope, type-written address...I'll wipe my prints off it and post it from...from a long way from where I live, won't be traced to me... It'll definitely be there on the Saturday.'

Parsloe slid his hand across the table and held her hand. 'Virginia...eighteen months, it's a long time to...'

'No!' She pulled her hand away as if jolted by an electric charge. 'Whatever happened between us is over...do you hear? Do you understand? Over, finished...we'll never see each other again after today.'

A look of anger entered Parsloe's eyes. 'Three thousand? I might need more. You know what I'm saying?'

'Yes, I know what you're saying and it won't do you any good, any good at all. If you go to the police, you'll only be dropping yourself in it. You'll be confessing to attempted murder, and it's only your word against mine and you are a convicted felon.' She paused. 'You know, you are not meant to know this, but very recently, a week or so ago, I was present when a man was acquitted of murder, even though he was guilty, the weight of evidence just was not there, the Crown just did not prove its case. I've been very cautious, it'll be your word against mine.' Again she paused. 'You've got a lot going for you, you'll pull through. Did you make contacts inside?'

'A few.'

'So you've got street-cred amongst the blaggers, you could use that. Can't see you going straight, the money's too easy on the wrong side of the law, and the only crime you mustn't commit is the crime of getting caught. Remember that.' She looked up. 'Where's the damn food?'

Virginia Woolley dropped Shane Parsloe off at the entrance to the Halton Dial estate saying that she'd like to drop him at his parents' door but the "Dial" is no place to take a Mercedes Benz, even in daylight. Then she said, 'You keep your mouth shut, for your sake and mine...and I will keep my word about a weekly envelope arriving on Friday or Saturday.' She drove away slowly, drove across the city to Cardigan Road, parked neatly in a cul-de-sac off the main road and walked up to the door of a large Victorian era house. At the door she pressed the bell beside the name "C Elms".

She warmed at the look of unconcealed delight, which rose across Christopher Elms' face as he opened the door in response to her ringing his doorbell. 'Hello.' She allowed her voice to warble with warmth. 'I didn't think you'd mind if I called unexpectedly. I hope you are not entertaining any of your other female admirers.' She stepped forward; they kissed then embraced.

'Oh yes,' he said when his mouth was free of hers, 'they're all here...care to meet them?'

'I think I'd better, make sure they measure up, nothing but the best for my young man.'

Sitting on the floor in his cramped flat, sipping coffee, he called out, 'I've been working on the drawings. I think I can come up with something that will impress your husband.'

Virginia Woolley returned from the bedroom in response to his call. 'There's no hurry, and forget him anyway.' She placed her mug of coffee in a space on the bookshelf and stood in front of him, running her fingers through his hair. 'When did you last change the linen on your bed?'

'I don't know...a few weeks...'

'A few weeks! Men!' She began to unbutton his shirt. 'Never mind, it'll have to do.'

'You mean...?'

'Yes, Christopher, I mean a woman doesn't call on her lover in the middle of the day for coffee...she has other things in mind.'

Later, afterwards, they lay side by side in silence, listening to the steady rumble of traffic on Cardigan Road, which was punctuated once by the blues and twos of an emergency vehicle dashing to the scene of some crime or some tragedy.

'We couldn't have done that at any other time,' he spoke softly, turning towards her.

'No...I am an anytime sort of woman, any place as well. We'll have to do it out of doors soon, while the summer's with us...it's often more fun...never as comfortable as in a bed, but more fun.'

'No, I mean the noise you make. In the house in the Lake District, in Windermere, that's one thing, but here...we are the only people in the building at the moment but soon...soon they'll be returning...the other tenants. I swear you'd think you and they were in the same room.'

'I see. I don't like stifling my screams...we'll have to bear that in mind, midweek, midday is our time...until we go away again.'

He smiled. 'Yes, I'm not in a hurry to get a job now, that can wait.'

'Especially since Maurice will commission you to redesign the garden in Windermere.'

'You think he will?'

'I know he will. What sort of fee will you charge?'

'For a full set of drawings for a garden of that scale...about three thousand pounds. That'll keep me in kebabs and other takeaway delicacies for a few months.'

She ran her fingers over his ribcage. 'I'll cook up another meal for us.'

'When?'

'Later this week, possibly next. I can't call every day. I'm on my way back from Armley, my route went right by this building and so...'

'Armley?'

'The prison, I'm a prison visitor. You can smell the testosterone in a male prison...made me randy, so I pressed your doorbell.'

'And I thought you were interested in me for my mind.'

'I am...as well.'

'As well?'

'As well as your delicious, young, firm and slender body. It is especially desirable if you are saddled with a husband like my husband. Oh, and the fact that you don't drink much at all...Maurice – it's probably about 4 p.m. – he'll be comatose by now. He'd be able to strip paint with his breath if he wasn't sleeping it off.'

There fell another period of silence, broken when Christopher Elms asked, 'Virginia, how long does it take to fall in love?'

'About as long as a piece of string. It can happen quite quickly, in my experience. Takes less time to fall out of love.'

'What does it feel like? Love, I mean...what does it feel like?'

'You'll know when you are in love.'

'Virginia, I think I am there now.'

She smiled. He saw her smile and returned the smile. He did not, could not, see her inner smile, much broader, much deeper than her outward smile, nor could he know that she was thinking, "You are my very good boy. My very good boy indeed". He did hear her say, 'Come…let's do it again, before your neighbours come home.'

An hour later they stood beside her Mercedes Benz in the cul-de-sac of Spring Road. The traffic on Cardigan Road was nose-to-tail. 'I've got to join that. Hate traffic.'

'You said we had to be discreet yet you wanted me to walk you to your car?'

'This is being discreet, Maurice won't come anywhere near here. You have to be careful if you are in the vicinity of the White House, that's where discretion comes in. You must not phone me, I will phone you. Keep your brain-fryer with you at all times.'

'Yes, ma'am!' Said with a smile. 'Well, you don't have to go yet. The university is down, the pubs round here will be empty, we could have a drink and a chat for an hour, the rush hour will be virtually over by then.'

She glanced at her watch, then at the stationary traffic. 'Probably won't be home any earlier, will I? Alright. Where shall we go?' She glanced about her at the small copse that was Sparrow Wood in full, glorious foliage, which somehow had miraculously escaped having its railings removed at the outbreak of war in 1939. She listened to the birdsong, and looked up at the blue sky, the airliner flying low overhead, undercarriage lowered on its final approach to Leeds Bradford Airport. The blue sky beyond, vast, cloudless.

'I like living near an airport.' Christopher Elms followed her gaze. 'Planes landing fascinate me, they are losing a dimension.'

'A dimension?' She hooked her arm inside his. 'Explain.'

'Well, a plane, when flying, is in three dimensions: it can go side to side, forwards, up or down, but upon landing is loses the up and down dimension…fascinates me.'

She smiled a warm smile, with hugely dilated pupils. 'You are very clever, I wouldn't have thought of that.'

'Or a railway line. I could rather fancy living next to a railway line. The sound of trains is very soothing.'

'Well, where are we going for a drink? Beer for you, I dare say, dare say you've earned it…fruit juice for me.'

'We'll go up the Oak, there is a pleasant absence of loud music in the Oak this time of day.'

Virginia Woolley reached the White House just as her sister-in-law was about to take her leave. Mabel waited by her car as Virginia Woolley approached and stopped her car by the front door. She got out, stern-faced, both women stood staring at each other, standing as far from each other as a normal speaking voice would permit. Any further apart, Virginia Woolley thought, and they'd have to raise their voices to communicate.

'I was hoping to avoid you,' the elder of the two women said icily. She would be seen, perhaps, as middle-aged, a little overweight but by no means obese, a short cropped, functional hairstyle, sensible summer shoes, an equally sensible, age appropriate, light blue dress. She wore an expensive looking watch and a chunky gold necklace dangled round her neck. She held a bunch of car keys in her right hand.

'Can't say I'm overjoyed at meeting you.' Virginia Woolley stood still, holding her ground.

'Been visiting your sister, I suppose?' The elder woman opened the driver's door of a silver volvo. She shrank back from the blast of hot air and bent down to open the window.

'No. Armley Prison, if you must know.'

'Armley? That's a man's prison. The likes of you belong in Wood Hall.'

'I know it's a man's prison. I'm a prison visitor.'

'You!' The elder woman snorted with derision. 'You a do-gooder? Don't make me laugh.'

'Happens to be true.'

'Don't think I don't know what you are about...visiting your sister...I'll get the proof of exactly what that means.'

Virginia Woolley remained stone-faced. Inwardly she smiled and thought, "So it's you. I should have guessed. Mind you, with your background, your contacts, you could have hired someone who knew what he was doing. But thanks anyway, I can turn that to my advantage." She then said, after a period of silence. 'I doubt it will make any difference, I think I know my husband better than you know your brother.'

'Remarkable, isn't it? My brother has never been able to attract any female. Not once in his life has he had a partner, no girlfriend, no lover, no one. Then at his age, suddenly, a glamour piece easily young enough to be his daughter falls into his lap professing...professing...professing whatever it is Maurice wants to hear. You and I know why you're interested in Maurice. You've got eight million reasons why you are interested in him.'

'Perhaps you are right,' Virginia Woolley sniffed. 'Let's just say you are right, does that make me any different from you, Mrs Strong?'

'What's that supposed to mean?' Mabel Strong snarled her question.

'Maurice told me about you...ashamed of him, hiding him from your friends, telling him not to attend your wedding. Even despite that he gave you a million pounds, but that didn't satisfy you, did it? Now you don't leave him alone. I bet I can also think of eight million reasons why you are suddenly the very concerned, very protective, little sister. You see we are not so different, you and I, we are both driven by the same greed...except I am a lot closer than you, and that's what you don't like.'

'You admit it?'

'Of course,' Virginia Woolley smiled. 'There's no one to hear us...your word against mine.'

'I could be taping you.'

'But you are not. You haven't tried to provoke me into saying something I'll regret, and you said yourself you were hoping to avoid me...so perhaps you're right...or perhaps you are wrong. I might even be the doting, loving wife you doubt I am. But either way, all I have to do is to wait until Maurice kicks the bucket and then this house and what is left of the eight million will be mine. Not yours. Maurice let me read his will.'

'His will?'

'Yes. I am the only person that has shown him any affection, or respect in his life...it all goes to me, a proper reward for a dutiful wife.'

'All to you...all?'

Virginia Woolley nodded. 'All. You don't even get a mention. All I have to do is wait...his age...the extent to which he drinks so as to fill up an empty life. I won't have to wait too long. In the interim my needs are adequately met by visiting my sister in Hull.'

'Your sister! That damned publicity...No sooner has his win been made public than you arrive from nowhere with a cock and bull, hard luck story about being a grieving widow, and you just happen to bump into my brother when he's buying everybody drinks in the King's Arms. How convenient... How very contrived, I say.'

'Dorset.'

'What?'

'Dorset. I didn't come from anywhere, I came up from Dorset...too many memories there...And I am a widow, my late husband, Mr Woostencroft, he drowned.'

'So you told us.'

'He didn't leave me much. Came north to make a new start.'

'My heart bleeds for you.'

Virginia Woolley smiled. 'Thank you, I appreciate your sympathy, but if you'll excuse me, I have to go make my husband's dinner.'

The following morning Virginia Woolley left the White House and drove slowly to Christopher Elms' address. The small white van followed her immediately she left the grounds of the White House and, on this occasion, Virginia Woolley made no attempt to shake it off. On that morning she wanted her movements to be catalogued.

She drove to the city, to Cardigan Road, and parked in Spring Road, followed by the small white van, always a few cars behind. She parked her car and walked towards the building in which Christopher Elms had rented rooms and reached the door just as the white van turned off Cardigan Road and parked near to where she had parked her car.

One and a half hours later, she and Christopher Elms emerged from the house, arm in arm, wearing light summer clothing, very content in each other's company, so a passerby might think, and would probably be amused and pleased for them, by turns, that they were not at all troubled by their evident age gap. As she stepped over the threshold of the house Virginia Woolley saw that the white van had not moved and pondered the pleasure she had had in the last ninety minutes compared with the ninety minutes of discomfort which the private investigator had spent sitting in the rear of the van, waiting like a preying paparazzo for her to break cover. She imagined the repeated click, click, click as the PI took photographs, lots of photographs, from behind the one-way mirror that was the glass in the rear door of the van.

The private investigator revealed himself to be a man, perhaps, she thought, in his forties, casually dressed, short hair, clipped moustache, for that was the image of the man who joined them in the Oak and who sat close enough to them to hear their conversation, despite the fact that at just before midday the pub was still largely free of patrons.

She thought him an amateur in the lowest, most ill-used sense of the word; not one who does something for the love of it, rather as an untalented novice. But she was using him and he made it easy for her to do so. After talking idly about little of concern, she noticed both their glasses were empty. She stood and asked, 'Same again?'

'I shouldn't really drink at lunchtime. I also don't like you buying all the time. Doesn't feel right.'

'Doesn't feel wrong either.' She smiled and walked to the bar and ordered a lager for him and tonic water for her, then she turned and called from the bar, 'Are you a bit peckish, Chris? A bag of nuts between us won't ruin lunch.' She turned to the barman in his "Oak" emblazoned T-shirt and said, 'And a packet of dry roasted please.' She turned from the bar as the private investigator stood and left the pub, doubtless, she thought, believing himself to have come up with the goods that morning, photographic evidence of a liaison of a romantic nature, and a Christian name. He would walk back to the doorway from which he had earlier photographed her and Christopher Elms stepping out, and would read the names against each of the thirteen doorbells. She had earlier noticed that of all the names, only one had the initial "C". He would shortly report to Mabel Strong, showing photographs of her sister-in-law and a young man who lives at this address and whose name is Christopher Elms, and who appears to be either unemployed or is self employed. Either way, he has much free time during the day to devote to the entertainment of Virginia Woolley. Doubtless she would then be obliged to pay handsomely for his services, but for Mrs Strong, mused Virginia Woolley, money was no object.

That day they took lunch in a small bistro and strolled about heady Headingley, which, despite it being midsummer when the universities were "down", still had a vibrancy about it. They went into the charity shops, Virginia Woolley declaring herself to be a "charity shop junkie". 'The way some folk can't pass a bookshop, or an antique shop...the way some men, and some women, can't pass a pub,' she said. 'I just can't pass a charity shop...never know what sort of knicknack you're going to find for sale at a fraction of its value.'

'Me,' Christopher Elms smiled and shrugged, 'me, I need them to live, they're my only source of clothing and other stuff.'

'Oh...poor you.' She hugged his arm in hers. 'We'll really have to get you kitted out.'

'No...the shoes were really generous, but there's a limit to what I can accept.'

'I don't want to make you uncomfortable but we'll see what you need as and when you need it.'

They walked on in silence. It was broken when Christopher Elms said, 'Virginia, I can't help what I feel...I just wish you were not married.'

'Well, I am.'

'We could be together all the time.'

'We have to snatch what time we can. Ha...Help the Aged, I have found them to be very well stocked... Come on.'

Half an hour later, with Christopher Elms carrying a bag full of stainless steel cooking utensils, which Virginia Woolley had pounced on and gladly paid the asking price of five pounds for, they passed a travel agent's in the parade of shops that was the street level of the Arndale Centre. Virginia Woolley stopped. 'All these far flung places, such bargains... Look, Los Angeles for less than three hundred pounds...and that's return.'

'Have you travelled much?'

'Just in Europe, the Mediterranean mainly, just love the sun. You...?'

'Never been out of England,' Christopher Elms smiled sheepishly, 'and I mean England. Never been to Scotland or Wales or Ireland, or the Channel Islands or the Isle of Man, ever.'

'Oh, you have never felt that wanderlust? All young people feel that, especially young men.'

'Felt it, of course, and lust is the right word. Nearly got to Scotland once. At Newcastle, the crowd I was with "did" Scotland in a day.'

'In one day!' She glanced at him with a look of incredulity.

'Well, it was the sort of thing students will do...very early train from Newcastle, breakfast in Edinburgh, after looking round the centre of Edinburgh they took the shuttle to Glasgow and had lunch there...started drinking about three p.m.. Took the shuttle back to Edinburgh for an evening meal. Then took the train back to Newcastle in time for the last hour in the Black Swan...that was the pub we used. But I was ill, there was 'flu going round at the time. I spent that day sitting in front of the gas fire watching daytime television. They all went down with it a few days later. So, I nearly got out of England. Once.'

'Oh, now, that we will have to do something about. Do you have a passport?'

'Yes...?' There was a note of query in his voice.

'Let's see...look for Malta, we just need a last minute cancellation.'

'Malta?'

'Malta...just look for Malta.'

'There,' Elms pointed. 'Two persons – half board.'

'Where?'

'There...a week, seven nights.'

'That's the week after next...perfect...perfect.'

Christopher Elms found it to be a hard week, a long and a slow seven days. He found focusing difficult, and he found himself looking for tasks to be done so as to delay commencing work on the plans for Virginia's husband's garden in Windermere. An acquaintance who called unannounced commented that he had never known Elms' flat to be so neat and tidy. And when he could no longer delay settling to work on the plans for the garden, he found his attention span to be diminished to fifteen minutes or less. He became irritable. He went out for long walks alone, just walking the streets, just to get out of his flat. Once he had been content to remain in the flat throughout the day, but he now found himself suffering from what he believed the Americans called "cabin fever", a need to get out of the oppressive space that was his two roomed cell. He told this to the acquaintance who had called and commented about the neatness of his flat to which said acquaintance had responded, 'You know what's wrong with you, don't you? You're in love.' To which Christopher Elms had replied, 'I know.'

At her insistence they were not to see each other for a whole week. He was not to phone her. If she was going to persuade Maurice Woolley to agree that she could "visit her sister" for a week, then she had to spend that same amount of time at home. She promised to phone him when she could, when her husband was not within earshot, but there must be no contact. 'Patience and we visit Gozo,' she had said, running her fingers through his hair. 'Or put it another way, impatience or Gozo – choose one.'

'Patience,' he had said, 'patience, patience, patience.'

'Good boy,' had been her response before kissing him.

'But it will be hard.'

'I know.' They had been standing by her Mercedes after

returning from their tour of the charity shops and the travel agent, wherein they had bought the package offered, seven days half board in Malta. She had noticed the small white van with blacked out rear windows still sitting there. She hoped that she was providing the private investigator, and her sister-in-law, with what they wanted. She had then driven away, returning to the White House, leaving Christopher Elms to learn about patience. She had rewarded him that week just once with a phone call, explaining that it had been difficult for her to get even a minute away from her husband.

He had believed her, but her husband's reported possessiveness did not seem to Elms to be in keeping with the image she had created of him as being a man with a liberal attitude to his marriage. He didn't ponder the apparent contradiction but gave his energy to getting through the awful week, taking one hour, even one minute at a time: cleaning his flat and going for walks, cleaning his flat again and going for more walks, trying to work and failing to apply himself; retiring early to bed so as to bring on sleep and escape, in an attempt to speed the coming of the morrow which meant that one day of his wait had elapsed, and he was thus one day nearer to being with Virginia again.

He would remember it as "that week", though in fact the period of absence from each other lasted fully ten days. On the evening of the tenth day she made a second, brief and hushed telephone call to him. 'I'll pick you up tomorrow at 1 p.m. Our flight's at three but we have to check in at two…You just need your passport, I'll buy you everything you need when we get there.'

The flight, Elms' first ever, was smooth and uneventful, he and Virginia Woolley reclining, hand in hand as the RyanAir Boeing 737 took them deeper into the evening. By the time they had cleared arrivals at Luqa airport Virginia Woolley advised that it was by then too late to travel on to Gozo and that they had to spend the night at the hotel that had been booked as part of their package. They hailed a taxi, which took them to the hotel, the appearance of which caused Virginia Woolley to sniff with distaste adding, 'It's only for a night anyway'. Their room on the first floor had two single beds, a cramped shower and toilet area, and over-looked a building site.

'The couple who cancelled this at the last minute don't know how lucky they were. What a narrow escape...'

'I can breathe the air.' Christopher Elms stood at the window. 'First time out of England...I can breathe the air. Seems strange,' he smiled, 'I'm out of England at last...not a virgin any more and with the woman I love... I am in heaven.'

'Do you?' She returned the smile as she casually, matter-of-factly, stripped to her underwear. 'Do you love me, Chris?'

He nodded. 'Yes.' He crossed the short distance of floor that separated them and they embraced. 'Well,' she said, wrestling free of his passion, 'we'll have to work this week...'

'Work?'

'Yes...work...We'll have to work out what this means for us.' She opened her suitcase and took out a dress, which she slipped on over her head and smoothed down over her body. 'If love comes into this, we can't go on snatching a few days here and there to be with each other. This is either going to go somewhere...or it's going nowhere.'

'You feel the same...about me?'

'No,' she smiled. 'I am older, more cautious, been scarred a few times...but...I could love you...if there is a way for-ward for us, but if we can't identify a way forward, well, I will hold my emotions in check until we can find a path for us to follow...together. Come, you must be hungry. I don't know this part of Malta but there has to be a restaurant somewhere.'

The following morning they took a bus into Valetta,

where Virginia Woolley bought sufficient clothing to last Christopher Elms the six days that remained. After a lunch of seafood in a street-side café, they took the bus to Cirkewwa and there caught the ferry to Gozo. A further grey and red bus took them from the ferry terminal at Mgarr to the village of Gharb.

'Quite barren,' she said, as the bus laboured along the narrow, winding road. 'Greener than Malta, but still quite barren. We used to be in Greece...but here they speak English.'

Christopher Elms' eye was caught by the image of a young boy tending a flock of goats and, in his mind, he was transported back to biblical times. 'Aye,' he said, 'it's very dry and hot.' Beads of sweat ran off his forehead. 'Didn't know it could be so hot.'

She slid her hand into his. 'The villa's cool. I phoned the lady who looks after it for us when we are in England. There'll be chilled beer in the fridge for you and a cleaned pool for me...and you, as well, of course...a cleaned pool for both of us.'

'You didn't buy me any bathing trunks.'

She threw him a pained glance.

'Well, it has the benefit of working odd hours,' Pulleyne said. 'You get free time when most folk are working.'

'Yes.' The woman seemed lacklustre. He couldn't tell whether she was just as dull as ditchwater or just very uninterested in him.

'I can go to the pubs when they're like this...quiet.'

'Yes.'

The woman, he thought, was a little overweight, not quite the average build that she had described herself as being in her ad. She was about his age, and had described herself as a civil servant. Unmarried.

'I like being a police officer. Pays the bills.'

'Divorces are expensive, I hear.'

Pulleyne nodded. He would look to a passing stranger like a man in his forties, a little unkempt, in need of care and attention, like an old house, or an old car. 'Yes...as I am finding out.' He forced a smile. 'As are children. They are with their mother but I am still paying through the nose.'

'How many have you got?' The woman sat stiffly, hand-bag perched on her lap. She had asked for an orange juice, which was still untouched as Pulleyne neared the end of his second pint.

'Two...both girls.'

'Ages?'

'Twelve and fourteen.'

'Nice.' A smile, brief, but it was there.

Half an hour later Pulleyne and the woman, who said her name was Jenny excused themselves from each other's company. They were not for each other and they both knew it. It was, he had found, sometimes just the way of it.

'So this is her sister?' Mabel Strong sat in the small office and looked at the coarse-grain black and white prints that Philip Wood, private investigator, had handed her. 'The little minx. I knew it...I knew it... And look at his age...he's a little boy. Who is he, do you know?'

'A bloke called Christopher Elms.'

'Is he employed?'

'He doesn't appear to be.'

'She's away somewhere at the moment...in a little love nest somewhere with this...this...infant. What is that expression...toy...something?'

'Boy,' Wood offered, 'toyboy, I think is the expression.'

'Yes, that's it, that's the expression. She wants my brother's money but seeks her pleasure well away from the marriage bed.'

'I see it all the time, Mrs Strong, but that's a good investment: your brother can force a good divorce settlement with those photographs, that's why hiring a private investigator pays for itself. It's a bit pricey at the time but the settlement that can be forced with proof of infidelity more than pays for the PI's fee.'

'Yes…this is excellent. I want you to keep tabs on them. I want more photographs like this. I'll let you know when she deigns to return to her husband. I knew it…her sister indeed!'

'I'll be happy to, Mrs Strong.' Wood had paused. 'My fee has now reached one thousand pounds. We agreed that once it reached that sum…'

'Yes…of course.' Mabel Strong opened her handbag and flourished her chequebook. 'Money's not a problem…not a problem at all…anything to nail that vixen. Anything.'

On the first afternoon Christopher Elms explored the villa. It was, he found, a renovated farmhouse rather than a newly constructed building. It had an L shaped floor plan and was of two storeys. Inside it was fully refurbished, and was clean and airy, with pine furniture. There were three bedrooms; one with a double bed, the other two contained bunk beds. The flat roof could be accessed and, being bounded by metal railings, offered itself as a safe sun terrace. The rear door of the villa opened onto a tiled area in which there was a swimming pool, and the high stone walls surrounding the rear of the villa assured complete privacy for any in the pool or around it.

Early that evening Elms explored Gharb village, in which the villa stood. It had a dry and a dusty feel as was, he reasoned, only to be expected during the summer months in the Mediterranean. The buildings were slab sided, he noted, fronting vertically onto the street, without protruding balconies or bay windows and were, like Virginia's husband's villa, of two storeys. A traditional red British telephone box, standing next to a monument, which had been placed to one side of the street, made him feel at home.

Using the bus service, they spent the week exploring the

island. 'Otherwise,' Virginia had said, 'we may as well be in any villa anywhere in the Med.' They visited the vast, for Gozo, rotunda church at Xewkija and its buildings of modest proportions; and the industrious glass factory where items of blown glass were sold to tourists. He recalled a wind-powered water pump, identical to the ones he had seen in photographs of the buildings of Australian sheep stations. It was a tall, metal framework structure against a vast blue sky. The steep-sided Ghasri Valley, accessed after a long walk from the nearest bus stop, he found impressive, as, he found, was the temple of Ggantija, which Virginia Woolley told him was reputed to be older even than the pyramids at Giza. Victoria, the capital of the island, must, he thought, be the smallest town to achieve capital status, and was also probably one of the most peaceful of capitals in the western world. They would return to the villa in the late afternoon and wash off the dust of that day's travelling by swimming naked in the pool. Their evening meal was taken in a relaxed silence with a minimum of wine, at Virginia's insistence, so as not to dull performance, and they would retire to their bedroom long before tiredness set in. It was on the evening of their last full day on the island, the day they visited Marsalfom Bay, with what Elms thought to be a brutal hotel development right on the shoreline, that Christopher Elms levered himself out of the pool, wrapped a towel round his waist and padded softly into the kitchen where Virginia Woolley stood, wearing a long cheesecloth dress, in front of the cooker, preparing the meal. She turned and smiled as he entered the kitchen. 'You're in early, time for a bit longer in the pool if you wish. Won't be ready for another twenty minutes.'

'I've been thinking...' Elms approached her and slid his arm round her, relishing her scent. 'I know what we have to do.'

'Oh?'

'Yes, it's the only thing we can do.'

'What's that?'

'We have to kill Maurice…we have to kill your husband.'

She remained motionless. She didn't respond. She did not eagerly embrace the idea…but equally, she didn't fling up her arms in horror. Elms pressed home his argument, realising that part of her, at least, was receptive to the idea. 'With him out of the way, we can be together.'

'Yes,' she squeezed him, 'but it's not so simple…things can go wrong…things do go wrong and we need his money. I can't just leave him for you, we're both penniless. You cannot profit from a crime, no matter what provision he has made for me in his will. If I have anything to do with his murder, I won't inherit anything. Let's sit down and talk about this.' They released their embrace and sat at the kitchen table.

'I thought you'd be shocked.' Elms forced a smile.

'Well…' she avoided eye contact with him, 'since you have been so open and honest, I can only be the same with you, and I confess that I have been thinking along those lines.' She slid her hand across the tabletop and held his. 'You're right, Chris, it could be so good. If we are to get the money, I can't be involved, I have to have an unbreakable alibi…and nothing can connect you to it…the murder.'

'You see, that's the beauty of it, I am not known to him. I have no connection with him. We can make it look like a burglary gone wrong…it happens all the time…the police will look for known burglars. I'll wear gloves and, even if I do leave a fingerprint, that doesn't matter because my prints are not on record.'

'They might be in future, the slightest offence and they'll take your prints then match them to the burglary.'

'I'll have to be careful not to commit an offence…I mean, what offence am I going to commit if I am living here with you or in the house in the Lake District?'

'Or even in the White House.' She paused. 'But can you do it? Can you kill? It isn't easy.'

'You know, do you?'

'So I have heard. For every psychopath that can kill, and does kill, and enjoys killing, I imagine there are ten thousand who couldn't go through with it.' She looked him in the eye. 'Could you, Chris? Could you kill? Could you kill a man you don't even know? Do it close up and personal, with a knife?'

'Who said I'd use a knife?'

'It was an assumption...you haven't got a gun.'

'I could batter him in his bed.'

'You could.'

'Knock him unconscious...put a plastic bag over his head. That would do the trick.'

'It would...but you still don't convince me that you could go through with it. You are too innocent...too gentle, a small town boy, just out of university. I am the only woman you've slept with. You've never been out of England until this week. Hardly the school of hard knocks...you're hardly a man of the world.' She squeezed his hand. 'There just isn't that sense of a survivor about you...you haven't got that edge that makes a man a killer.'

'Perhaps,' he glanced down at the floor, 'perhaps I'm more ruthless than you think. Perhaps you underestimate me and what I lack in ruthlessness, I make up for in passion.'

'You really do love me, don't you?'

'Yes...yes...yes...'

'I believe you.' She ran her thumb in a circling motion over the back of his hand. 'If it works...if we can do it...we'll be together, with all the money we'll ever need.'

'Is he a strong man?'

She shook her head. 'No, he's smaller than you and he's weaker than you...I should know. He's likely to be drunk as well.'

'So I won't have to attack him?'

'Probably not. Just pull the plastic bag over his head and

leave the house. He'll be brain dead in less than three minutes; totally life extinct in ten…there won't be anybody around to revive him anyway. You know, this really could work.'

'If I didn't think it could work, I wouldn't have suggested it…and, like the trial, it's still a question of what can be proved. That guy did murder his wife, his smile said so, but you were right, we still brought in the correct verdict in light of the evidence that was offered.'

'Now,' she smiled, 'now you're thinking like a killer. Now you are beginning to convince me that you really can do it.'

'I can,' he nodded and squeezed her hand, 'I can do it. I will do it… I'll do it for you, Virginia.'

'You'll do it for both of us.'

'That's what I meant…for both of us.'

'You'll have to do two things.'

'Name them.'

'Well first, I want you to familiarise yourself with the house, its grounds…study it from the road. I'll hire a car for you. You can drive?'

'Yes.'

'Good. Then you'll have to get in the house…it's alarmed but I think I know how to get you in…that's for me to sort out.'

'When shall we do it?'

'When shall you do it, you mean?'

'Yes.'

'A few days. I can anticipate when he's likely to be drunk. I can tip you off. I'll have to sort out my alibi…you'll have to study the front of the house. I'll hire a car for a few days…no, no I won't. I'll give you the cash to hire the car, you should drive to and from your flat to the White House until you know every inch of the route.'

'Yes.'

'I can describe the inside of the house.'

'Any dogs?'

'No. Maurice doesn't like them.'

'So…just an alarm. How are we going to get round that?'

'There's a small ground floor window. It isn't alarmed because it has been painted up…doesn't open. If it did, it would allow access to a scullery which is always kept locked. Anyway, both Maurice and the company that installed the alarm thought it was a risk worth taking, so long as we made a point of keeping the scullery door locked. Which we do.'

'So, if you could free off that window and leave the scullery unlocked, I could get in?'

'Yes, easily.'

'And out?'

'Leave by the main door.'

'That'll set the alarm off?'

'Yes…but nobody takes any notice…nobody near enough to hear. The alarm works by scaring intruders before they break in…as a deterrent.'

'I see.'

'It's not linked to the police station. You could walk out of the house…drive away. It will ring only for about twenty minutes, then it will switch off. I will come home the following morning to find the front door open and my husband murdered.'

'It's going to work.'

'Yes…You'll have to take a bag with you, a sports bag, take some items of value. It has to look like a burglary.'

'Of course.'

'Which is why a plastic bag over his head isn't a good idea.'

'No?'

'No, a burglar wouldn't do that…but someone who wanted to murder Maurice would.'

'Of course, I wasn't thinking.'

'Neither was I. It's got to be a more violent death, as if the burglar was defending himself as Maurice attacked him.'

'Yes…so a blunt object or a knife.'

'Yes.' She smiled and glanced at the cooker. 'You know, I am not particularly hungry anymore.'

'Nor me.' He squeezed her hand.

'Let's go up,' she said, and thought, "Oh you are such a good boy".

Three days later Christopher Elms received a phone call. He strode nervously across the floor of his living room and picked up the phone. 'Hi?'

'You alone?' It was Virginia Woolley.

'Yes.'

'You sound nervous.'

'I am. Wouldn't you be?'

'Well, you've got to want to go through with this, really want it.'

'I do.'

'Good. I want you to do it as well, so don't bottle out on me now…don't bottle out on us.'

'No.'

'Good. Did you get the money?'

'Yes. It arrived this morning. Elms Landscape Designs, the postie had to work out which box he had to put it in but he guessed correctly…typed address, postmarked Hull. You drove all the way to Hull to post a letter?'

'Nothing will go wrong if we are careful…my handwriting on an envelope addressed to you, postmarked Knaresborough, if that fell into the wrong hands…'

'And the money in used notes…'

'Same reason. Took me a long time to launder that money…two withdrawals of two hundred and fifty pounds each from my credit cards, went on a spending spree buying things for less than five pounds and apologising for having nothing smaller than a twenty pound note…but eventually, many magazines and newspapers and cups of coffees in Starbucks later – I had three hundred and fifty pounds in untraceable notes.'

'You took a risk not to record it or register it. I've never seen so much money in my life...just lying in my letter box.'

'The risk was worth it, money can be replaced, but recording or registering it can have been dangerous, even if I used a false name, I would still have had to sign for it.'

'You have it all thought out.'

'I hope so. So tell me what you are going to do with the money?'

'I'm...' he paused as he heard a roar in the background. When it had died away, he asked, 'What was that?'

'A juggernaut carrying sheep, each one destined for somebody's Sunday lunch...don't often get them on this road.'

'You're not using your mobile?'

'Nope...phone box, near York.'

'You are not taking any chances at all.'

'No...and neither should you, my sweet pet. Neither should you.'

'I'll do my best.'

'Well, make sure your best is good enough.'

'It will be.'

'Good. Now, what are you going to do with the money?'

'Buy a large bag, like a sports bag, from a charity shop...a dark jacket and a pair of gloves.'

'Good. Then...?'

'Hire a car. Drive out to the White House...study it...get to know it from the road.'

'Good. I'll phone you again, let you know when he's likely to be drunk...he's drinking at the moment...then there'll be two or three days self pitying "I'm never going to do that again", then he'll get thirsty and demolish another bottle of Scotch, all by himself, all in one go. So, two or three days from now...give me time to free up the small window. I'll mark it for you. We have an old wheelbarrow. I'll leave it propped up against the wall beside the window. So just look for the wheelbarrow then jemmy open the nearest window to it.'

'Okay. You're sure he'll be drunk?'

'Yes. I'll phone you when he starts to drink. It'll be about three or four in the afternoon. You should plan to arrive at about 9 p.m. He'll be sleeping by then.'

'Alright.'

'Then it's a smash on the head with something good and heavy.'

'That's going to be the hard part.'

'Alright, listen, I'll tell you what to do...once you're out of the scullery you'll be in the kitchen...plenty of teacloths around...pick one up. Maurice will be in the living room lying on the couch, put the cloth over his face and then do the business...that'll make it easier for you.'

'Yes, Virginia. Just wish that there was some other way round this...'

'Well, there isn't. If you want us to be together, permanently, then this is the only way...understand?'

'Yes.'

'Look, he's elderly, he's had his life...and he won't know anything about it...for him it'll be like he went in his sleep.'

'I suppose I could look at it that way...he won't feel anything...he won't know anything.'

'No, he won't, keep thinking that, Christopher...I want you to keep thinking that.'

'Okay.'

'After you have done the job, go to the display cabinet...it's in the same room, it's full of his collection of gentlemen's pocket watches...smash the glass and put the watches in the bag.'

'A sports bag for just a few watches?'

'You're right...get a smaller bag...one of those small rucksacks that folk use when going out for the day.'

'I know the type.'

'Good...one of those...'

'Then leave by the front door. Oh, and you'll need a knife to jemmy open the window.'

'Yes.'

'Don't use one from your flat, buy one from the charity shops. Has to have a strong blade...a small carver will do.'

'Alright.'

'Then what? I want to make sure you remember.'

'I drive away, dump the watches in the river...and the knife too.'

'Don't forget...never take the gloves off.'

'I won't.' He forced a smile, which he knew could be "heard" down a phone line.

'Well, you'd be surprised how many do. I spoke to the police officer who attended our last burglary, he told me that burglars are often in a state of high anxiety when they are inside people's houses and in their anxiety, they forget themselves and remove their gloves. So even if the point of entry shows evidence of gloved hands, he said, it was still worth examining the rest of the house. So don't forget yourself.'

'No, Virginia.'

'Once you have got rid of the bag and the knife, return home. Return the hire car and wait for me to contact you.'

'Okay.'

'I'll be with my sister. I'll return home the next day and discover the body...then I'll play it by ear. That'll be my job. Your work is all up to the murder...mine is all after. You just lie low and act as though nothing has happened.'

'Alright...alright, I'll just stay in...stay at home.'

'So that's agreed...anytime you like.'

'If I can hire a car today, I'll be able to start to study the house this evening, plenty of light up until about eight or eight-thirty.'

'Good. So one more phone call from me to tell you when he's drinking.'

'Yes.'

'Good. Don't worry, it's going to go like clockwork.'

'If you say so, Virginia...I love you.'

'Love you too. Now go and hire that car.'

Virginia Woolley replaced the handset and walked from the phone box to her car. She drove to the M62 and drove west towards Leeds, leaving Hull behind her. She later joined the A1 and followed it north to Boroughbridge, where she picked up the A655 and followed it home to the White House. The small white van which had followed her as she left the house earlier that day, and which she had easily lost on the M62 had, she saw, returned to its usual position at the entrance of the drive of the that which stood on the far side of the road from the White House. 'You just stay there,' she said as she turned into the drive of the White House, 'until about eight o'clock this evening...just be patient...you can do it.'

Philip Wood sat in the van. The seat was getting hard. The van was stuffy even with the window down; the air in the van was becoming difficult to breathe. It hadn't been a good day – no result at all. He felt hungry, he wanted a shower, clean clothes and a chilled lager. The latter he felt would go down without touching the sides of his throat. He glanced at his watch, 6 p.m. He doubted "madam" was going out again that day. He was getting to know her; she seemed to be a day bird, not a night owl. He was about to start the engine when he saw a small car pull into the kerb and stop. A young man got out and looked at the White House, which stood a few hundred metres distant. He stared at the house. To Philip Wood, he seemed to be studying it. 'Well, well, well,' Wood said to himself as he recognised the young man and reached for his camera with its 300mm lens. 'This is interesting...this is very interesting indeed. Might have a result today, after all.'

* * *

Virginia and Maurice Woolley sat together in the drawing room of the White House, seated in armchairs separated by a large amount of floor space. He sat with his back to the window, through which she could see the well-manicured lawn at the rear of the house, surrounded by the ivy covered wall, verdant under a canopy of blue, fleeced with a trace of white.

'I don't mind.' He reached for the bottle and unscrewed the cap, breaking the thin, metallic seal.

'Mind what, darling?'

'You going with your sister.'

'Well, she is my sister.'

He poured a generous measure of whisky into a large tumbler. 'Of course.' He swallowed deeply, drinking the alcohol as another might drink a glass of water. 'Your sister...don't think I don't know what that means,' he stiffened as the alcohol reached his system. 'I am not that stupid.'

'Darling...'

'But you return, that's the important thing. If I didn't let you go...if I didn't let you have your shenanigans, you'd go away and not return.'

She remained silent.

'That's what I said to our Mabel.'

'You discuss our relationship with your sister?'

'We have no relationship to discuss, but I do discuss our marriage. I like you in the house. I like you in my bed.' He took another deep swallow. 'If not every night, that's better than not at all.'

'You are very open-minded, darling.' She blew a kiss at him.

'Just realistic, I'd say.'

'Yes.' She stood and walked slowly, elegantly out of the room, carrying herself in that manner which she knew pleased him: the finishing touch to his impressive house. She returned a few moments later carrying a second bottle of scotch. She placed it on the table beside him and leant forward and kissed his forehead. 'Something tells me you're going on a session, husband of mine, just thought I'd save you a walk…a stagger rather, to the drinks cabinet.'

'A stagger?' He sniggered. 'And you don't nag me about the booze, that's something else you can visit your sister for. Will you be in tonight?'

'Probably. But I'm going out now.'

'To your sister's?'

'Yes. But I'll be back later.'

She drove away from the White House and was dutifully followed, lost sheep like, by the white van, which she allowed to follow her as she drove sedately south on the A1. When she turned onto the M62 eastbound, the driver of the van made no attempt to follow, clearly having learned from experience that he would soon lose her, and doubtless, she believed, would return to his lonely vigil, barely concealed, opposite the gates of the White House. As she approached Hull, she left the motorway and found a public call box in Anlaby.

The phone seemed to have an unusually shrill ring to it. He believed it was his nerves that made it seem so. With a reluctance, with a sense of dread, with a hollowness in the pit of his stomach, he picked up the phone. 'Yes? Hello.'

'It's me.'

'Virginia! Where are you?'

'In Dorset. Tonight's the night.'

'How do you know?'

'Just phoned him…he's well on, speech slurred…What time is it now? Just after four…he'll be out of it by nine. I have done what I said, wheelbarrow in place, window freed off.'

'Okay. Jesus…I'm scared.'

'You'll be fine. He'll be in the drawing room, just follow the sounds of snoring and the smell of his breath. The house lights will be on…won't need a torch.'

'Alright. I'm sweating and shivering at the same time.'

'Just remember the goal…the prize.'

'You and me?'

'Yes, Chris, you and me. It'll be good, so unbelievably good.'

'Yes.' He swallowed. 'Yes, I believe that. I believe it will.'

'Now, I'm going to plan my return for about midday tomorrow.'

'Okay.'

'I am going to try and get away from the house. I won't be under suspicion. I'll just say that I want to go for a drive. Once I am sure that I am not being followed, I will come to you. Right…so we know what's happening.'

'Yes.'

'Right, I'll be round your house tomorrow, then there'll be no contact between us for a few weeks.'

'A few weeks!'

'Yes, but I'll post you some cash from time to time, you can't survive on what the dole gives you. Okay. You psych yourself up now, drive away from your house at dusk.'

'Yes, Virginia.'

'That way you'll be at the White House just after dark.'

'Yes…love you.'

'Love you too, Chris.' She replaced the phone. She then rapidly redialled his number and the instant he answered, she hung up. She did not think he was likely to dial 1471 to check the origin of her call but she felt that the risk was too great to take. She drove on into Hull, to East Hull, near the prison, to Portobello Street. She parked her car on the main road and walked up to the front door of a terraced house two doors down from a corner fish and chip shop, opposite a scrubby area of green on which children played with a ball and where a lean man walked a hungry looking dog. Hull, HU9.

* * *

'Yes?' Said the woman, who flung the door open at Virginia Woolley's second, insistent ring on the bell. 'Oh...you...'

'Hi.'

'Fallen from grace, have we?'

'No, just keeping in touch with family. We haven't quarrelled, have we? Just been a few years.'

'Come in.' The woman stepped aside. 'How's life among the gentry?'

'Awful, and we don't mix with the gentry, just got a big house.'

'The big house,' the woman echoed, 'that's what Rigger calls prison.'

'How is he?'

'He's inside again. Doing a three stretch for receiving.'

'A three? He'll do that on his back.' Virginia Woolley walked into the entrance hall of the house. It seemed so cramped to her after the cavernous nature of the White House. She turned into the living room, which had two chairs and a television on a table in the corner, and space for little else.

'Yes. He's not worried. He'll be out in less than two. He's got a couple of mates in there, and he's not complaining because the busies only found about a tenth of what he'd already received and moved. So we have money in the bank right now.'

'Good. Do you still have the spare room at the back?'

'Our Dan's room? Aye...'

'I'd like it for the night.'

'Okay. Want a break from that fossil of a husband of yours?'

'Just need to be somewhere else for the night.'

'Fine. You'll have to make up the bed. I can let you have some sheets and that...and you'll have to share it with a motorbike.'

'A motorbike?'

'Yes, it's in bits on the bedroom floor. Well, the engine

and wheels, the frame's in the backyard. His room was the only place he could work on the engine during the winter, just left them there when he went to live with a girl in London. They'll be there for him to clean away when he gets back, I'm not touching them.'

'Thanks. So, we'll go out for a few this evening?'

'Yes. They've refurbished the Hull Mariner. You'll hardly recognise it.'

'The Mariner...be nice to be in the old Mariner again, it's been a few years. Can we later, rather than earlier? I want to do something about nine o'clock.'

'Fine, the pubs are never crowded in East Hull, even at last orders, no one round here has enough money, and Rigger says I've not to flash the money around too much.'

'Sensible.' She put her bag down on one of the armchairs. 'And speaking of money,' she took out a building society passbook from her bag and handed it to her sister. 'Can you keep this for me?'

'Yes.' The woman opened the book. 'It's in your maiden name.'

'Yes, a little nest egg. I want it kept safe.'

'A hundred thousand pounds!' Her sister gasped as she read the final entry. 'Some nest egg.'

'I want something.'

'You have the house in Windermere, the villa on Gozo...Rigger still talks about that holiday we had, the busies looking down every rat hole in Hull and all the while he was sunning himself in the villa...and you didn't take a penny off us.' She paused. 'You're up to something.'

Virginia Woolley pursed her lips and raised her eyebrows.

'You've found a way of getting your hands on his fortune, haven't you?'

'Possibly. But if it goes pear-shaped, I'll be for the Big House myself, and not for a three stretch. That's why I want that to come out to.' She pointed to the building society passbook. 'It's in a high yield account, so it'll grow while I eat porridge, if it comes to that. If it works out, there'll be a serious drink in it for you and Rigger. If the busies come by, just tell them the truth. That I spent the night here.'

'Okay,' her sister nodded. 'I'll wrap this up and put it in the fridge.'

'The fridge!'

'Yep.' Her sister smiled. 'We have a lot of valuables in the fridge in an old margarine tub. Rigger says the fridge is the last place a burglar looks.'

'And he should know!' Virginia Woolley and her sister laughed in mutual contentment.

Later that evening, the two women went to the police station in central Hull to report the theft of Virginia Woolley's handbag. 'We were walking down Portobello Street, this hard little street turk runs up from behind, snatches my bag, runs off...'

'Did you get a good look at him?' asked the duty constable.

'White youth,' offered Virginia Woolley.

'Dark hair,' added her sister.

'Yeah...jeans, really too dark to see much more.'

'So quick too.'

'What was in the bag?'

'About forty pounds in cash...credit cards...usual stuff.'

'Well, all I can do is take a note of it, record the incident.'

'Appreciate that. Could I have a crime number? I can possibly make an insurance claim.'

Christopher Elms halted the car, shaking with fear. He got out, walked to the roadside and vomited. He walked a little way from the car and sat down on the grass verge. It was night, no other cars in sight. An owl hooted. He heard the rustle of a nocturnal animal prowling the woods behind him.

So he'd done it.

He had killed. Taken life.

It hadn't gone like she had said it would go. It had been a mess. Very bloody, very messy, and he experienced what he had most wanted to avoid: eye contact at the moment of death.

The first stages had gone according to plan. He had parked the hire car at the top of the drive to the White House, near the gates. The house seemed to have an eerie look; in the night it looked different from in the daytime, the garden in darkness under a night sky, and it being painted white, it looked to him like a solid, square-shaped iceberg. Lights burned in the downstairs rooms. He had moved noiselessly round the side of the house, to the rear. He had glanced once at the spread of the rear garden and then searched for the wheelbarrow. He saw it just as she had said it would be: propped up against the wall of the house. He had moved closer to it, found the window and inserted the blade of the knife between the window and the frame. It had opened easily. He resisted the urge to peel the gloves off. His palms were sweating, he desperately needed to take the gloves off but he was able to overcome the urge. He had opened the window and had slithered inside the house and sat in the cool and the dark of the scullery.

Listening.

He heard nothing.

He had moved to the door, pressing his eye against the keyhole. The light was on in the kitchen and, so far as he could tell, it was empty, as she had promised it would be. Slowly, gently, he had tried the scullery door. It opened silently. She had clearly played her part; she had done all she said she would do. Now he knew it was up to him. He also knew that if he was going to turn back, then that was the time. But what would be his life if he turned back? No Virginia, no employment. It was only a matter of time before his landlord discovered that he was unemployed, then he'd be on the street, looking for accommodation with the druggies and other lowlifes, or going back to Batley, to his room at the back of his parents' council house, staying in his room while the rain poured outside. That terrible feeling that the world was going on without him, that life was going past him...some local boy made good, and his parents would know the truth of his "success" in life. A good degree from Newcastle University and all he had to show for it was a life on the dole. One year's employment and then the dole. For life. But if he went through with it, he would be with Virginia, she would support him financially, he'd get his design company off the ground.

No contest.

He had opened the scullery door and stepped into the kitchen. He stood for a moment, allowing his eyes to become accustomed to the light. He took a tea towel from the work surface beside the sink and looked for something heavy to use as the murder weapon. He had opened drawers but found only cutlery, until he opened a drawer that contained items and tools of household maintenance: spare light bulbs, small batteries, screwdrivers, and a hammer. It was only a small hammer. He thought that hammers hardly got smaller, a hammer for driving in panel pins rather than nails, but it would do. He put the knife in his pocket and picked up the hammer.

He had crept out of the kitchen, up a flight of stairs and into what was evidently the entrance hall of the house. It was then that he heard the man's snoring. Just as she said he would. He also began to detect the stale odour of alcohol-laden breath. He had turned a corner and saw that the door to the drawing room was open.

He had paused. It was still not too late to turn back. But to turn back was something he could not find it in himself to do. They were in it together, she and him. She had fulfilled her part of the contract. He had to fulfil his. He had knelt on all fours, not wanting to be standing as he entered the room. He had inched his head round the door at floor level and saw with no small measure of relief that the curtains had been closed. No one could see in the house. He scanned the floor area. No one else was in the room, just he and the snoring man. Elms left the bag at the door and stood holding the cloth in one hand and the hammer in the other. He saw Maurice Woolley lying on the couch, his head near to Elms. "That makes it easier," he had thought, "just creep up and drop the towel over his face."

When Elms moved on Maurice Woolley, he moved quickly, darting up to the man, dropping the cloth over his head and hitting, hitting, hitting with the hammer. Hitting until the cloth was red. Hitting until the hammer made a squelching rather than a thudding sound. He dropped the hammer in repulsion, staggered back and sat in an armchair.

Maurice Woolley no longer snored. He lay quite still.

Christopher Elms then began to collect himself. He knelt and picked up the hammer and walked to the display cabinet and began to smash the glass so as to retrieve the watches therein.

It was then, at that point, that things had started to go wrong. Horribly, horribly wrong.

'Not again...' the harsh rasping voice came from behind Elms. He had turned, and standing over him, swaying unsteadily from the alcohol and the concussion, was the nightmare vision of Maurice Woolley with a blood smeared face, and one eye bloated and shut. 'Not again...not again.' He advanced on Elms, arms outstretched, a man defending his property, and taller and heavier than Virginia had described him. Elms stood and instinctively reached for the knife in his pocket. Woolley had advanced, closed on Elms, Elms pushed the knife into Woolley's stomach, heard the man groan and collapse forward. He stabbed again, and then again. The third time he had stabbed Maurice Woolley in the chest, Woolley's head raised, and with his one good eye, he had looked into Elms' eyes, from about six inches distant, as at the same instant Elms had felt Woolley's last moments of life quiver in the handle of the knife.

Then he had run out of the room, taking the knife with him, into the entrance hall, opened the front door, triggering the burglar alarm. He remembered himself sufficiently to keep to the drive rather than run the risk of leaving footprints on the lawn or in the flowerbeds, reached the car, started it and drove, just drove, down narrow country roads, until he could no longer keep the contents of his stomach down, whereupon he halted by a river by a small wood bathed in moonlight. He flung the knife into the river.

He sat on the grass verge until the first sliver of dawn rent the night sky, whereupon he stood and walked on weak-feeling legs, back to the car. He remembered the man's breath, the smell of it, the smell of blood, the look in the man's eye as life left him, life that he, Christopher Elms, son of a bus driver, university graduate, had taken. He glanced up at the dawn and pondered the saying that only those who stay up all night can truly see the dawn, and yet it seemed to him that his night was just beginning.

Maurice agreed to that. He just doesn't want to employ anyone, anyone at all. He is very principled like that.'

'I see.' The constable tapped his notepad with his ballpoint. 'You phoned us as soon as you found your husband?'

'Yes…immediately.'

'You didn't see anybody at all? I mean, anyone else around the house?'

'None. I wasn't really looking for anybody when I arrived, and after…well, I was in a bit of a state.'

'I can understand that. Seems to me to be a burglary gone badly wrong.'

'The house is alarmed. Oh! I didn't check to see if the alarm had been triggered. It will ring for twenty minutes but still needs to be re-set.'

'Something we can check.' The constable glanced over his left shoulder. 'Oh…here's my boss.'

Virginia Woolley looked to her left and saw two unmarked cars turn into the drive. The constable got out of the car and waited for them to approach. In the car Virginia Woolley continued to think herself into the shocked and distraught state of the suddenly and unexpectedly widowed. She continued to sit facing forwards as she heard two cars halt, three car doors open and shut and further heard the murmur of hushed conversation. She then saw the constable lead three people past her and towards the house. The first was a finely built, youthful looking man, who carried a black Gladstone bag, the second was a taller, well-built man dressed in a light summer suit whom she thought to be in his late forties. Following him was a sensibly dressed woman in her early thirties. The constable lifted the blue and white tape and the three other persons bent and walked beneath it, while the constable remained at the door. He had clearly given directions.

She waited in the car, window fully wound down, as the temperature of the day began to rise. She noticed the young man carrying the black Gladstone bag leave the house and walk past her without acknowledging her. She heard a car door open and shut and listened as the engine fired and the car reversed, turned and then drove away. Moments later the sensibly dressed female emerged from the house, slid athletically under the tape, talking into a mobile phone as she did so. She then switched the phone off and walked towards the police car in which Virginia Woolley sat.

'Mrs Woolley?' She smiled as she approached.

'Yes.'

'I am afraid your husband is deceased, as you thought. The police surgeon has just pronounced life extinct.'

'Life extinct.' She echoed the phrase.

'Yes...sorry, it's not very sensitive but that's the expression. I am sorry if it upsets you.'

'No, it doesn't upset me, I have more to be upset about than the terms you use.'

'It seems he disturbed an intruder. It sometimes happens. Burglars can get violent in their panic, very violent indeed.'

'So I believe. What happens now?'

'Well, my boss, Mr Hirst, he's looking round your house. It's a crime scene, we don't need a warrant.'

'I wouldn't insist on one, we have nothing to hide.'

'Good...well, doubtless he'll also be wanting to talk to you at a later date. Anyway, what will happen now is that I am going to take you to the police station in Harrogate. We'll take a statement from you.'

'You are going to take me? To drive me?'

'Yes. Why? Is that a problem?'

'No...no...Sorry, I am still a little shocked.'

'Well that's understandable. Dare say you could use a hot cup of tea.'

Virginia Woolley nodded. 'Yes...that sounds...lovely.'

'Good. Would you like to get out of this car? We'll go to Harrogate in Mr Hirst's car.'

* * *

The SOCO laid a path of aluminium platforms, each about a foot square, from the front door of the White House to the drawing room, as the crime scene photographer followed, stepping on the platforms and photographing whatever the scene of crime officer drew his attention to, notably what appeared to be bloodstained footprints on the tiled floor of the foyer. Further photographs were taken in the drawing room, in black and white, and colour, of the deceased from all angles. Clive Hirst, having toured the house room by room, was satisfied that all criminal activity had been confined to the drawing room and the point of entry, which he had rapidly determined to be the small window in the scullery. He had walked out of the house and round the rear of the building and examined the window externally. The frame had clearly been forced with a knife or some similar instrument, and with his hand safely encased in a latex glove, he gently, carefully opened it further and saw that it afforded a route into the house that could be negotiated by a slightly built person. Below the window was a course of gravel, which ran round the perimeter of the house. No footprints there. He returned to the front of the house as Richard Pulleyne arrived in his car, followed by a minibus containing uniformed officers. Hirst walked up to Pulleyne as Pulleyne got out of his car. 'Morning, Dick.'

'Morning, sir.'

'Lovely day for a murder.'

'Isn't it, sir, and is that what we have?'

'Oh yes, murder most foul…elderly bloke, disturbed a burglar…blood everywhere.'

'Ought to prove useful.'

'Yes…they'll be bloodstains all over the felon's clothing. I think we'll wrap this one up quite quickly.' They walked towards the house. 'Entry appears to have been gained at the back of the house. There's a small window that has been forced.'

'Not alarmed?'

'No, strangely enough.' They ducked under the tape as it was raised for them by the constable. 'There is an alarm system in the house which appears to have been triggered, but the window wasn't part of the system, it has no metal contacts which, if separated, trigger the alarm.'

'Odd oversight.' Pulleyne stepped on the aluminium platform behind Hirst. 'Footmarks,' he said.

'Yes, we've photographed them, of course, it's those and things like that which makes me believe we'll have someone in custody for this very soon. And this is ye victim.'

'Oh, my...' Pulleyne looked at the body of Maurice Woolley. 'What a mess. Poor old boy, nearer the end of his life than the beginning, but even so, no one deserves to be butchered like that...wearing day clothing, I note.'

'Yes, I observed that. So a break-in during the evening rather than during the night, that's odd as well...summer...light nights. I mean, this is around the longest day. Two things will keep a burglar away from houses: wet, cold wintry weather and very light nights... Well, they will make the prospect of committing a burglary less attractive, but my sister was burgled on a summer's afternoon once.'

'Oh, aye, they'll get in if they want in. Just got to make your home less of an inviting proposition than your neighbour's.'

'Indeed. No dogs, too. House like this and no dogs.'

'That's odd. Who found the body, sir?'

'The wife...now the widow...she's at the station. DC Lucas is interviewing her. She told the constable who responded to her call that she discovered the body when she returned home this morning. She had spent the previous night with her sister in Hull.'

'Easy enough to check that alibi, sir.'

'Yes. She's not in the frame at all. I mean, look at those injuries, that's a struggle between two men, and there was no blood on her clothing and, as you say, the person who did that will be massively bloodstained. We are just waiting for the pathologist to arrive... So, Dick, can you organise a search of the grounds, please?'

'Consider it done, boss.' Pulleyne turned and walked on the aluminium platforms out of the house.

'My sergeant's right,' Hirst found himself addressing the corpse of Maurice Woolley, 'no one should be butchered...you have been butchered. Don't worry; we'll get the animal that did this. He'll go down for life alright.'

Virginia Woolley sipped her tea as DC Lucas opened the statement pad. 'Before we start...'

'Yes?' DC Lucas smiled at Virginia Woolley.

'I have two favours to ask.'

'Yes?'

'Well...my husband has a sister...a Mrs Strong, Mrs Mabel Strong.'

'Yes...'

'Well, she should know as soon as possible, but we don't see eye to eye...you know sisters-in-law...and if I am going to be here anyway, I wonder, could the police inform her? She lives close by.'

'Yes,' Lucas nodded. 'Strictly speaking, in this case you are the next of kin so we can notify your sister-in-law by phone. Yes, we can do that, if you'd give us her number.'

'Thanks.' Virginia Woolley opened her handbag and searched for her address book. 'And the other thing, I don't want to go back to the house tonight. Can I go and stay with my sister?' She leafed through the address book.

'I can understand that. I can not see it being a problem, you'll just have to let us know your sister's address and phone number.'

'Of course. Ah...here is my sister-in-law's number.'

Ten minutes later DC Lucas returned to the interview room and sat in the polished pine upright chair and rested her forearms on the similarly polished pine tabletop. She glanced up at the opaque glass window. 'Not an easy phone call to make,' she said, 'but they never are.'

'I can imagine. Some job you have.'

'Rewarding and frustrating by turns...some we win and some we don't, but Mr Hirst...that's DCI Hirst, he is confident we'll make an early arrest in this case. It was a botched break-in, very clumsy; people who do that leave a trail that leads right to their front door. So, let's take a statement.' She smiled.

'You're not from round here?' Virginia Woolley returned the smile. 'I used to live in Dorset, your accent sounds familiar.'

'Close...Hampshire. I'm a good Hampshire girl.'

'Okay.'

'So, you said you spent the night with your sister?'

'Yes, in East Hull.'

'We'll have to check that...just a formality.'

'Yes...of course.'

'And you returned home this morning and found your husband's body?'

'Yes, as I said...phoned the police straightaway. Was it this morning? It seems like a different lifetime.'

'Shock does that,' DC Lucas explained. 'We often encounter it. I don't suppose you'd know of anyone who'd want to harm your husband?'

'No. No one. He wasn't one to make enemies. He was a gentle soul.'

'As we said, it looks like he disturbed a burglar. Did you notice anyone loitering about the house in the previous few days? Burglars often sight up a property before breaking in.'

'No, I didn't, and Maurice didn't mention seeing anyone acting like that.'

'Alright.' Lucas paused. 'Your husband was obviously a wealthy man...that house...your car. What did he do for a living?'

'He was retired. I dare say that's the best way to put it.'

'What was his occupation before he retired?'

'I don't know.'

René Lucas looked puzzled. Virginia Woolley steeled herself. It was now she realised, now, at this point, that clouds of suspicion would begin to gather over her, it was here that the thin ice starts. From here on she had to tread lightly and above all, not rush to give information that might indicate her innocence, that information is for the police to tease out slowly, over time, like reporting her handbag stolen to the police in Hull, she knew she mustn't be too eager to tell them that.

'I don't understand.' DC Lucas turned the pen over in her hand. 'He was your husband yet you don't know what his occupation was?'

'I don't think he had much of an occupation. You may as well know now...he won the Lotto.'

'Ah...'

'Nine million pounds.' Virginia Woolley raised an eyebrow. 'Someone has to win.'

'I see,' René Lucas said slowly. 'Had you been married long?'

'A little under three years.'

And that was it. The look in the policewoman's eyes, the silence...Virginia Woolley knew then that she was in the frame. No suspicion about her being involved in the actual murder...but conspiracy before the fact, facilitating it, it still carries the same life sentence. She realised that this young, but clearly experienced policewoman knew that she had conspired to murder her husband. The hardening of the look in her eyes, the sudden coldness of manner, the evaporation of all sympathy for the recently widowed. Two women, both possessed of feminine intuition stronger, more finely honed than the male instinct, and in that instant they both knew that one of them was a cold and calculating killer who had covered her tracks well, had probably left nothing that could link her to the murder, and they also both knew that all the other had to do was prove the case against the first. The silence between them lasted fully twenty seconds.

'I see.' DC Lucas broke the silence. 'Well, we'll just get this down in the form of a statement. Then we'll drive you back to your house, you can pick up your car and go to your sister's.' Her voice was cold, distant.

Gwendoline Fay, having followed the directions she had been given, turned her car into the driveway of the White House. She saw a collection of vehicles at the top of the driveway close to the house; marked police vehicles, unmarked cars, and the ominous presence of the black windowless mortuary van seemed to her to underline the reason for their presence being requested. She also saw the line of white shirted police constables, both men and women, walking slowly across the lawn, carefully searching the grass in front of them as they did so. She halted her car behind the mortuary van and walked with her bag to the front door of the house. The constable recognised her and nodded a salute then lifted the tape to allow her ingress.

She stepped into the foyer and looked about her, absorbing its space, its dimensions. She noticed a scene of crime officer photographing something on the floor; she thought it might be a footprint in what appeared to be blood. She walked on the stepping-stones of aluminium platforms and entered the drawing room. 'Just following my nose,' she said cheerily. She was a tall, slender woman in her mid-forties who wore her blonde hair short. She was always found by those who worked with her to be of a cheerful disposition. 'This makes quite a change from a damp council house.'

'Morning, Dr Fay.' Hirst greeted her warmly. 'Yes, indeed it does...indeed it does. Well, one deceased of the male sex, pronounced life extinct by the police surgeon at ten past ten this forenoon.'

'I see.' Gwen Fay viewed the corpse. 'Looks like quite a fight he put up. Haven't seen a face as battered as that for some time. Usually indicates an attack driven by passion.'

'Yes.'

'Somebody who doesn't have a personal axe to grind against his victim will attack the body but an attacker fuelled with hate will attack his or her victim's face.'

Clive Hirst nodded. 'That's a good point. We have assumed up to now that he disturbed a burglary, but the damage to his face, as you say, that points to a personal motive. We should have seen that. This might be more complicated after all.'

'Well, we'll see.' Gwendoline Fay knelt by the body as she snapped on a pair of latex gloves. 'You'll be wanting the time of death.'

'It would be useful.'

'Well, the time of death, Detective Chief Inspector, is between the time he was last seen alive by an independent witness and the time he was found deceased. Frankly, that is as accurate as any scientific measurement will tell you. Too many variables...but day clothing...'

'Yes, we noted that...managed to do that.'

'Blood beginning to congeal...this time of year...this turn went down late yesterday evening. And that's as close as I'll commit to in respect of time. Too much blood just for a facial battering, a lot on the shirt.' She unbuttoned the front of the shirt. 'Ah...stab wounds, that's where the blood has come from, and this one here...' she pointed to an incision at the bottom of the ribcage, 'if this has an upward plane and if the blade was of sufficient length, it may well have penetrated the aorta...instant death. The wounds to the stomach would have caused a slower death if he couldn't have been hospitalised in time. Any weapon found?'

'A hammer...quite a small hammer, hardly the classic

blunt object, not heavy enough to do any damage I would have thought...and a tea towel soaked in blood, can't fit that into the jigsaw. I can't see anybody wiping up the blood.'

'No, that is strange. So, have you taken all the pics you need to take?'

'Yes, all done.'

'And there is a positive identification?' Fay looked up at Hirst.

'Again, yes, one Maurice Woolley aged sixty-seven years.'

'And a heavy drinker.'

'Yes...the bottle...and even in death he reeks of the stuff.'

'Yes, indeed.' Gwendoline Fay stood. 'Might have been a little easier for him. If he was drunk he might not have felt the terror he would have done had he been sober. Like those poor boys in the trenches in the First World War,' Gwendoline Fay grimaced. 'They had to get them drunk in order to get them to leave the trench and attack the German lines.'

'Really?'

'Yes. I never knew my grandfather, I was a bit of a late baby, unplanned, but my father often told me that he and hence me and my brothers are only here because his father got drunk. You see, they were standing round the dixie of rum, proper naval rum I believe, it had been diluted the navy way, and my grandfather just happened to be standing next to a Salvationist who had signed the pledge, and the Salvationist offered his tot of rum to my grandfather so he got two tots...double ration.'

'Lucky man,' Hirst smiled.

'Well, as you'll hear, luck is not the word. Anyway, the whistle blew and they all scrambled out of the trench, over the parapet, eighteen, nineteen, twenty something...such a waste...and my grandfather, having had double rum ration, ran for about six paces, so the story goes, and keeled over, comatose through alcohol excess. I mean, it shows you how strong a tot of rum was if two tots could do that to a serving soldier, a young man in the peak of physical condition.'

'They must have been out of their skulls.'

'Makes you angry. Anyway, he came to a few hours later with a mother and father of a hangover feeling very fragile and crawled back to the British lines and found out he was the only one of his platoon to have survived the charge, and he went on to survive the war.'

'Blimey.'

'Yes, as you say. If he hadn't been standing next to the Salvationist, or if the Salvationist had turned to the man on the other side... Well, my grandfather was a hard drinking man all his life and I think it blighted my father's childhood. My grandfather would apparently say that the stuff saved his life, so what harm could it do him? My father, like the children of many alcoholics, doesn't drink, but unlike other children of alcoholics, he doesn't hate alcohol. He has few good memories of his childhood because of alcohol, but he has never been able to escape the fact that it is only because of alcohol that he, and subsequently his children and his grandchildren, are alive. He has an ambivalence towards it that has never left him. I, too, have that same ambivalence, probably felt less keenly than my father because my childhood wasn't blighted in the same way his was, but I don't like dwelling on the narrow escape our family line had, especially when I look at my own children. They are alive, giving me such joy, because of a tot of rum consumed nearly a hundred years ago. Makes me feel very insecure to dwell on it.'

'Quite a story.'

'Yes.' She nodded to the bottle of whisky 'I'm here only because of that stuff. Well, if you'd care to remove our dear departed from here to York District, I'll conduct the postmortem this afternoon. Will you be observing for the police?'

'I dare say,' Clive Hirst smiled, 'for my sins. Yes, I'll be observing.'

'Boss!' Richard Pulleyne stepped into the drawing room. 'Found something...a bloodstained knife.'

Virginia Woolley drove to Christopher Elms' flat, stopping at a branch of Safeways en route. She searched the immediate area for the white van and, not seeing it nor any other parked vehicle that looked as though it may contain a photographer behind its darkened windows, she deemed it safe to ring his doorbell. She heard him bound down the stairs towards the door. He flung it open and she stepped forward and bundled him inside. 'Careful,' she said, pressing him against the wall with bulging plastic bags in each hand. 'Careful.' She kicked the front door shut behind her.

'Virginia...Virginia...' He clutched her, shaking. She thought him close to tears. 'It was horrible...horrible...I've killed someone.'

'Shut up!' She gripped his shoulder. 'Quiet...don't you see,' she hissed, 'that's just the sort of talk that will finish us? Come on upstairs, I've brought food for you. Get a grip...calm yourself...upstairs.'

In his flat she sat on the settee, put three plastic bags containing food beside her, a fourth bag she placed on the floor out of his view. 'But you did it though...'

'Yes, but it was messy. I thought I'd done him with the hammer but he got up, came at me from behind. I stabbed him...there was blood everywhere.'

'Alright...try and keep calm. Did you get rid of the knife?'

'Yes. I threw it into a river, it looked deep and muddy, no one will ever find it.'

'Good. So far, so good. If we keep calm, we'll get away with it.'

'Yes...keep calm, have to keep calm...just pacing up and down in here, like an animal in a cage. It's horrible, you have no idea.'

'Just be strong, lie low. I've brought you some food, mostly in tins, but enough for a week or two. So why don't you put this in the kitchen?' she patted the three plastic bags, 'and while you are in there, put the kettle on. We both need a strong cup of tea. I'll tell you what I told the police.'

'The police have spoken to you already?'

'Of course they have. I found the body, didn't I? Come on. I'd help you ordinarily, but it's important for you to do something, so come on, get this fodder in the kitchen.'

Christopher Elms picked up the three bags and carried them into the kitchen. As soon as he had disappeared from view and was heard putting cans on shelves, Virginia Woolley leaned to one side and opened the plastic bag she had laid on the floor. From it she took the pair of shoes she had acquired from Christopher Elms and wearing which she had stepped into her husband's blood. She slipped the shoes under the settee, pushing them well out of sight. She folded the plastic bag and put it in her handbag, then breathed a sigh of relief. That manoeuvre had gone easier than expected.

A matter of minutes later Christopher Elms emerged from the kitchen carrying two mugs of steaming tea. He handed one to Virginia Woolley.

'Well...' she held the mug in both hands and sat forward. 'It's all going to plan, there's nothing to connect you with the murder.'

'The murder?' He spoke with evident despair. 'What have I done? What have I done? Never been in trouble with the police, ever, then I commit the worst... It's not happening...it's a dream.'

'No...it is happening and it's very real...but you don't have to do anything else, just stay indoors...and stay calm.'

'It's easy for you to say, you haven't murdered anyone.'

Virginia Woolley thought, 'Oh, how wrong you are...not as messily as you did it...but how wrong you are,' but said, 'No, I haven't, but it's alright, the police believe that my husband disturbed a burglar, so they'll be looking at known felons with a record for housebreaking. Alright?'

'Yes, Virginia.'

'You wore the gloves throughout?'

'Yes.'

'The knife has gone?'

'Yes, thrown away. Like I said, no one will find it.'

'Good. If you have any bloodstained clothing you should put it in a plastic bag and take it to the laundrette in a few days' time.'

'A few days?'

'Yes...this is one minute, one hour, one day at a time...understood?'

'Yes, Virginia.'

'Don't go to the pub, alcohol will loosen your tongue and if you blurt something out the way you did down in the hallway just now, well, we're both finished,' she stood. 'So stay calm. I'm going now.'

'Back there?'

'No. To my sister's.'

'Down in Dorset?'

'Yes. The police drove me back to the house, I picked up my car...told them where I'd be. I am not under suspicion. They understood that I don't want to be in the house, not for a few days and I think they rather liked the idea of me being out of the way. I'll contact you.'

'When?'

'A few weeks.'

'Weeks!'

'Yes, I have already told you that. Look, Chris, do you want a life with me, the villa in Gozo in the winter, the house in Windermere during the summer?'

'Yes, of course I do, that is the plan.'

'Good, because I want that too...but we must earn it. Not contacting each other is the next phase of the plan. One day at a time. I'll see myself out. You be good for me and keep your head.'

In the hallway she opened the door gingerly, looking for the white van. Not seeing it or any possible stand-in vehicle, she walked calmly to her car and drove to Hull, where she and her sister spent the remainder of the afternoon and much of the evening in the Hull Mariner, two girls together, laughing and planning their futures.

Clive Hirst opened the door and walked into the room. As he did so, all conversation stopped. 'Sorry I am late.' He stood in front of the whiteboard and put his briefcase on the desk. 'Just come from the post-mortem...smell of formaldehyde.' He glanced at those present: PC Deere, Detective Constable Lucas, DS Dickie Pulleyne. 'Dare say I'll catch hell from my wife when I get home. She does complain about me bringing the smell of death into the house...the smell of preservation fluid isn't quite the same, but try telling her that.' There was a hum of softened laughter, just sufficient to break the tension. Hirst sat in the chair and reached for the whiteboard marker. 'Right, what have we got? Remember, this is not presenting the case in the court, here everything goes into the pot, anything at all...observations, suspicions, intuition...you know the score by now. So, PC Deere...'

'Sir?'

'You were the first on the scene, anything to offer?'

'I don't think so, sir. She did seem quite genuine to me.'

'Yes.' Hirst stood and wrote the date on the whiteboard, below which he wrote "Maurice Woolley, Murder". 'See anything relevant to the inquiry?'

'Didn't, sir, just the deceased.'

Hirst smiled. 'Yes, that's relevant, I dare say,' there was a second hum of laughter, 'but nothing else?' He wrote 118/120 under the word murder. 'That's the case number. Please take a note of it.' Three pens were lifted to three notebooks. 'Alright,' Hirst resumed his seat, 'let's start with

the facts so as to give everybody an overview. The deceased
is Mr Maurice Woolley, sixty-seven years; he was, we
believe, a lotto winner. His sister has phoned me in
response to a call DC Lucas made to her notifying her of
her brother's murder. She gave a little information on the
phone, that's how I know he's a Lotto winner. She is anxious to talk to me, very anxious, but kindly agreed to delay
coming up from South Yorkshire, where she lives. She
seemed to understand the importance of the first 24 hours
following a murder, probably watches a lot of television,'
again a hum of laughter. 'But she claims to have something
to tell us, but what she has to tell us will wait, she said.'
Hirst paused. He glanced out of the window at the rooftops
of well-set Harrogate basking under a blue, early evening
sky. 'The post-mortem has been concluded. Dr Fay has
found, as she suspected, that death was due to a knife being
thrust into the deceased's heart. Other knife wounds to the
stomach would have led to his death, but it was the single
upward thrust into his chest cavity that killed him. There is
evidence that he was a hardened drinker, but Dr Fay was
puzzled by the absence of damage to his liver and kidneys,
suggesting that he had hit the bottle late in life, but that is
probably not relevant. What is relevant is that, as well as the
knife wounds, there was massive damage to the face. The
front of the deceased's skull was fractured in many places,
cheek bones, teeth smashed, one eye practically destroyed,
jaw smashed. We found a small hammer at the scene and
also a blood-soaked tea towel.' Hirst paused. 'Dr Fay said
that the wounds to the head, well, rather to the face of the
deceased, were consistent with blows from the type of hammer found and she suggests that what might have been the
scenario was that the deceased was lying sleeping, probably
quite drunk, and the attacker covered Mr Woolley's head
with the cloth then rained blows upon him. Thinking then
he was at least incapacitated, the attacker began to break
into the display cabinet whereupon Mr Woolley came to,

because the blows were not to his skull, and so did not render him unconscious, as the attacker had clearly hoped. He then confronted the attacker, who stabbed him in the ensuing fight. Gloves appear to have been worn throughout; no prints on the hammer, or the cabinet. The hammer and the teacloth are at the forensic science laboratory at Wetherby, where the blood will be analysed, but it is doubtless that it will be matched to the deceased's blood.' Hirst paused. 'Entry to the property appeared to have been via a small downstairs window which, for some reason, is not alarmed. Perhaps Mrs Woolley will be able to explain why that is the case. Exit was via the front door which, when opened, triggered the alarm. The alarm system itself has recorded that it was the opening of the front door that set the alarm off, at exactly 11.37 p.m. That would be the time of the murder, no need to put upon the good Dr Fay for once. The murderer didn't hang around after he had stabbed Maurice Woolley. Nothing was stolen...he fled in panic...no fingerprints, but Dick, I think you have something for us?'

'Yes, sir.' Richard Pulleyne sat forward. 'Lovely footprint in the flowerbed. Couldn't be clearer...we've taken a cast of it. There's also a footprint in the blood in the house.'

'Good.'

'And possibly the murder weapon itself. A knife covered in blood was found on the lawn as if thrown away in panic. It appears to have been removed from the nest of knives in the kitchen. Interestingly, it appears to have fingerprints.'

'Possibly the householder's?' Hirst raised an eyebrow.

'It's possible, of course, it's even likely, but what does make these latents interesting is that they were not smudged. If the latents were those of the householder, and if the murderer wore gloves, you'd expect the prints to be smudged.'

'But they're not?'

'Nope.'

'Possible explanation?'

'Killer took off his gloves as he ran from the house in panic. Without thinking he held the knife for a brief instant with an un-gloved hand before throwing it away.'

'Plausible,' Hirst nodded. 'Quite possible. We all know what folk are capable of doing in panic.'

'No match on the prints as of now, sir. Knife has gone to the forensic science laboratory to have the blood analysed. As you said with the hammer and the teacloth, it will doubtless prove to be that of the deceased.'

'Thanks, Dickie. I feel a sense of early progress.' Hirst looked at DC Lucas. 'Anything for us, René?'

'Yes, sir. I interviewed Mrs Woolley. She…' DC Lucas sat back in her chair.

'Something has occurred to you, I think, René?' Hirst's expression was warm, approving.

'It has…it did and it hasn't left me, in fact over the last hour or so the conviction has strengthened.'

'The conviction?'

'The conviction that she is a conspirator in the murder.'

Hirst sensed a sudden tension in the room. He held the pause and then said, 'Alright, in your own time, René.'

'Thank you, sir. Well, in terms of the information she gave, she was with her sister in Hull last night, visiting, she said, and staying overnight. Sounded to be a regular thing that she did. An easily checked alibi anyway, unless said sister is in on it, and that is if I am right, but…'

'It's alright, René, not presenting a case to a jury, as I said, anything and everything goes into the pot.' Hirst rested his elbows on the table.

'Very good, sir. Well, it's a number of things really; number one, she impressed as being very skilled in terms of her presentation, didn't overact, didn't come on as the grieving widow, seemed shocked but not overly so and she wasn't in a hurry to provide information that would point to her absence of involvement, which would have been very suspicious. So, in terms of her manner, she is an actor of consummate skill and is happy to be under suspicion, or I am way out in left-field and she is genuinely uninvolved in the murder.' Lucas paused. 'But there's more. There is the fact that her husband is a Lotto winner, as you said, to the tune of nine million pounds.' Again she paused as the sound of gasps filled the room. 'So, she's a wealthy woman as of now. We can safely assume that, and there is an age gap of thirty years between her and the deceased, and they were married for less than three years. It wasn't said in so many words, sir, but the strong impression was that they married after the Lotto win. Easy to check anyway.'

'Very easy.'

'It comes down to intuition. I have learned to listen to my intuition.'

'And I have learned not to underestimate female intuition,' Hirst grinned. 'But do carry on, this is good.'

'That's it, really, sir. I just felt that I was in the presence of a cold, calculating, manipulative, cruel person. One who is well capable of orchestrating a murder but keeping herself well distanced.'

'Orchestrating,' Hirst echoed. He thought it a perfect choice of word, but then he thought he would expect nothing less from a graduate in English Literature. 'Controlling from a distance...you felt she was capable of that?'

'Oh, yes, sir. Very much.'

'Interesting. Where is she now, do we know?'

'Hull, back with her sister, so she said. Didn't want to spend the night in the house. I could understand that, so, after taking her statement, I drove her back to the family home, the White House, would you believe?' There was a little suppressed laughter. 'Anyway, she drove off in her Merc. No reason to detain her, sir.'

'None. She's still not under suspicion and she's not of the criminal milieu...she won't be able to hide.'

'Don't think she wants to, sir. If I am correct about her, she seems to be content to weather the storm of suspicion in order to collect nine million at the end of it, or whatever her share will be in accordance with his will, and if he died intestate, she'll get everything.'

'Quite some motivation.' Hirst leaned back in his chair. 'I don't think you are off in left-field at all. I think we ought to get to know this lady a little better. Her sister-in-law is coming to see me tomorrow, we'll see what she has to say. Well, thank you all, and thank you especially if you have, as you have, PC Deere, worked into overtime to be here. We'll pick this up tomorrow. This meeting is concluded.' Hirst tapped his pen on the desk.

That evening René Lucas walked into a pub. It was something that, like most women, she rarely did alone, but she needed somewhere else to go, other than her cramped flat, and the pub offered the illusion of companionship and human warmth. She ordered a gin, and then another and still another.

To stay or to return? House prices were rising, indeed rocketing, the money in the bank from her own house sale wasn't much, she had had a little equity but it wasn't working for her where it was. She knew she had to put it into bricks and mortar soon, very soon, but bricks and mortar up here? Or home? Again she fondled and rummaged in her handbag for her phone, and finding it, held it, just held it, as she ordered more alcohol.

Clive Hirst thought Mabel Strong to be an aptly named woman. She was, he saw, round of face, buxom, hair in a perm, no decoration except for an engagement and wedding ring, a necklace, a functional looking watch, tweed twin set, sensible shoes, no make-up save for a little lipstick, a Yorkshire accent. She just was a "Mabel". She was also strong. She seemed to have a physical strength. She looked to have strong arms and was large-boned and taller than the average woman, and she also impressed Hirst as being strong in the emotional, psychological sense; there was a look of steely determination in her eyes. She would, he thought, make a formidable opponent.

'Thank you,' Hirst spoke, trying to relax his posture while he noted Mrs Strong remained sitting upright as though being interviewed for a job or having just received a "sit up straight in your chair" admonition. She held a brown paper envelope in her hands, which she kept, held together, on her lap. 'Few members of the public seem to know the value of keeping out of the way during the first twenty-four hours of a murder inquiry, unless of course, they have vital information, and thank you for travelling up to see us.'

'Well, I should tell you that I am an ex-girl in blue.'

'Really?' Hirst beamed at her.

'Yes, really. I was a detective constable with the South Yorkshire police, so I know how things work, and have no problem about travelling. Barnsley isn't really far away and it's a pleasant drive. I haven't been to Harrogate for many a long year. I just wish the circumstances could have been different.'

'Yes, it can't be pleasant. I am sorry about Mr Woolley. You can perhaps answer a few questions for us, but first I understand you have information that is, you believe, pertinent to the inquiry?'

'Yes. Dare say you could say that.' She held up the envelope and handed it to Hirst. 'The photographs in there are
of my sister-in-law and her young lover, "toyboy", is, I
believe, the expression. His name is Christopher Elms and
he murdered my brother.'

Hirst held eye contact with Mabel Strong. He cupped his
chin in his hand. 'If you'd care to tell me what you know?'

'I don't know where to begin,' she glanced round the
small room. 'This is more comfortable than the interview
rooms in my last nick...light, airy, even have carpets...we
had lino and no source of natural light.'

Hirst let her speak. He knew she was finding her own
words. He knew it was her way of preventing herself from
freezing.

'It was that damned lotto win.'

'Damned win? I know people who survive on a day-by-
day basis in the hope that they might win the next lottery.'

'As we all do, and my husband and I did well out of the
win, but it ruined Maurice. You may as well know the truth
of it. Maurice was my brother, a full fifteen years older than
me, and I loved him but he was a disappointment to our
parents and an embarrassment to our family. He couldn't
hold a job down, had massive periods of unemployment
punctuated by a job here and a job there. The longest job he
held was as a dishwasher in a Chinese restaurant...that
lasted about two months. He lived in private rented accommodation, dingy flats with the low-lifes of this world...folk
who die and their bodies are found weeks later when the
landlord forces entry to find out why his rent is
overdue...people with nobody, people who are buried in a
pauper's grave, three coffins to a plot. He lived his life
amongst them.'

'Yet you turned out to be successful. Do you know why?'

'No...nature, not nurture, in Maurice's case, he just never
seemed to connect with the world...head in the air...feet
permanently eighteen inches off the ground, that was just

our Maurice. He was my brother but he was a waste of space. Then about three years ago now…the way he tells it is that he was ambling down the street, not due any welfare for another two days, but had food enough in his bedsit to survive. He had a pound in his pocket…so it was half a pint of beer or a lotto ticket.'

'And he won the lotto?'

'Nine million pounds. I knew it would be the end of him…just didn't realise how final it would be.'

'That explains something that puzzled me.'

'Oh?'

'Yes. Yesterday I walked round the White House…'

'Yes, the name amuses many folk but it in fact has always been called the White House, from the mid-eighteenth century. The first owner had the corners of the house painted white, a subsequent owner had the whole lot painted white, so it was called by its present name, but it does predate the more famous White House in Washington DC, it even predates the first White House.'

'The first White House?'

'The present White House in Washington DC was built in the 1860s. The first one was a much smaller affair and was burned by the British in 1801, I think it was.'

'Didn't know that.'

'Just one of those things I happen to know. Anyway, Maurice's house was built in 1770, before America became the United States, so it's safe to assume that his White House, Maurice's White House, predates even the original White House in Washington.'

'Well, you live, you learn…but what puzzled me as I walked round Mr Woolley's house was how unlived in it felt…so many unused and empty rooms…and the rooms that were used seemed to have new furniture.'

'Yes, well, if you've just come from a bedsit you don't have a great deal with which to furnish and fill a twenty-roomed country house.'

'The collection of watches?'

'All bought by Maurice over the last three years.'

'I see.'

'And the new furniture for the rooms that were used, well, he had to fill it with something.'

'Of course.'

'He was stupid enough to agree to publicity and no sooner than the publicity machine had done its bit, than did madam arrive from the south of England.'

'Mrs Virginia Woolley?'

'The little tart...and I mean tart. You know her, she has convictions for soliciting.'

'Really?'

'Yes, really. You'd hardly credit it, would you? She was Mrs Virginia Woostencroft, very classy, fitted her name...but I was still with the police then, I obtained her fingerprints and did some checks. She is a.k.a. Vera Wortley and has two convictions for soliciting for purposes of prostitution. Fined ten pounds by the Hull magistrates, nearly twenty years ago now, she was a teenager at the time. Straight out of school and onto Waterhouse Lane.'

'That's the red light district in Hull?'

'Yes, that's where the girls stand looking for passing trade...at least they did then.'

'I don't know Hull, I confess.'

'You are missing little. It isn't my favourite city. A very strange place, it's not just the relentless wind off the North Sea, and that can be a biter in winter, it's something I can't put my finger on, it's all there and yet the city hasn't got that spark that makes it work. Each time I go to Hull I have a feeling that I am descending down into something and each time I leave I have the opposite feeling...that I am climbing out of something. But maybe that's just me.'

'As I say, I can't comment.'

'Anyway, once I realised madam's game, I did some digging, tried to warn Maurice, but Maurice, he had never had a girlfriend in his life and then suddenly out of the blue there's Miss Class Act from the southern counties offering matrimonial bliss…and got what she wanted, all eight million.'

'Eight?'

'Yes. Maurice gave a million to me and my husband.'

'I see.'

'I won't pretend it didn't help us. I never amounted to anything in the police…early fifties, still a detective constable and in the Child Protection Unit…a "kiddie cop" as we were called. Got paid the same as a DC in the drug squad or the serious crime squad, but we didn't get the prestige. You know what police canteen culture is…and my husband, he was a primary school teacher, never got the headship he felt he deserved. So the million enabled us to take early retirement, it enabled us to sell our ailing and ageing Nissan and buy a new Volvo. We sold our little three-bedroom semi and bought a five-bedroom detached house with an acre of garden and we haven't even scratched the surface of the million, house prices around Barnsely being as low as they are.'

'You wouldn't,' Hirst smiled.

'The rest is put by for our children and their children. But Maurice started to drink; he had nothing to fill in his days so he hit the bottle. Never was a drinker before…no money…but after the Lotto win he was sinking a bottle in a single day, then drying out for a day or two, then sinking another bottle.'

'Yes…the pathologist commented on the absence of liver and kidney damage, given his age and apparent alcohol consumption.'

'Because he had only been drinking heavily for a few years.'

'And you were suspicious of Mrs Woolley's motives?' Hirst leafed through the photographs Strong had handed him. 'With good reason, it seems.'

'Suspicion isn't the word. Her motivation was transparent, she just couldn't wait for him to die of natural causes, she wanted her lolly now.'

'If we can prove her involvement, Maurice Woolley's money would go where? Do you know?'

'No, I don't. The will has yet to be read though I believe he left it all to her. But if you can prove her involvement, she won't be allowed to inherit anything he might leave her...can't profit from a crime, so I dare say what he might have left her will come to me as his only surviving relative...' She drew a deep breath, 'but I want to make it plain that is not my motivation for pointing an accusing finger at her. I want you to know that, Mr Hirst.'

'Understood.'

'It's not that I want it, it's more that I don't want her to have it. I don't want to win. I want her to lose. I'm probably not making a lot of sense...'

'I think I know what you are saying, Mabel. You don't mind if I call you Mabel?'

'Not at all.'

'Call me Clive, if you like...two cops.'

'Ex-cop.'

'Near enough.'

'Thanks, Clive.'

'So, did you take these snaps yourself? They're very good.'

'Heavens, no...I hired a private investigator, told him of my suspicions...he followed her.'

'I'm interested in these photographs,' Hirst held up the photographs showing Christopher Elms looking across the field which separated the road from the White House, 'he looks like he's sighting up the property.'

'Yes, the private investigator recognised him, he was waiting there in case Virginia left the house, thought it curious and took the photographs.'

'I see...and Mr Elms lives at this address you have here?'

'Yes...so the private detective informs me...haven't been there myself.'

'Okay...now, what about the alarm system.'

'Yes, we thought of that, he must have steamed in...nobody takes any notice of those alarms, not even the intruder...my husband says.'

'Actually, it's more intriguing than that,' Hirst interrupted her. 'We found the point of entry, a small ground floor window at the back of the house. For some reason it was not alarmed. The alarm appears to have been triggered when the burglar, whom you claim to be Christopher Elms, escaped the premises via the front door.'

'An un-alarmed window?' Mabel Strong frowned. 'That is interesting...puzzling...that's news to me. They had an earlier break-in not long after they were first married.'

'Did they?'

'Yes. Maurice overpowered the burglar and sat on him until the police arrived...a nasty called Parsloe, Shane Parsloe.'

'Was Mrs Woolley at home at the time?'

'No...no...she wasn't.' Mabel Strong's voice seemed to Hirst to falter, as though she was remembering or realising something. 'Just like this burglary...and he was a young man too, in his early twenties...just like Mr Elms.'

'Most burglars are in their late teens or early twenties, can't read anything into that.'

'No, but what is interesting is that he came from east Leeds, I believe.'

'A long way to travel to turn a window.'

'That's what I thought, it was as if he had help in targeting the house.'

'I see where your suspicions are leading, Mabel.'

'Well, after that Maurice had the house alarmed. But an un-alarmed window, that's news to me.'

'Do you know how Parsloe effected entry?' Hirst wrote Parsloe's name on his pad.

'A window at the rear of the house, not a small one though, a large sash window. He just slid it up and in he went.'

'I see. We'll pay him a call anyway, as you say, the similarities are...interesting.'

'Very interesting, I'd say. Puts someone up to murder Maurice, doesn't work...waits, then tries again...successfully.'

'Yes. I didn't want to say so in so many words but...yes, it does seem that could be a possibility. Just one more point, did you say that Mrs Woolley claimed to be widowed?'

'So she said. Widowed twice before she's forty, very tragic or very convenient if her first husband was as wealthy as Maurice, depends how you look at it. She certainly had money...those clothes, the Cartier watch...it was probably her way of telling Maurice that she really wasn't a gold digger, that might have been her ploy.'

'We'll have to do some digging, turn over a stone or two. What was the marriage like?'

'It wasn't. She kept going off to "visit her sister", so she claimed. Off with a man somewhere.'

'You think?'

'Well, a week or so ago she "visited her sister" for a week and came home with a sun tan.'

'And your brother accepted that?'

'Yes.'

'He did?'

'Yes. Yes, he did. I even showed him the photographs the private detective took and he said he knew, he knew what was going on when she was "visiting her sister" but he said if he stopped her, she'd go anyway but wouldn't return. This way, he said, at least she came back. I think he was content that she was there to set the house off, like an ornament for his enjoyment. They shared the same bed but...well, I don't know, that doesn't mean anything.'

'She was Mrs Woostencroft?'

'I believe so…might have been Woostenholme.' Mabel Strong paused, searching her memory. 'No…no…I am as certain as I can be that she was Woostencroft. Yes, yes it was Woostencroft. Certain.'

'Where did she live before coming to Yorkshire?'

'Dorset. Minster something…or something Minster.'

'It'll be Wimborne Minster, boss.' René Lucas tapped her pen on the arm of her chair as she sat with Hirst and Pulleyne in the conference suite. The room was too large for their purposes but it was the only room in the building that they could find which wasn't being used. Consequently they "borrowed" it, to confer. 'I spent my life in Hampshire before coming north, it shares a border with Dorset. There will doubtless be other Minsters in Dorset but Wimborne Minster is the one that springs to mind.'

'Right.' Hirst jabbed a finger in René Lucas' direction. 'You start phoning, find out what you can about the death of a prominent man named Woostencroft in the Wimborne Minster area. Don't know when but possibly within the last five years.'

'Will do, boss.'

'Play your cards right and there might be a trip to the beautiful south in it for you.'

'Great!' Lucas smiled. 'I could rather fancy that. It will save the money sending me: I'd stay with my parents. They live in Hampshire, as I said, only about half an hour's drive from Wimborne.'

'Mutually convenient. You, Dickie…'

'Yes, boss.'

'You and I will go and arrest Christopher Elms on suspicion of murder. We'll get a warrant to search his flat before we go…these photographs…Mabel Strong's statement, it's more than enough for a warrant.'

René Lucas sat at her desk, stirring the sugar in her coffee with her pen as the screensaver wandered mesmerically, gently, around the monitor screen of her computer. She pressed the phone to her ear with her left shoulder, holding, as she had been asked to hold. The line clicked and what was for her a homely southern accent, said, 'Hello, DS Moon speaking.'

'Hi, DC Lucas, North Yorkshire CID.'

'Hello.' The voice was warm.

'Hello. The reason I am calling is to enquire if you have any knowledge of a local bigwig, that is, local to the Wimborne Minster area, a local bigwig called Woostencroft who died a few years ago in circumstances that may have been suspicious?'

'Yes...that rings bells. It's often the details of the case you remember, but the names tend to evaporate from your memory, unless of course they are major cases in which all the details get logged in the brain box, but that name... Wait a mo...' Lucas listened as DS Moon appealed to the office in which he was sitting. 'Anyone here recall a local fat cat called Woostencroft who died a few years ago...possible suspicious circumstances?'

'The old guy in the swimming pool?' a male voice shouted from some distance.

'Yes...left a lot of dosh.'

'That's it...young widow.'

'Remember it well.' Then to Lucas he said, 'You there?'

'Yes.'

'Dare say you heard that?'

'About the swimming pool?'

'Yes. Old boy, swimming in his indoor pool. He died of a heart attack while swimming. Nothing suspicious in that, but there were very slight whiffs of suspicion that only a copper's nose could pick up.'

'Oh?'

'Well...the old boy was healthy, no history of heart disease. The heart was healthy when examined by our pathologist but he explained that fear could induce a coronary in a healthy heart.'

'So I believe.'

'Then there was the money. He was a financier...left his house and over a million in realisable assets, stocks and shares and property to his wife who was thirty years his junior and to whom he had been married for less than eighteen months.'

'Yes.'

'Finally, there were the scarves.'

'The scarves?'

'Yes...two silk scarves...knotted and also cut, found by the brother of the deceased in the waste bin in the kitchen. He didn't report them for a few days, by which time they had been put outside by the widow with the rest of the contents of the bin, in a bin liner and had then been collected by the council...irretrievable...so their significance, if any, couldn't be assessed.'

'I see.'

'So it was death by misadventure. Case closed.'

'Yes...name of a state in the USA'

'Virginia,' a voice called from the room in which Moon sat.

'Thanks,' Moon said. 'Hear that?'

'Yes. Virginia. When did Mr Woostencroft drown?'

'About four years ago. Probably nearer five.'

'So Virginia Woostencroft would have been about thirty-two years old?'

'Yes. About. Quite a nice age to come into a cool million or two. And greed is the oldest of motives.'

'As you say.'

'Why the interest, can I ask?'

'Well, we largely suspect that milady might have put in a repeat performance up here in the frozen north.'

'Really?'

'Yes, except she's polishing her act, probably getting

someone to do her dirty work for her and probably vastly increasing her gains. Not a million plus in realisable assets this time, would you believe, but a cool eight million.'

'Eight million!'

'Yep. First and only wife of a lotto winner thirty years her senior.'

'This is looking like an established pattern.'

'Isn't it just,' said René Lucas, 'isn't it just.'

In Clive Hirst's experience, no two arrests are ever the same: there are those who come quietly, instantly compliant; there are those who do what they can to ingratiate themselves with the arresting officers, cracking jokes during the ride down town and at the charge bar; there are those who run; there are those who resist violently; but the arrest of Christopher Elms was totally outside Hirst's experience. The ringing of the doorbell, the wait, the footsteps on the stairs – sounding a little nervous, thought Hirst – the timid opening of the door, the colour draining from Elms' face as he clearly recognised Hirst and Pulleyne for the police officers that they were, the buckling of the legs at the knees, the futile attempt to slam the door as tears burst from Elms' eyes and his face crumpled like a paper bag being screwed up, the crying of 'no...no...no...no...'. It was not a resisting of arrest in Hirst's eyes, it was more, he thought, in the manner of psychological denial; the young man just could not take on board what he had done. Pulleyne, too, Hirst realised, saw what he saw: saw Elms' reaction for what it was and he, not Hirst, took control of the situation, gently pushing the door against Elms' weak resistance and, in a fatherly-like gesture, putting his arm round Elms' hunched shoulders and guiding him, coaxing him out of the house, softly saying, 'Come on, Christopher...come on,' and into the rear of a waiting police vehicle, whereupon he was handcuffed to a police constable and conveyed to the police station in Harrogate.

Hirst and Pulleyne searched Elms' flat, rapidly finding

the old pair of shoes under the settee with what appeared to be soil and blood impressed into the pattern of the soles, and in the laundry basket they found jeans and a shirt stained with what appeared to be blood. All items of interest were bagged and tagged and sent by courier to the forensic science laboratory at Wetherby.

René Lucas declined the offer of a cup of tea. It was her distinct impression that she was in the presence of two extremely unpleasant women. 'So, you'll confirm Mrs Woolley's alibi, Mrs Roberts? That your sister was here with you on the night in question?'

'Yes.' Mrs Roberts smiled gleefully as she replied.

Lucas averted her gaze; it was too damn gleeful, in her opinion.

'Any other person that could confirm the alibi?'

'Pub full of punters…we spent the night in the Mariner.'

'Anybody who knows you personally?'

Both women shook their heads slowly, then Mrs Roberts said, 'Wait a minute,' she looked at her sister, 'wasn't that the night…? It was, course it was, that was the night that your handbag got nicked.'

'Yes,' Mrs Woolley gasped, 'yes, it was. Yes, my handbag was stolen from me, right outside the door, a little street turk grabbed it and ran. He was only about ten.'

'If that…'

'You saw the incident?'

'Yes,' Mrs Roberts nodded, 'but the point is that it was reported, wasn't it, sis?'

'Yes…we reported it to the police in Hull. At Queen's Gardens police station.'

"How very convenient," thought René Lucas, "so damn convenient it smells like Hull Fish Market at the end of a trading day in high summer." The report of the crime would be genuine enough but the crime itself would probably be a work of fiction. Like an insurance scam in the days before insurance companies started to give tokens to replace stolen items instead of a single cash lump sum in settlement. In those days a homeowner could force entry into his own property, having removed any items of value to a safe place, report the crime, obtain a crime number, obtain an insurance payment to replace what was "lost". The "stolen" items then miraculously find their way back into the person's house and the homeowner has money for a very pleasant summer holiday. Can't do it too often...but once every five or six years... It was the case, Lucas knew, that when insurance companies started to give tokens that could be exchanged in shops to replace stolen items, burglaries in Britain were much reduced in frequency. And here, in front of her, was much the same scam, an invented crime, not for any insurance compensation, but so as to give Mrs Woolley the cast iron alibi of all time. At about the time her husband was murdered, she was in a police station fifty miles away, giving a statement and obtaining a crime number. Very neat. Checking her claim would have to be done, but it would, Lucas was fully aware, be a formality. Mrs Woolley needed an alibi and the Humberside Police provided it for her. 'Well, that's easily checked.'

The two sisters smiled.

'Mrs Woolley, I understand you were previously married?' René Lucas enjoyed the look of shock that crossed Virginia Woolley's face.

'What's that got to do with Maurice's death?'

'Probably nothing.' René Lucas noticed that Mrs Roberts also looked unnerved at her question. 'But we won't know until we have investigated.'

'My husband had a heart attack. My first husband, that is.'

'Where was that?'

'At home...at our house.'

'Where was that?'

'Dorset. Wimborne Minster.'

'Ah...I know it, lovely little town. I'm from Hampshire, if you remember.'

'Aye. I was never really happy there; I grew up in East Hull. Dorset's a bit too chocolate-boxy. I could only ever see Wimborne as a toy town...no docks...no fishing industry.'

'I can understand that. I've come across northerners who have moved to the south and come to feel that they are cheating; life just isn't hard enough down there. They feel they are getting away with it. Whatever "it" is.' Lucas wanted to encourage dialogue; she felt her question might have caused the sisters to put up their guard. She wanted it down. She wanted them to believe they were in control. Her father had taught her the valuable lesson: "It is possible to win by allowing the other person to think that they have won, so be aware of a victory which comes too easily, for therein may lie your defeat." So had often said her lovely, lovely father, whom she might see again one day soon, courtesy of the calculating Mrs Virginia Woolley. 'So what was your address in Wimborne?'

Virginia Woolley paused. 'There was an inquest. My first husband died by misadventure.'

'Yes...I am sure there is no relevancy, Mrs Woolley, but we do need to obtain background information in murder inquiries...so, address, please'

'Torrington.'

'Just Torrington?'

'Torrington, New Forest Way, Wimborne.'

'Sounds a big house.'

'It was a newly built luxury home. Henry was a financier.'

'Henry?'

'My first husband. Mr Woostencroft.'

'Quite a tragedy. I mean, being widowed twice and while still in your thirties.'

'Yes...I will not be looking to get married again. It's too painful.'

'Has its compensations though,' René Lucas smiled. 'I mean, your husband being as wealthy as he was.'

'Yes, I had a good standard of living. I did have that.'

'I was really thinking of what you might inherit.'

'Ah, well...' Virginia Woolley shrugged. 'That depends on what his will says.'

'When will you know that?'

'Later on this afternoon. The will is lodged with a firm of solicitors in York. We'll be going there after visiting my sister's husband.'

'Oh...is he in hospital? I am sorry.'

'No,' Mrs Roberts answered, 'he's in prison.'

Clive Hirst would remember it as an array of vivid colours, like, he thought, the colours on a painter's palette.

Green was the grass and foliage that stood before them and all around them as he, Pulleyne and Lucas watched from a discreet distance, but made no attempt to conceal themselves.

Brown was the colour of the coffin lowered into the grave.

White was the cassock of the priest.

Black was the clothing of the pallbearers and the mourners, just three mourners, Mr and Mrs Strong who stood together, and Virginia Woolley who stood apart, all in black; shoes, nylons, two piece suit, handbag, veil and wide brimmed hat.

Grey was the colour of the small and very old church, which lay beyond the grave.

Blue was the sky, vast and cloudless.

'She moved south and went native.' The Mint took a long drag on the nail and exhaled through her nose. 'Her words, not mine. "I've moved south, she said, and I've gone native".'

René Lucas had left Mrs Roberts' house on Portobello Street and had driven to Queen's Gardens Police Station in

Central Hull. She'd identified herself and was immediately invited beyond the enquiry desk. She asked about Mr Roberts of Portobello Road, Hull. A plain-clothed WPC, whom Lucas found to be very warm-natured, typed what details she could into the computer that stood on her desk.

'Oh...*that* Roberts,' she said. 'Richard "Rigger" Roberts, three years for receiving, he's in Hull Prison. He'll walk home when he's released. Three years...that's a holiday for him, and your Mrs Woolley is related to him?'

'By marriage, but she didn't seem to object. She wasn't at all embarrassed by her brother-in-law being inside.' Lucas looked around her, officers in uniform and plain clothes were busy at their desks or walking rapidly about. She was reminded of the joke about the best way to impress your boss: walk rapidly past his office holding apiece of paper in your hand. The building in Hull was newer and more airy than the station in Harrogate but the ethos of the workplace seemed to be similar. A police station is a police station is a police station. 'I was really looking for information about Virginia Woolley, she's apparently known to you under the name Vera Wortley.'

Mary Plowright typed "Vera Wortley" into the database.

'Ah, yes...two convictions for soliciting for prostitution, years ago...she was seventeen...nothing since. Sorry we can't be of more help.' She pursed her lips, glanced at her watch. 'I tell you who might... The Mint might be able to help.'

'The Mint?' Lucas smiled.

'Sandra Minto, she's about Virginia Woolley's age and she's been working Waterhouse Lane since she left school, though now the girls stand on Castle Street in the main or Great Thornton, Street but CCTV keeps them well dispersed. If Virginia Woolley has convictions for soliciting...'

'Which she has.'

'Then The Mint will know her. She takes her refreshment at the Bay Horse. Not too far from here. I'll take you.'

The two women walked in silence, but comfortably so, happy in each other's company through the centre of Hull. They turned into The Land of Green Ginger. Lucas remarked on the name of the road, which she described as 'amazing'. The road was narrow with four- and five-storey buildings, blackened with industrial fallout.

'Yes, this is Old Hull. The streetname is a reference to the spice trade of the eighteenth century. Hull had its snout well into that trough, helped establish the city's wealth base. The Museum of Slavery is near here, Wilberforce House. It's in the house where Sir William Wilberforce was born and grew up...a pleasant place to visit if you're interested in whips and manacles.'

'Not especially,' Lucas grinned.

'That's an aspect of Hull's history that we're less proud of. Hull was one of the ports from which slavers set sail from on the first passage to the Bight of Benin.'

'The slave triangle. Yes, I have heard of that. They made a lot of money, apparently.'

'Not as much as you'd think. The real profit was made from plantation produce...not from dealing in "black ivory".'

'You seem to know what you're talking about.'

'More than some, less than others. I left school with no qualifications, took a degree in history from the Open University. Now I am doing a part-time MA at Hull University.'

'Well done, you.'

'Yes...I am quite pleased and proud. Read an article once about a snow called the *Africa*.'

'A snow?'

'A rig of a sailing ship, akin to a schooner or a ketch or a brigantine. I don't know what the sail configuration is that makes or made a sailing ship a snow but anyway, this ship was bought by merchants in Bristol, the crew were hired, all manner of goodies were purchased and loaded to use to trade for slaves. So they set sail, did the first and the middle passage alright, sold the slaves in the West Indies but couldn't get a return cargo…nothing rots a ship like being in harbour. The crew were being paid for doing nothing and were getting fractious. Still no scent of a cargo in the offing after some weeks, so the captain decided to cut his losses and return to England in ballast. The ship was sold for much less than it was bought for because by then it was in need of a refit, the money for the ship plus the money obtained from the sale of the slaves wasn't sufficient to pay the crew and recover the cost of the goodies carried out on the first passage. So the merchants lost money on the venture – serve 'em right you might think, but it's interesting that that trading triangle depended on a paying cargo for the third passage if it was to be profitable.'

'It is…that had never occurred to me.'

'But as I said, that's part of our city's history which we are less proud of. Ah…here we are, lovely old pub.'

The two women walked into the Bay Horse and René Lucas found it as Mary Plowright had described. It was, she thought, both lovely and old. The entrance was narrow and low and, from the pavement, a patron walked straight onto wooden floorboards within a narrow panelled passageway.

'If The Mint isn't in her seat,' Mary Plowright turned to René Lucas, 'she's not in the pub. Simple as that.' Mary Plowright opened a door to her right and entered a snug with panelled walls, circular tables, a bench against the wall with polished wooden armrests at intervals and wooden chairs in front of the tables. A woman sat in the corner in front of a schooner of sherry. She was slight, slender, and René Lucas thought she had a hard and a used look about her. She also thought she looked ten years older than Virginia Woolley but then, she pondered, that's what a life working the streets does to a woman. She smiled and nodded at Mary Plowright. 'Hello, Sandra.' Plowright's voice was warm, affectionate. Her manner, observed Lucas, was affable, not threatening in the least.

'Miss Plowright, haven't seen you since my last appearance.'

'This is Miss Lucas, she's a copper too. Can we join you?'

'Take a seat.' Sandra "The Mint" Minto drained her glass.

'Same again?' Lucas asked.

'Yes, please, pet. Double sherry, please.'

'Mary?'

'Orange juice, please.'

When the three women were seated, the two officers, sipping fruit juice, and The Mint eagerly eyeing her new schooner of sherry, but waiting before she drank it, Plowright asked how The Mints' girls were doing.

'Fine...growing up fine, thanks, one's nearly sixteen, the other two are about to turn fifteen...they're twins, you see,' she explained to Lucas.

'I gathered,' René Lucas smiled.

'They'll be ready for the street soon.'

Lucas gasped. 'You are going to prostitute your own daughters?'

Plowright remained impassive. She clearly knew of The Mint's plan.

'No, they're going to prostitute themselves. I'm not a pimp. They'll keep all the money they make.'

'But...'

'But nothing, pet. For girls like I was at sixteen and for girls like my daughters, it's either stacking shelves or it's the street. There's more money on the street and the hours are better. So long as they are not working to feed a habit, and mine aren't, I saw to that. Lucy, my eldest, she got hold of some blow once and...well, the hiding I gave her...all round the house. I had to keep her off school for a week until the bruising went otherwise I'd have the welfare busies knocking on the door, but it worked, she's never been near drugs since and neither have the other two 'cos they saw what I did to our Lucy... And they've kept their virginity...I made sure of that. A sixteen-year-old virgin in this town, that's like finding a nugget of gold. Most girls have started by the time they're fourteen...many younger than that.'

'That's true.' Mary Plowright sipped her drink.

'Now that they can sell...I've got regulars already bidding...clean men, professional men, family men...offering serious money, high four's...low fives.'

'That much!' Lucas again gasped.

'Well, these punters have got that sort of money and for the virginity of a pretty sixteen-year-old, they'll spend it. But they won't do anything illegal; they've got positions to keep. I'm talking doctors, lawyers, business men, scared of doing wrong...but taking a sixteen year old away to their little love nest for a weekend, the first weekend after her sixteenth birthday...that's okay. I'm going to introduce Lucy to an accountant, a big name in this town...unless, of course, somebody tops his bid between now and then.'

'Of course,' Lucas replied dryly. 'You don't want a good marriage for your daughters?'

'You wed, pet? I don't see a ring.'

'No...'

'Bit uncomfortable, that question?' The Mint smiled.

'Yes.'

'Failed romance?'

Lucas nodded.

'Well, lucky you. There's no such thing as a good marriage. All men are scum. My girls will be better off on the street. I know what I'm talking about. I've done alright by the street,' she began to drink the sherry. 'Bought my house, fully paid off mortgage, got money in the bank...but you didn't seek The Mint out to talk about her family?'

'No.' Lucas spoke. 'I want to ask you about a girl you may have known once, a girl called Vera Wortley.'

'Vera!' The Mints' craggy face seemed to Lucas to light up at the mention of the name. 'Beetle! I haven't heard that

name for...must be twenty years. She left Hull and went to
the south. Came back about two years later when her
mother was ill, didn't hardly recognise her. She said she'd
moved south and gone native.'

'Gone native?'

'Got posh. See me and her grew up together, her dad was
bin man, left the same crummy council school together. She
was "Beetle" 'cos of her initials VW, like the car...you know,
the Volkswagen Beetle.' The Mint inhaled deeply, manlike.
The Mints' gestures, Lucas observed, were all manlike.

'Yes, I had worked that out,' Lucas thought.

'I was The Mint and we started on the street together on
Waterhouse Lane. Then, after a couple of years, she bought
a bus ticket and went south. She came back a couple of
years later and had she changed. She'd let all those posh
ways rub off on her. We had a drink together. She told me
how she did it. She went to Plymouth or Portsmouth, one
or the other, where there's plenty of sailors, but not like the
sailors in Hull. In Hull they're all trawler men, they want a
girl before they get drunk and they don't like paying for
it...really make a girl work. Me, I never knew any different
anyway, but Vera, she said the Royal Navy sailors get drunk
before they want a girl and throw their money away like
confetti. It's a lot easier, she said. They pay upfront and
then can't do it because of the drink. She told me she collected money for nothing sometimes...paid for her flat and
her clothes. Changed her name to Virginia, said 'Vera' was
too common, started to listen to Radio Four and let all
those educated accents rub off on her as well. Began to hang
around the posh places, watching how posh women go
on...the walk, the speaking voice. Began to go to wine bars,
got picked up by classy guys, learning as she went. If money
got tight, she'd go and work the naval dockyard for a few
nights. She suggested I join her...I was tempted, I really
was, the clothes she was wearing, the money in her handbag...but I hadn't got her acting ability. She was in plays at

school. She did have a talent to act...that must have helped her...couldn't have harmed her. She told me she hadn't quite mastered it yet, the posh act, still slipped into East Hull walk and talk, but she was well on her way. She said she was looking for a rich old man and once she'd pulled him she'd always ensure the stairs were kept well greased.'

'She said that?' Lucas asked.

'Yes...nothing in it. A lot of girls say that, "marry a rich man and keep the stairs greased".' She paused to sip her sherry. 'Bumped into her sister, Penny Roberts, married Rigger.' The Mint turned to Mary Plowright. 'You'll know Rigger?' She again drew heavily on the nail.

'Yes.'

'He's inside again right now, receiving, I think. Anyway, Penny told us that Vera, or Virginia, had done it: married an older guy and was living in the big house in the south somewhere. Interestingly she kept her initials...was VW before marriage and was VW after marriage.'

'Do you know when she got married?'

'Be in her early thirties...thirty-one, thirty two...not much older. A girl like Vera wasn't going to throw her twenties away on a loveless marriage, she'd want a good time first. Never knew what happened after that.'

'She was widowed. No harm in telling you that.'

'Really? Did her husband leave her much?'

'I think she did alright. She remarried.'

'Did she?' The Mint smiled. 'So she lost her initials after all?'

'No, strangely enough, by pure coincidence her second husband was also a "W". She kept her initials. No harm in telling you that either.'

'Well...she grew up as VW and after two marriages, she was still VW. That's Vera.' The Mint sipped her sherry and dogged the nail in the ashtray. 'That's Vera. She had this knack of getting what she wanted, and keeping what she wanted. I wouldn't put it past her to be attracted to men whose surnames began with a "W" so she could keep a bit of herself to herself in some way, despite being wed. Did she do alright with husband number two? Rich man is he...? Anyway, why the interest in Vera?'

'That we can't tell you.'

Virginia Woolley and Penny Roberts stepped out of the chambers of Thackery, Holmes and Duffy into the bright and warm late afternoon sun. An open-topped bus hummed slowly along St Leonard's Place, followed by an open topped horse drawn carriage containing excited children and two proud parents. The two women looked at each other, open-mouthed.

'The lot,' gasped Penny Roberts.

'Everything. Everything.' Virginia Woolley was equally shaken. 'I thought he might leave some to his sister...but everything...everything to 'my dear wife', just as he once told me.'

'Some dear wife you were.'

The two women laughed.

'You're made.' Penny Roberts stopped laughing and did so suddenly. She fixed her sister with a serious gaze. 'You've done it. You've pulled it off.'

Virginia Woolley shook her head. 'I'm not out of the woods yet, that female cop, she was reading me. She's a shrewd cow...I could tell. Maybe I should have stopped with Henry? I got enough out of him. Maybe I've been too greedy? Have to box clever...got to box really clever.'

'But it's yours. He's transferring the deeds of the White House to your name...the money goes into your bank account.'

'Yes, but if I can be linked to his murder,' she spoke in a whisper, 'then I lose everything he left me in the will. That's the law. Look, we'll go back to Hull, spend the night in the Mariner...but keep the real celebration on hold, I don't like counting chickens...'

Chapter Seven

Elms put his hand to his forehead. The blue shirt and denims were ill fitting.

'This is not happening to me, my parents…they thought I was doing so well. What can I do?'

Hirst pushed his chair back, the feet scraped across the hard floor of the agents' room. The walls were tiled, the window high and opaque. It was a hard, harsh room, designed to focus discussion.

'What can you do?' Hirst took a packet of cigarettes from his pocket, opened the packet and offered it to Elms, who snatched at a cigarette hungrily. 'I don't smoke myself but I have learned a packet of twenty Benson and Hedges goes down very well in situations like this. We left you for a few days after you were remanded to think about things.' He lit a disposable lighter and held the flame for Elms to light the nail. 'Have you absorbed the fact that you are looking at a life sentence?'

'Life…' Elms echoed.

'Nominally…you could be out in less than ten years…accept guilt…show remorse.'

'I'll be thirty-three.'

'Yes, you'll spend the rest of your twenties in the slammer, that's foregone, you have to decide if you are going to spend your thirties inside as well.'

'Even your forties,' Pulleyne added.

'But you have to prove it.'

'Yes, we know that and we can.'

Elms glanced up at Hirst, a look of alarm in his eyes.

Hirst nodded. 'We can prove it.'

'But…'

'But what, Chris? But you thought you had covered your tracks? You didn't think we'd find the knife? Didn't make a thorough job of getting rid of it did you? And the

shoes...hiding them under the settee in your flat, that was-
n't very smart.'

'Under the settee?' Elms gasped. He was wide-eyed.

Hirst paused. 'Look, Chris...you don't mind if I call you
Chris?'

Elms shook his head. 'Under the settee?'

'Under the settee.'

'But that's not possible.'

'It isn't? Why?'

'Because...no you're trying to trap me, I won't fall for
tricks.'

'No tricks, Chris,' Hirst held eye contact with Elms, 'no
tricks at all. Look, I've been a copper for a long time, I can
read people and you're not a bad lad...not in yourself, you
are not a bad lad. Despite what you did.'

'I didn't do anything,' Elms pleaded.

'Now look!' Hirst banged his hand on the tabletop.
'Refusing to admit guilt because you think we can't prove
anything is one thing, but don't get into a state of denial in
your own mind. If you enter that state of denial, you'll
never get out. You are a university graduate...Newcastle, no
less.'

'A lot of good it did me.'

Hirst reached down to his left side and picked up his
briefcase, opened it and extracted a brown paper envelope.
He put the briefcase back on the floor and felt inside the
envelope. He took out a black and white photograph and
laid it on the table. The photograph showed a knife lying
against a ruler. 'Recognise the knife, Chris?'

'No.'

'Sure?'

'Yes.'

'Look again.'

'It's a knife...there's plenty like it.'

'Yes, but this knife is special, it's quite unique. You see
the stains on the blade? That is Mr Woolley's, Mr Maurice

Woolley's blood. No question of a mistake...and you see that powdery stuff on the handle? That's the remains of aluminium powder that was spread on the handle and which adhered to guess whose fingerprints?'

'Not mine.'

'Wrong...yours, Chris. Right thumb and first and second finger of the right hand, just the way you'd hold a knife if using it to stab someone.'

'See, you've a problem, Chris,' Pulleyne probed. 'That knife was found on the lawn outside the White House...where you flung it in panic. The knife was the murder weapon...right size blade for the wounds to Mr Woolley's chest and, as Mr Hirst has just said, the blood is that of the deceased. Perfect DNA match.'

'That would be difficult for you to explain. Did you visit the White House as a guest of Mr and Mrs Woolley?'

Elms paused as if thinking, as if searching for another trap being laid for him. Then he shook his head and said, 'No'.

'Never been in their kitchen except on the night of the murder?'

'I was never ever in their kitchen.'

'You see, that makes things even more difficult for you, easier for us...more difficult for you, because that knife is one of a nest of knives which are kept in the Woolleys' kitchen. You picked up the knife as you passed through the kitchen to murder Mr Woolley because you were infatuated with his wife and wanted her for yourself. Despite the age gap.'

'No...no...'

'No? Look at this photograph.' Hirst laid the photograph of a footprint on the table. 'Old pair of sneakers, or train-ers...a bit worn but with distinct damage to the sole. Only one pair of shoes could have made that print, it's one of a number of prints leading from the murder scene to the front door. What makes the print is blood, Mr Woolley's blood. The killer got Mr Woolley's blood on the soles of his shoes and left a trail of bloody footprints leading away from the corpse.'

Elms was ashen-faced.

'In the garden we found another lovely footprint in the soft earth of the flowerbed, left by the killer as he ran from the house, across the lawn...same shoe...see the damage? Now, have a look at this photograph.' Hirst laid a photograph of a pair of trainers on the table. 'Recognise them?'

Elms gasped.

'They were found under your settee, Chris. They have the same damage to the sole as the shoes that made the earlier prints that were left inside the White House and in the flowerbed. The soles had traces of Mr Maurice Woolley's blood on them and also soil from the Woolleys' flowerbed.'

Elms' head sagged forward.

'And now have a look at these snaps of a happy couple...you and Mrs Woolley clearly liking each other very much...and of you on the road that runs past the White House, taking a keen interest in the building, sighting it up.'

'How...?'

'A private detective. Someone hired him to follow Mrs Woolley because it was believed she was having an affair outside her marriage and she was...with you. So you see your problem, don't you, Chris? You had the motive to murder Mr Woolley, the murder weapon was found with your prints on it and your shoes put you at the scene of the crime and at the time of the crime. All you can do is go G.'

'Go "G"?'

'Go guilty. It's futile to fight this. Just digging yourself deeper if you do. Ask any lag in here, they'll all say the same. The first step to an early parole is a cough...a guilty plea.' Hirst thought Elms seemed to be feeling as if he was falling into a bottomless pit. 'We've been doing some research about your lover...'

Elms looked at him questioningly. 'Virginia?'

'Yes,' Hirst nodded. 'There are a few things you should know. If you don't already, that is.' Hirst paused. 'No...look, you tell us about Virginia Woolley.'

After a pause, Elms said. 'Well, she's a lady in her thirties, locked in a marriage that wasn't going anywhere. Her husband was a lot older than her.'

'Yes, so far that's true.'

'Well, she's from the south of England, where her sister lives. Went to a private school...doesn't like being called "Beetle" because that was her nickname...at school I mean...'

'What did she tell you her husband did for a living?'

'She just said that he was good with numbers. So I presumed he was an accountant...or a financial trader.'

Hirst and Pulleyne glanced at each other. 'Good with numbers,' Hirst coughed with laughter. 'I suppose that's one way of looking at it, one way of putting it.'

'Aye.' Pulleyne's chest similarly heaved with amusement.

Hirst sat forwards, rested his elbows on the table, pyramided his fingers, inclined them towards Elms and spoke solemnly, quietly. 'Chris, I'll tell you what we have found out about your lady love. I'll start at the beginning of her life.'

'She was Virginia Woostencroft before she married...'

'Yes she was...that is before *this* marriage, but she began life not in the soft and gentle south of England but up here, in the north, in Yorkshire.'

'In Yorkshire? But the way she speaks...'

'She grew up in East Hull. She went to a council school and her name then was Vera Wortley...a dustman's daughter. She was known as "Beetle" because of her initials but it wasn't in the dormitory of some private school in the south, which for some reason seems to impress you, it was in the yard in a comprehensive school in Hull. She left school and went onto the streets, never worked at all. By the time she was seventeen she had convictions for soliciting. She moved south and began to learn all the airs and graces of the upper classes; she had a knack for it. But what we are learning about Mrs Woolley is that it's a case of taking a girl from the street but being unable to take the street from the girl.'

'What it means, Chris,' Pulleyne sat back as he spoke, 'is that once somebody has become ruthless, once they have experienced that fear for their own existence and have become a survivor – that ruthless survival at all costs and willingness to exploit others for their own ends – it never leaves them, no matter what situation you put them in.'

Elms listened intently with dilated pupils. Hirst and Pulleyne knew that they were reaching him.

'So having cultivated the classy way of acting...speech...body movements...she married, by which time she was Virginia not Vera. Dare say she thought "Vera" to be as common as muck. Being Virginia suited her purposes better. She married a wealthy older man...who died. At the time there did not appear to be any suspicious circumstances but we'll be taking another look at his death. But anyway, she became monied, moved north and ingratiated herself with Maurice Woolley, who had been an embarrassment to his family all his life. The longest job he had held down was as a dishwasher in a Chinese restaurant...held that for a few weeks.'

'His money?' Elms pleaded.

'A Lotto win...nine million pounds. I dare say that's what she meant by her husband being good with figures.'

'Oh...' Elms' head sagged.

'So by your actions you have probably made Virginia Woolley, a.k.a. Vera Wortley, a very wealthy woman. The will has been read but we don't yet know the details, but even if she had been left but a tenth of his estate, well, she'll not be short of money.'

'Some favour you did her, Chris.' Pulleyne retained his

relaxed posture. 'You carry the can...she laughs all the way to the bank. Is that what happened, or is she wholly innocent and unaware of your actions?'

Elms remained silent, looking at Hirst, then Pulleyne and back to Hirst again. 'I thought she was posh...classy,' he said softly, 'it added something. Can't put my finger on it, but if you come from Batley...' He dogged the cigarette in the ashtray.

'I can understand that,' Hirst smiled. In his own youth he too had experienced the frisson of seducing a woman of superior social class. He had never understood the British class system but it was there, and very real, and he was the son of a railway worker, and she had been the daughter of a very senior clergyman in the Anglican Church. In the event he had married, happily and successfully, a sweet girl who had caught his eye when she was working as a secretary in the police station typing pool, but the memory of the summer he had spent with the adorable and appropriately named Felicity Goodyear, remained golden.

'Well, this is it, Chris.' Hirst leaned back and relaxed his posture. 'You see, either one of two things has happened here.' He paused. 'Either...either you acted alone out of infatuation for Virginia Woolley, murdering her husband so as to have her and her wealth to yourself...and that motivation is as old as the hills: get rid of her husband, pretend to have no knowledge of the murder, be full of sympathy, be her rock in time of distress, and Mrs Woolley genuinely knows nothing of your hand in her husband's murder. Either that happened, or there was a conspiracy between you, and that is as old as the hills as well, and Virginia Woolley is up to her neck in it...and if that, the second possibility, is what has happened, then there are two possible motivations for Mrs Woolley's involvement. Either she is as fond of you as you are of her and wants nothing but a life spent with you, or you have been manipulated into doing her dirty work for her and she's going to let you hang out to dry.'

'No...' Elms shook his head.

'You see, Christopher,' Pulleyne raised his eyebrows. 'If Mr Hirst is correct, if she intends to let you hang out to dry once she has her hands on her husband's estate, then that would explain how the trail of evidence led from the murder scene right to the underneath of your settee.'

Elms remained silent, as if absorbing some dread possibility.

Pulleyne pressed his point. 'You might be interested in knowing that there appears to have been an earlier attempt on Mr Woolley's life. Another young man attempted to do what you succeeded in doing. Mr Woolley overpowered him...no evidence then that he intended to kill Mr Woolley, so he went down for burglary. He's out now, but it was because of that that the burglar alarm was fitted, but one window wasn't connected to the system...the window you used to get into the house. Do you know why it wasn't connected to the burglar alarm system?'

Elms nodded. 'It was painted over, it couldn't be opened. She said she'd free it off for me...she said she'd prop a wheelbarrow up against the wall beside the window so I would know which one it was.'

Hirst took the packet of cigarettes and offered Elms one. 'Good boy...' he said. 'Let's take a statement from you. You've done yourself a big favour.'

Elms took the cigarette. 'That's what she used to say,' he put the cigarette to the flame of Hirst's lighter. 'Good boy. Used to call me a good boy.'

One hour later Hirst and Pulleyne stepped out of Armley gaol and fell into step with each other as they walked towards Hirst's car.

'Going to lift her, boss?' Pulleyne asked.

'Yes...yes...' Hirst fumbled in his jacket pocket for his car keys, 'but not yet. I think we should go softly, softly, catchee monkee on this...she's not going anywhere. She seems strong enough to weather suspicion. I want to talk to this fellow, Parsloe, and I want to wait and see what René brings back from the south on the death of the first husband. I don't want to put Virginia Woolley under pressure...not for a while yet.

The following day Hirst and Pulleyne drove to Halton Dial in Leeds. They turned into the Dial and drove to Palmer Street, where they parked outside a council house with an untended front garden. An overweight woman answered the door; she smelled of stale tobacco. A strong smell of damp, despite it being high summer, wafted from the interior of the house.

'You just can't leave him alone, can you?' she snarled, clearly having no difficulty recognising Hirst and Pulleyne as being police officers. 'He's not been out a month and here you are harassing him.'

'He's not in trouble, Mrs Parsloe, we want to chat to him. We think he can help us.'

'He's in bed.'

'Well, get him up.'

'He doesn't get up till lunchtime.'

'We could get a warrant.'

The woman scowled. 'You're not getting in the house.'

'Just get him up and outside in ten minutes,' Hirst snarled.

'Or we'll be back at seven tomorrow morning,' Pulleyne added, 'with a warrant. And if you obstruct us, we'll be doing you as well.'

The woman slammed the door shut. Hirst and Pulleyne glanced at each other and grinned.

'Never changes, the Dial, I mean.' Hirst glanced around him. The police activity was already attracting attention, children began to gather, adults stood in doorways or sat at upstairs windows. 'Our own little Dodge City, here in West Yorks.'

Minutes passed. Pulleyne said, 'That's ten minutes, boss.'

'Give him another five. He's making a point not just to us but to his neighbours. He's got to live here, we haven't.'

Moments later the door of the house opened. Shane Parsloe stood on the threshold. Trainers, new jeans, T-shirt, gold watch. 'What?' he asked with the same hostility his mother had earlier demonstrated.

'S'ok, Shane,' Hirst said. 'You're not in trouble. We want your help.'

Parsloe paused. He looked about him. 'Alright. One of you walk ahead, one walk behind and we'll sit in your car. I can't be seen to be too ready to talk to you.'

'Fair enough.' Hirst turned, Parsloe followed him. Pulleyne followed Parsloe. Hirst opened the rear door of the car and Parsloe slid inside. Hirst and Pulleyne occupied the front seats. Hirst asked. 'Would it be better if we drove off?'

'Aye,' Parsloe grunted. 'Make it look like I'm being lifted. We won't get a brick through our windows, then.'

Hirst drove off the Dial, turned left onto New York Road, drove out past Seacroft and turned into the car park of a Little Chef near the motorway. Over coffee Hirst asked him about Virginia Woolley.

'Who?'

'The wife of the man whose house you burgled.'

Parsloe shrugged. 'Is that her name? What about her?'

'Any contact with her?'

'No.'

'Any truth in the rumour that there was more planned than just the burglary?'

'What rumour?'

'The rumour that you went to the house to murder Mr Woolley, make it look like a burglary gone wrong?'

Parsloe laughed as he poured an excessive amount of sugar into his coffee. 'I'm really going to cough to that...I don't think.'

'Well, what you failed to do, someone else has just done.'

'You don't say?' He lifted the cup to his lips.

'Yes, we do say. How long were you her toy boy for before she put you up to murdering her husband?'

Parsloe winked, but said nothing. It told Hirst and Pulleyne much.

'I see. How did you break in? It'll be in the file, but remind me.'

'Pushed up a sash window. Easiest house I've ever entered...and believe me I have turned a lot of windows, a lot more than you'll ever know.'

'Oh, we believe you. Serial offenders get away with more crimes than they are convicted for.'

'Yes...turn nine windows, get done for the tenth. It's like paying tax...so long as you earn more than you lose. Win some, lose some, but win more than you lose, that way you're on top.'

'You on top, Shane?'

Parsloe pursed his lips. 'Doing alright.'

Which, Hirst thought, was either bravado or the truth. 'Been busy since you got out of Full Sutton?'

'That's for me to know and for you to find out.' He drank the coffee. 'You know the rules as well as me.'

'Nice trainers,' Pulleyne commented. 'Designer jeans...nice looking watch. T-shirt doesn't look cheap...not bad for a guy living on the dole.'

'Guy needs good gear.'

'Where did the money come from?'

Parsloe smiled. 'I refer the honourable gentleman to my previous answer,' he paused, 'about me knowing and you finding out.'

'Yes, I thought that's what you meant.' Pulleyne eyed Parsloe with distaste. 'It wouldn't be the case that a certain person is paying you for your silence?'

'What is it?' Hirst was more friendly, 'a few hundred a month?'

Parsloe put the cup down. 'Look, you can think what you like, I'm only scared of what you can prove. I'm saying nothing – "cough to nowt" – that's the rule.' He glanced at his watch. 'Pubs are opening and the good cop, bad cop act doesn't wash anymore, not with me, but...' Parsloe looked pleased with himself, 'let's just say you might be right...but only might be.'

Hirst nodded. He had believed Parsloe would be unable to resist boasting.

'But, as I said, I'm coughing to nowt. I mean, look at it from my point of view, if I cough I get done for attempted murder and I lose a nice source of income. So, no statement, and I just didn't say that.'

'Two of us heard it.'

'Two of you heard nothing. A hint...a suggestion.' He drained his cup. 'You can drop me at the Cricketer's Arms, they do a good lunch at the Cricketers.'

'Get a taxi.' Hirst stood.

Pulleyne did likewise. 'You can afford it.'

Driving back towards Harrogate Hirst said, 'He's right, we'll not pin anything on him for this but he told us that what we suspected is happening is what is happening. Virginia Woolley put him up to murder her husband, it didn't come off, but he can't blackmail her without being done for attempted murder. So she's paying him for his effort but not his silence. An envelope in the post once every few weeks.'

'Aye...' Pulleyne glanced to his left across open fields bountiful with the summer crop of golden wheat, beneath a blue sky. 'Aye, that wasn't a wasted visit, not a wasted visit at all.'

'Won't be able to prove anything, in either case, but you're right...not a wasted morning.'

* * *

'Daniel phoned us.' John Lucas, white-haired, wearing an open woollen cardigan, slacks and slippers, stooped to place another piece of wood on the fire.

'Oh?' René Lucas tried to sound uninterested. She doubted that she managed it.

'Yes...he seemed to know that you were coming home.' He stepped away from the open fire and warmth flooded the room. Sap issued forth from the fresh piece of wood in a high-pitched hissing sound. John Lucas sat in "his" armchair. 'I still don't understand you two splitting up.'

René Lucas had enjoyed the drive south. It was as if her car had an urgency about it, as if it knew it was going home. In recent weeks she had found herself forcing her foot to keep the accelerator pressed down as she journeyed north, feeling as if the car was dragging a weight behind it, but the journey south, by contrast, had come to be done with elation. She left the M1 at Daventry and driven past Oxford and Banbury and onto Salisbury and beyond. South of Salisbury, she was home, the gentle rolling countryside of Hampshire and Dorset, the signposts to such familiar places as Chandlers Ford, Eastleigh, Bishops Waltham, Shirrell Heath. She drove slowly through Hundred Acres, feeling a glow of warmth each time she saw a pub selling "Badger Beer", and then continued into North Boarhunt. Beyond North Boarhunt she turned into the drive of a white-painted house, which stood in its own grounds. It reminded her of the White House in Yorkshire, except that this house had the softer, more intriguing name of Pick in the Putty and it was also on a much smaller, much more modest scale.

She ate a full and wholesome meal with her parents and later sat with her father in the drawing room in front of the log fire, her mother going out for the evening to the bridge club. She knew her father was curious, she knew it was his curiosity that prompted him to tell her that Daniel had phoned.

'Did you tell him that you were coming home for a day or two?'

It wasn't really any of her father's business but she answered anyway. 'Yes...yes, I did.'

Her father smiled. 'Good. I hope you'll be able to see him before you return north, back to the frozen wastelands.'

'It's as warm as it is down here.'

'Probably...but it's time you came home.'

René Lucas said nothing, then stood and excused herself, saying she had a busy day tomorrow and wanted an early night.

Virginia Woolley drove back to Hull being further disinclined to spend the night alone in the White House. It was a large house for a woman, for anyone, to feel at ease in, and now that her possessions had been packed into the large cardboard boxes the removal and storage company had left for her to use, the building was even more prone to echoing. She drove down the drive as dusk gathered and glanced with satisfaction at the large "For Sale" sign that had been fastened to one of the front gateposts. She, too, had a busy day upon the morrow.

'I need at least six of these before I can function in the mornings.' DC Lyall pointed to his mug of tea. 'I am a caffeine junkie.'

'Well, let's just say it's more than welcome.' René Lucas blinked as the morning sun caught her eyes.

'Sorry...' Lyall stood and lowered the blind. 'The sun moves round to the other side of the building as the day goes on, but we get it in the mornings.' He was a man in his forties, old for a detective constable, thought Lucas, but his jovial attitude was probably the reason for his lack of advancement. Just not emotionally mature enough to progress beyond the rank of detective constable. He sat down again and picked up a file. 'Well, here it is, all three pages of it...not a lot in it, really, old boy had a seizure in his swimming pool. We opened the file because his brother screamed "foul play" but there was no indication of that.' He handed Lucas the file. 'All the evidence pointed to natural causes, and that was the coroner's verdict, or misadventure, if I remember. His stomach was full, went swimming after a heavy evening meal...a bit silly...well, his ticker gave out under the strain, a man of his age...'

'Do you know why the brother of the deceased...Mr Woostencroft...why his brother should cry "foul"?'

'No hard evidence, just thought Mrs Woostencroft was a bit "iffy"...many years his junior, came from nowhere, no background, nobody from her side at the wedding, which, on her insistence, was a quick registry office affair...not married long, then he dies, leaving her everything. A large amount of money plus three properties, the house here in Dorset...a vast new build bungalow, a cottage in the Lake District and a villa in the Mediterranean. I don't mean in the sea,' he grinned at his own joke. 'On Cyprus or Crete or some place like that, is what I mean.'

René Lucas returned the grin as politeness dictated, but thought it was easy to see why Lyall hadn't made promotion. Such a cavalier attitude wouldn't go down well with any board. 'So she did well out of it and a few days later...it's mentioned there...brother phones us up to say he'd found some knotted silk scarves in the waste bin in the kitchen, hadn't seen the significance at the time, the significance being that they might have been used to restrain Mr Woostencroft in some way, causing him to have a heart attack.'

'Tied up in the pool, you mean?'

'Yes. He'd panic...he'd begin to drown, then his heart would gave out, so it would looked like natural causes.'

'I see.'

'Anyway, by the time we got there, the rubbish had been collected by the council and taken to a landfill site.'

'You didn't search the site?'

'No, thank goodness.'

'Thank goodness?'

'Have you ever searched a landfill site?'

'No.'

'I have...very unpleasant. But we didn't because we took advice from the CPS. They said the scarves wouldn't prove anything unless they were seen tied to the body or could be linked to the house in some way. They stopped being evidence once they had reached the landfill site. So it would be a massive waste of police time for no purpose at all.'

'I see.'

'Well, you'll be wanting to visit his brother.'

'Yes.' Lucas closed the file. 'It's the other reason for my trip.'

'I'll give you directions to Low Burnham.'

'Thanks,' Lucas stood, 'but I'm from these parts. I know exactly where it is.'

'Thought you sounded local. Quite surprised. Thought you'd be a black pudding and mushy peas sort of lassie...you know, a real coalminer's daughter.'

'Well, there you go. I'll find my own way out.'

'We served different gods.' The Reverend Woostencroft received René Lucas in the vestry of All Saints Church in the parish of Low Burnham. She found him a solemn man, serious minded. A man in his sixties, she thought he well suited a clerical collar. She had first called at the vicarage and had been told by a cleaner to try the church. ''E's got a funeral this afternoon, 'e's likely preparing for it, dear...' So she had tried the church, successfully, having been escorted to the vestry by a lady who was arranging the flowers around the base of the lectern. 'I serve mine...he served Mammon.'

'Confess I was surprised to read that you were a clergyman. I mean, given your late brother's lifestyle.'

'Yes...we were different.'

'So you suspect your sister-in-law of foul play in respect of your brother's death?'

'Yes.' Reverend Woostencroft stroked his chin, 'I am afraid, suspect is all I can do. She arrived suddenly...out of the blue...much younger than Henry, married with indecent haste...so indecently hurried that I thought there might have been a child on the way. How wrong I was.'

'Oh?'

'Yes, the marriage was doomed to fail...the age gap...the absence of any spiritual values in the union, and then the issue of children arose.'

'She wanted children?'

'Oh no...he did...she didn't. We talked one day. Even though we had different callings we were still brothers and kept in close contact. "Last chance I have to have children. I won't be the youngest father in the world, but I'll be the best," he said, "but each time I raise the question of children she just walks away. I've built it all...I've got no one to leave it to". He drowned a week later.'

'To whom did he leave it?'

'Well, Henry's will vastly favoured Virginia...his money in excess of one million plus three properties. The ludicrously named "Henry's Perch", being their house here, the house where he drowned, and a large house in Windermere and a villa on Gozo, off Malta.'

'Yes, I know and "Henry's Perch" isn't such a ludicrous name. I grew up in a house called "Pick in the Putty".'

'Pick in the Putty?' The Reverend Woostencroft smiled.

'My father, he was a yachtsman and yachtsmen don't talk about "dropping the anchor", they talk about "dropping the pick", or "putting the pick in the putty".'

'I see.'

'So when father's wanderings were behind him, he looked for a place to settle, found the house he wanted to bring up his family in and put his "pick in the putty".'

'I rather like that, it's an endearing name for a house, bet-

ter than Henry's Perch, which is just silly.'

'Well...not for me to comment.'

'We...myself and Barbara, my wife, got some, quite a sub-stantial amount by our standards, it will enable us to leave something to our children. Not many clergymen can leave much in the way of material possessions to their children, but, thanks to Henry, we will be able to do so...but the lion's share of it went to Virginia. She sold Henry's Perch and left the area. Don't know if she sold the other two houses, never saw her at all after the funeral.'

'I see. So tell me about the silk scarves?'

'I will, if you'll tell me why the sudden police interest?'

René Lucas sat forward. The old wooden chair in which she sat creaked. 'Well, without giving any details, Mrs Woostencroft remarried.'

'She did?'

'Yes, she did...and her second husband also met an untimely death, also leaving her much in his will. Her hus-band...her second husband's death was clearly suspicious, so we are taking a fresh look at your brother's death...sometimes it's like that.'

'Well, well, well.' The Reverend Woostencroft glanced up at a stained-glass window set in the ancient stone walls of the vestry, through which sunlight was streaming. 'You'd think one million pounds and three houses would be suffi-cient, but greed might be her undoing.'

'It might. So...the scarves?'

'Ah...the scarves...the scarves.' The Reverend Woosten-croft opened both palms. 'What can I say? Well, clergymen are like judges, we are expected to be magnanimous, merci-ful, yet cannot afford to be naïve. It's a difficult path to tread at times. It's that, plus a combination of unwillingness to think that my brother was playing the sort of sex games that he might have been playing. The sum of those two was greater than its constituent parts.'

'Sex games?'

'It is, I fear, the only explanation. I visited the house the day after my brother died…she was there, the grieving widow, all in black, a little eager to wear black I thought. I made us both a pot of tea and, after we chatted, I cleared up the cups and took them to the kitchen to wash them and put the teabags into the bin in the kitchen. It's one of those where you pressed a pedal and up pops the lid.'

'Yes…'

'It was then that I saw the scarves, about three, possibly four. I saw that they had been knotted together and also cut neatly, cleanly, as with a pair of scissors. I thought nothing of them at the time, I was in shock… I was grieving…and in my striving for high-mindedness, again, the sum was greater than the constituent parts, well, it was fully three days before the possible significance occurred to me. Henry would not go swimming after his evening meal, he had to have been incapacitated in some way, lured to the pool, tied up and pushed in. He wouldn't have been overpowered, not by her, and there was no evidence of any other person having been in the house that night.'

'So he allowed himself to be tied up by Virginia as a sex game?'

'It's the only explanation. I also found a dog collar and lead, but they didn't have a dog.'

'He must have walked willingly to the swimming pool.'

The Reverend Woostencroft nodded. 'Yes…at what point his hands and feet were tied we'll never know, unless she confesses…which I doubt.'

'Which I doubt, too. She's not the type to 'fess up to anything.'

'"'Fess up"? That's a term I haven't heard before.' Woostencroft forced a smile. 'Anyway, I went to the police with my suspicions about the scarves, they called at Henry's Perch but by the time they arrived the council had collected all the refuse from the houses in that area.'

'So I believe.'

'They explained that the scarves were not evidence of anything anyway, but they were sympathetic to my theory...uncomfortable as it might be to think that Henry played such games.'

'Well, believe me, Reverend, police officers don't get paid much but we see life and I can tell you, sir, that your brother's sex game was mild in comparison to some we have encountered.'

'Thank you, I can take comfort from that.' The Reverend Woostencroft held eye contact with René Lucas. 'Thank you.'

Virginia Woolley, wearing a low cut blouse and figure hugging jeans, stood on the steps watching the removal of the contents of the White House from the building into the van. Six men were employed upon the job, all muscular, but two particularly caught her eye, both handsome, she thought, both in their twenties, both stripped to the waist and, conveniently, they worked together. When they passed her carrying a large cardboard box, she stopped them. 'What's your name?' She ran a finger over the biceps of the first youth, the youth who had walked backwards down the steps. She thought him to be particularly "decorative".

'Tony.' He grinned at her. She knew he was taken by her.

'And you?' She turned to the other youth.

'Christopher.'

'Another Christopher...'

'Another?' He too grinned at her.

'Nothing...a recent episode in my life. Would you two boys like to work for me?'

'Doing what?'

'Mmm...just being...useful...just being yourselves.' She pushed a piece of paper into the pocket of Christopher's jeans. 'That's my telephone number...phone me this evening. I'll pay you twice what you're earning now plus all found.'

'All found?'

'Yes...so it will all be spending money and there's the prospect of foreign travel...all at my expense.'

'Travel?' Tony seemed to her to be particularly keen.

'The Med...my villa...look, just phone me after five o'clock this evening...after five, before seven. I'll explain then. But I warn you, I have an obstacle to overcome before I can employ you both. I'll explain this evening.'

René Lucas sat with Daniel Hay in the wine bar. He slid his hand across the table and held hers gently.

'Thank you,' he said.

She looked at him questioningly.

'For not withdrawing your hand.'

'Part of me still wants to.'

'I know...I can imagine. I have felt sick since you went away...so angry with myself.'

'We just let that woman come between us.'

'Yes...it was the silence...daily contact with you and then nothing for three weeks, in the midst of which I was told you were seen having dinner with another man.'

'By her...'

'Yes. I thought it was your way of cutting me loose...she caught me on the rebound.'

'I understand that now...and I transferred to the north of England...feeling betrayed by you. I was so hurt. I went from a state of bliss to feeling that my heart had been torn out of me. But I should have contacted you to let you know I couldn't see you for a week or two...the job asks that of us sometimes...and at short notice...and my machine went down, couldn't email...I could and should have phoned you.'

'All so stupid, such a silly, stupid, stupid misunderstanding.'

'I know...we could have sorted it out so easily. We both let it blow up into something it wasn't and we've both been damaged by the experience. I didn't realise how much I need you until I thought I'd lost you.'

'I felt the same.' He squeezed her hand. 'I felt hollow...for months I felt hollow.'

She smiled. 'I know that feeling. Are you going back to London tonight?'

'I don't have to...'

'Then don't...this is Bournemouth...if we can't get a hotel room here, we can't get one anywhere...even in the middle of summer...and tomorrow you can come and re-meet Mummy and Daddy. They were so upset when they found out we had split up. They'll be delighted to see you.'

'Do you mean it...about tonight?'

'Yes.' She squeezed his hand. 'Yes...I mean it.'

'So you're coming home?'

'Yes...oh yes, I want a life with you. It'll be some weeks yet...'

'Weeks?'

'Yes, we're in the middle of a big case...I want to see it through. In fact. it's because of the case that I came home for a couple of days. Had to interview someone...read an old file. Strange...'

'What is?'

'We are back together because of the actions of the most callous and calculating cow I have ever met. If I had not had to come down south, I wouldn't have phoned you.'

Chapter Eight

'Silk?' Gwendoline Fay asked.

'Yes, so it was reported.' René Lucas sat in Fay's cramped office.

'Well...ideal...ideal material...lovely material, but ideal for what you have hypothesised...doesn't cause bruising you see. It's one of the material's magical qualities. You can use silk to tie somebody up and no matter how tight the bonds, it will not bruise the flesh. It's also fairly easy to untie...but it's also very easy to cut, so yes, the silk scarves that were reported knotted and also cut in the home of a man who allegedly drowned in his indoor swimming pool...yes, very significant. Very significant indeed...as significant as a smoking gun.'

René Lucas stood. 'Thank you, Dr Fay. That's very helpful.'

Wendy Forrest ran three miles with a weighted knapsack on her back. One and a half miles out, and then retraced her steps. She jogged the same route each lunchtime during the working week, up hill out and thus easier on the return leg. Upon reaching her place of employment, she stripped, showered, dressed in her pinstripe suit and slid on a pair of metal-framed spectacles. Her black hair was tied back and hung to her shoulders in a glossy ponytail. She was then no longer a trim, athletic female jogger, but Wendy Forrest, solicitor, employed by the Crown Prosecution Service. She sat at the head of the table in the conference room; she held eye contact with Hirst, Pulleyne and, finally, René Lucas. 'I'm prepared to run with it,' she said, glancing to her left at the view afforded by the conference room window of the busy metropolitan skyline. 'It's a weak case. As it is, it's one of those cases which depends on wholly circumstantial evidence...but the weight of said evidence might be sufficient to sway the jury.'

'We thought as much,' Hirst rested his forearms on the table, 'but we've taken it as far as we can. We won't get a confession...we'll try our damndest, but we won't.'

'You'll have to charge her with both murders in order to allow the issue of the silk scarves to be introduced.'

'Understood.'

'The motivation is powerful and the statement of Christopher Elms is...well, also powerful. I can't help feeling sorry for him.'

'I know what you mean,' Pulleyne growled. 'Daft lad, but at his age, in his circumstances, I can see many others doing the same. Deadlier than the male, alright.'

'So Elms has confessed and he'll stick to his statement in court? He won't retract that?'

'No...he's come down to earth, no longer "Johnny Head in Air", his infatuation with Woolley is now replaced with hatred.'

'Good. He'll make a strong witness.' She tapped her pen on the desk. 'You know we could pull this off. I've gone with weaker cases and secured a conviction. I suggest we try them separately. Elms first. He'll be up and down again within a minute.'

'A minute?' Hirst smiled.

'Well, the shortest murder trial in British Criminal history lasted sixty seconds. The charge was read, the felon said "Guilty", the Judge said "Life" and down he went, that was at Nottingham some years ago. Christopher Elms' trial will be about the same length and then he can start working towards his parole. He could be out in five years...then start doing what he can to draw order out of the chaos he has turned his life into. Whatever he manages, he'll always lead a badly eclipsed life...not easy to explain away a murder conviction to a prospective employer, and he can forget about being allowed visas for foreign travel. Like I said, part of me feels very sorry for him. But, this Virginia Wooley...I don't want to appear vindictive but her...her I would like to see convicted.'

'I think we all feel the same on that score.' Hirst leaned back. He looked out of the window and allowed his eyes to follow the track of a small airliner on its final approach to the airport, the fuselage and wings glinting in the sun, doubtless, he thought, returning a cargo of bronzed holidaymakers from two weeks somewhere south of the 44th parallel. When the aircraft had been consumed from his view by the skyline, he said, 'We'll do our damnedest. I really do not want to see her walk.'

'Right.' Wendy Forrest opened her briefcase. 'I'll go to the judge in chambers, I'll have a warrant for her arrest within the hour. If you could contact the Dorset police, let them know of this development.'

Virginia Woolley reminded Hirst of the iconographic photograph of Myra Hindley; that same indignant expression, those hard eyes, that set jaw, angry that she had been arrested. 'The time is 17.32 hours, the date July 23rd, the place is Harrogate police station, North Yorkshire,. I am Detective Chief Inspector Clive Hirst, North Yorkshire Police. I am now going to ask the other people present in the room to identify themselves.'

'Detective Sergeant Pulleyne, North Yorkshire Police.'

'Gavin Lowe, solicitor of Mulrine and Wilson and Company, representing Mrs Virginia Woolley in accordance with the Police and Criminal Evidence Act of 1985.'

'Virginia Woolley, here under protest.'

Lowe turned to Woolley and held up a finger as if to say "Quiet". Woolley nodded.

Hirst saw the admonition, he also saw Woolley's acknowledgement of it and knew then that this was going to be an uphill battle.

'Mrs Woolley,' Hirst began, 'you have been arrested in connection with the murder of your second husband, and also in connection with the death of your first husband, whose death is now viewed as suspicious.'

'I understand Mrs Woolley's first husband lived in the south of England,' Lowe interrupted.

'Dorset. Yes.'

'And he died there?'

'Yes.'

'Well, in that case, I challenge your authority to question my client about the death of her first husband.'

'We have been in contact with our colleagues in the Dorset police. I can tell you that this is now a joint investigation involving both forces. I can also tell you that Dorset officers will be travelling north, probably tomorrow, to interview Mrs Woolley at greater depth in respect of the suspicious death of her first husband. We feel that the suspicious death of her first husband is germane to the murder of her second. On that basis, I feel it is within my authority to question Mrs Woolley about the death of her first husband.'

Lowe turned to Virginia Woolley. 'Alright,' Lowe was a young man, in Hirst's eyes; he also seemed very serious minded, 'you can answer questions about your first husband.'

'Silk scarves were seen in your house in Dorset, in the waste bin in the kitchen. They were cut and knotted...they were seen the day after your husband died in his swimming pool. What do you know of them?'

'Nothing.' Her voice was calm, controlled.

'You deny they were there?'

'No.'

'How did they get there?'

'I have no idea.'

'You didn't put them there?'

'No.'

'I suggest you used silk because you knew it wouldn't cause bruising. We have taken expert advice about the merits of using silk to restrain someone.'

'No.'

'You did very well out of the death of your first husband, didn't you?'

'Please make a question, Chief Inspector.' Lowe spoke softly but with quiet authority.

'Did your husband leave you three properties in his will?'

'Yes.'

'And a substantial amount of money.'

'No.'

'No?'

'No.'

'We were led to believe that you were worth one million pounds upon the death of Henry Woostencroft.'

'I was...'

'I see. You mean the one million was the total value of the properties?'

'Yes, and he also had stocks and shares, which I sold along with the house in Dorset. In total I raised another million'

'Which you inherited?' Pulleyne observed.

'Quite some motivation,' Hirst added.

Lowe turned to her. 'Don't respond to that. Only answer clear questions.'

Virginia Woolley nodded.

'Then worth two million pounds, you moved north.'

Virginia Woolley remained silent.

'And married again with what some might see as indecent haste, to another wealthy man, who, like your first husband, was considerably older than you. Made quite a living out of being a trophy wife, haven't you?'

'Please confine yourself to asking my client questions, Chief Inspector.' Again spoken softly but his words carried weight.

'I like older men.'

Lowe glanced at Virginia Woolley as if to say, "Don't say anything you don't have to".

'You also like younger men. You've ruined Christopher Elms' life.'

'He ruined his own life.'

'You manipulated him...you danced him like a puppet on a string. You obtained possession of his shoes, walked in them in your husband's blood and managed to secrete them back into his flat.'

'Did I?'

'Yes, you did.'

'No, I didn't.' She remained calm.

'You told him about the window that wasn't alarmed...'

'Yes.'

'You did?' Hirst's heart leapt, he had tripped her.

'Yes, I did.'

'So that he could use the un-alarmed window to access the house?'

'No,' she shook her head, 'no, I mentioned it in passing. I told him about the window that wasn't alarmed because when the building was alarmed, that window was painted over. Subsequently my husband freed it off but we still were not concerned; it led to a scullery which was always locked.'

'Except that it wasn't locked on the night your husband was murdered.'

'Apparently not. Poor Christopher was lucky.'

'Or unlucky...depends which way you look at it.'

'Whatever...but what Christopher did he did off his own bat. The poor boy was infatuated with me. He probably thought that if he murdered Maurice, he could have me all to his silly little self. He was nothing to me...Christopher, I mean, he had a small use...but other than that he was on the edge of my life.'

Lowe looked uncomfortable. He clearly didn't like Virginia Woolley speaking so freely. Hirst, on the other hand, loved it.

'So,' Hirst continued, 'tell me about Shane Parsloe.'

'Who?' She raised her eyebrows.

'The other young man you sent to kill your husband...but that went wrong, didn't it?'

'The name means nothing to me.'

'Paying him for his effort?'

'Paying who?'

'Parsloe...mind you, he's hardly going to confess to attempted murder, so it's safe to assume his mouth will remain shut. But a bit of sugar is deserved, is that what you think?'

Virginia Woolley remained silent.

'So, your two husbands died in about as many years and you are now worth...what? Ten million?'

Virginia Woolley shrugged. 'I really don't know. I have an accountant handling my money.'

'I imagine you have...I imagine you have.'

'You really don't seem to have anything more than circumstantial evidence against my client, Chief Inspector.'

'We haven't.'

Lowe smiled. 'Well, in that case, I will have to ask you to release Mrs Woolley, she has no case to answer.'

'Well, that's for a jury to decide, Mr Lowe, and our solicitor in the CPS is of the opinion that the evidence in this case, albeit circumstantial, is still sufficient to convict. So, Mrs Woolley, you will be taken from this room to the charge bar, where you'll be charged with conspiracy to murder Maurice Woolley. The Dorset police will decide whether you are to be charged with the murder of your first husband following their interview with you. You will appear before magistrates in the morning and we will oppose bail.'

Lowe turned to her. 'I'll try and get Peregrine Lamyman for you. Do not confess to anything.'

'Who?' Virginia Woolley was ashen faced.

'Lamyman...he's about the best defence barrister in this circuit.' Lowe turned to Hirst. 'Where will my client be detained?'

'The cells in the police station tonight, and if the magistrates don't allow bail, then she'll be transferred to New Hall Women's Prison until her trial.'

'How long will that take? The trial, I mean?' Virginia Woolley appealed to Hirst.

'Months.' Hirst reached for the on/off button of the tape recorder. 'You'll be inside for Christmas.'

Virginia Woolley's head slumped.

'The time is now 18.37 hours. The interview is concluded.' Hirst switched the machine off. He pressed the eject button and the twin cassette holders eased open. He took the cassettes out and put each in a Perspex cover and handed one to Gavin Lowe.

On a February morning the following year the judge summed up for the jury. 'Ladies and gentlemen of the jury,' he spoke in clear but solemn tones, reading from prepared notes, 'there is not one shred of evidence which connects the defendant to the death, in what might have been suspicious circumstances, of her first husband, Mr Henry Woostencroft, in their family home in Dorset. There similarly is not one shred of evidence which connects her to the murder of her second husband, Mr Maurice Woolley. We have heard only her strong and insistent denial of any involvement in either murder. All the Crown's evidence in this case has been wholly circumstantial. We remember that upon the death of her first husband, after only a few months of marriage, the defendant inherited an estate valued at approximately two million pounds. There was, therefore, you may feel, motive. We remember the testimony of the brother of Mr Woostencroft, the very credible Reverend Woostencroft, who recalls finding a number of silk scarves in the kitchen waste bin of Woostencroft's home in Dorset, the scarves having been knotted, and having been cut with scissors. He also found a dog collar and leash in the same bin, yet there was no dog in the house, either as a pet or as a guard dog. It was as if some sex game, which many would find distasteful, and which involved restraint, had been played, and it is the assertion of the Crown that while thus restrained, Mr Woostencroft had by some means been lured into the area of the indoor swimming pool and introduced into the water, whereupon he drowned. The evidence given by the pathologist, Dr Fay, to the effect that silk bonds will not cause bruising to the flesh lends further credibility to the Crown's assertion that the defendant, having waited until her husband was deceased, entered the water, cut the silk scarves from his wrists and ankles and disposed of them and the dog lead, quite carelessly, but sufficiently thoroughly that they were not found by the police who attended the scene. What the police found was the corpse of a late middle-aged man floating in the swimming pool. There were no signs of a struggle, no signs of violence, and the police were content to accept the death as an unfortunate accident. When the post-mortem found that the gentleman's death was caused by a massive coronary, the case was closed. In the light of subsequent disclosure, it is the Crown's case that Mr Woostencroft's coronary was induced by the panic and terror, and the realisation that his new young wife was murdering him. The Crown's argument, you may feel, has some credibility.'

He paused and sipped from a glass of water. 'We remember the testimony of Mr Christopher Elms who pleaded guilty to the murder of the defendant's second husband, Mr Maurice Woolley, and who collected a mandatory life sentence. Mr Elms impressed as a genuinely contrite young man when called as a witness for the prosecution, telling how the defendant had told him how to enter the house without triggering the alarm system, and who but the householders, you might think, would know how to do that? Having murdered Mr Woolley, he claimed he did as instructed by the defendant and so thoroughly disposed of the murder weapon so that it could not be recovered, even to support his confession and subsequent testimony. Yet clothing and footwear with the deceased's blood upon it and them was found in his flat, and a knife which could have caused the injuries to Mr Woolley by virtue of the nature and size of the blade was found in the grounds of the house and was further found to have Christopher Elms' fingerprints upon it, as if discarded in a panic as he fled the scene. Christopher Elms' claim that the defendant obtained his footwear, contaminated it with the blood of her deceased husband and then, by some means, reintroduced it to his flat and placed it where it was found by the police is for you to believe or disbelieve. Similarly, Christopher Elms claims that the defendant inveigled him into putting his fingerprints on the knife in question by asking him to carve a joint of meat, which she had prepared for them during their involvement, and which knife she pointedly took away, with other cutlery, without washing it, is again for you to believe or disbelieve. But whatever the truth of the planning of this murder, the defendant inherited eight million pounds upon the death of her husband. Again, a motive is present. That the deceased was not in the vicinity of her home when her husband was murdered, but some fifty miles away visiting a relative in Kingston upon Hull, is not in dispute, but her alibi, provided by the police themselves in the form of a statement taken from her in respect of a reportedly snatched handbag at the time of her husband's murder in West Yorkshire, is both convenient and suspicious.' Again he paused and sipped from the tumbler of water. 'We now turn to the personality of the defendant. She informed both the Woostencroft and Woolley families that she was the only daughter of wealthy parents, now deceased, and had been educated privately at a prestigious public school. It explained why both her marriages were very quick registry office ceremonies attended only by her husband's close relatives. The defendant was clearly able to carry off the deception with polished manners and with a freshly acquired upper class accent, probably garnered through simple social observation and mimicry. The truth of her background is rather different. She grew up in Hull, one of four children of a refuse collector, and left her local authority school at sixteen with no qualifications. She has living relatives, but she kept them from both her husbands and her husbands' families by the simple expedient of not telling her own relatives that she was getting married. She is therefore a woman capable of lying and the jury may care to ponder upon that when considering her denials. The defendant is also a woman whose sexual tastes attract her to younger men, yet her first husband was twenty years her senior, and her second husband was a full thirty years older than she. The jury may care to ponder, then, her motivation for marriage, that it might have been something other than passion. It is certainly the case that both marriages ended in the sudden death of her husband, and both marriages lasted for a period most conveniently measured in months, rather than years.'

The judge paused, then continued. 'Yet, as I said, the prosecution's case remains wholly circumstantial, but there comes a point when the accumulation of circumstantial evidence becomes compelling and is sufficient to convict. It is now for the jury to decide whether the weight of circumstantial evidence in this case is sufficient to allow a safe conviction. The jury is invited rise and consider its verdict.'

Peregrine Lamyman, short and slightly built, entered the cell in which Virginia Woolley sat. She glanced up at him. 'Well,' he took the seat opposite her. 'It's now in the lap of the gods.'

'No, it's not,' she smiled. 'It's in the lap of twelve people who are too stupid to avoid doing jury service. How can people who are too dim-witted to avoid losing weeks of their lives decide whether I should lose years of mine? Mind you, I did jury service once...'

'That's the way it has always been and always will be until

someone can think of a better alternative. But remember, the longer the jury stay out, the greater the chance of acquittal.'

'Really?'

'Yes, as a rule of thumb, and if goes against you, don't despair, we can appeal. As His Lordship said, the evidence is wholly circumstantial, that in itself is grounds for an appeal. I also felt that his Lordship's summing up was quite biased against you.'

'I thought that too. It was as if he was telling them to convict without actually saying it.'

'Yes, it seemed that way, but that's good in a sense; it will make the appeal argument much stronger, circumstantial evidence and a biased summing up.'

Virginia Woolley sat looking round the holding cell; drab green with no artificial light. 'So how long between conviction and appeal?'

'Three years, four perhaps, if we lodge immediately upon conviction, which of course we will do.'

She shook her head. 'Three more years in New Hall...there are some hard women in there; they hate me for being posh...though I show I'm not, but it doesn't help. They read the papers, they catch the news. I was attacked in the showers. They know everybody's business. So, if I am convicted...what will it be...life?'

'Probably. Conspiracy to murder does not necessarily mean life, it depends on the degree of conspiracy, but in this case a high level of conspiracy is alleged, so don't be surprised if you receive a life sentence.'

Virginia Woolley sank her head into her hands. 'What can I do?'

'Well, if you accept the verdict, don't appeal, you could be out in less than ten years.'

'I might do that...better than rotting in there until I am an old maid.'

* * *

At the close of the first day of the jury's deliberation she was escorted with other females on remand to New Hall gaol. At night she lay in her cell listening to the screams of angry or distressed inmates, wondering how she could cope with ten years of this, ten years of the same, possibly even longer...thirty-seven now...nearly fifty when she gets out, at least...but the jury had still not returned after a full day's deliberation and what was it that Peregrine Lamyman had said? 'The longer they are out, the better chance of acquittal,' something like that...a full day and still no verdict. She decided to accept guilt if the appeal failed...no reason not to. She had lost the money anyway. If she gets out early enough, she might still be attractive enough to remarry and she had that one hundred thousand pounds to come out to anyway, in a high yield account in her maiden name, paid in with hard cash taken from her married name account...utterly untraceable. Should have put more in...should have done this, should not have done that... She had rapidly found that all the prisoner can do is allow the past and all its regrets whirl to about in her mind, until sleep, merciful sleep, rescued her from her demons. The following morning she was returned to the High Court and sat all day in a cell in the basement of the building, uncomfortable in her smart clothing. Eventually she removed the constricting outer clothing and sat in her lingerie, having folded her clothing into a neat pile and placed them on the very clean floor. When the large turnkey brought her her lunch, she enjoyed the woman's look of surprise. 'Why not?' She stood to accept the tray. 'It's warm, no point in being uncomfortable...won't take me a minute to claw it all back on.'

'Yes why not?' The turnkey smiled; yet cast an envious glance over Virginia Woolley's figure. 'Why not, indeed?' She pulled the door shut behind her.

Still the minutes ticked by. Each minute brought with it a greater chance of acquittal. At 5 p.m. the turnkey opened her cell and told her to dress, she was going back to New Hall. Virginia Woolley raised her eyebrows and was unable to conceal a smile. Two full days without a verdict. Hope, she found, was indeed springing eternal. That night was the same hell as the last; the hell that is a women's prison.

Richard Pulleyne left the library, turning his collar up against the rain and walked slowly home. Again he thought, it was always worse when they don't turn up at all.

On the morning of the third day's deliberation, and dressed elegantly, Virginia Woolley stepped across the threshold of the cell in the Court building and peeled off her outer clothing and tugged off her pinching heels. She sat for an hour, feeling sick with worry, yet, at the same time, resigned to her fate. There was, after all, now nothing she could do. After what she thought was about a sixty-minute period the turnkey unlocked the cell and asked her to get dressed. Trembling with fear, she dressed and was led by the turnkey to the entrance to the cell section, where she was handed over to the custody of the court bailiff. The bailiff took her through the maze of corridors and stairs used to convey the accused and the convicted to and from the court. It was, she had found, a very lonely walk, just her and the court bailiff who didn't speak, no natural light throughout the journey, plain, drably painted walls, the clicking of heels and the jangling of keys being the only echoing sounds. She emerged from the corridor and was escorted into the dock of the court. She projected herself in a demure manner, continuing as she had done throughout the trial as an image of innocence, as a woman cruelly, wrongly accused. This was the verdict, this was it...the clerk was there, the legal teams, solemn in their black gowns and white wigs, the jury, twelve good men and women true...seven men, five women... The male-dominated jury might favour her, so had said Peregrine Lamyman; more sympathy from a male-dominated jury towards a female accused. Women, on the other hand, would be merciless to a female accused who had no defence that they could sympathise with such, as reacting to years of domestic abuse. Virginia Woolley looked towards Peregrine Lamyman who, with his junior behind him, sat just beneath and to one side of her. He did not look at her.

There was a tap on the door behind the judges bench, a female usher entered and said, 'All rise'. The court stood as the judge, in scarlet and ermine, looking again, she thought, like an unintentional caricature of Santa Claus, entered the room. He shuffled in front of his chair and bowed to the court, and each official in the well of the court returned the bow and sat when the judge had seated himself.

'Members of the jury,' the judge addressed the jury box. 'You have been retired for two days and have clearly been unable to reach a unanimous verdict. After this length of time, I am entitled to accept a majority verdict. I wish you to return to the jury room and return with a majority verdict with which at least ten of you are in agreement.' He stood, bowed to the court and left the room. The court bailiff tugged at the sleeve of Virginia Woolley's jacket and she was led back to the cells, handed over to the turnkey. 'Majority verdict,' Virginia Woolley said.

'I'd keep your clothes on.' The turnkey led her to her cell. 'In my experience, the jury won't be long in coming back, not after a majority verdict has been asked for.'

Thirty minutes later she returned and opened the cell door. 'What did I tell you?'

Virginia Woolley stood. 'So this is it?'

'This is it.'

The turnkey led her down the cell corridor and once again handed her over to the stern-faced court bailiff, who escorted her to the dock where she stood, as the judge entered, bowed, and sat. The jury was led into the court by an usher and filed into their seats. On this final occasion they were led into the jury box by a bearded, bespectacled man who, throughout the trial, had sat on the second row. This time he sat on the front row, in the seat nearest the judge. He had clearly been chosen as the foreperson. Virginia Woolley looked at him; it was his voice that was to determine her fate. The jury sat down.

The court clerk stood and faced the jury. 'Will the foreperson please stand.'

The bearded, bespectacled man stood.

'Have you reached a verdict?' asked the court clerk.

'Yes.'

'Do you find the accused guilty or not guilty?'

'Not guilty.'

Virginia Woolley caught eye contact with the foreman and smirked. She watched as the foreperson seemed to bend forward, as if he had been punched in the stomach, and sink, as his knees seemed to buckle. She watched as a turbulence of realisation rippled through the jury box, hands went to foreheads, heads sank.

'Is that your majority verdict?' The court clerk's voice betrayed his clear disappointment.

'Yes. By a majority of eleven,' the foreman stammered.

A female juror sitting in the second row, middle aged and quite prim seeming, thought Virginia Woolley, said in complete defiance of protocol, in a voice loud enough to carry across the well of the court. 'What did I tell you? What did I say? I told you it would be a safe conviction.'

Clive Hirst stood at the window of the living room looking out at the relentlessly falling rain. He became aware of his wife's presence beside and a little behind him.

'It's life giving,' she said, 'look at it that way…better than drought.'

'The rain? Yes. I know it's well set in, we'll take the car to the golf club this evening, but I wasn't thinking that. It's that trial. I can understand why they didn't convict, though I could have understood more if they *had* convicted…but she got away with it, and she's unlikely to re-offend, so we won't be nailing her for anything…we won't even have that compensation. She murdered one man, orchestrated, as DC Lucas put it, the murder of another and ruined a young man's life in the process. She wins herself millions of pounds and all she collects is a few months on remand in New Hall. I know that police work is a matter of "win some, lose some", but when you lose something so big…'

His wife remained silent. She just didn't know what to say.

Christopher Elms lay on his bed in Armley Prison. The cell door was unlocked and another prisoner entered the cell carrying a cardboard box containing his possessions under one arm and a set of blankets under the other. The door was closed behind him and locked. Christopher Elms had seen the other prisoner before, he was large, bald-headed, missing a few teeth. He had seen him staring at him in the showers. He was the one they called "Animal". The man looked down at Elms as if devouring him with his eyes.

'Crowded nick,' said Animal. 'They put me in here with you…just the two of us.' He began to snigger. Christopher Elms wept uncontrollably.

On Gozo Virginia Woolley stepped from the shade of her villa and walked by the swimming pool towards four young, bronzed and muscled men. She wore high-heeled mules and a sarong. As she approached, the young men stopped talking and stood in a line, like a group of soldiers "falling in". Virginia Woolley stopped walking when she was about ten feet from the young men and looked at each of them in turn. Then she said, 'Tony,' and turned and walked back towards the villa, with Tony following in her wake. She turned to him and smiled. 'Good boy,' she said. 'Very good boy.'

SPEAK
FOR THE
DEAD

SPEAK

FOR THE

DEAD

AMY TECTOR

WITHDRAWN

A DOMINION ARCHIVES MYSTERY

KEYLIGHT
BOOKS

KEYLIGHT BOOKS

AN IMPRINT OF TURNER PUBLISHING COMPANY

Nashville, Tennessee

www.turnerpublishing.com

Cover design by Emily Mahon

Book design by William Ruoto

Library of Congress Cataloging-in-Publication Data

Names: Tector, Amy, author.

Title: Speak for the dead : a novel / Amy Tector.

Description: Nashville, Tenn. : Keylight Books, [2023]

Identifiers: LCCN 2021060180 (print) | LCCN 2021060181 (ebook) | ISBN
9781684428861 (paperback) | ISBN 9781684428878 (hardcover) | ISBN
9781684428885 (epub)

Subjects: LCSH: Coroners—Ontario—Ottawa—Fiction. | Murder—Ontario—
Ottawa—Fiction. | LCGFT: Detective and mystery fiction.

Classification: LCC PR9199.4.T393 S64 2023 (print) | LCC PR9199.4.T393
(ebook) | DDC 813/.6—dc23/eng/20220519

LC record available at https://lccn.loc.gov/2021060180

LC ebook record available at https://lccn.loc.gov/2021060181

Printed in the United States of America

To Susie

SPEAK

FOR THE

DEAD

THE WOMAN DANGLED IN THE CENTER OF THE ROOM, HANGING A FOOT OFF the floor. Though small, her body dominated the narrow vault. Floor-to-ceiling shelving, stacked with neat cardboard boxes, lined both walls. It made the cell-like space feel more cramped. Confined spaces triggered Cate Spencer's claustrophobia, but she had a job to do. The yellow rope around the woman's neck was tied to a pipe in the ceiling. It was braided polypropylene, common in hardware stores. It cut deeply into the woman's throat, leaving mauve-black bruising. A stool lay kicked over at her feet.

Cate could have reached out and touched the body, but she knew better. Instead, she took a deep breath, shoving away her sense that the walls were closing in. Muffled thunder rumbled outside. The summer storm that was threatening as she drove over the rutted road of the Canadian Forces Base Eastview had arrived.

She took another breath, her claustrophobia receding. An unusual smell—sharp and chemical—permeated the air. The victim's face was purple and her mouth spotted with blood. Curly hair sprang from her head, a dynamic sign of life amid the horror of death. She was young, early twenties. Her jean jacket hung open, and her T-shirt was some kind of artisanal thing with a wide neck and stenciled birds. A pair of tortoiseshell eyeglasses lay cracked on the cement floor. "Ident been through?" Cate asked. She couldn't touch anything until they took their photographs.

Detective Dominic Baker stood at the vault's entrance with a knot of others. She didn't need to turn around to know that remnants of

Sausage McMuffin clung to his shaggy gray mustache and that he looked impatient.

Normally she found his brusque manner frustrating. Her job was to review every aspect of death until she understood precisely what had happened. Baker tended to rush the coroners, anxious to get clearance so he could concentrate on the next unexpected death. In the past, she'd doubled down on her own meticulousness, ordering extra tests, interviewing additional witnesses just to annoy him. These days she welcomed the idea of a quick case, uncomplicated by police overzealousness.

"Ident was here over an hour ago," Baker said.

Cate ignored the implied criticism that she was late to get to the scene. She struggled to move quickly lately; everything felt hard.

She pulled on a pair of latex gloves and reached up, feeling along the woman's jaw. The lips did not part, the muscles locked. Next, she turned to the right arm, gently trying to move the thin limb, testing to see if she could flex or extend.

There was no give to the arm; the victim was in full rigor mortis. Normally this would mean death occurred at least four hours ago, but surprisingly for such an out-of-the-way and derelict-looking building, the air-conditioning was at meat locker chill. Given how cold it was, rigor would set in much faster. The victim could have died as little as two hours ago.

Usually this was where she would feel a small zing of professional pleasure. She had a puzzle to solve: the challenge of understanding someone's final hours with the clues only medicine could yield.

These weren't normal times, however. Nothing was normal since she learned the news about Jason's accident. Today was her birthday, and it felt appropriate that she was spending it with death. She tried to be grateful that she was out of the house. Better than sitting in front of the TV, mystified that people could care about traffic or a Kardashian, rather than the only thing that mattered: her brother Jason was dead.

"Can someone find out what the exact temperature is?" she asked without looking back at the three men clustered at the door. Besides Baker, a young uniformed officer and a tall straight-backed guy whose name she hadn't caught hovered at the entrance.

She heard footsteps walking away and assumed the officer was looking for the answer. She waited twenty seconds and spoke again, without turning. "I'll also need a stepladder."

Baker cursed, and she heard him leave. She smiled. Make the lazy bugger work.

All was silent except for the soothing hum of the air-conditioning. Cate jotted down a few notes.

"She's so young, isn't she?" the remaining man asked.

Cate stiffened. He wasn't police, then. Cops knew better than to interrupt while she was doing her examination.

Given his upright bearing and crewcut, she'd bet he was military. That would make sense. While she hadn't gone through the base's main gate on her drive across the fields, she wouldn't be surprised if this weird building was part of the Air Force. "Yes," she said, not turning around. "She's young."

She slid off one of the woman's shoes and pressed the firm flesh of her foot. The blood pooled there, and the skin remained purple. Lividity was fixed.

"Why would someone so young take her own life? Tragic." The man's voice was deep, but almost plaintive, like a child's.

She scowled. "Well, bad stuff happens." Jason's plane had crashed into the jungle. Her breath caught in her throat. She put a hand on one of the metal shelves to steady herself. Even through her glove, she could feel its biting coolness.

"You OK?"

The man's solicitous tone nearly brought her to tears. "I'm fine," she said. "Where's that goddamn ladder?"

"Unknot your panties, Cate. I've got one." She turned. Baker held a small ladder.

The junior officer had returned as well. "It's four degrees Celsius," he reported.

She turned back to the victim, but for a crazy moment it was Jason—his face distended and purple, his eyes bulging. She blinked, and the image was gone.

CHAPTER TWO

"HAS ANYONE MOVED THE BODY?" CATE ASKED. THE ANSWER WAS AN obvious "no," but she had to ask.

"According to the paramedics, she was clearly dead when they arrived. They knew not to disturb the scene," Baker responded, remaining in the hallway.

"That's good," Cate said. It was always better to examine the body in situ. She climbed the ladder and continued her scan, moving her fingers over the woman's head, feeling and looking for signs of trauma. Nothing obvious. Folding back the woman's right ear, she searched to see where the rope came to a point. The coolness of the vault would slow the development of bruising. It was difficult to tell if the wounds were consistent with asphyxiation secondary to hanging.

She paused to make notes. The deceased chose hanging, one of the worst ways to die. Despite the strongest death wish, the body clung to life, involuntarily thrashing against the slow denial of air. Cate had seen necks almost cut in half from the body's refusal to quit.

Baker's voice broke into her thoughts. "Her name is Molly Johnson. An employee at the Dominion Archives." His voice softened. "She was twenty-three." Baker could be a dick, but he always treated the dead with respect.

Cate looked at the body again, seeing the fragility of Molly's collarbones jutting out from her T-shirt. Flushing, she was overwhelmed with anger. Twenty-three was ridiculously young. This girl must have hated her existence. Had she felt a yawning loneliness? Wondered what the point was?

Cate stepped off the ladder and turned her back on those thoughts. Baker and the two others stared at her expectantly, but she couldn't find any words.

"Suicide, obviously," Baker said.

His statement returned her focus. "Without analysis of the bruising, it's impossible to be definitive." She frowned. Something about the scene troubled her.

"Come on," Baker said. "It's clearly suicide."

A ruling of suicide meant that this was a coroner's case, and she was in charge, with assistance from the police. If she found the death suspicious, then it would be the other way around. She looked at the scene again. A somber quiet hung over the vault; a muted despair that belied the ferocious struggle Cate knew must have taken place not too long before. "Is there a note?" she asked.

The junior officer piped up. "We haven't found one yet."

Baker glared at the younger man, then shrugged. "Manner of death is your call, of course, doctor."

He was annoyed. Undoubtedly, he didn't want another homicide added to his caseload. His irritation wasn't Cate's problem.

She stepped out of the vault, relieved to escape the tight space and join Baker and the others in the hallway. Bare fluorescent bulbs lit a long, wide corridor. Metallic doors ran down both sides at five-foot intervals. Presumably, each led to similar tiny rooms. At the far end of the hallway stood a big steel door and the office area she had initially come through. There were no windows. The floor and ceiling were cement. The door to the vault she'd been in was at least half a foot of solid metal. It reminded Cate of a prison.

"What is this place, anyway?" she asked, pulling off her gloves.

"It's a nitrate film storage facility," the military guy said with a smile, almost as if he were apologizing for his answer.

"What's that?" she asked.

The tall soldier shrugged, the gesture loosening his posture, making him appear boyish, even though he was pushing fifty. "I'm no expert, but it's old film. They stopped making it in the fifties. The Archives stores it out here."

"Why?" she asked. The Dominion Archives had a huge building in downtown Ottawa.

The soldier smiled again. "Good question."

Cate frowned. Why was he grinning at her like that? He needed to settle down.

He continued, "Nitrate is highly flammable and can spontaneously combust if it gets overheated. They wanted it well away from the rest of their archival collection."

"OK," she said. "That must be why they keep it so cold."

Baker spoke. "Yeah, it's quite something. They deliberately built this place far from civilization because the nitrate is so dangerous." Baker, in his usual brown jacket, Looney Tunes tie, and wrinkled dress shirt, looked like the stereotypical cop, but he talked about the science of nitrate film with surprising enthusiasm and authority. "They store it in such small vaults on purpose, so that if one negative goes boom, it limits the damage—each vault has a metal blast door designed to withstand fifty kilograms of explosives." He pointed behind him to the emergency exit door. Next to it was a case containing two large fire extinguishers, suppression blankets, and a firefighter's ax.

She looked down the length of the hallway. There were at least twenty metal doors, each containing highly volatile explosive material. One spark could ignite a firestorm. She shivered, anxious to leave. "I've got what I need." She injected a brisk note into her voice. If she went now, she could visit her father and be home in time for a hot shower and a smooth scotch.

She started walking up the long hallway toward the entrance, and the military guy hurried to catch up. "We didn't officially meet," he said.

Cate didn't want to be here, chitchatting with this joker. Then again, there was nowhere else she wanted to be, either. Maybe Molly Johnson, hanging in that vault, had the right idea.

"I'm Major Peter Harrison." He stuck out a hand and smiled yet again.

"Dr. Cate Spencer." Despite herself, she was curious. Yesterday was her day off, and she'd pulled the blinds on the July sunshine, spending it chain-smoking in front of the television. The upside of that river of cable news and nicotine was that she was up to speed on the latest happenings. After a decade of legal wrangling with environmentalists and Indigenous activists, the government had sold off Canadian Forces Base Eastview to TDR Enterprises. It was the biggest land deal in Ottawa history. The groundbreaking ceremony on a billion-dollar housing development and nine-hole golf course was sometime this month.

She shook Harrison's hand. His grip was firm, and his eyes were a clear blue in his weathered face.

"I'm second in command, CFB Eastview."

"You won't have much to command soon," she remarked.

The major's laugh was a bark. "You're right. We're down to one crew for the final move, and we've got to get cracking. Mothballing one hundred years of history."

Lots of people were unhappy with the development. Indeed, demonstrators had set up a permanent protest site at the turnoff to the base. She'd driven past them on her way to the nitrate facility. The group was well away from the main gate, maybe to ensure better visibility from busy Turcotte Road. There were about thirty people, waving signs bearing slogans like "Stop the Rape of the Land," "Social Housing, Not Two-Car Garages," and "We Were Here First!"

"So, this building is part of the base, then?"

"No," Harrison said, a note of apology in his voice. "Even though it's right on the property's edge, it belongs to the Archives. The first police officer on the scene wasn't sure whether this was our jurisdiction or not, so I got the call." He shrugged.

Cate would have expected the second-in-command at a base like Eastview to be authoritative and autocratic, but Harrison was an eager puppy. He was clearly some kind of paper-pusher, promoted for his ability to file reports on time and kiss the right ass.

"The major's right. The Ottawa PD are the lucky winners of this case." Baker had caught up to them. The junior officer was left standing alone by the open door to the vault. Cate noted that he was careful to face away from the suspended corpse.

She wondered why Baker was allowing Harrison access to the death scene if he wasn't involved in the case. In the past, she would have called him out on this sloppiness, but now she mentally shrugged. If Baker couldn't be bothered to follow protocol, why should she worry?

They'd reached the entrance to the anteroom. Cate had spotted a couple of work rooms on her way into the vault area. She could commandeer one of those for the necessary paperwork. "I'll get my warrants signed. Then you can move the body," she said to Baker.

He grunted in approval. "Good, I want to cut our girl down."

She met his eyes and nodded. She felt the same way: a desire to restore Molly to dignity and a semblance of peace.

"Glad you caught this call, and not that douche, Williams," Baker said gruffly.

Dr. Sylvester Williams had been an Ottawa coroner for twenty years, and what he didn't know about the job was not worth knowing, at least according to him. This was the closest Baker had ever come to complimenting her, and Cate was surprised to find herself flattered.

"I'll need the victim's particulars to finish up the paperwork." She took out her phone and dialed dispatch to let them know she was wrapping up. The call failed.

Baker laughed. "Don't bother. There's no cell reception here."

The ever-helpful Harrison chimed in. "This whole area is a bit of a dead zone. You usually have to drive back to the main road to get a signal."

"Fine," Cate said.

Baker handed her a sheet. "We got the deceased's name and DOB from the girl who discovered the body. She was a coworker. Stowe's interviewing her. He can collect your paperwork." Detective Stowe was Baker's partner, slick and smooth where Baker was rumpled and abrupt.

Cate nodded. "Have you contacted the family? I'll need the next of kin details."

Baker held up an old flip-type cell phone. "This was in her pocket. It's only got work numbers, so we'll look at her employment file."

"Good," Cate said. Thankfully, she didn't have to inform Molly's family, but she did need to speak with them and answer their questions about the manner of death.

Nodding to Baker and Major Harrison, Cate pushed through the door to the anteroom. The air was warmer, and the soothing noise of the rain against the windows was a comforting change from the coldness of the vaults. The deluge was already easing; nothing so fleeting as a summer storm. Stowe and the witness were nowhere in sight.

Unlike the vaults, this room was chaotic. Boxes were scattered on the floor and every surface. Cate cleared a place at the table and sat down to fill out the forms.

She needed to make notes for her preliminary report. She thought back to the image of Molly's body hanging there—a brutal note of discord in an otherwise well-ordered scene. There was no sign of struggle. No boxes knocked over or kicked in. That didn't jibe with suicide by hanging.

Was there more to this? In Cate's experience, death was almost always straightforward. Murder mysteries only existed in novels or on TV. During five years on the job, no one had ever tried to mask a murder through suicide. Her stomach knotted: at least none that she had caught.

CHAPTER THREE

SHE WAS BEING RIDICULOUS. WHILE MURDER MYSTERIES FLOURISHED IN popular culture—seemingly every quaint British village had hosted at least one murderous vicar—Cate knew they didn't happen in real life. Murder, when it occurred, was depressingly un-mysterious: look to the partner (almost always male); look to the gang associates (almost always high); and then call it a day.

This was her first suicide since Jason's death. She hadn't expected to be unsettled like this. The idea that Molly had chosen to end her life was so heartbreaking, final—and seductive. Cate frowned. Was she actively hoping the death was murder rather than suicide so that she wouldn't have to face her own bullshit? Technically, she shouldn't even be on this case. Her shift had been over for five minutes when Dispatch called. She could have said no, but somehow spending time with a corpse was more appealing than the alternative: staring at the television until it was time to go to her father's for the obligatory birthday visit. Her first birthday without Jason.

She'd never been good at self-awareness. She'd relied on Jason to call her out on her unique crazy. Cate closed her eyes briefly and pulled the paperwork to her, turning to the job's routine. Until she signed a warrant to take possession of the body, it couldn't be removed to the morgue. Similarly, no autopsy would be performed without her signature. She filled out and signed her two warrants and the small tag that would be placed on Molly Johnson's toe to keep her identity straight at the morgue.

Stowe still hadn't returned. She didn't want to go back into that icy cold vault and deal with Baker. She'd give his partner two more minutes. The boxes surrounding her were all the same size, but some were brand-new, with white barcodes in the right-hand corners and indecipherable codes printed above them. Others were older, yellowed, and squashed. Restless, Cate opened one of the newer ones. A row of stacked white envelopes greeted her. She pulled one out. The top-right corner of each envelope was labeled. "R1455, Portrait Series. L.M. Montgomery." The Archives had collected negatives related to the author of *Anne of Green Gables*.

She placed the envelope back in the box and turned to an old container. Its cardboard edges were battered. It wasn't barcoded, and someone had scrawled across its front with a Sharpie: "For Destruction."

A strong smell, like rotting socks, hit her as she opened this box. Instead of a neat row of envelopes, it contained a jumble of loose photographic negatives. Some were curled up tightly like little cigarettes. Others had a thick whitish stain covering them. Others were gooey, as if they were melting. Still others were almost iridescent. These were beautiful. She put on a pair of the nearby white cotton gloves and picked one up. It was a polarized image; the light and dark areas reversed. It had been years since Cate saw an image like this. Looking at it reminded her of going to the shopping center as a kid to pick up a roll of film that had been developed, that moment of excitement as you waited to see how your photographs had turned out. Now that anticipation was gone forever, though she supposed today's teenagers had Snapchat or TikTok pleasures she couldn't begin to fathom.

These negatives were different from the ones she'd fetched from the mall. Rather than small strips of images, they were individual, each about four by five inches. The negative in her hand was of a ghostly woman in an old-fashioned dress staring at the camera, her hair in a tight bun, her eyes humorless. The switch between black and white made it challenging to interpret. Cate strained to understand what she was seeing.

The polarization of the image, the dress so dark against the whiteness of the background, made the woman stand out, alone and bereft in an unadorned room. The world might pity this lonely-looking woman, someone who couldn't build a family, or keep relationships, but her very isolation was her source of strength. This woman would never be left devastated and gasping over a lost relationship. Cate was sure the woman in the photograph, her eyes so uncompromising, was a survivor.

The film's deterioration was fascinating. A shimmery stain covered half the image, its rainbow colors blending eerily with the woman's figure. Cate held the negative up, studying it to see how the chemical decomposition was happening. Squinting at the light, the pounding thrum of a headache surged forward, and her stomach heaved. The suddenness of her reaction alarmed her. She remembered the strong odor when she opened the box.

She put her hands on the table to catch her breath and in that moment heard a shattering sound. She looked up to see a rock bounce through the window into the office, followed seconds later by a cherry bomb, its fuse aflame.

CHAPTER FOUR

Cate dropped to her knees, pressing her body against the wall. Heart thudding, she waited, but no other projectiles came through the window. She turned toward the voice. A young woman, perhaps twenty-five, was crouched in the doorway. She was Asian, slight and fine-boned like a pixie, or maybe that was just her haircut. She was wearing jeans and a black T-shirt emblazoned with "I'm a cutie pie" in pink. Her face was pale and her eyes huge. She looked terrified.

Cate thought she heard retreating footsteps outside. It was hard to be certain over the pounding of her heart. The younger woman dashed forward to stamp out the cherry bomb.

Cate crunched across the broken glass, picking up the rock that had come through the window.

The pixie girl spoke. "We have to evacuate."

Before Cate could say anything, the other woman leaped over a couple of boxes to yank the fire alarm on the wall. An earsplitting wail filled the room, reverberating throughout the old building. The noise was like a physical force pounding Cate's body. Her headache increased with a vengeance. The blare left no choice but to leave.

The younger woman was already at the fire exit at the back of the room. "Hurry," she called.

"Wait." Cate grabbed the folder that contained her paperwork.

"Hurry," the girl repeated, making an impatient gesture with her hand.

Cate hesitated at the door. The noise was brutal, but she didn't like to be rushed. The girl, surprisingly strong, shoved her through the exit and closed the door behind them.

They emerged at the back of the building. The rain had eased to a drizzle. An empty field lay before them leading to a gentle hill. There was no sign of anyone. Cate's adrenaline surge turned to anger. She'd like to give the idiot who threw the cherry bomb a piece of her mind. She also needed a cigarette. She patted her pockets before remembering she'd left her smokes in the car.

"Come on," the younger woman said and hurried toward the hill.

"Where are you going?" Cate asked.

"We've got to get to the fire-safety perimeter."

Other than the alarm, now muffled by the closed door, all was quiet. Baker and the others must have used the exit by the vaults.

"I'm going to walk around to the parking lot," Cate called after the woman. There was no way she was following that pixie into some field when her car and her cigarettes were on the other side of the building.

"No," the woman said. "Let's go. We must get to the safety perimeter."

"In case you forgot, there is no fire. You're the one who pulled the alarm. In reaction to a defused cherry bomb, I might add, not exactly dynamite."

Now the woman turned and strode back, speaking with a fierceness that caught Cate off guard. "Do you know what happens when nitrose cellulose starts to deteriorate? It off-gasses and gets increasingly volatile. Eventually, if the conditions are right—say, a cherry bomb landing in the middle of it all—that gas will spark and start to burn." The woman's voice became more urgent. "Nitrate film burns fifteen times faster than wood. It produces its own oxygen as it's burning. Nothing—not water, not smothering, not anguished prayers to God—is going to stop it. It will burn for days with an intensity that will literally suck your breath away."

Cate blinked and looked back at the building. "To the safety perimeter it is."

They picked their way across the field. Cate kept an eye out for the bomb thrower, but aside from the occasional damp groundhog, they were alone. The other woman set a brisk pace. As her lungs began to clog and her breathing grew labored, Cate struggled to keep up. They stopped at the top of the hill and Cate doubled over, as if pulled toward the earth by the heaviness of her lungs. Her coughs shook her frame; great, unpleasant hacks that left her seeing stars.

"You should quit," the woman said.

"Huh?" Cate croaked.

"My grandpa smoked, and he died wheezing and coughing like you. Every day of his last year was a struggle to get his breath. By the end he couldn't talk—he'd just stare at you with these sad, pleading eyes. It was horrible."

"Thanks for your concern," Cate said, finally able to stand upright and breathe. "How long do we have to stay here?"

"Until the fire department gives the all-clear."

Cate strained to hear the wail of the trucks approaching, but all was quiet. She looked around. Below her was the base's perimeter fence, marching off into the distance. On its other side was a scene of pastoral beauty. A creek, oxbowing in an undulating pattern, fed into a small lake. Ancient willow trees bent down as if to sip from the clear blue water. A boulder thrust up from the middle of the lake. She blinked. Through the soft rain, it looked like a fairy tale world, unreal and magical.

"Pretty, isn't it? That's Lake Mitchell. Molly and I ate lunch on this spot when we worked out here."

"You're the coworker who discovered the body," Cate deduced.

The woman winced, and Cate regretted her bluntness. To her credit, though, the other woman carried on and introduced herself.

"Rose Li."

Cate took a deep breath. As unorthodox as this situation was, she was talking to someone who knew the victim, and she had to regain both her professionalism and her compassion. "I'm sorry for your loss," Cate said. "I'm Dr. Spencer."

"Doctor?" Rose asked.

Cate was accustomed to puzzlement. With a violent or sudden demise, people always expected the cops, but no one anticipated the bureaucracy. "I'm the coroner. I have to certify the death."

Rose's eyes widened.

Cate could see all the usual questions forming in her mind. "Yes, I'm a real doctor. No, I don't do autopsies or solve crimes. My role is to determine manner of death."

"Oh," Rose said softly. "What are you going to say about Molly?"

Cate glimpsed the pain behind her eyes, and it reminded her of her own bewilderment at Jason's death. She didn't want to deal with this now. "The case is still open, so I can't discuss it. Certainly not with the person who discovered the body." Once again, she was harsher than she intended.

Rose crossed her arms. "That 'body' was my friend a few hours ago." She hugged herself. "Yesterday Molly was complaining that there wasn't any skim milk for her coffee. She said that one teaspoon of cream would go straight to her ass. Now you come along and call her 'the body' like she's some piece of meat."

Cate was impressed. This soon after the demise, survivors often had trouble accepting reality; they couldn't face the finality of death. Her conversations with loved ones usually revolved around confirming the death and equivocating about how painless it had been. Rose didn't seem to need that kind of comfort.

"I don't consider . . ." Cate closed her eyes, searching for Molly's last name. "Miss Johnson to be a 'piece of meat.' I want to find out what happened to her and lay her to rest."

Rose wasn't listening. She stared down at the lake. "I should have stopped this. I should have helped her."

If Rose's acceptance of Molly's death was unusual, her feelings of inadequacy were not. "It's quite common to feel guilty when someone dies suddenly. To feel like you could have done more to prevent it." Cate paused. Jason had died thousands of kilometers away from her, alone in a foreign country. She cleared her throat and continued. "The truth is, we're powerless, and that's terrifying."

"Except Molly didn't 'die suddenly.' She was murdered."

CHAPTER FIVE

CATE STARED AT ROSE. "MURDERED?" SHE REPEATED. HER INSTINCTS
were right. "What's the evidence?"

"Molly was happy. We had plans to catch a movie tomorrow night.
Who makes plans when they're going to kill themselves? Who worries
about their ass getting fat?"

Cate was annoyed she'd let herself think Rose might have proof
of a crime. No one wanted to admit that stopping life's pain once and
for all was a viable, and sometimes rational, option. It was too desta-
bilizing for everyone else who had to keep plodding on. She adopted
her most soothing voice, the one she had used in her previous life as
a family doctor to tell a woman she'd felt a lump. "Finding a body
can be traumatic. I'm sure Detective Stowe has discussed counseling
options with you. There are specific programs for witnesses to violent
death."

"Cut the crap," Rose snapped. Her voice broke, but she didn't cry,
instead becoming aggressive. "You're idiots if you think it's suicide."

Cate's head throbbed. "I understand your pain, but you were her
coworker. You don't know what her home life was like or what issues
she may have been dealing with or what had happened in her past.
Who knows why she felt the way she did?" Cate heard her voice rising
but couldn't stop the words. "Maybe she was sick of getting up every
goddamn day and trudging through life only to fall into bed every
goddamn night." Anger, or perhaps something else, choked in her
throat and she couldn't speak. She turned back to the building. There
was no smoke. No fire. She wanted to get away from this girl. She
headed down the hill.

Rose followed her.

"Shouldn't you stay in your safety zone?" Cate asked snidely.

Rose ignored her tone. "Please. I'm sorry. I know Molly didn't kill herself, she wouldn't. I tried to tell Detective Stowe, but he didn't seem to care."

Cate stopped. She was only a few hundred meters from silence, solitude, and a cigarette. "Look, I'm the one deciding on manner of death, not detectives Stowe or Baker."

"Killing herself is the last thing she would do. Not like that."

No, Cate hesitated, not like that. She had spent a week in a Toronto hotel as part of her coroner training, learning about decomposition rates, accidental drownings, Sudden Infant Death Syndrome . . . and suicide. Men favored firearms, women poison. Statistically speaking, it was relatively rare for a woman to hang herself. So rare, she now recalled the instructor saying, such deaths should raise a red flag.

"You don't think Molly killed herself. I can tell by your face," Rose said.

Cate spoke with professional crispness. "I'll do my investigation. I'll get the autopsy results. Then I'll make a decision based on evidence."

"But Dr. Spencer—"

Cate interrupted, anxious to get away from the insistent woman. "Sudden death is horrible, but it happens. Go see the police-assigned counselor, and try to move on."

"But—"

Cate put up a hand. "I can't discuss it further." She strode away as fast as she could. Of course, that cardio-fit pixie could catch up to her, if she wanted to, but Rose stayed behind in the drizzle, standing forlornly in the field.

Cate moved briskly back to the building and tried the door they had exited through. It was locked. Going around the building to the right wasn't an option; the CFB Eastview fence ran right up to the building.

Going left meant walking the length of that long row of vaults to the very end, where the body was, and back up the other side. A scrubby tangle of bushes and trees had sprung up, although there was a rough path through the brush. The canopy protected her from the light rain and birds sang above her head. She could hear the alarm faintly, but it did not disturb the natural setting.

Cate had been called to a few murders over the years. They were always straightforward, with the guilty party often still there, in handcuffs, sobbing over what they had done. If this was homicide, it was more premeditated than the usual intoxicated rage. Cate shook her head. Speculating was not her job. She was trained to be professional and distant from the everyday business of death. She wanted her usual numbness. She needed a drink.

The trees were mostly beech with an occasional maple. The air smelled earthy and fresh. She took a couple of deep breaths. The smell reminded her of boarding school and the years she spent living in the countryside. When was the last time she was in the woods? Probably five years ago in Gatineau Park with her ex. Toward the end, their hikes were one of the few bright spots in the marriage. The sound of a bird chirping, high and clear, made her smile. Her headache receded.

Cate rounded the end of the building. The body, presumably not yet removed, was through that wall. A scattering of rubbish lay among the trees: old cardboard boxes sodden from rain, a single sneaker, a muddy-looking sleeping bag, some smashed wine bottles, and even a used condom, looking like a large white slug. The path widened, and she saw the tracks of many pairs of shoes in front of the emergency door. Rather than exit through the office entrance by the parking lot, Baker and the others must have left through here. She paused. Unlike the door she and Rose had used, this one, the one leading directly to Molly's body, was ajar.

CHAPTER SIX

DAMN IT. BAKER WAS SLOPPY. WHAT OFFICER LEFT A DEATH SCENE UN-secured? Cate walked toward the parking lot and then paused. She thought of Molly's body hanging there, unattended and vulnerable. She should secure the scene. There was no sign of fire or the cherry bomb thrower. Surely, it was safe to enter. She poked her head into the building. The hallway of vaults stretched before her, somehow dim even under fluorescent lights. The alarm deafened, echoing in the confined space. She rubbed her head.

She turned to the vault containing the body. Molly's open eyes stared with the dead gaze of a porcelain doll, refusing to reveal what had happened. Cate drew on her years of analyzing such scenes and examined the rest of the space. If someone had intruded, they didn't seem to have touched anything. The shelves at Molly's hand and foot level were undisturbed, the boxes still neatly arranged, their barcodes facing outward.

It was obvious Molly hadn't struggled in death. Cate thought through the implication. A killer would have strangled her and staged the hanging to hide his crime. Is that what had happened here? Baker was swamped and wanted a nice, simple suicide. God, it would be easy to let this go. She was so tired.

Molly's broken glasses lay on the floor before her, still untouched. Cate's job was to make sure that lives taken in sudden and unexpected ways were honored and their deaths understood. She wouldn't let Baker pressure her into an easy finding of suicide. Molly deserved the truth.

Cate left, closing the door securely behind her. The parking lot was empty of people, and for a moment Cate was surprised, but then she remembered the safety perimeter. Getting into her car, she sighed as she reached for the Tylenol in her purse. She swallowed a couple of pills and stared at the building.

It was one-story and ramshackle, practically leaning against the upright CFB Eastview fence. In any other part of Ottawa, such a desolate building would have invited graffiti, but this spot was too lonely even for vandals. She reached for her smokes, but then a couple of fire trucks roared up.

An enormous man in a yellow jacket and helmet jogged toward her. He looked like a tired, rumpled bear. She rolled down her window.

"You Dr. Spencer?" he asked. "Detective Baker told us you were unaccounted for. Where's the girl?"

She explained that she and Rose had evacuated on the other side of the building. "I don't think there's an actual fire." She told him about the cherry bomb and the decaying film. She added, "The death scene is at the last vault by the fire exit—please don't disturb it." She drove away, leaving the firefighters cautiously approaching the main door.

Baker, Stowe, a couple of junior officers, and Major Harrison stood in a huddle further up the laneway. *This must be the limit of the safety perimeter*, she thought as she pulled over. The police were surrounding a tall, skinny kid, maybe twenty, with spiky brown hair and ear stretchers distending his earlobes so much that Cate could have passed her thumbs through the holes. His jean jacket was covered in pins: Greenpeace, PETA, Rainforest Alliance, and a little cartoon monkey.

She nodded to Stowe and handed him her folder of paperwork. He flashed a warm smile back. "Thanks, Cate."

She and Stowe—stocky, Black, and very handsome—had gone on one horrible date, a year after her divorce. Coffee and a walk along the Rideau Canal. She had only agreed to it because Jason threatened to sign her up to an online dating site unless she "got back out there." Cate spent the entire date making sarcastic digs at poor Freddy Stowe and hating herself for being such an asshole. She'd called Jason afterward and told him to butt out of her love life. She must have sounded fierce, because for once he respected her boundary and never bugged her about dating again. Stowe was married now and had two little kids and a house in Barrhaven. Whenever they met, Cate suspected he was relieved at his escape.

"Where have you been?" Baker asked. "We worried you and the girl might be trapped in a fiery inferno."

"And you were all set to race in and save us?" she asked.

Baker shrugged. "I knew you wouldn't let a little fire stop you from getting home."

"We exited on the other side of the building. By the way, you left your emergency door open. Someone could have tampered with the scene."

"Motherfucker." Baker turned back to the boy. "You'd better not have gone in there."

The kid rolled his eyes. "One word: lawyer."

Baker's hand curled into a fist, and the two younger officers took a step closer to the young man, glowering at him. Stowe looked on with an amused grin. The kid looked small next to the angry police officers, but his smirk didn't show any fear.

Harrison stepped forward. "We're waiting to get the all-clear from the fire department. Then I believe Detective Baker will be returning to the police station with this young man." His words, spoken with calm authority, reminded the cops to stand down. He turned to Cate and smiled. "I'm glad you're OK. I worried when I heard the alarm go off. Detective Baker insisted we follow protocol, or I would have gone back for you."

His earnest look made her nervous. "Thanks." She gestured to the young man. "Who's this?"

"Simon Thatcher," Harrison said. "One of the activists who have been protesting since TDR announced they're breaking ground imminently. You probably passed some of them when you came in."

Cate nodded. "What's he done?"

"We bumped into him skulking in the woods when we evacuated. Baker grabbed him as a precautionary measure. I don't think he likes those things in his ears."

"Baker's instincts might have been right," Cate said. Could this surly looking boy have strangled Molly and staged her suicide? She walked over to Baker and Stowe and told them about the rock and cherry bomb.

Stowe looked thoughtful at the news, but Baker turned to the kid, his voice booming. "Oh good. That's trespassing, damage to property, and mischief. That lawyer you want so bad is going to have his work cut out for him."

Again, the boy's smirk widened, and he shrugged. There was something immensely irritating about Simon's smug self-assurance.

Cate tugged on Baker's arm, pulling him and Stowe away from the others. "There's more." She spoke in a low voice. "There's no suicide note and no sign of a disturbance at the scene—usually hanging victims struggle. I suspect..."

Baker held up a hand. "You suspect?" He raised an eyebrow at Stowe, who didn't respond. Baker was undeterred. "Hold your horses. Your job isn't to suspect anyone."

Cate wouldn't be dissuaded. "Maybe Thatcher knew Molly. If this is a homicide, he might be implicated."

Baker chuckled. "You worry about the autopsy results and give me your verdict on whether it was suicide. Leave the actual investigating to police officers."

His patronizing tone set her teeth on edge. "I'm not investigating, Baker."

Stowe intervened. "Cate, we all want to get to the truth. Just like any other case, we'll await your findings and proceed. For now"— he looked sincerely regretful—"we have to work under the assumption of suicide."

Stowe was as dismissive as Baker, only smoother about it. They couldn't mollify her with a second-rate good cop/bad cop routine. "I've done my job and given you useful information. I couldn't give a rat's ass what you do with it."

Baker gave a satisfied grunt. "That's right," he repeated. "You do your job, and we'll do ours."

Before she could reply, a red Prius pulled up alongside Cate's car. A tall man, a bit stooped around the shoulders, stepped out. He wore a Tilley hat and a checked shirt.

One of the young officers approached him. "I'm sorry, sir, but there is a police investigation underway. You'll have to turn back."

Harrison stepped forward, an ingratiating smile on his face, and extended his hand. "Good to see you again, Mr. Wakefield." He turned to the officer. "This is Terry Wakefield. He's the CEO of TDR Enterprises. As of next week he's the owner of these four hundred acres of prime real estate."

Simon Thatcher lurched forward, but one of the officers grabbed him in a firm grip.

Wakefield nodded at them. "I heard the police were called out here."

Advancing, Baker flashed his badge. "Detective Baker, Ottawa Police. How did you hear that?"

Wakefield smiled. "This is a billion-dollar investment. People are paid to tell us when a bird sings off-key out here."

Cate stared at him. She'd read news stories from Indigenous/ environmentalist development protests about private security firms that used counter-terrorism methods, including infiltration and propaganda, to destabilize activists. She wondered if one of those protesters she had passed was secretly on Wakefield's payroll.

Simon obviously thought the same thing, because he spat on the ground. "Goddamn rats," he muttered.

"There's been a suicide at the Archives," Baker said.

Cate noted that he made no mention of the cherry bomb.

"Suicide?" Wakefield said.

"Manner of death pending my final report, of course." She stepped forward. "I'm the coroner, Dr. Cate Spencer."

Behind his affable exterior, Wakefield's eyes were sharp and assessing. Absurdly, she found herself hoping she measured up.

"Pleasure to meet you, doctor. What a terribly sad way to start our project."

"Yes indeed," she said. In his floppy hat, dad jeans, and commendable car, Wakefield didn't look like a billionaire.

Baker's chest had puffed out, and she could see he was about to launch into full bloviating mode. Now wasn't the time to talk to him or Stowe about Molly's death. Besides, her father was waiting. "Well, it looks like you men have everything in hand. Baker, I'll be following up on some details."

The detective raised an eyebrow but said nothing.

Cate walked back to her car, surprised when Major Harrison hurried over to her.

"It was nice meeting you," he said.

"Likewise." What did this guy want?

"Can I give you my number?"

She crossed her arms.

"In case you have any questions about the base or anything." He thrust a business card at her.

"OK." Was this flirting? It had been so long she didn't even know anymore.

CHAPTER SEVEN

THE PROTESTERS HAD LEFT TURCOTTE ROAD, AND CATE'S DRIVE ACROSS the fields was quiet. She lit a cigarette, trying to shake off her uneasy feeling. It wasn't so much the death itself but the idea of dying in that creepy old building, with the echoing hall and thick prison-like doors. Its contents, too, were eerie—those old, polarized images staring out from thousands of boxes, all capable of bursting into flame. The whole place was unsettling.

Cate shivered, pushing the thoughts from her mind. She was good at compartmentalizing. You had to be with this job. She saw a lot of death, some of it the gruesome stuff of horror films. If she hadn't learned to shut off those images and seal them away, she would have gone crazy or quit years ago. She took another drag. The fingers of her right hand were stained brownish-yellow, the nails darkened from yesterday's chain-smoking binge. Jason had nagged her for years to quit. Turned out that saving lives in the Congo was more hazardous to your health than a pack-a-day habit. He would have appreciated the irony.

Instead of heading home, she turned in the direction of Rockcliffe Park, toward her father. The pattern they'd established was three duty visits a year: Thanksgiving, Christmas, and her birthday. Christmas was the best one, because at the end of it she could close his front door, knowing that she didn't have to return to that house for seven beautiful months.

Jason's death disrupted that awkward tradition. When she'd seen her father at the small memorial, she'd been unnerved. He hardly spoke, hardly moved. All her life he was a lion: powerful, terrifying, unpredictable. It was strange to see him so shattered—defanged.

She reached Rockcliffe and turned off the Parkway onto Acacia Street. This was her childhood, these streets of mansions, guesthouses, and BMWs. She had longed for subdivisions and ballparks instead of roads that were too steep to bicycle up and lawns guarded by wrought-iron fences. She pulled into her father's driveway. Even through the drizzle, the house looked immaculate; the old stones glowed golden and warm, misleadingly inviting.

He grudgingly let her in, and she was shocked by what she saw. Empty glasses littered the mahogany coffee table. Old newspapers lay tossed in heaps on the Persian rug, and the television was moved from the basement rec room to a place of awkward prominence in front of the couch.

"Marie-Pierre has been slacking," Cate said.

"I fired her."

"What? She's worked for you for twenty years. Why would you fire her?"

"Stealing."

Cate stared at her father. He was even smaller and frailer than she remembered, but the old belligerence was still there. He glared at her, daring her to make a comment, and she changed the subject.

"Any word about the return of Jason's remains?" she asked. His ashes were still in Kinshasa, tied up in red tape. Unsurprisingly there was trouble coordinating their return, even with the assistance of his organization, Medical Aid International.

"You should have gone to get them," he said.

Guilt warred with anger. "Daddy, you know I wanted to. The Medical Aid people advised against it. They said the area was too unstable."

"He would have gone for you."

She winced. That was true. Jason had spent his life looking out for her. One more way she had messed things up. "I've called the Congolese embassy dozens of times, but I only get voice mail."

Her father closed his eyes and sighed.

She felt a pang of sympathy for the old bastard. "I'll go to the embassy in person and straighten this out. I know something about the kind of paperwork involved."

His eyes snapped open, as if sensing her pity. "What kind of doctor knows more about bureaucracy and death than about curing sickness?" An easy jibe, one he'd made many times before.

"I help the living find answers."

He blew his nose. "It's ghoulish and a waste of your education. You're supposed to save lives. Look at my career. Look at your brother. We were physicians." He seemed to get taller, as if belittling her made him grow. "You should never have closed your general practice."

The old, old feelings, a charming mixture of defiance and fear, tightened her gut. "When I was a GP, you called me a glorified nurse."

"That was before I knew the alternative," he said. "Thirty-eight years old today and you've got a morbid profession and a failed marriage to your credit."

He'd never forgiven her for leaving Matthew, calling it a family shame. "I only divorced him, Daddy. It's not like I murdered someone." Cate regretted the retort as soon as it left her mouth.

Her father took a step toward her. She shrank back. "Remember you are in my house, Catherine. I demand respect."

You don't demand respect, you earn it. That's what Jason had whispered to her after one of her father's tirades. They'd never dared say that to his face, though.

"Yes, Daddy." There was a long silence as Cate battled down a choking anger. Jason had abandoned her with this poisonous old man.

Her father eased himself down on the couch and flipped on the TV. She took a deep breath and tried another tack. "I had an interesting case today. A woman hanged herself." She waited a beat and plowed on through his silence. "It's very rare for women to kill themselves that way. When a woman is found hanging, it can often be something else."

Her father turned up the volume on the TV.

Cate raised her voice. "In those instances, it's not suicide. It's murder." Speaking her suspicions aloud made them more solid. Despite what Stowe and Baker might want to think, Molly could not have hanged herself without disturbing the scene.

Her father looked up, the crafty intelligence lurking behind his tired eyes. "Aren't you being a bit dramatic? I certainly never read such statistics."

He was never going to admit she knew something he didn't. "No, I suppose you wouldn't have. You were a thoracic surgeon." He didn't pick up on her mild dig. She sat down on the loveseat beside the couch and watched his profile watching the screen.

At a commercial he turned to her. "Happy birthday," he said, handing her a paper bag. Her mouth fell open. It was years since he gave her a present. She was annoyed at the eagerness she felt. Suddenly she was twelve years old again and scrambling for signs of his love. "Thank you."

She opened the bag, uncertain what to expect. It was a jumble of jewelry. She took each item out, laying them on the table beside her. There was her mother's engagement and wedding rings, an emerald brooch, diamond stud earrings, and several pendants. She held up a wide platinum bracelet, the metal shining brightly even in the dimly lit home. She remembered her mother wearing it. She'd called it her Wonder Woman cuff. Five-year-old Cate imagined it gave her mother special powers.

"This is all of mum's jewelry," she said.

The commercial break was over, and her father's attention was fixed on the screen. "You're all that's left, now."

Cate stared at him. Was that an acknowledgment of familial bonds or a statement of despair?

Her father changed the channel to the news network. The television blared an unending stream of stories, each more urgent than the last. The announcers' faces filled the screen, all teeth, hair gel, and scripted empathy. The anchorwoman was reporting from CFB Eastview. Cate sat up straighter. When someone died from suspected suicide, the news usually reported the death as "unexplained." This was a deliberate decision on the part of responsible media outlets, because a proven correlation existed between extensively reported suicides and a rise in copycat deaths.

The story wasn't about Molly Johnson, however. The screen showed footage of the protesters at CFB Eastview followed by a cut to the airport. "We turn to Toronto's Pearson Airport, where police have arrested one of the organizers of the demonstrations against Terry Wakefield's planned development. Protest leader Liam Westin was apprehended boarding a flight to Ottawa when child pornography was discovered on his laptop." There was now a shot of a young bearded man being led away in handcuffs. She wondered if Simon Thatcher, the boy with the ear distenders, knew Westin. How would his arrest affect the protest? The report continued: "Westin has been a prominent environmental activist for the past five years and is a vocal opponent of the TDR development."

Her father snorted, "Disgusting," and turned the channel to a cooking show. After another twenty minutes of silence, Cate left with her usual sigh of relief.

CHAPTER EIGHT

CATE WENT HOME TO SANDY HILL AND STRAIGHT TO THE LIQUOR CABI-
net. Happy birthday to her. The first glass of scotch burned like hell, but the second comforted and began to numb.

Opening her email, she was pleased to see that Baker had sent her the next of kin info, identifying Fabienne Aubin as Molly's "lesbian lover." Cate could imagine the cop's prurient delight in discovering that tidbit. She emailed Fabienne, setting up a time to meet the next day.

She was surprised to see a message from Dr. Marcoux, the Regional Supervising Coroner for Eastern Ontario, and her boss. He was generally a hands-off supervisor, having confidence in his team's judgment and professionalism. He'd needed to chide her for being tardy with her reports a couple of times over the years, but she normally went weeks without hearing from him. While his emails always bore the Ontario Coroner's motto on the right-hand side: "We Speak for the Dead to Protect the Living," they were usually filled with cat memes and puns about his passion, genealogy.

This message was unusual, not only for its lack of smiley faces but also because Marcoux had asked for an update on the "TDR" case. She shifted in her seat and sipped her scotch. The request for a case update wasn't strange, but Marcoux's wording was odd. This wasn't the TDR case; it was the Molly Johnson case. She wondered if Terry Wakefield's long reach extended all the way to pressuring her boss for inside information. Was the developer that worried about bad publicity? She hesitated before replying, eventually promising to keep him updated as usual. She had nothing concrete to report now, anyway.

Her last task done, she poured another scotch. She wandered over to the wooden shelving system where the old record player sat. She hadn't used it in years. One of her few memories of her mother was of her dancing around the kitchen as she cooked dinner—spaghetti and meatballs, Cate's favorite. Her mother's hair was in a ponytail, the sunlight streamed through the window, and Leonard was singing about a lady named Suzanne feeding you tea and oranges.

She'd laid claim to her mother's record player and albums when she had returned from medical school in British Columbia. Jason didn't object—he knew that the music was Cate's connection to their mum. "It's all yours, Kit Kat," he had said to her. She hadn't played an album in years, though. She ran her fingers over the turntable. She thought of that warm, fuzzy, comforting sound emerging like a miracle from a piece of plastic. Someone once told her that a record player's needle was made from a tiny sliver of diamond—that seemed right. You'd need something precious to call up that kind of sound. She couldn't bear to listen to the old records now. Not on her birthday. Too maudlin even for her.

Cate turned away and gulped her drink, remembering to eat: Pad Thai, consumed from the takeout container while staring at the TV. The alcohol softened her, and she found her thoughts drifting back to her mother again.

She was five when her mother died—a car crash and she was gone. Cate didn't remember anything about the accident or even the weeks following her death. Her first clear memory after her mother's demise was of a Sunday evening. The housekeeper was gone, and it was just the three of them. Her father made grilled cheese sandwiches. It was actually nice, rain pouring outside, the low sound of a fire crackling in the living room hearth, and CBC's *Cross Country Checkup* a murmur in the background. Her father put her plate in front of her, and she spoke without thinking: "The crusts are burned." As soon as the words were out, she tensed, expecting the plate to be flung across the room. Daddy didn't tolerate sass.

Instead, it was worse. Her father's face caved in, and his shoulders slumped forward. He stumbled to a kitchen chair, placed his head in his hands, and sobbed. This was wrong. Daddy always knew what to do. The knot returned, tighter than before. It was a heavy anchor in the pit of her stomach, a remorseless, dragging weight. If loving someone could destroy her powerful father, what would it do to her?

Cate lit another cigarette. She stared at her lighter's flame, thinking of Rose's dread of fire. Molly's body hanging in the air, heavy and leaden; the eerie luminescence of the negative as it played off the light; the rock crashing through the window. She took a deep drag.

Butting out her cigarette, she noticed the overflowing ashtray. It really was a disgusting habit. She recalled Rose's warning to quit or end up like Grandpa. Jason would also be happy with her decision, all his nagging finally paying off. Cate rose unsteadily from the couch and searched out her carton of smokes. She had three packs left. She stood over the toilet and broke every single one of the cigarettes in half. She peed on them for good measure. Back to the living room to celebrate with another scotch.

CHAPTER NINE

CATE'S PLANE PLUMMETED THROUGH THE AIR, DROPPING LIKE A ROCK toward the earth. The fire from the engine was licking her seat, the heat unimaginably fierce. The walls of the cabin squeezed in on her. She was in the nitrate vault with the concrete walls closing in, tighter, tighter. Her lungs compressed. She couldn't breathe.

She awoke with a gasp. The plane crash nightmares she'd had for three weeks since Jason's death were changing, now including a fun claustrophobic element. Was this progress? She didn't need a shrink to trace the source of her panic. Her father used to punish her by making her stand in the broom closet. A tight, enclosed space, dark and filled with murky shapes and smells. Sometimes she'd be in there for hours. It was always Jason who rescued her, whispering that it was safe to come out, that their father's rage had subsided.

Jason.

He'd been so happy to be re-posted to Congo. It was a snowy March evening, and they were at Cate's place—the kitchen tidied before his arrival, the scotch stowed in a back cupboard out of sight. She'd even held off smoking in front of him, although by the time he left at ten o'clock she was tense and itching for nicotine. Maybe that's why she'd been such a bitch. "Ebola," she'd said toward the end of the night, after he'd told her about the outbreak and his expected role. "You're really perfecting that martyr complex, aren't you?"

He'd stiffened. The frown line between his eyes deepened, and his expression turned into a glower. For an instant he looked exactly like their father. When had her brother gotten so old?

"I'm no martyr," Jason snapped, and she knew she'd found a vulnerable spot.

"That's exactly the kind of saintly comment a martyr would make, though, isn't it?" She easily slipped into the role of annoying little sister.

"I like to help. Does that make me a bad person?"

Yes, she wanted to scream, when it takes you away from the people who really need you and puts you in the path of a freaky, infectious disease. Instead, she said, "Do you even hear yourself? You sound like a sanctimonious tool."

Instead of rising to her bait, he'd tightened his lips and left. Cate retrieved the scotch bottle and drank a few glasses. By the next day, she'd tamped down all her anxieties about this latest mission, and they never discussed the argument. She even drove him to the airport.

Cate heaved herself out of bed and padded downstairs, unable to remember much about the night before. This morning the Laphroaig bottle was almost empty, and it appeared that she'd gone to bed with the front door slightly ajar. She was pouring herself a coffee when her landline rang.

"Dr. Spencer?"

"Yes?"

"It's Rose Li."

"How did you get this number?" Cate asked. It was unlisted. Almost no one had it.

"I'm an archivist. We're trained to find out information."

"You shouldn't be calling me," Cate said, unsettled.

"I'm sorry, but listen. I think I've found a clue."

"What are you talking about?"

"A clue. I was going through Molly's agenda at work, and she met this guy, Albert Owl, at this weird address in Vanier." Vanier was a poorer neighborhood in Ottawa's east end, home to a recurring prostitution problem and a thriving meth trade. "She triple-starred his name and underlined it."

"This is highly inappropriate. I'm the coroner, I don't investigate. I decide on—"

"The manner of death, I know," interrupted Rose. "But if you sign off on a suicide, no one will investigate. Besides, you're the only one who will take me seriously."

"You need to contact Detective Baker. He's leading this case."

"I did. He literally told me not to worry my pretty little head about it."

"Damn it," Cate muttered, unable to stop herself. Molly's death was still officially undetermined, so Baker should be receptive to all possibilities. Had he even arrested Thatcher? "What's so unusual about this address, then?"

"It's 164 Marier. I googled it. That's—"

"The Marier Residence, a nursing home," Cate finished for her. As a professional necessity, she knew every old-age residence and funeral parlor in the city. "Maybe Mr. Owl is a grandparent or family friend."

"No, Molly was from Vancouver. All her family is there. She literally knew no one when she moved here."

Cate was exasperated. "Well, maybe she was volunteering."

"One of the appointments is at eight p.m.; another is at eight in the morning. There's no pattern. Plus, she was there on Monday. The day she died. She went on her lunch break."

This caught Cate's attention. She rubbed her face. "All right, I'll talk to Baker."

Rose groaned in frustration. "He's not going to listen. I need to prove Molly was murdered, and I'll go myself if I have to." Her voice was urgent, implacable.

Cate hesitated. She could see Rose showing up at the long-term care facility and causing a disturbance. If Molly was murdered, Rose's interference would harm any investigation. "Sit tight, OK? I'll call Baker, and I'll get him to meet with you. He'll listen to me." She had no confidence in that.

The younger woman agreed reluctantly, and they hung up. Cate reached for her cigarettes before remembering last night's grand gesture.

Quitting now seemed like a foolish idea, but regret didn't get her a nicotine fix.

She picked up the landline and punched in the number for the Ottawa Police Department, hoping to distract herself from her craving. Baker wasn't there, but she left a message asking him to call her back right away. She didn't have much time before she was due to meet Molly's next of kin, but she needed to review the notes Baker sent. The details she'd read last night were a little fuzzy.

Fabienne Aubin was listed on Molly's personnel file as her emergency contact. She was a schoolteacher who lived in Gatineau, the neighboring city across the river in the province of Quebec.

In a normal case, after meeting with the family, Cate reviewed the forensic pathologist's autopsy results and wrote her own report, pronouncing manner of death. Then the case, from her point of view, would be closed. That was an enormously satisfying feeling. You could never achieve the same sense of finality in family medicine because the only time your patients' demands stopped was if you failed and they died. By the end of her marriage, those never-ending needs had become oppressive. That general practitioner work was another aspect of her life she shed with the divorce.

Cate's intention to quickly accomplish the next of kin interview was thwarted before she even left the house. She couldn't find her damn cell phone. She looked everywhere, but by the time she abandoned the search, she was half an hour late. She drove quickly, annoyed with herself. Just how drunk was she last night?

CHAPTER TEN

FABIENNE AUBIN LIVED ON A GENEROUS LOT OVERLOOKING THE LAZY
waters of Brewer Creek. On the Ottawa side of the river, an adorable
brick house like hers would have been worth a small fortune, but the
province of Quebec's semi-regular threat of separation managed to
burst any housing bubbles before they formed. People were leery of
accidentally investing in North America's newest breakaway nation.

A well-dressed woman in her early thirties answered the door. Her
black hair was pulled into a sleek bun. The woman's subtle makeup
highlighted her big brown eyes, and her glossy lipstick emphasized
full lips.

"Miss Aubin? I'm Dr. Spencer. We spoke on the phone. I'm sorry
for being late."

"It is OK." She spoke with a strong French accent, but it had a
Caribbean, rather than Quebecois, inflection. Cate wondered if Fabienne was Haitian. Many people from the troubled island had immi-
grated to Quebec, attracted to its prosperity and shared language. The
government was happy with the influx of French speakers, although
the population was sometimes less enthused about the newcomers'
skin color.

Fabienne led Cate to a sunny living room with thick carpeting and
honey-colored walls. The room gave off an aura of assured good taste
that made Cate edgy.

They sat in plush armchairs, facing one another. Fabienne appeared calm and well rested, like a human version of the room.

"I'm very sorry for your loss. It must have come as quite a
shock."

Fabienne briefly closed her eyes. "Oui."

"Like I told you over the phone, this visit is strictly routine. As the coroner, it's my duty to certify the manner of death. I am also here to answer your questions about procedures for claiming the body and preparing for the funeral."

Fabienne spoke calmly. "I won't be making any decisions about Molly's funeral. I will leave that to her parents. They will certainly want her body returned to Vancouver."

"Sorry, I don't understand. I thought you were Molly's partner."

"Yes, but we'd only been dating for a few months."

"Molly listed you as 'family' under her emergency contact number."

"Family? Vraiement?" Fabienne's voice shook, and a flash of what looked like anger passed over her face. It was gone so quickly, Cate wondered if she had imagined it.

Fabienne continued, "Molly should not have done that."

This was not the reaction Cate was expecting. "Why not?"

Fabienne hesitated and then said, "Molly only moved in with me in May because her landlord was giving her troubles. We were not so serious. I can't make such big decisions about her funeral. That's for her parents, not me."

Cate was at a loss. Something about Fabienne was off. She spoke without thinking. "Since I'm here, I'd like to ask a few further questions."

"Of course," Fabienne said with a regal nod.

Cate didn't know what she wanted to ask. She had never interviewed a potential murder suspect before. "How did you and Molly meet?"

"Online, of course. Is there any other way?"

Was that really the only method to meet someone now? Since that one date with Freddy Stowe, Cate hadn't even contemplated a relationship. The world's longest dry spell was infinitely preferable to the complicated alternative. "Good," she said. Now what was she supposed to ask? "What was Molly like?"

Fabienne replied without a trace of emotion. "She was full of energy. Very direct. Passionate. She liked to communicate. That's very different from me. She was always on her iPhone, texting, emailing. I am not so interested in the computers, but Molly is branché—wired." She paused to correct herself. "Was. Molly was wired."

Cate paused for a moment in case the other woman needed to collect herself, but Fabienne gazed at her, awaiting her next question. She recalled the meager information Baker had given her. "You're a teacher, right?"

"Oui."

"It must be nice to be on break right now."

"I'm teaching the summer school session." Fabienne crossed her arms. "I don't mean to be rude, but I am due there this afternoon."

"Understood," Cate said. Usually the bereaved wanted to keep her talking as long as possible because she was their last link to the departed. "Have you been in touch with Molly's parents? Informed them of her death?"

Fabienne shook her head. "No, I think that policeman Baker will do so. He was here last night. I gave him her parents' phone number."

"Baker was here?" That was odd. Normally he'd send a sergeant to inform the next of kin. The uniform was calming for people. It helped them accept the finality of what they were being told and reassured them that something official was being done for their loved one. "Did you tell him that you weren't comfortable making the funeral arrangements?" If Baker had known Fabienne wasn't next of kin and sent Cate here on a fool's errand, she'd kill him.

Fabienne furrowed her brow, obviously trying to recall. "Non. I don't think that came up. He spent two hours with me. Asking many questions."

"Really?" That was thorough.

Fabienne shrugged. "I think he was interested in our relationship."

When Cate looked quizzical, Fabienne clarified. "That Molly and I were lovers."

Cate struggled not to roll her eyes.

Fabienne lit a cigarette and Cate tilted her head slightly, breathing in the dirty, wonderful smell. "Want one?" Fabienne asked, gesturing with her pack.

It was tempting. Surely a cigarette would ease the headache that lingered behind her eyes. Cate shook her head. "No. I've quit."

Fabienne snorted. "You Anglos are always quitting things. Try sticking around once in a while."

Cate laughed. "You're funny."

Fabienne shrugged again. "It's a, how do you say, a mécanisme de survie."

"Coping mechanism," Cate said.

Fabienne nodded. "Yes, that seems right. It's mechanical. I'm a robot. No feeling. Like nothing is different, but everything is."

Cate let her words hang there for a moment. Fabienne's calmness could be a mask for deep pain, or the chilling serenity of a murderer without conscience. It was impossible to know which. "Was Molly on any medication?"

"Oui. Ritalin and antidepressants."

"She was suffering from depression?"

"I don't think so. These days everyone is on something. She'd been on Ritalin since she had twelve years."

Cate leaned forward, unable to prevent herself from asking the question, "Do you think she killed herself?"

Again the shrug. "That's what Detective Baker said. Who knows? Life isn't easy. Molly could get sad sometimes. Maybe it was too much." Fabienne gazed at Cate, her hands folded in her lap.

She had learned of her girlfriend's death last night, but Fabienne had no friends and family around her now. Her face was perfectly made up and her shirt ironed. She was heading into work soon. In all her years as a coroner, Cate had never held such a subdued interview with a victim's lover.

"Can I see Molly's prescriptions?" Cate asked.

"Certainement," Fabienne said, butting out her cigarette. "They are in the bathroom. One moment." She stood, and Cate followed her.

Fabienne stopped. "I will bring them to you."

"That's fine," Cate said. "I'll save you the trip." While her interview technique wasn't great, working with cops had taught her that as long as you remained reasonable and spoke firmly most people would do what you wanted. She stared at the other woman, waiting for her to acquiesce.

Annoyance flashed in Fabienne's eyes, but she gave in. "The bathroom is here. It's very small. Have a look." Fabienne flipped on the light and stepped out of the way.

The other woman was right; it was a tiny space, painted a soothing green. The room gleamed, and Cate smelled the strong odor of bleach. Fabienne had cleaned it recently.

Cate took her time opening the medicine cabinet. She didn't know what she was looking for, but she examined her surroundings carefully. The garbage was nearly empty. Plastic disposable contact lenses, floss. Not a lot of Kleenex. If Fabienne had been sobbing her eyes out, she hadn't been throwing the tissues in here.

The meds with Molly's name were standard: Celexa for depression and anxiety. Ritalin for everything else. The doses were relatively low, and the bottles were almost full.

"Was this everything she took?"

Fabienne hesitated and shrugged. "She had a prescription for medical marijuana. She would get migraines—it helped."

This was becoming a more common approach for migraine treatment, although the science wasn't strong on its effectiveness. "In what form did she take it?"

"A vaporizer." Fabienne pointed to it in the medicine cabinet. "She only used it when she felt a headache coming. Molly wasn't into drugs."

"Did the same doctor prescribe the marijuana as the other medication?" Cate asked.

Fabienne nodded. Cate reached for her phone to note the physician's name, then remembered she'd lost it. "Do you have a pen and paper?"

The other woman disappeared. Cate glanced around the room.

She was discouragingly bad at looking for clues. Feeling a little fool-ish, she pulled back the shower curtain. What was she hoping to find, evidence of grout rot? She was surprised by the colorful scene be-fore her. Someone had painted a series of vivid monkeys, arms inter-twined, on the tiles around the spout so it looked like the animals were pouring out of the faucet. "These are charming," she said when Fabienne returned.

The other woman smiled, her features softening. "Molly said she needed to leave her mark. She complained that this house was too per-fect. I needed to let her be a little silly somewhere." Fabienne handed her a notepad and pen.

Molly was given one spot, hidden behind the shower curtain, to "leave her mark." Was Fabienne as controlling in the rest of the rela-tionship as she seemed to be about her house? Cate jotted down the physician's name and the dosages.

They walked back to the living room. Neither woman sat.

It was time to go, but Cate couldn't leave without trying to crack Fabienne's veneer. "Were you and Molly happy?"

Fabienne's response was quick. "Of course." She crossed her arms over her chest.

The answer was too fast and too short. This was normally the opening the grief-stricken seized. The opportunity to remember their loved one. To start framing their relationship as a story. Cate didn't respond right away, letting Fabienne's abrupt answer hang in the air. This was another trick she had learned from the police.

"Molly was young. She was still experimenting. She'd had many boyfriends in the past, but she was interested in trying a relationship with a woman. She thought being gay was wonderful. Exciting." Fa-bienne pulled out another cigarette and lit up. "We loved each other."

"You hadn't had any fights lately, no problems?"

Fabienne shook her head.

"Did her parents know about your relationship?"

"Oui, Molly told them when we moved in together."

"How did they react?"

"They were good, better than mine ever would be. They are from Vancouver, you know—des vrais hippies." Fabienne's tone was condescending.

"What do you mean?" Cate asked.

"They are vegetarians, peace activists. Her mother is a lawyer who represents the homeless. Her father runs a consultancy about saving trees or whales or something."

"They were open to having a gay daughter?"

"Open?" Fabienne laughed. "They loved it. It bothered Molly sometimes, that her parents were so pleased. It gave them one more thing to feel smug about, she said."

"Was Molly looking to rebel against them?"

Fabienne's gaze sharpened. "You think she was only with me to irritate her parents?"

Cate was startled by the intensity of the question. "I didn't say that."

Fabienne's cool demeanor returned. Cate wondered if she imagined the anger. "I think you have everything you came for. I have answered your questions, yes?"

Cate had overstayed her welcome. "Thank you for your time."

Fabienne walked her to the door and watched as she got into her car. Cate recalled the monkeys pouring out of the faucet, the only sign of life, or of Molly, in that house. Fabienne was lying about something. She would bet on it.

CHAPTER ELEVEN

THE CONGOLESE EMBASSY WAS SITUATED IN THE KIND OF HOUSE WHERE, in another neighborhood, you'd expect to have congenial chats with the owner while grilling steaks or mulching the garden. Instead, located as it was on Range Road, Ottawa's unofficial embassy district, chummy neighborliness was a rarity. Instead, the norm was iron fences, black Range Rovers with tinted windows, and security cameras perched on high walls like crows.

Cate entered an anteroom smelling overwhelmingly of lemon floor polish. A wooden door led to a large room with three counters. About a dozen straight-backed wooden chairs stood against the far wall. Cate approached the only occupied kiosk. A slim Black woman, her hair braided into an elaborate twist, sat behind the counter. "Excuse me," Cate said. "I've been leaving messages for three weeks, but no one returns my calls. I need to make arrangements—"

The woman put up her hand and asked in lightly accented English, "Did you take a number?"

"What?" Cate looked around. They were the only two people in the room.

"Please take a number." The woman pointed one finger, nail painted a bright red, at the machine dispensing tickets. "You will be called in due time."

Cate opened her mouth to protest, but the woman gave her a steely look, and Cate realized it was futile. She marched over and took a number—212—and sat in one of the chairs. In front of her the words "Embassy of the Democratic Republic of the Congo" were emblazoned on the wall. A huge logo featured a leopard's head bordered by an elephant tusk and spear, beneath which were the words "Justice, Paix, Travail."

Cate stared at that image for a full ten minutes, becoming angrier with every tick of the large clock. The clerk was literally filing her nails behind the counter. Cate's head pounded and her stomach roiled. She coughed. Damn, she could use a cigarette. Her irritability mounted.

Finally, a number was called. "Numéro deux-cent dix. Number two hundred and ten?" the clerk called. She and Cate stared at each other. The woman called the number again, waited for a response, and returned to managing her cuticles.

Cate didn't even have her phone to pass the minutes. By the time her number was called, her patience, limited at the best of times, was exhausted by both the circumstances and nicotine withdrawal.

She spoke briskly. "I want to repatriate my brother's body. He died working for Medical Aid International. His plane crashed, and I want to bring him home." Despite her frustration, she managed to keep her voice steady. "The information you sent my father indicated that he died outside of Kinshasa. His remains are held in that city."

The woman took down the details of Jason's death, the same ones Cate had left on every single message, serenely telling her that someone would be in touch shortly.

"Shortly? What exactly does 'shortly' mean?" This was not how mourners were supposed to be handled. Bumbling bureaucratic ineptitude did not comfort survivors. Straight answers delivered in a compassionate manner were how you helped people accept and move on. Irritation snapped into Cate's voice. "I've been calling you for three weeks."

The woman shrugged. "I will relay your message to one of our analysts."

"That isn't good enough. We've been waiting too long already."

The shrug again.

"Listen, if I don't get an answer soon, I am going to raise holy hell. I'm going to my city councillor, my MP, and the goddamn prime minister." She was shouting now. It felt so good to release some of the tension building up behind her eyes. "I'll call every goddamn radio and TV station in this city and let them know what kind of shitshow you are running. Why is this taking so long? I'll have this whole thing investigated and exposed."

The woman had obviously pressed a panic button, because the next thing that Cate knew, she was flanked by two guards. They grabbed her by the elbows and in seconds carried her through the anteroom and into the sunshine. The embassy door slammed behind her.

Cate blinked as the red tide of rage ebbed from her vision. She took a deep breath, then let out a long, hacking cough. When it subsided, she was hollow-chested and exhausted.

She was still shaky when she stepped off the curb to get to her car. A horn blared, and she leaped back. One of the embassy's Range Rovers barreled past. She stared after its red ambassadorial license plates. Diplomatic immunity meant that embassy personnel couldn't be prosecuted in Canada. Years ago, a drunk-driving Russian diplomat had killed a woman not far from here. He never saw the inside of a courtroom, let alone a jail cell. His only punishment was a return to Russia. There was no justice for that victim's family.

CHAPTER TWELVE

BACK AT HOME, CATE STILL COULDN'T FIND HER CELL PHONE, AND THERE was no message from Baker on her landline. However, there were three from Rose, each more urgent than the last. The final said, "I'm not waiting around anymore. I'm going to talk to this guy right now." Rose left that message fifteen minutes ago. It wasn't far to Vanier. Cate could get to the nursing home and do some damage control.

The Marier Residence was a white institutional building set back from the road. It loomed over the houses surrounding it like a cruise ship next to fishing boats. Cate pulled into a parking spot as Rose finished locking a red bike with a wicker basket to the building's railing. It was a hot day, and Rose's short hair was sweat-slicked, her cheeks pink from exertion. She looked incredibly youthful. Detective Stowe's notes on her, which Baker shared, indicated that she was twenty-four, was born in Ottawa, and had been working at the Archives for less than a year.

Rose approached the car, grinning broadly. When was the last time anyone had looked that happy to see her? Cate's grip on the wheel clenched. She reached for her cigarettes. Goddamn it.

"I was hoping you'd come," Rose said. "I knew you didn't believe Molly killed herself."

The gratitude in Rose's voice unnerved Cate, and she spoke crisply. "Don't count your chickens. Even if the autopsy proves conclusively that Molly was murdered, solving her death will be difficult." Cate certainly wasn't going to reveal her suspicions to Rose.

"What do you mean?"

"If Molly was murdered, the killer made a lot of effort to cover up their crime. That's not the normal MO. Overwhelmingly, when a woman is murdered, her partner is to blame."

"Isn't that usually with male partners, though?" Rose asked. "That's not the case with Molly."

Cate thought about Fabienne's strange reaction to her girlfriend's death. She wouldn't be so quick to strike that woman from the suspect list. She bit her lip. Something else about her interview with Fabienne niggled at her. She turned to Rose, changing the conversation. "Did you cycle over from the nitrate facility?" It was only a kilometer further east.

Rose shook her head. "The cops have closed the building, pending the determination of manner of death."

At least Baker managed to do that. "Are you off work, then?" Given the shock Rose had received yesterday, it wouldn't be surprising.

"No, Molly and I don't . . . I mean, I don't work full time at the facility. Most of the time it's locked up tight and empty."

That squared with Cate's impression of the place.

Rose continued, "I'm based at the main Archives' building downtown. It's horrible there, though, everyone talking about Molly, speculating about why she did it." Rose shivered despite the heat. "Apparently there was a murder at the Archives, like, ten years ago. A commissionaire was killed and his body was squished in the stacks. Now everyone is talking about that one, plus Molly's death. Speculating. I was glad to get away."

Cate felt for the woman, but it wasn't her place to console her.

Rose glanced at her watch. "Visiting hours start in ten minutes. I've got a list of questions to ask Mr. Owl."

Cate opened her mouth to warn Rose against interfering with a police investigation but instead found herself asking, "What do you know about this man?"

Rose's face lit up. "Albert Owl. He doesn't have any internet presence, no Facebook, no LinkedIn, no Insta, although if he's old enough to live here, that's not surprising. From his name, I'd guess he's Indigenous. He's been here for ten years. Pays for it via a small veterans' pension."

Cate raised an eyebrow, and Rose shrugged. "Like I said, I'm good at finding things out."

Despite herself, Cate was intrigued. What Rose had said earlier appeared true—there was no obvious connection between Molly Johnson and Albert Owl. What were they meeting about?

The day was thickly humid. Cate had stuffed her hair into a ponytail, but she could practically feel it expanding into a thick frizz at the nape of her neck. They walked toward the building's entrance and stopped in the shade of a Norway maple.

"So what do you do at the facility?" Cate asked as they waited for visiting hours to start.

"We're prepping the collection for the move."

"What move?"

Rose stared. "You don't know about this?"

Cate shrugged.

"We've got to shift the entire nitrate collection—six decades worth of photographic negatives and film—to make way for TDR's big development." Rose's voice was bitter.

Cate furrowed her brow. "Why? The nitrate facility isn't even on Eastview land. TDR doesn't own it, do they?"

"No, but Terry Wakefield doesn't want his precious luxury homes sitting next to a powder keg."

Cate thought of the fizzling cherry bomb. "Is the fire risk really that serious?"

"Back in the sixties, thousands of cans of deteriorating National Film Board nitrate spontaneously combusted. The fire lasted for days, and you could smell the toxic stench months afterward. Some people still remember that, and some of them buy million-dollar homes, so TDR gave us the boot."

Cate clenched her jaw. She hated bullies. "How can TDR dictate who its neighbors are?"

"They've got money and lawyers. They cited a million different bylaws and regulations. They said we were leaching toxins into the soil, which is total bullshit, and they told the city that if we moved, they'd clean up everything for free." Rose's eyes shone with indignation, and for a moment she reminded Cate of Jason, when he was fired up about the latest injustice he'd witnessed. Rose was still speaking. "Basically, they came up with every excuse under the sun. TDR wants to sell picture-perfect homes, and our facility isn't part of the vision. They said we had to be out before they break ground."

Cate recalled the battered box of negatives marked "Destroy" that she peered into yesterday. If a quick whiff of the fumes made her feel sick, what would a whole building do? Maybe Wakefield had a point, not that she'd say so to Rose.

"You sound really annoyed," Cate said.

"They barely gave us any warning, just told us we've got to go. We have to store all of the negs in some crappy warehouse where they will deteriorate even further while we look for permanent storage. We're not taking care of our history. We're failing our mandate." Rose's eyes filled with tears, but she blinked them away and wiped her hand under her nose.

Everything was shitty. Bullies always won. Good people like Jason died. "Nothing is fair," Cate said bitterly.

Rose gave her a piercing glance but didn't comment. Instead, she looked at her watch. "Visiting hours have started. Let's go." She walked to the door.

Cate followed behind, nursing doubts about the wisdom of this plan. If Baker found out Cate was doing this, he would throw a fit. She smiled. Actually, that would be kind of entertaining.

CHAPTER THIRTEEN

LAMINATE FLOORING, PUCE WALLS, FLUORESCENT LIGHTING, THE FAINT smell of urine and disinfectant—the Marier Residence was like most of the city's long-term care facilities. It was chronically underfunded, understaffed, and overfilled. Cate's regular visits to these places, combined with the chaos of the pandemic, had opened her eyes to the importance of conscientious saving. There was no way she wanted to end up somewhere like this when she got old. She led them to reception.

"Dr. Spencer," said the admitting nurse at the front desk, recognizing Cate from previous visits. "That was quick."

Cate blinked at the odd greeting. "I'm here to see Albert Owl."

"Yes, I know, but we only called it in twenty minutes ago. Were you in the neighborhood?"

Cate was about to explain that she wasn't on duty when the implication sunk in. "He's dead?" She shot a quick glance at Rose. Her eyes reflected Cate's own questions.

The nurse looked at her oddly. "Yes, heart attack. That's why you're here, isn't it?"

Rose interrupted. "Yes, that's right. I'm a student of Dr. Spencer's. I'm shadowing her to learn how to, uh, coroner."

The nurse looked at Rose in her Converse high-tops and vintage "Free Mandela" T-shirt but said nothing. "His room is this way." She turned and walked down the hall.

Cate let her get out of earshot. "What are you doing?" she whispered to Rose.

"It's too much of a coincidence. There must be a connection between his death and Molly," she whispered back.

"We can't do this." Interviewing a living person was entirely different from playing on-duty coroner at a death scene.

"Five minutes, tops. I want to look around his room. Besides, what could you say to the nurse now that would even make sense?"

Cate hesitated. Rose had a point. She was committed to this foolhardy endeavor. If they'd called in the death less than half an hour ago, they had time before the legitimate coroner showed up.

The nurse stopped at the far end of the hall in front of a closed door. Albert's room was next to the dining room, which smelled of greasy fish and overcooked vegetables. The nurse was impatient. "Mr. Owl wasn't at breakfast, but he often liked to sleep in. When he didn't appear for morning snack, one of our nurse's aides checked on him. He had a heart condition, of course, so I guess his time had finally come."

The room was only large enough to fit a single bed, a bedside table, and a small desk. A large, framed watercolor of a bucolic scene—a river winding into a deep blue lake—took pride of place above the bed. A bark basket sat on the desk beside the television, a TV guide next to it. Cate was surprised those were still being published.

Albert Owl was lying on the bed, dressed in pale blue pajamas, a polyester blanket covering his lower half and a sheet pulled up to his chin. His eyes were closed, and a prominent nose overshadowed his sunken mouth. He looked asleep.

Stepping into the room behind Cate, Rose made a small sound when she saw the body. Cate wondered if it was her first sight of a dead person, but then remembered what had happened yesterday.

Cate turned to the nurse. "Did he have family in the area?"

"No family, I don't think, but he often had visitors. He's an Indian, you know. Not India Indian, but a real one. Lots of them came to see him, but they never gave us any trouble. I always treated them like any other visitor."

"That was very good of you," Cate said, but the sarcasm was lost.

"What would they talk about?" Rose asked. "His visitors, I mean?"

The nurse shrugged. "I don't know. Half the time they talked in their language."

"How old was he?" Cate asked.

"Ninety-eight."

"He doesn't look it," Rose exclaimed.

They all glanced down where Albert lay.

"Oh yes, he had quite the life. Traveled this whole country. I think he grew up in the Depression and might have been what they call a 'hobo'—you know, rode the rails, all that."

Rose was impatient with the nurse's reminiscences. "Did he have any other visitors recently? People who weren't Indigenous, maybe?"

"Funny, a young woman did stop by a couple of times in the past few weeks. Sweet girl with glasses."

Cate leaned forward.

The nurse continued, "I'm not sure what their connection was, but they mostly seemed friendly."

"Mostly?" Cate asked.

"I walked in once to change his sheets, and they were arguing."

"About what?" Rose asked.

"The young lady was trying to persuade him to do something, but Mr. Owl would have none of it. He could be quite stubborn—we'd practically have to chase him around the home when it was time to clip his toenails."

"You didn't hear them mention anything specific?" Rose pressed.

The nurse looked surprised, and Cate realized that if they kept questioning her, they'd blow their already thin cover. "OK, well, I think we have enough information, thank you." Cate said. "I'll examine the body and issue the death certificate,"

"OK. Call me if you need anything."

As soon as the nurse left, Rose turned excitedly to Cate. "See, Molly needed something from Albert Owl. If we figure out why she visited him, we'll find out why she was murdered. I'm sure of it."

"Not necessarily, and I'm not saying it was murder," Cate said. "I'm waiting for the autopsy."

Cate might be off duty, but her training took over. She looked over the body. His hands were crossed over his chest. Nursing home staff could not be dissuaded from placing the corpse in a respectful position after death, despite Dr. Marcoux's sternly worded emails. Cate didn't mind, actually. She liked that they cared enough to make death more reverential.

She donned a pair of the latex gloves she always carried in her purse. Albert's face looked waxen. She gently opened his eye. His pupil was fixed and dilated. She tugged on his jaw. It didn't open, consistent with rigor mortis. She examined his arms. There were no puncture marks or stiffness. She pulled the sheet back and studied his body. There were no outward signs of trauma.

Before she could continue, a voice boomed from the hallway. "I told you, nurse; I'm on the roster, and I'm meant to be here."

Cate knew that rich baritone. She closed her eyes. Of course it would have to be Sylvester Williams on duty. Of course he would arrive less than an hour after receiving the call. Williams was an uptight, upright, sanctimonious douche, but he was punctual.

"Rose!" Cate called. The other woman was rifling through the desk. "We've got to get out of here."

She dropped the paper she was holding, and they hurried to the door. As they were leaving, Rose stopped and stared at the painting above the bed. "Oh," she said and took a step closer to the artwork, snapping a photo with her phone.

"Rose," Cate said more urgently, and they stepped out of the room. At the far end of the hallway they could see Williams, a tall man with a goatee, remonstrating with the nurse who stood in front of him with her hands on her hips.

"This way," Cate said decisively. They turned in the opposite direction and went out the service door behind the dining room.

"Well, that was too close for comfort," Cate said. Now that she was outside, she couldn't believe what she had done. What a ridiculous risk to take. How would she have explained herself to Williams? She was shaky and would have bitten off her own arm for one drag.

"Are you going to get in trouble?" Rose asked.

Cate bit her lip. Showing up at a death scene off duty and with a non-coroner in tow was definitely irregular. She could go back in and try explaining things, but the thought of confessing to that preening turd Williams was more than she could stomach.

If Williams reported it, Marcoux was unlikely to get upset. The angriest she'd ever seen him was when they'd had a rare work party at the Rideau Carleton Raceway. He had shouted, "Gosh darn it!" and slammed his lemonade down when "Dandy Suitor" had outrun "Wots Up Doc."

The bright sun made Cate squint, intensifying her headache. "It will be fine. Let's go."

"So, what do you think about our investigation?" Rose asked as they walked back to the front parking lot.

Cate shrugged. "Mr. Owl appears to have died of natural causes. At his age, it's probably coronary artery disease. I'll request Williams's preliminary report as soon as it's done." Williams was thorough and quick. His report would undoubtedly be submitted today.

Rose grinned. "Maybe you didn't learn much, but I did."

"We were only in there for five minutes."

"Didn't you recognize the painting? It was Lake Mitchell, at Eastview." She brandished her phone, and Cate stared at the screen. Now that Rose pointed it out, Cate saw the distinctive curve of the river. Underneath the painting, Rose had captured the title in black ink: "Lake Nigamo: Singing Water."

"That must be its Indigenous name," Rose hypothesized.

"Yeah," said Cate thoughtfully. It looked like Molly and Albert Owl had a connection after all.

CHAPTER FOURTEEN

CATE UNLOCKED HER DOOR, AND THE HOUSE'S COOL AIR WASHED OVER her like a welcome friend. She flipped the alarm cover to disarm it, but it was blinking green. The LCD screen displayed the stark word "Disabled."

She had set it before she left. She was sure of it. Her skin prickled. Cate stepped into the kitchen. A small inner voice told her it was stupid to walk into her house containing a possible intruder, but another voice, one that sounded like her father's, told her to get in there and sort this out.

"Hello?" She tensed, listening for the slightest noise. "Anyone here?" Nothing was disturbed in the kitchen. She grabbed the big steel flashlight from under the sink and headed for the stairs. The steps creaked. She paused. Was that a muffled footfall on the floor above? Her mouth was dry. She mounted the rest of the stairs in a rush, brandishing the flashlight. There were only three rooms on the second floor: a never-used guest room, her bedroom, and a bathroom with a tub big enough to swim backstroke. All three were empty. Cate checked her closets before she relaxed. She flopped on her bed, stretched out. She must have forgotten to turn the alarm on. She felt foolish.

Between last night's drinking and the nicotine withdrawal, it was good to lie down. She could hear children calling to one another, the distant drone of a lawnmower. She closed her eyes, and for a few moments she floated in that precious space between consciousness and sleep.

The familiar buzz of her phone made her jump. Where was the stupid thing? She located it under her bed, a dim memory of last night's drunken game of Candy Crush swimming back to mind. She'd missed a call from Baker.

As she sat on the bed, another thought occurred to her: why could she hear the lawnmower and children so clearly? Her bedroom window was ajar. Had she opened it last night? Cate looked out. Because her house was built into a hill, it was a short-ish drop to her backyard. Immediately below was her neglected flowerbed, home to hundreds of dandelions and remorseless feelings of guilt and inadequacy. It would make a soft landing for an athletic intruder.

She hurried downstairs and went outside to inspect it. There were no footprints in the earth, still soft from yesterday's rain, but a couple of dandelions looked bent. She stared up at her window. Was she being paranoid, or had someone been here? Her headache returned, and with it a powerful desire for a cigarette.

Cate went back inside to inventory her valuables. It didn't take long. Her engagement and wedding rings were still in the jewelry box where they sat with the items her father gave her last night. She checked her ground floor office. The paperwork associated with her job—her reports and analyses, copies of autopsy results, notes on cases—was securely locked in the filing cabinet. Her laptop sat on her desk. If there was an intruder, he'd left empty-handed. Her mind eased, she listened to Baker's message. He wanted to meet at police headquarters on Elgin Street.

Cate parked in a semi-legal spot in front of the building. It was usually tricky to find parking on Elgin. Police HQ was a block-wide concrete compound. It reminded Cate of a bunker, embodying the police's increasingly defensive posture in the wake of various scandals around their treatment of Black and Indigenous populations. She was always edgy in here—so much testosterone, and all of it armed.

The first time she'd seen Baker's desk, Cate was caught off guard. She'd expected a pigsty—papers scattered everywhere, old coffee cups, and a calendar with half-naked women on the wall, maybe even an overflowing ashtray in defiance of city bylaw. Instead, color-coded file folders were neatly stacked on the surface, and a philodendron thrived on the corner. Today the classical strains of Radio Canada's *Espace Musique* played from his computer speakers.

Cate took a seat opposite his desk.

"Did you meet the dyke?" Baker grinned.

"You're a complete asshole," Cate said. "Fabienne's not the next of kin. She's not responsible for the funeral. You could have told me that before I went out there. We still need to inform the parents."

"I know. She called me this morning after you'd been by. Said that you'd taken notes on Molly Johnson's prescriptions. Nice work. Thorough." His voice held grudging respect.

He continued, "I got the info on her parents." He scrawled it on a piece of paper and passed it to her. "They live in Vancouver. Mom's a hotshot lawyer, dad's a consultant." He tugged at his mustache.

"You think I'm going to inform them?" That was way beyond her job description. She came in after, when the first emotional shitstorm had passed, to answer questions about the death.

He surprised her again by shaking his head. "No, I fucked up by not breaking it to them right away, so I called them myself."

She had to give him kudos for making such a terrible phone call. Normal protocol would have been for Baker to pawn off the job on the Vancouver PD. They'd send a uniform over to tell the bereaved.

"Remember the time difference when you call. I woke them up to tell them their daughter was dead." He grimaced.

"How did they take the news?"

"They were doing fucking cartwheels. What do you think?"

"Did they seem surprised? Were they expecting this?"

Baker gave the question some thought. "They weren't expecting it. Even over the phone, I could tell. Mrs. Johnson was stunned."

"What about the father?"

Baker raised an eyebrow. "You're taking quite an interest in this case."

"Like I told you at the facility, I don't think it was suicide."

"What the fuck, Cate? She hanged herself. She was on antidepressants. Why would it be anything else?"

"No note and her death throes should have disturbed the scene."

Baker snorted. "None of that is compelling. I know the reason you're chapping my ass. You talked to that pain-in-the-butt friend . . ." He flipped open his notebook. "Rose Li. She told you the sob story about how her buddy couldn't possibly have killed herself. Come on, Cate. I thought you had a decent bullshit detector."

"I don't care what you think, Baker. I'm not signing off on manner of death until I get more information."

Baker shook his head. "This is your first suicide since your brother's accident. People have been saying you're taking it hard. I thought you were too tough to go squirrely, but maybe I was wrong."

Cate's head reared back at the mention of Jason and her chest tightened. "My brother has nothing to do with this. You're a lazy cop, and you don't want to do your goddamn job."

Baker didn't rise to her insult; he just leaned back in his chair and smiled. "And you think you can do better? Stowe and I have four other active cases. I've got a hemorrhoid bigger than a double-glazed donut and no manpower for a flimsy case that is obviously suicide."

Cate wondered if she should tell Baker about visiting the Marier Residence. He'd be furious, and what did she have to report except a watercolor of a lake?

"From the people I've talked to, it doesn't appear that Molly Johnson was depressed. She was medicating; she was stable. Why would she kill herself?"

Baker shook his head. "You met her girlfriend. Wouldn't you off yourself if you had to live with that?"

"Fabienne might be in shock." Cate's defense of the other woman was a knee-jerk reaction in the face of Baker's rudeness.

Baker shrugged. "Maybe. Have you ever seen that kind of reaction from a lover before?"

"No one that self-composed," she admitted.

Baker leaned forward. "Don't overcomplicate this. It was suicide, and my hunch is that living with the Ice Queen drove Miss Johnson to it."

Even if Molly and Fabienne didn't have a great relationship, it didn't explain why Molly chose hanging, especially with easy access to her own medication for a painless overdose. There didn't seem much point in trying to convince Baker. "What about that kid you arrested yesterday? What's his story?"

"Simon Thatcher? He lawyered up right away and wouldn't say a word. We charged him with trespassing, had to release him. He threw that cherry bomb, though. I'm sure of it."

"Why?"

"He's a troublemaker. Been questioned a bunch of times for property damage at environmental protests. Doing stuff against pipelines, that sort of shit. He was detained once in the States at an anti-Trump thing. Now he can't cross the border. He was arrested at a rally in Halifax a couple of years ago . . . He'd probably chained himself to a seal, for all I know."

"He sounds like a committed activist."

Baker snorted. "He's an entitled little prick. His parents are big movers and shakers and throwing cherry bombs is his way of working out his daddy issues."

Cate felt a pang of empathy. "Can I talk to him?"

"You think he's going to help you determine manner of death? I can see him marching in the street singing Kumbaya, but I can't see him analyzing forensics."

"Maybe he saw something when he was prowling around. Did you ask him that?"

"You really have lost your marbles, Cate."

She glared at him.

"Go to town. Ask him anything you want. Like I said, he refused to talk to me." He wrote down a number on a notepaper and pushed it to her. "Before you go rushing off to CSI him, have a look at this."

He shoved an envelope across the table.

She flipped it open. It was the preliminary autopsy report, back from the forensic pathologist. "Goddamn it. They should have sent this directly to me. Why did you get it?"

"I don't know. Maybe the lab realizes that it's cops who solve cases, not coroners."

"Have you read it?"

He shrugged. "Seems open-and-shut suicide."

She stood. There was nothing more she could get from Baker. "I'll review the report and let you know my final decision on manner of death."

Baker rolled his eyes, and Cate clenched her fists to resist slapping him.

She walked out of his office. Wending her way to the main entrance, Cate realized she felt excited . . . energized. She may have made zero progress with Baker, but there was something to this case, and she could contribute. She stepped into the lobby, blinking at the bright fluorescent lights.

She saw him before he saw her. He was as tall and broad as ever, but his hair was graying at the temples. He wore a sharp suit, much fancier than anything he'd owned when she knew him. His walk had that same confident swing, almost a strut. She spun back toward the door she'd exited, hoping he wouldn't notice her.

"Cate!" His voice, calling her name.

She breathed deeply, readying herself for the panic attack, like the one she'd experienced before meeting him that last time at the lawyer's office. Her heart rate remained steady, though, her breathing even.

She turned.

CHAPTER FIFTEEN

MATTHEW TOMKINS JOGGED TOWARD HER, GRINNING AN OPEN, BOYISH smile.

Cate couldn't help smiling back. God, he really was attractive. "Matthew. It's been a long time."

"Yeah." His eyes drank her in. "You look good. Really good."

She'd forgotten about the force of his charm, the warmth of his voice, that sheer sexiness. This reminder made her feel a bit better. Maybe she shouldn't have spent so many years beating herself up for staying with him. He was awfully hard to say no to. "Ditto," she said. There was a thick gold band on his ring finger that she hadn't put there. The size of it announced his bride's proud possession . . . or deep insecurity.

"God, it's been years, eh?"

"Five," she said. Damn. Now it looked like she was counting.

"I can't believe it's been that long. We never bump into each other."

Cate shrugged. "The instant we separated, I threw out my high heels. I haven't been to a cocktail party or a restaurant that serves caramelized anything since."

Matthew threw back his head and laughed, a happy, unselfconscious sound. "I've missed your sense of humor."

Cate flushed with pleasure and was immediately annoyed with herself.

"What are you doing here, anyway?" he asked. "Paying off the usual mountain of parking tickets?"

"No. Work, actually."

"What, you're a cop, now?" Matthew chuckled.

"No, a coroner."

He looked taken aback. "You don't have your practice anymore? You loved family medicine."

Cate folded her arms. "Things change."

"Was it the divorce?"

Anger, that faithful friend, swept over her. "Believe it or not, I don't make my life decisions based on your screwups."

Matthew's face darkened, and he seemed about to yell at her. Cate took a step back, waiting for his anger. The last months of their marriage were nothing but fights. Had she married Matthew because she was unconsciously seeking the same dynamic she grew up with—an angry man who did not tolerate dissent? She had wrestled with that question and others in post-divorce therapy. She never reached a definitive answer.

Before Matthew could respond, a group of men, a wall of expensive suits, came up behind him. "Are we ready to go in?" A tall man with a balding head and a kindly smile clapped Matthew on the back. It took Cate a moment to recognize Terry Wakefield without his Tilley hat. He didn't have the same trouble placing her. "Dr. Spencer." He smiled and extended a hand. "What a pleasure to see you again."

"Mr. Wakefield," she said.

Matthew interrupted. "You two know each other?"

"We met yesterday at the nitrate facility," Wakefield explained.

"What in God's name were you doing there?" Matthew asked Cate.

She shrugged. "I'm the coroner. There was a death. Why do you care?"

"I'm lead counsel representing TDR. We want to ensure this incident doesn't delay the groundbreaking and party this Saturday." He was speaking more for Wakefield's benefit than hers.

The last time she had seen Matthew, he'd been a junior lawyer still struggling to make his way in Main, Pinder & Thibodeau, the city's biggest corporate firm. He must have climbed fast. "It's not an 'incident,' Matthew. It's a young woman's death."

Wakefield turned to talk to the other men, and Matthew stepped toward her, speaking in a low tone. "Relax, Cate. We're all on the same side." He touched her arm.

She jerked it away. Her breathing quickened. "Do not come near me, Matthew," she said in a fierce whisper.

He put his hands up, his eyes searching her face. "All right, all right."

"Sorry to interrupt, Tomkins, but we don't want to keep Detective Baker waiting." Wakefield nodded goodbye to her.

"Right." Matthew rubbed the back of his neck. "Nice seeing you, Cate."

The group turned and passed through the door she had just exited, like a murder of well-dressed crows.

Cate's legs were leaden. She stumbled out of police headquarters and searched her purse fruitlessly for any sign of a cigarette—she'd take a half-broken stub at this point. She left her car. She could barely manage to put one foot in front of the other right now, let alone operate a motor vehicle. She walked up Elgin Street, the cafés and patios spilling over with students in tank tops and sundresses. She stared at them, wondering how they afforded their eight-dollar Frappuccinos. Anything to stop thinking about Matthew.

It wasn't easy to avoid seeing someone for five years in a small city like Ottawa. The first couple of years after the divorce, she had worked hard at it. She'd dropped any mutual friends, which meant almost all of them, stopped going to their shared gym, and moved to Sandy Hill, which was as far from their Westboro home as she could get without leaving downtown. Now here he was, turning up at her work like a cancer, poised to destroy everything she had built.

She walked the length of the street to the Lord Elgin Hotel, its solid stone façade promising a safe haven. She entered the cool, dim foyer and beelined to the bar.

She found a quiet seat and ordered a double scotch with no ice. Cate swirled the glass in front of her, staring at the amber liquid, breathing in its astringent, purifying smell. She would have to give up the case. There was no way she could handle the emotional chaos Matthew's presence unleashed.

Cate allowed her mind to drift back to memories she rarely entertained. She was a different person when she was married. A GP with a practice she was committed to and friends she'd have over for dinner or go on weekend hikes with. After the divorce, she could no longer manage the emotional baggage people brought to their family doctor. She cut everyone out of her life, even old school friends she'd known before the marriage. She'd wanted to quit medicine entirely, but Jason convinced her otherwise. "You're tougher than you think, Kit Kat. Don't let that bastard get to you." Jason encouraged her to take a job as a coroner. To her surprise, Cate found the work was a good fit. She analyzed scenes, gave families the answers they craved, and walked away. No mess. Maybe she smoked too much, drank too much, and spent too much time alone, but when Jason was home from his latest mission, they'd get takeout and spend hours catching up and laughing. That had been enough.

Sorrow pushed into her throat. All she wanted to do was lay her head on the bar and weep. What would she do without Jason? She had a flash of his face, his crooked grin, and his stupid floppy hair that he was so vain about. She mustn't let the hard knot in her chest loosen. If she did, she'd never be able to pull it closed again.

She focused on the file folder in front of her. Inside would be the information she needed to determine manner of death: graphic photographs of Molly Johnson's corpse and a careful analysis of the factors contributing to her demise. If she gave up on this case, some other coroner would take over, and who knew if they'd entertain the homicide angle. Molly's death would be labeled suicide, and her murderer would walk. Cate recalled the Ontario Coroner's motto—she must speak for the dead. This was her calling. The girl deserved justice.

Cate pushed her drink away and flipped open the autopsy report. It was thin, as preliminary reports often were, only two pages. Molly's death was attributable to asphyxiation. The pathologist noted ligature marks and bruising "not inconsistent with hanging." Time of death was between four p.m. and seven. As dry and unsparing as the language was, something was off. She read it over again, pausing over the wording: "not inconsistent" was different from "consistent." It left room for doubt. She looked to see who had performed the autopsy. Her heart lifted. Naomi Gold: she was smart, thorough, and painstaking. If she wrote "not inconsistent," it was for a reason. She must have some small doubt about the death. Cate called her office. Naomi was not expected until Monday. Cate made an appointment to see her then.

That felt good. She left the bar, the rest of her scotch untouched.

Back in her car, Cate decided to capitalize on her momentum. This morning's visit to the embassy had been a disaster. After her temper tantrum, she doubted she'd hear from the Congolese again; but there were other avenues to bring Jason's remains home. She pulled out her phone and made a call.

CHAPTER SIXTEEN

CATE PARKED ON A QUIET STREET IN OTTAWA'S WESTERN SUBURBS IN front of the unassuming offices of Medical Aid International. She never visited Jason when he'd worked out of these offices between assignments. Instead, he'd come to her house most nights he was in the city. He'd flop on her couch and demand to know what they were ordering for dinner. She loved when he was home, and they would slip into easy familiarity—teasing each other, watching TV, and making bad jokes about their shitty childhood. Things hadn't been easy as kids. With every passing year, their father's grief at their mother's death had grown meaner and harder. It was a relief when Jason was nine and she was seven and they'd been packed off to a boarding school. Most kids would have hated the adjustment, but Cate remembered her time at Canterbury Day and Boarding School with fondness. It was a reprieve from their father's unrelenting anger, and of course, she wasn't alone. She had Jason.

Medical Aid International was located with a group of other internationally focused charities, including an adoption program and an anti-malaria intiaitve. Its offices were small but bright and crisply air-conditioned, giving welcome relief from the humidity. She presented herself to the receptionist responsible for all three charities. "I'm Cate Spencer. I called earlier. I want to talk to someone about my brother, Jason Spencer."

The woman stood. "You're Jason's sister? Follow me. The director is expecting you." They walked to an office with a sign on the door reading "M.A.I., Canadian Operations." The receptionist paused. "We really miss your brother." Her eyes filled with tears. "He was a wonderful man."

Cate looked away, unable to say more. She took a deep breath and entered the office. A slim Black man rose from behind the desk, extending his hand. "Dr. Spencer?" he asked with a melodious accent. "I am Brilliant Aduba."

Cate couldn't stop herself. "Brilliant?"

He nodded, as if expecting the question. "In the Igbo tradition, there is a saying, 'when a person is given a name, his gods accept it.'"

Cate thought about that for a moment. "So your name is destiny?"

Brilliant shrugged. "My older brother is named Gospel, but he's not in the church. The youngest of us six kids is named Nomatter, because my parents were simply too tired."

Cate laughed. "Igbo, is that Nigerian?"

"I am impressed. Most westerners don't realize that there is more than one nation in Africa, let alone which tribes are found in which country."

"Jason talked a lot about Nigeria. I think it was his favorite place to work."

Brilliant pointed to a leather chair opposite his desk. "Yes, he and I had many chats about my country. It was lovely to talk with your brother, because he saw the beauty of the landscape, the pride and humor of the people. It was refreshing to discuss the good things, instead of dwelling on corruption and other problems."

"Yes." Cate's mouth twisted. "Jason was good at focusing on the positive."

"I am so very sorry for your loss. It was a blow to all of us when his plane went down."

"That's why I'm here," Cate said, eager to put an end to any further sympathy. "I've been trying to repatriate his ashes. According to the paperwork the Congolese embassy sent my father, he was working in Kinshasa, but they won't share any details about the accident."

Brilliant shook his head. "First thing you need to know is that you mustn't trust the government. Jason's plane went down outside of Kinshasa, yes, but he wasn't working there. Instead, he was returning from some leave he took in western Congo. His actual worksite was in Goma. That is in the east. Nearly at the Rwandan border."

Cate tilted her head to one side. "Why would they lie about that?"

Brilliant lowered his voice, even though they were the only two in the room. "It's rumored that the government is running illegal manganese mines in the east. It's an incredibly rare metal, very valuable. They want to draw as little attention as possible to their activities."

"What's that got to do with Jason? He was a doctor."

"Of course. Medical Aid International is strictly non-partisan. We never take sides. The problem is that the whole area is very dangerous." Brilliant sipped a glass of water. "The aftereffects of the Rwandan genocide are alive and well in eastern Congo. Hutu and Tutsi rebels continue to fight, tacitly aided by governments of neighboring countries. It is a quiet, simmering war. Meanwhile, the region has some of the richest ore deposits in the world—gold of course, plus rare minerals like manganese and cobalt—that are essential for modern technology. A dangerous place."

Cate could no longer keep quiet; the anger that was building as he spoke exploded. "You sent him there? He was a doctor, not some kind of soldier or mercenary. What were you thinking?"

Brilliant didn't even blink at her outburst. "It's true, it was very dangerous, but Jason knew this. He asked for the assignment. He was one of our best doctors, always willing to go where the need was highest. Not a soldier, but a healer—that was his calling."

Her anger intensified. Jason and his goddamn savior complex. "They lied to me about where he was. I'm going back to that embassy to demand answers."

He put up his hand. "I advise you to proceed with caution. Do not cause a stir or push too hard."

Cate told him about her angry outburst there this morning.

Brilliant shook his head. "You will have better results with them if you offer enticements. They do not respond well to threats."

"Enticements, like bribes?" Cate didn't have the faintest idea how you bribed someone. Who should she give it to? The woman with the red nails at the reception?

Brilliant didn't answer her question. "Let me work some contacts and see if I can get things moving. The family of Jason Spencer deserves closure."

"How do we even know he died in a plane crash?" she asked. "If they lied about the location, they could be lying about everything."

"Unfortunately, the crash most certainly happened. It was a small airplane, and it killed a locally engaged nurse and the pilot as well. There was only one survivor, a Congolese aid worker. I have the accident and autopsy reports here." He tapped a manila envelope on his desk.

She moved to pick them up, but Brilliant placed a hand over the documents. "You're welcome to take copies, but they are upsetting."

"I want to see," she said. "I can handle it. I'm a coroner."

"Of course," Brilliant said.

A few minutes later, Cate sat in her car, an envelope with copies of Jason's accident report on the passenger seat. What had his final moments been like? She could visualize the tiny plane flying above the green forests of the Congo. Did the engine fail, or was their pilot incompetent? Did a storm bring them down? Her job was to figure out manner of death, and she had no idea what happened to Jason. Did he die of smoke inhalation, impact, or a post-crash fire? Tears pushed at her throat, threatening to choke her. She pressed the back of her hand to her mouth to physically stop the sob. The answers were in the file by her side, but she wasn't sure she was ready to face them.

CHAPTER SEVENTEEN

THE MORNING SUN WAS NOT YET STRONG WHEN CATE PULLED INTO THE
Dominion Archives parking lot. The hulking edifice, ten stories of
concrete and cement, took up an entire city block at the west end of
Wellington Street. Its importance was signaled by its closest neigh-
bors: the austere Supreme Court building and the gothic towers of
Parliament.

Cate's joints ached and her head was heavy with exhaustion. When
she got home yesterday, she spent a sober hour staring at the envelope
containing the details of Jason's death. She couldn't open it. It was one
thing to review a fatality scene for professional purposes, another to
confront her only brother's death in graphic, intimate detail. In the
end, she stowed the file in a desk drawer and turned in for the night.

It had been a long time since she'd gone to bed without a little nip—even before Jason's death and the nightmares, she'd found
scotch a useful way to fall asleep. Last night she tried it sober, and she
had tossed and turned. Was it possible to forget how to fall asleep?

Fatigue wasn't helping her nicotine withdrawal, which was kicking in
big-time. Her shoulders and neck were tense and her hands shook slightly.
She dug into the bag of carrots she'd bought to help with cravings. The
crunch was satisfying, but she missed her tar and tobacco.

Cate signed in at the visitors desk and made her way to the Reading Room. She'd been in the building once for work. A homeless man
was discovered dead in one of the bathrooms. It really was depressing
how often people died on the throne. Rose had mentioned a murder
at the Archives, but that was before Cate's time as a coroner, and she
didn't know anything about that case.

She chose a chair at a table overlooking the Ottawa River. It was a gorgeous view. The water twinkled under the sun, and Cate idled a few minutes watching tourists stroll along the path on the opposite bank.

"Sorry I'm late," Rose said, sitting down beside her. Today she wore a pink headband and bright blue eyeshadow all the way up to her eyebrows. On anyone else, it would have seemed insane, but Rose was able to pull it off through brazen force of will.

"What did you want to see me about?" Yesterday Baker hadn't objected to her talking to Simon Thatcher. She interpreted that as license to continue investigating as she saw fit.

"I want to show you a few things." Rose stood. "I've been doing some digging."

Cate raised an eyebrow but followed the younger woman. They passed through the heavy glass doors into the foyer. "My office is a few floors up." Rose punched the elevator button.

The doors opened, and a thin man in his fifties stepped back to let them in. "Hello, Rose," he said.

"This is good timing." Rose turned to Cate. "I wanted you to meet my boss. Gerry MacIntyre, this is Dr. Cate Spencer."

They nodded at one another. "Dr. Spencer . . . Are you at the university?"

Rose replied. "No, Gerry, she's not a professor. She's a doctor—a medical doctor."

"Oh. I didn't think you folks still made house calls," he said with a feeble laugh.

"I'm a coroner," Cate said.

"A coroner," he repeated.

Cate noted the surreptitious way he inched further away from her, not an unusual reaction. Even people who knew better could revert to primal superstition when confronted with death.

The elevator doors opened on the fifth floor, and the trio stepped into a quiet, dim hallway that smelled of old paper.

"I'm determining the manner of Molly Johnson's death," she explained.

"Manner of death? I understood it was suicide."

"I have to make that determination."

Gerry swallowed hard, his Adam's apple bobbing in his thin throat. "This is an official visit, then? I should clear your investigation with my superiors. They'll want to know that you're here and that the proper protocols are implemented. Let me make some calls; then I can answer your questions myself."

She didn't want to be subjected to endless bureaucratic double-speak. "That's very kind but not necessary."

"No, it's impossible for you to be here talking to Rose like this. It's not the correct protocol at all." His hands fluttered as he spoke.

"As the coroner, I can talk with whomever I please during my investigation. I have been given that power by the government of Ontario."

Gerry blinked and opened his mouth before shutting it again and offering no further protests.

Cate got the impression he was used to being told what to do.

"Gerry was Molly's boss too," Rose explained. "He hired us at the same time."

"When was that?" Cate asked.

Gerry coughed. "I'm not sure. Maybe six months ago?"

Rose nodded. "Remember? It was February and freezing cold? Molly wore this crazy scarf that she knit herself. It went way down to her knees."

Gerry hesitated. "I don't remember that scarf."

"Yeah, it was all sorts of colors and covered in little knit mon-keys—super elaborate."

"I said I don't remember that scarf." His voice rose. He flushed, and there was an awkward pause.

"Were you surprised to learn of Molly's death?" Cate asked.

He crossed his arms, still flustered. "Of course. Why wouldn't I be? It was shocking. Shocking."

"She hadn't changed her behavior lately? Maybe started to come in later or shown less interest in her work?"

"Molly was an exemplary employee. She always gave one hundred and ten percent." He twisted his hands together. "If you'll excuse me, I have to make some phone calls."

They watched him walk through a set of doors to the left, his gait agitated. "What was that about?" Cate asked.

Rose shrugged. "I don't know. He didn't really react to Molly's death yesterday. Maybe it's only hitting him now."

"Maybe," Cate said.

"Our office is this way." They turned and went through a set of doors on the other side of the hall. The office was small and cramped. It was filled with books on photography, boxes, bundles of white cotton gloves, and two rickety desks set against opposite walls. Both held computers so old they must have been made when Bill Gates was only a millionaire.

"I shared this with Molly. That's her computer."

"Has Baker looked at it?"

Rose shrugged. "I told him about it, obviously, but he didn't seem interested. Besides, I've already checked her account."

"Isn't it password protected?"

Rose raised an eyebrow. "I hacked it. Her password was 'monkey.' She had a thing for them."

"If her death is a murder, breaking into her account might be tampering with evidence."

Rose tossed her head. "Molly and I were working on the same project. If anyone asks, I'll tell them I needed to see some files."

Cate hesitated for a moment, but curiosity won out. "What did you find?"

Rose shut the office door. "I'll show you." She sat in Molly's chair and turned the computer on. It made a deep whirring sound, and Cate thought she smelled the faintest odor of burning before the login screen came up. A slow boot-up later, they were in Molly's calendar. "She had it synced to her phone, so anything in there will show up here." Rose pointed to the screen. "See, there's her appointment with Albert Owl on Monday. She'd also put that in her paper agenda."

Cate saw the note on the screen, with Owl's name and the address for noon on the day of her death.

"Look here, though," said Rose impatiently. "She also had a 4:30 p.m. appointment on the same day. What if she was meeting the person who killed her?"

That was in line with the time of death. "Who's the appointment with?" Cate asked.

"Doesn't say, but it's at the nitrate facility."

"It's work-related, then."

Rose shook her head. "No, we were both doing the exact same thing, preparing the collection for the move. We usually left at four p.m., so she deliberately scheduled a meeting for after I was gone."

"How did she explain staying late on Monday?"

"That's the funny thing. She didn't say anything about it. She got ready to go at four p.m., same as me. When I left, I had the impression she'd be following right behind. She wanted me to think she was leaving too."

Cate rubbed her head, speaking more to herself than to Rose. "If it isn't suicide, it comes back to who would want to murder her. I see three options: someone from her private life, someone from her professional life, or a random stranger."

"It's got to have something to do with Eastview, don't you think? That painting in Albert's room connects him to Molly."

Cate considered. "Albert's death appeared to be natural causes. He was ninety-eight."

"What if it wasn't, though?"

Wanting to rule out that possibility, Cate made a mental note to call Sylvester Williams.

Rose continued. "Even if the death has nothing to do with Eastview, I doubt the killer could be some random crazy. The facility is always locked—it happens automatically as you leave the building. There's no way in without a key. We're very conscientious because we're in the middle of nowhere and all those demonstrators were by Turcotte Road."

Cate considered Simon Thatcher. "Did she know any of the protesters?"

Rose furrowed her brow. "She started bringing them Timbits and coffee on the days we went out to the facility."

"When did she begin doing that, do you remember?"

"Last Wednesday. I know because that was the day we saw the herons in Lake Mitchell."

Five days before her death. "Why had she become friendlier?"

"We drove by them three times a week for months. I think she admired them. They're out there, rain or shine, and it's a lost cause."

"She sympathized with them?"

"Yeah, I think so. Also, she might have been lonely. She'd only recently moved from Vancouver."

Cate's heart squeezed. It wasn't easy to carve out a life for yourself in a new city. She had tried in British Columbia when she went to medical school, but she had met Matthew almost immediately, and somehow, they had ended up back in Ottawa. What would her life be like if she had never met that man?

Rose continued, "I should have been a better friend to her. She was always trying to do stuff, but most of the time I was busy. I've got my family here and my university friends." Rose blinked back tears. "She was trying to connect, you know?"

Cate didn't know what to say and made an inadequate soothing noise.

Rose blew her nose, and her voice became businesslike. "I could have been a better friend to her in life. I'm not going to let her down in death. Maybe Molly met a protester and for whatever reason he or she killed her at the facility."

"Maybe," Cate said. Privately she didn't think that sounded likely, but she was eager to steer the conversation away from Rose's grief. "Could there be a connection to the project you're working on?"

Now it was Rose's turn to sound doubtful. "There aren't usually a lot of motives for murder in the Archives. I can't see anyone getting too riled up unless it's a genealogist who finds a transcription error in the 1921 census."

Seeing Cate's blank reaction, Rose spoke. "Sorry, that's an insider joke. See, genealogists are, like, intensely passionate about our records, and the 1921 census—"

"So, no possible connection with the job, then?" interrupted Cate. She didn't tell Rose that coroners had a few nerdy jokes of their own. Her boss had a bumper sticker that read, "Only a coroner would like you for what's on the inside."

"I'm not sure," said Rose. "Right now we're preparing the nitrate to move to temporary storage. Eventually we're going to have a purpose-built center."

"OK, so what does that involve?"

"We go through all the photos, making lists. The stuff that's too deteriorated gets segregated, although that's a total nightmare because we can't find a contractor to dispose of it. We've been looking ever since it was clear we'd have to move."

"But the base sold the land ten years ago." Living in Ottawa, the seat of federal government, Cate was familiar with bureaucracy, but this struck her as completely ridiculous.

"There aren't many waste management companies willing to take a risk with nitrate, especially the really unstable deteriorated stuff. It's incredibly volatile. Provincial fire regulations dictate it can't be moved in temperatures over twenty-six degrees Celsius. It's got to travel in an air-conditioned truck on a cool day. The preference is to dispose of it in situ. That comes with a ton of regulations, and most companies can't be bothered. Meanwhile all the film that's unreadable keeps piling up in 'for destruction' boxes that never get destroyed."

Cate thought of that long hallway with the vaults, each one packed with boxes. There must be thousands of containers in there. "The two of you were going through every box of photographs? That's a huge project."

"We've been at it the whole six months, and it will take another month to finish—longer now that it's only me." Rose's voice broke, as the reality of Molly's death hit her anew.

Cate spoke, hoping to distract Rose. "Could it have been a robbery gone wrong, someone trying to steal some of the negatives? You've got some old stuff, surely some of it is rare, maybe valuable?"

Rose squared her shoulders. "I doubt it. Generally speaking, negatives aren't worth that much. I mean, negs belonging to super famous photographers like Ansel Adams or Annie Leibovitz might get a good price, but that's the exception. Normally the expensive item in photography is prints." Rose's gestures became animated as she warmed to the topic. "Prints are where you see the photographer's mastery of the medium and their artistry. They demonstrate their dark room skills. Basically, only archival institutions collect photographic negatives on a mass basis because we like to document the process and get the unique record. It's really, really difficult to change or forge a film negative. Negatives are the originals."

"Hmm," said Cate. None of this was particularly helpful in establishing a motive.

As if reading Cate's mind, Rose injected her voice with enthusiasm. "If there's nothing valuable, maybe Molly found a secret that somebody would want to protect or hide. Something incriminating."

Cate considered. "Like a naked picture of a politician or evidence of a crime?"

"Yes," Rose agreed. "Although now that I think about it, it doesn't seem likely. I mean, nitrate film stopped being produced in the 1950s, so any crime would have to be really old."

Cate was frustrated. "If we want Baker to take this seriously, we need to come up with a plausible motive for murder. As it stands, we have nothing but some nursing home visits and a coincidental meeting time. If we don't have motive, maybe Molly did kill herself."

Rose turned to Cate. "You don't really believe that."

Cate allowed herself to fantasize about writing "suicide" on the report and walking away. "It would certainly be easier if I did."

Rose broke out into a grin. "Something tells me you don't take the easy way out, Dr. Spencer."

Cate stared at Rose. Once that was true. She had fought to go to BC for her degree, fought to get top marks in medical school, fought to save her relationship with Matthew. All the fight had gone out of her since the divorce. Cate sighed, and it must have been deeper and more heartfelt than she realized, because Rose looked at her with concern. She made an effort to speak forcefully. "Something is off about Molly's death, and you and I are the only two who seem to recognize it."

Rose nodded emphatically. Cate was beginning to feel a kinship with the younger woman, the two of them battling long odds together. The power of that connection caught her off guard, and for a moment, she glimpsed the depths of her own loneliness.

"What's the next step in our investigation, then?" Rose asked.

Cate blinked, imagining Baker overhearing them. "Slow down. You're not investigating anything."

Rose opened her mouth to protest, but the ringing of Cate's cell stopped her. She was on the duty roster, and a body had been discovered in Britannia. Cate noted the address and turned to Rose. "I've got to go, but I'm serious. No more looking into things on your own." Rose nodded, but Cate wasn't convinced by the other woman. "Listen to me, Rose. You can do more harm than good."

"Don't worry, Dr. Spencer. I'll be the height of discretion."

Cate, looking at her sky-blue eyeshadow, was not convinced.

CHAPTER EIGHTEEN

THE SICKLY-SWEET ODOR OF DECOMPOSITION HIT CATE AS SHE STEPPED out of the elevator. It filled the shabby hallway, indicating someone had been dead for a while. A young officer met her at the door. He looked unsettled. Seeing cocky new cops get queasy on a scene as they realized that bodies sometimes needed to be removed with shovels and plastic bags rather than gurneys was a grim pleasure of the job.

Cate took in the scene. The cramped apartment was what she expected in these kinds of calls. Stacks of old magazines, piles of clothing, and bundles of newspapers filled the space. Every flat surface held an overflowing ashtray, and the smell of tobacco was a low, gritty base note in the overwhelming scent of rotting human flesh. Bottles of cheap vodka were scattered on the floor, suggesting what might have contributed to cause of death. Often at such scenes, the individual was some kind of addict, lonely and isolated, with only booze or pills for company at the end. She shivered, for once not actively craving a cigarette.

Someone had mercifully opened the door to the small balcony, and the smell, though strong, was not overpowering. She could hear the sergeant in the bedroom, rummaging through drawers. Probably looking for an address to contact the family.

The man hadn't died on the toilet, at least, but eased out of the world slumped in his armchair, with the remote fallen from his hand and the TV still blaring. He was in his underwear, and his thin chest was covered in gray hair. Cate hoped he was watching something he liked when he died. Terrible to go out watching a bad reality show or the braying of canned sitcom laughter.

She pulled on her latex gloves and did her preliminary examination, finding nothing untoward.

"Can you give me a hand here?" she asked the young officer by the door.

He swallowed hard as she handed him a pair of gloves.

"I'm going to need you to help me move him."

The young man glanced at the bedroom door, obviously hoping the sergeant would emerge and relieve him of this duty. Cate could have told him that the senior officers knew to make themselves scarce when it was time to examine the body.

She didn't want the officer fainting, so she spoke matter-of-factly, trying to relieve him of his dread. "We're going to lean him forward."

The officer grasped the man by the shoulder. Cate grabbed the other shoulder. She met his eye, and they edged the body away from the chair. The skin was soft, squishy in her hand: evidence of bloating. As his head advanced, a trickle of burgundy decomposition fluid dripped from his mouth and nose, landing on the officer's shoe.

"Fuck," he shouted, leaping away and letting the body fall with a soft thud to the floor.

"For God's sake," Cate said. "Show some respect."

The officer wasn't paying attention to her, however. He stared in horror at the armchair. A thin sheet of grayish white skin had remained attached to the upholstery, waving in the slight breeze coming from the balcony. A few maggots, fat and well fed, wriggled, wondering where their dinner had gone.

The officer's green color deepened, and Cate barked: "Go to the balcony now and get some fresh air."

By the time she finished her examination the sergeant had emerged from the bedroom. She discussed the relevant details with him.

"This one looks pretty straightforward," she said. "Natural causes. I imagine alcohol was a contributing factor."

He nodded. "I've talked to the neighbors. Apparently, he was a grumpy bastard. Alcoholic, surviving on a small disability benefit from a back injury about fifteen years ago. They never saw any family visiting or anyone coming in, for that matter. According to the neighbor, he watched TV all day and drank. They called it in when the smell got bad."

Cate shivered again. Now that Jason was gone, would this be her fate? An unmissed death in front of *Love is Blind*? "Well, he died doing what he loved," she said, gesturing to the television.

The sergeant guffawed, and Cate felt an unreasonable flash of anger at his laughter.

"Do you have a next of kin?"

The sergeant shrugged. "I didn't find any names or addresses yet. I'll canvass more neighbors."

Cate looked around. She could see no landline. "Is there a phone in his bedroom?"

The sergeant shook his head.

"He must have a cell, then," Cate said.

The sergeant looked dubious. "I doubt this guy—"

Cate cut him off. "Everyone has a cell phone." She strode to the coatrack and rummaged through the jackets that hung there until she hit the jackpot. The phone was a cheap brand a few years old. It reminded her of the one they'd found on Molly Johnson. She gave it to the officer with a smug smile. Baker was wrong if he thought she couldn't handle a little police work. She finished filling out her forms, handed them to the sergeant, and left the building.

On her way to the car, she bumped into Detective Stowe. "What are you doing here?" she asked, sounding more aggressive than she meant to.

Stowe shrugged. "I heard a body called in and was out this way. I thought I'd stop by and see if I could lend a hand."

"I don't think there's anything here for you. Seems like straightforward natural causes."

"Good," he said. "You're not going to overcomplicate this one, now, are you?"

She put her hands on her hips. "What does that mean?"

"Baker told me you're trying to be cute with the suicide at the Archives."

"I'm not being 'cute,' I'm determining manner of death. It's my goddamn job."

Stowe put up his hands, smiling. "Easy, easy. I'm telling you what Baker told me. He's in a world of hurt from those TDR guys. Apparently, the CEO came at him with a bunch of lawyers yesterday. They want the case resolved before their groundbreaking soiree this Saturday."

She could see Matthew smiling his charming smile while letting Baker know in no uncertain terms that his career would be severely limited if he didn't do what TDR wanted. "I suppose he collapsed like a cream puff?"

Stowe laughed again. "Nah, Baker hates corporate bullshit. He likes to remind suits that when it comes to police cases, he's the big swinging dick. I'm sure he told them to fuck right off, possibly even in those words."

Cate felt a twinge of affection for Baker. She would have enjoyed seeing the testosterone battle between him and Matthew. She wasn't sure where she would put her money.

Stowe entered the building, and Cate turned back to her car. She paused. Something about the victim's phone . . . She recalled Baker saying that Molly's phone held only work numbers, but Rose said that her friend kept her phone synced with her computer. You couldn't do that with a cheap flip phone like the one Baker found. Fabienne said Molly was always on her phone. Had she said what kind? Cate paused, unable to remember her exact phrasing.

She dialed a number. "Rose," she said when the other woman answered. "It's Dr. Spencer. What kind of phone did Molly have?"

If Rose was startled by the intensity of Cate's question, she didn't show it. "An iPhone, why?"

"But there was an old cell phone found in her pocket at the facility."

"Oh yeah, that's the crappy phone they give us for work. We've all got them. I think they were built in 1995. Molly hardly used hers. She always had her smartphone."

Cate's heart was pounding. "There was no iPhone found on Molly's body."

There was a pause as Rose absorbed her words, then she said exactly what Cate was thinking. "Whoever killed Molly took her phone."

SYLVESTER WILLIAMS WAS ONE OF THOSE MEN WHO WAS NATURALLY slim all his life until middle age suddenly slammed the brakes on his metabolism and a round, maternal belly popped out, almost overnight.

"Something about your story isn't adding up." Williams tapped his teeth with a slender finger. They were sitting on a terrace in the ByWard Market. A beautiful, sunny Friday, tourists in sneakers and baseball caps milled about the outdoor stalls, contemplating the purchase of miniature Mountie statues, Canada T-shirts, and every manner of maple product.

"I explained to you my interest in the case, Williams." Cate refused to call him by his preferred nickname, "Sly." She glanced at her phone. She'd called Baker yesterday, as soon as she'd learned about Molly's cell phone, but the detective hadn't returned her call.

The waitress handed over their drinks. Williams had ordered a coffee, laboriously explaining that he wanted almond rather than soy milk for various annoying reasons. It was a sunny day, and Cate had treated herself to a gin and tonic. She had second thoughts as the waitress placed it in front of her, however. Apart from one sip of scotch at the Lord Elgin on Tuesday, she'd gone over twenty-four hours without a drink. She didn't want to think how long it had been since she'd done that. Maybe she could make it a streak.

"Yes, but I don't see why you were at the Marier Residence in the first place. The nurse was adamant she'd shown you and a student into Mr. Owl's room."

Cate had already resolved to bluff it out. If there was one thing she excelled at, it was denial. She raised an eyebrow. "Obviously I wasn't there. None of this makes sense. You know coroners don't take students on. It's ridiculous."

"And yet, here you are, asking me about that very case," Williams noted triumphantly.

She wanted to wipe the smug look from his face, but she wanted information more, so Cate bit back an angry retort. She shrugged. "I don't know what to tell you. It's a coincidence."

"I wonder if Dr. Marcoux will think it's a coincidence," he remarked.

"Really, Williams? You're going to involve the boss?" Cate rolled her eyes and played with the straw in her glass. She wasn't too concerned. The worst she'd get from Marcoux would be a lecture, followed by another enthusiastic discussion of his family tree.

"You're right, we shouldn't pester him with our little squabble." Williams adopted a sanctimonious tone, which was even worse than the smug one. "Lord knows that man is getting on in years, and he's certainly had his share of problems. I'm not sure he's handling stress very well, lately."

Now Cate was more than irritated. It was common knowledge that Williams was angling to take over as Regional Supervising Coroner when Marcoux retired. Had he stepped up his campaign and started actively smearing Dr. Marcoux?

Williams didn't notice her anger and continued talking. "I mean, his wife died years ago, but it's like he's still mourning her. Plus, of course, he must cope with that deeply troubled son on his own." Williams shook his head sorrowfully.

Dr. Marcoux's son had severe schizophrenia, which must pose challenges, but the way Williams said "deeply troubled," it was like Marcoux's forty-year-old son was nothing but a crushing burden rather than a beloved child. "I think Dr. Marcoux is doing great," she said staunchly.

Williams raised an eyebrow in a truly infuriating fashion. His dismissive attitude toward anyone who wasn't perfect always maddened

Cate. She wasn't as efficient as he. She took her time talking to families, trying to help them come to terms with the death, whether the deceased was a homeless drug addict or a pillar of the community. Williams's lack of empathy made him a bad coroner, no matter how thorough his reports were.

He sipped his coffee and said placidly, "Anyway, I don't see how your hanging case could relate to Mr. Owl's death."

"I can't explain it to you without violating confidentiality," Cate explained again.

"And yet I'm meant to divulge the details of *my* case? Your request really is absurd."

"Come on. All I'm asking is for a heads-up."

"About what?"

This was the reason she had endured Williams's ten-minute disquisition on the merits of his paleo-diet and the joys of his Tesla. She leaned forward and spoke in a hushed tone. "Did Albert Owl die of natural causes?"

Williams brayed out a laugh. "Good lord, woman. He was ninety-eight. Of course it was natural."

She could use Williams's sense of superiority against him. There was nothing he enjoyed more than making someone feel stupid. She adopted an innocent, slightly bewildered voice. "There was nothing suspicious? No signs of trauma? Nothing on the history or in his charts?"

Williams's chest expanded and his voice deepened as he delivered his response. "Cate, Cate, Cate . . . Owl was a routine Nursing Home Threshold investigation. He had a history of diabetes, hypertension, and a previous myocardial infarction. Neither the staff nor his family had any concerns."

Cate considered; all those elements aligned with a non-suspicious death.

Still chuckling at her perceived ignorance, Williams took a big sip of his coffee and stood. "It was natural causes, Cate. Trust me." He sauntered off, leaving her with the bill.

Williams was thorough, and a heart attack was entirely plausible. Rose was going to be disappointed, but Cate was relieved that the elderly man had met his death naturally.

She checked her phone in case she'd missed a call. This morning, on Brilliant's advice, she'd contacted the Canadian embassy in Kinshasa for help with the return of Jason's remains. They'd promised to get back to her, but she'd heard nothing yet.

Her stomach reminded her it was lunchtime. Cate signaled the waitress to bring her a menu, waved away the untouched gin, and ordered a Perrier instead.

She gazed across the street. A tall Black man in sunglasses wearing a baseball cap pulled low over his face was leaning by the entrance to the parking garage. There was nothing unusual in that, except for the intensity with which he was staring at her. The hairs on the back of her neck stood up. The waitress arrived with her drink, and when Cate looked over to the entrance again, the man was gone. Now regretting abandoning the gin, she took a long sip of water. She was edgy. It was three days since she'd had a cigarette, and carrot sticks were poor substitutes. Maybe she should pick up some gum or get the patch.

In the absence of a deep, satisfying pull on a cigarette, she drummed her fingers on the table, scrolled through her phone, and dialed Simon Thatcher's number, getting his voice mail. She'd already left a couple of messages. Another wouldn't hurt.

What else could she do? She remembered Major Harrison's business card and took it out of her wallet. He'd told her to call him if she had any questions. He might have some ideas about an Eastview connection between Molly and Albert. Harrison knew how the base operated, and unlike every other professional connected to this case, he was eager to talk to her.

She dialed the number.

A crisp voice answered. "Hello, Major Harrison's office."

Cate was flustered. She hadn't expected a secretary. She explained who she was.

There was a delay and then Harrison's voice. "Dr. Spencer?"

"Major Harrison, I'm calling to take you up on your offer."

There was a pause. "I'm sorry, I'm confused."

Cate could have sworn he was flirting with her at the facility, but obviously he didn't even remember their conversation. Her voice was tight, and her words came out in a rush. "When we met on Tuesday you had said you'd be happy to answer any of my questions about the base or the nitrate facility."

"Of course." He sounded distracted, and his voice was clipped. "I'm quite busy. The official handover to TDR is occurring Saturday, just before the groundbreaking gala."

"OK," Cate said. She was piqued at his disinterest and annoyed with herself for her annoyance. What did she want? She thought of Harrison as an overeager puppy and now she was bothered that he hadn't flirted? "Well, maybe next week, when things have settled down—"

"Have you had lunch?" he interrupted.

She stared at her Perrier. "No," she said.

"I could see you now. I haven't eaten yet. Since I'm short on time, can you come to the base?"

"Sounds perfect."

He gave her directions and they hung up. Her stomach gave a little flip. Hunger or excitement?

CHAPTER TWENTY

FOLLOWING HARRISON'S DIRECTIONS, CATE TURNED OFF TURCOTTE ROAD and cruised past the protesters, trying to spot Simon Thatcher. No luck. The track to the nitrate facility was to her right, and she was tempted to have another look, but she didn't want to keep the Major waiting. Besides, if Baker was doing his job, officers were still investigating the scene. She clicked her tongue in annoyance. Why hadn't he returned her call about the missing cell phone?

The back gate to the base was open and unguarded, just as Harrison said it would be, presumably because there was nothing to keep watch over anymore. She drove onto the property and noticed activity on a hill overlooking the nitrate facility and the lake, as workers erected a white marquee. This must be for tomorrow's TDR launch soiree—ten years in the making.

She kept driving. Occasionally, to her right, she spotted the glitter of the creek that wended its way below the nitrate facility to Lake Mitchell. What had the watercolor in Albert Owl's room been titled? Lake Nigamo? Singing Water. It was a fitting name for such a beautiful spot.

The narrow road passed fields, rifle ranges, and gray, utilitarian buildings whose use was obscured by their long abandonment. A thin, well-maintained airstrip kept her company for a while before petering out.

The road started to dip; she must be nearing the Ottawa River. More buildings cropped up. Rows of uniform and symmetrical white clapboard houses reminded Cate of soldiers standing in formation. Streets branched off the main drag, making it feel like she was on the outskirts of a small town. Occasionally she'd pass a sign of habitation: clothes fluttering on a line, a TV flickering in a living room, a moving van. These isolated signals of the last few families still here somehow made the base feel lonelier. The place seemed like the ghost town it was only twenty-four hours away from becoming.

Closer to the center where the administrative buildings were, this sense of loneliness was more pronounced. Here was the school, its windows already boarded up. A low, brown building proclaimed itself "Green Grocer and Laundromat," its letter *M* hanging askew. She pulled up to the three-story white clapboard headquarters dominating the little town center. A Canadian flag and a blue Royal Canadian Air Force flag fluttered in the breeze.

Several cars, a couple of army jeeps, and a big gray van filled up the parking lot. People bustled around, mostly in the blue uniform of the RCAF. No one stopped Cate to ask for ID. She walked down a long hall, peeking into rooms filled with moving boxes. She found Harrison's office without any trouble. It was the biggest one, in the back, with a huge window overlooking the Ottawa River.

The receptionist's office was empty, but she could see Harrison sitting at his desk. "Hello," she said, knocking on the doorframe.

"Dr. Spencer," he said, with a wide grin. "So great to see you."

She smiled back, easy and unforced. "Call me Cate, please."

He stood and walked toward her. He was skinnier than she had remembered, and taller.

"I'm Peter," he said. "If you don't mind, I thought we could go outside for lunch. I don't get to see the sun much these days." His voice was deep and carried a note of authority she hadn't noticed at the nitrate facility.

She nodded.

"Let's nip out the back way," he said. "If I walk through there"— he gestured to the hall—"a hundred people will stop me with questions, and we'll never eat." He held open the door for her and they stepped into the heat.

He shook the paper bag he was carrying. "I bought you a sandwich. I grabbed one turkey and one cheese, in case you were vegetarian."

"Thanks," she said. "I eat meat, but that was thoughtful of you."

He shrugged. "I'm a meticulous planner. Force of habit."

"I guess you need good organizational skills to succeed in the military." That sounded lame. Why was she suddenly self-conscious?

"Yes," he said. "Habits I learned in the Balkans. That was a messy time. Planning for every eventuality kept me alive."

He'd served in the Balkans? So much for her impression of him as a pencil-pusher.

A couple of young men in military uniform walked toward them, exchanging crisp salutes with Peter without breaking stride. Cate had never thought of herself as a particular fan of the military, but there was something very satisfying about the orderliness of those gestures. Everyone knew their place and played their part.

"I thought we could head up the little rise there." He gestured to a slight hill. "There's a bench and some shade. Great view of the base. You can see for miles. The whole place is spread out before you." His voice held a note of wistfulness.

"You're sad to be leaving," she said.

He turned slightly to her. "That's very perceptive."

She shrugged, self-conscious again.

"I was second-in-command for ten years. This was a small base, and we were a real community. Now we're scattered. Some folks went to Gander, Newfoundland, others to Victoria, British Columbia, and all points in between."

"That must be hard," she said.

"That's the Air Force. You obey orders."

She could see regret in his eyes. "And yet?"

"If this space was going to be used for something worthwhile, something meaningful, I wouldn't feel so sad."

"You agree with the protesters." She didn't bother hiding her surprise.

"Luxury homes for the city's mega-wealthy isn't the kind of cause most people rally behind."

"Did you fight the development?"

"I did. Years ago I made the case against selling the land. I argued the base still had a role. My pleas fell on deaf ears."

"If it was still viable, why didn't they listen?"

Peter snorted. "Terry Wakefield is a powerful man. He's friends with federal, provincial, and municipal politicians and every non-elected official in between. Plus, lots of the city's wealthy and even not-so-wealthy jumped on the investment bandwagon. Many people have gambled on TDR's success, and now they want to see development so they can get their payout."

Cate pursued this. "Do you think there was something corrupt about the sale?"

He put up two hands. "No, not corrupt, but this land is worth a fortune, and that trumps everything else."

She could hear the frustration in his voice. "There was no way to stop it?"

Peter smiled. "No, though I knew I had to go down fighting. And I am going down. They've suggested that I retire."

"Retire? How old are you?" she couldn't help blurting.

He grinned. "An advantage of military life, early retirement. I'm only forty-eight, but I'm too big a pain in the ass to keep around. With the base closing, my heart isn't in it. To be honest, it might even be broken."

Most of the men she knew would never confess to such vulnerability. It took more courage, she suddenly realized, to admit weakness than to bluster out some macho bullshit. "That's terrible."

"That's the military. Shut up and take your orders. Still, I wish they'd at least put up a plaque or something. There's so much history here."

"Really?"

"Some of the first aircraft to fly in Canada took off from the old airstrip. Charles Lindbergh landed there six weeks after crossing the

Atlantic. Thousands flocked here to glimpse his plane. They waited for hours in an icy drizzle."

"Amazing. I never knew."

"Oh yeah, it was a huge story." Peter's gestures expanded with the tale. "The Americans sent up twelve Curtis P1B's to escort him. There was a tragedy, though. Two of them had a mid-air collision, and an American lieutenant died trying to parachute to safety."

"My God." Cate could see the young pilot's terror, envision the plane plummeting to the earth. A fiery death from the sky. Just like Jason. Her head whirled for a moment.

Peter didn't notice her distress. "He died in front of all those spectators. It devastated the city. The prime minister ordered a state funeral." Peter's voice was hushed. "As the dead man's special funeral train chugged alongside the Rideau Canal, Lindbergh swooped over it scattering red rose petals from his plane."

Cate closed her eyes and imagined the sunlight gleaming off Lindbergh's wings as he dipped low over the black locomotive, scarlet petals falling like bloody tears from the sky. "What an incredible story."

Peter laughed self-consciously. "I guess I've been outed as a history nerd."

"There are worse things."

"You're easy to talk to, do you know that?"

"Maybe you're easy to listen to." Good lord, where had that come from? Cate was actually impressed with her own ability to flirt.

Peter continued, gesturing to the empty fields around them. "You wouldn't know it now, but during the Second World War, this place was humming. They did tons of very important, highly classified stuff here—trained elite fighters, had a chemical weaponry lab, even a spy school. A lot of that info is still classified. After the war, we were heavily involved in aeronautic experimentation." His tone was wistful. "Since the Cold War wound down, everything kind of fizzled out."

They fell into a companionable silence. Cate glanced over at Peter as they walked along the rutted road. A few hairs poked out from the top of his shirt. When had she gotten so old that she was interested in men with gray chest hair? Was she interested in Peter? The question made her heart thump, but she breathed out the panic.

They sat on the bench, the tree shading them from the sun. Peter passed her a sandwich, and they ate in silence. There was a slight breeze, and Cate realized she was in no hurry to talk about the case. Instead, she asked him why he'd joined the military. In other circumstances, she would have been reticent to pose such a personal question, but it felt natural.

"I was young. Nineteen. My parents were dead. I wasn't very good at school. It was the easiest thing to do."

"Most people wouldn't consider getting shot at in the Balkans the easy option."

He laughed. "I didn't say I was a smart kid, just all alone."

"How did your parents die?"

"Car accident. It was February. Freezing rain. They slid right into the Madawaska River."

"Oh, that's horrible. I'm so sorry," Cate said.

"You know what the poet Christina Rossetti called grief?"

She shook her head.

"'Gnawings that may not be fed.' I'm afraid it's true—I don't think you ever get over a loved one's death. It may fade, and the pain may lessen, but it's still there, an unhealed wound—gnawing."

Cate surprised herself by saying, "My mother was killed in a car accident when I was five."

"You poor kid." He looked at her with such compassion that she had to look away and blink back tears. "What happened?" he asked.

"Foggy night and she lost control. I was in the car. My brother and I both were. We didn't have a scratch on us. My grandmother called it a miracle. My father thought it was something else."

"Surely he didn't hold you responsible?"

Cate shrugged. "Who knows? I have no memory of the accident, but one of the first things I do remember is being grilled by my father. Had Jason and I been horsing around? Had we been yelling? Was I kicking her seat?"

"But it's insane to blame children," he said.

Cate's mouth twisted. "You haven't met my father. He was an angry man before the accident, but after that . . ." She stared up at the cloudless sky, thinking about airplanes and how they stay up. It was magical . . . until it wasn't.

"Did you want to talk about that young woman at the facility?" Peter's voice interrupted her thoughts. "Detective Baker mentioned you still hadn't ruled on manner of death."

Her back tensed. "Baker shouldn't be talking to you about the case."

"It was a courtesy. The facility isn't officially part of the base, but I've got to make sure that all the i's are dotted and the t's are crossed on this handover."

"Why does the successful launch matter to you?"

"It's my job. TDR is hypersensitive to bad publicity, and the brass is very anxious to accommodate Mr. Wakefield."

She stared into his face. "I think Molly Johnson was murdered. Whoever did it made it look like suicide."

Perhaps it was his military training, but Peter showed no surprise. "Do you have any proof?"

"I don't need proof for my report. It's based on available evidence and the balance of probabilities. It's the police's job to find proof. The evidence for suicide is inconclusive. Baker hasn't been very receptive to my doubts, though." He couldn't even be bothered to follow up about the missing phone. She thought of her own interview with Fabienne and her visit to the Marier Residence. "I'd like to have something concrete to point him to, but I'm not getting very far on my own."

"This case has gotten under your skin," he observed.

"I've seen plenty of homicides and suicides before, but this one is different. Something is off, and I can't let it go."

"I'm a big believer in instinct. If this case is giving you bad juju, you should listen to your gut. How can I help?"

She smiled but hesitated. Even when she'd made the appointment to meet with him, she'd known this was a fishing expedition. Now she didn't know where to start. "Does the base have a lot of interaction with the facility?" Maybe one of his men was nearby on the day of Molly's murder.

Peter shook his head. "No. For the past year we've been focused here, shutting up the buildings, winding things down. There's not much call to go out that way. The men go for swims in Lake Mitchell, of course, but that's about it."

"Lake Mitchell?" Cate asked. "What do you know about its history?"

"It's always been part of the Eastview. I've seen the original plans from 1921. We opened the base as an 'Air Harbor'—that's an airport for the military. We used to own the facility too, of course. That's where we stored the nitrate negs."

"Wait, I thought that was an Archives building."

"It was the RCAF's originally. Our pilots did most of the topographic surveying of Canada—photographing the whole country from the air. That created massive amounts of nitrate negatives. Initially we stored our own nitrate film there. Then for a while we used it for temporary holding cells."

Cate thought of those small, dark vaults. "They don't seem like pleasant places to be locked up."

"It was always only short-term. They'd chuck in the drunk and disorderlies for a few hours until they sobered up, slap someone in for joy-riding in a jeep, that sort of thing."

"Why'd the Air Force stop using it?"

Peter hesitated. "It's not a nice story."

"Come on," Cate urged. "You can't leave me hanging."

He shifted. "Back in sixty-one, a young corporal was thrown in the brig. He'd gotten drunk, and the idea was for him to sleep it off. Only the arresting officer was called away when his father died. He hadn't finished the paperwork when he left. There weren't any other prisoners at the facility at the time, and no one thought to check the place for a week."

Cate's hand flew to her mouth as the horror of the situation sunk in.

Peter continued, "He was dead when they found him. Dehydration. He'd ripped off all his nails in his attempts to pry open the steel door. He tried to write a final message on the wall by using the blood from his fingers. He must have been hallucinating, though, because it was gibberish."

Cate thought of those dark, forbidding vaults. They'd given off an air of menace and misery. She couldn't imagine how terrifying it must have been for the young soldier as he realized no one was coming to save him.

Peter continued. "The arresting sergeant, the one who forgot the boy, shot himself a week before his trial. They handed the building over to the Archives soon after that. No one had an appetite to keep using the vaults as cells."

There was a silence and then Cate cleared her throat, pushing the tragedy from her mind. "It seems like the more I find out about Molly's death, the further I get from understanding. I feel like I'm missing something obvious." Cate smacked her hand on the bench to emphasize her point. Her fingers brushed against his, and she drew them back as if burned.

They talked of inconsequential things until Peter rose. Cate took the hint, and together they walked back to her car.

He leaned down as she was putting on her seatbelt. "This might be weird, but the big TDR groundbreaking party is tomorrow night." He coughed. "I was wondering if you'd like to accompany me."

"Sure," she agreed.

He grinned. "It's a date."

Only as he walked away did she realize that it was, and only when he disappeared from view did she realize that she was happy about it.

CHAPTER TWENTY-ONE

THE SUN PUSHED THROUGH HER WINDOW THE NEXT MORNING, BUT FOR once Cate didn't resent its arrival. She opened her eyes and stretched luxuriously. If this was what waking up without a hangover felt like, she ought to try it more often. She sat up, ready for the morning ritual of lung-splitting hacks, but managed only a few anemic coughs. Maybe quitting would actually take. She grinned and slipped into her dressing gown. It was time to start thinking about taking up running again. That plus an organic veggie box, and she'd have rejoined the ranks of the smugly healthy.

Normally Cate dreaded Saturdays if she didn't have a coroner's shift. A long, empty weekend without the distraction of work was intolerable. Weekends were meant to be spent eating brunch with friends or fighting with your significant other at Ikea. She'd spent the last few since Jason's death buried in a movie theater; watching two and sometimes three films in a row, until she was queasy and her eyes ached.

Today was different, though. For one thing, she had a date to the hottest party in town. She was going to go shopping and buy herself a dress. When was the last time she did that? She smiled, surprised at how much anticipation she felt.

For another thing, she was going to make some progress on the case. After a lot of emails back and forth, she had managed to schedule an eleven o'clock phone call with Molly's parents. She needed to give them information on their daughter's death and hoped to learn more about the young woman's state of mind.

She checked her phone. It was dead, but even after charging, there was no reply from the Canadian embassy, Simon Thatcher, or Baker.

Her mood was too buoyant to be affected by this radio silence. She called Thatcher again. Now his phone didn't even ring, going directly to voice mail. She left another message. She'd follow up with the embassy and Brilliant on Monday.

Coffee brewing, she fetched the paper, ready to dive into the day's news. Professional interest demanded that she check the obituaries first. Albert Owl's funeral was being held Monday morning at Beechwood Cemetery. The only surviving relatives mentioned were a niece and a cousin. She circled the notice.

The front-page article in the Living section was usually devoted to profiling an Ottawan who had done something extraordinary. In such a small city, "extraordinary" was flexible. Sometimes it was a woman who designed dog snow pants; other times it was a mailman's crusade to save a bird with a broken wing. Today's edition brought her up short: "Beloved Ottawa Doctor Dies Saving Lives in the Congo." The photo of Jason was from about fifteen years ago, and he looked so young. It was taken after his first skydiving adventure. He was grinning into the camera, eyes crinkled, head thrown back, brimming with joy at what he had done. He'd told her that she ought to try it, that it was as close to flying as humans would ever come. She scoffed, reminding him that he was the risk-taker, and she was the plodder. He shook his head. "Just because that's what Daddy says, doesn't make it true." She was twenty-three at the time, and her father was still a god to her, an Old Testament deity—vengeful, petulant, unpredictable, and angry. Jason's comment wormed its way into her consciousness, though, and helped her find the strength a few months later to tell her father that she was going to the University of British Columbia instead of McGill for medical school.

The *Citizen* must have profiled Jason because of his charity work. She now remembered someone mentioning the possibility at the memorial. She traced the photograph with her finger. He wasn't coming back. He had left her to go to university in the States, and he'd left her a dozen times for Medical Aid International missions. Now he'd left her for good.

The tears she hadn't allowed herself to shed surged up. She cried with great, snotty sobs, howling at the pain she carried since that telephone call from her father. Her chest ached with the effort.

When her tears finally stopped, her coffee was cold, and her sadness was replaced by anger. Her father must have known about the article; the photo came from his mantelpiece, and as she scanned the text she saw quotes from Dr. Marcus Spencer, respected thoracic surgeon. Why hadn't he told her about this? Why was everything, even Jason's death, couched with malice and coldness? Her head ached. She was exhausted and in dire need of a cigarette. Screw quitting. She shrugged a sweater on over her pajamas and was heading for the store when her cell rang. She answered it without checking the call display.

"Cate, is that you?" The sound of Matthew's voice snapped her to attention.

"How did you get this number?"

"It was listed on the police report about that suicide at Eastview. Listen, I was reading the paper. Jason died?"

She nodded before realizing he couldn't see her. "Yes," she whispered. "Almost a month ago."

"Cate, I'm so sorry." His voice held real pain and deep compassion. He knew how important Jason was to her.

"It's OK," she said. "I'm coping."

"I want to see you."

"I don't think that's a good idea."

"I'm sorry to bother you, but I'm so bowled over by this news. Cate, please. I want to talk about Jason."

She was torn. Seeing Matthew again churned up all the old feelings, all the old pain. Yet Matthew had loved Jason, she knew that. The temptation to talk about her brother with someone who could share her memories was stronger than her anxiety.

He spoke again. "Please, Cate."

He would persist in this, she knew, and hound her until she agreed to meet. She didn't have the strength to fight him, but she wasn't a

fool. She wouldn't let him invade every aspect of her life. "Fine, but not here. I'll meet you at the Second Cup on Laurier in half an hour."

"Thank you," he said.

Hanging up, Cate prepared for battle. She pulled her hair, still thick, still dark, into a ponytail and applied mascara to her eyelashes, also still thick, also still dark, and chose shorts that showed off her legs and a T-shirt that emphasized her chest. Feeling good about herself was her best weapon against this particular enemy. She stood in front of the mirror. Something was missing. She pulled out the jewelry her father had given her on her birthday. Her mother's platinum Wonder Woman cuff. She slid it on her wrist and straightened her back. She was ready for combat.

CHAPTER TWENTY-TWO

a booth, facing the door. She wanted to be able to spot his approach. She wrapped her hands around the cup, grateful for its warmth in the over-air-conditioned room. She tapped her fingers on the table and thought savagely about how good a cigarette would be.

She watched Matthew walk in. He carried himself with more strength and assurance than Peter, and she was instantly annoyed with herself for comparing the two. Matthew's face had fleshed out, softening his strong nose and hard chin. That wasn't the only thing that had fleshed out. His loose polo shirt couldn't mask the small bulge of his stomach, and his eyes were deeply creased. He ordered a coffee in his quick, confident way and sat down.

His smell—that familiar scent of Dial soap and him—overwhelmed her, and for a moment she worried she'd be lost in long-ago emotions. She reined in her feelings, speaking in a detached voice. "Decaf?"

"Yeah, Tansy has me off all toxins. No alcohol, cigarettes, red meat, gluten, fluoride, and definitely no caffeine."

"Tansy?"

He twirled his wedding ring. "We got married a couple of years ago. She was my financial consultant. She knows all my secrets."

"Not all of them," Cate said. How long until Tansy discovered, or maybe she already knew, what kind of man he really was? She brought her cup to her lips, her hand trembling.

Matthew noticed the shaking. "Cate, I—"

She shook her head emphatically. "I don't want to rehash our marriage. Understand?"

"OK, I won't talk about it." He took a big swig of his coffee.

Cate was surprised at how quickly he acceded. The old Matthew would not have allowed her to take command like that. He would have challenged her, to remind her he was in charge.

"I can't believe Jason's dead." Matthew's voice cracked with emotion. "When I saw his face staring back at me from the paper, I was stunned. How did it happen? How are you doing? Jesus, how's the old man?"

"He was still working with Medical Aid International. This mission was an Ebola epidemic in the Congo. He always said the most dangerous part of the work was the planes they used." She rubbed her face, utterly drained. "He was right about that."

"Cate, I'm so sorry."

Looking at his eyes, filled with pain and sadness, she remembered how Matthew had worshipped Jason nearly as much as she did. A kid from rural Nova Scotia, he was dazzled by her brother's sophistication and confidence.

Matthew was reading her thoughts. "He was like the older brother I never had. First thing that flashed through my mind when I saw that photo was the time he helped us move in when we arrived from BC—remember that shithole apartment on Stewart?"

Cate recalled the basement one-bedroom. It always smelled of damp, and she'd once found a cockroach on her toothbrush.

Matthew was lost in his reminiscences. "We'd bought a ton of stuff from Ikea, only I didn't know how to put any of it together. We didn't have Ikea in Nova Scotia, and my old man had never taught me to use a hammer, let alone an Allen key." He laughed. "When Jason showed up with pizza, he saw I was struggling. He got right to work, and we did it all. He never made me feel stupid."

She smiled. It was good to talk about her brother with someone who had loved him. It was the kind of talk she should be able to have with her father.

"After you and I broke up, I tried to stay in touch," Matthew said. "I emailed him. I wanted to go for beers, to talk. To tell him my side."

"Oh?" Cate hugged her chest. Jason had never told her this.

"Yeah, he wouldn't answer me. I must have sent half a dozen emails. I guess I thought if I could convince him to forgive me, I could convince you."

She ignored that. "What happened?"

Matthew shrugged. "I finally called him. He told me never to contact him again. I was crushed."

A knot she didn't even notice forming in her chest loosened. Jason hadn't betrayed her. "One of my brother's many sterling qualities . . . loyalty."

"I always envied your relationship with him."

Cate knew that. It was one of the dozen sources of tension in their relationship. Matthew resented the time she spent with Jason. By the end of their marriage, he was making it so unpleasant to see her brother that she'd almost stopped altogether. Cate didn't voice those old accusations, though. "We had to look out for each other—God knows our father wasn't going to."

"How is he?"

"I don't know, honestly." Cate found herself telling him about her last visit. About the TV in the living room, firing the housekeeper, and his general confusion. In talking about her father, and Matthew's mother, whom she genuinely missed, they slipped back into the easy conversational rhythm of their marriage. Cate's shoulders loosened, and she surprised herself at the number of times she laughed. Matthew was older, more confident and calmer, and still knew how to make her laugh.

She took a sip from her mug. "This coffee is great. It's amazing how taste slowly returns after you quit smoking."

"Wait a minute, you were smoking? Self-righteous Cate with the lung-cancer statistics if I so much as looked at a pack?"

She thought of the year immediately after the divorce, when that first long drag of a cigarette was the only thing that got her out of bed in the morning. "I realize now that everyone's got to have a few weaknesses. It's what makes us human."

Matthew searched her face, seeing more than she would have liked. "Are you OK, Cate?"

She laughed, and it sounded high and false. "I'm peachy."

"You seem different," he ventured. "Angry."

"I wonder why that is."

He stared at her for a long moment, and she met his gaze. She would not burst into tears in front of him.

He spoke softly. "I'm sorry it took Jason's death to bring us together again, Cate. I'd like to be friends."

She shook her head. She might not be the most emotionally healthy person, but she knew enough to know that what he proposed was a bad idea. "We can't be friends, Matthew. We have too much history, and it's too ugly."

"That's not true, Cate, and you know it." His voice rose, a thread of anger adding an edge to his tone. "I miss you. I miss talking to you and hearing you laugh."

Her stomach clenched at his tone, the anger reminding her of things she'd rather forget. She crossed her arms. "No."

"Let's actually talk about that night. Let me explain. I've changed. I've—"

She interrupted him, surprised at how easy it was. "I told you I'm not discussing our relationship, Matthew. Bring it up again, and I'm leaving."

There was a long silence. Matthew had obviously learned to pick his battles. He took a sip and grimaced. "Decaf is disgusting."

She accepted the change of topic. "And you used to be such a coffee snob, even when we were completely broke."

"I've got to watch my health now. I've got responsibilities."

A thought, so sharp, so painful it took her breath away. "Do you have kids?" Her voice was husky.

He was stirring his coffee and didn't notice her intensity. "No, but I do have the mother of all mortgages."

She laughed. "I would have thought a big shot lawyer didn't worry about paying the bills."

He leaned away from the table, rubbing the back of his neck. The familiarity of the gesture jarred her. "I made partner two years ago, and then we landed TDR. One of the senior partners was handling all their accounts. They're so huge we've had to hire more staff. Anyway, he's retiring soon. He handed TDR off to me this week. This client will make my career."

He was always ambitious, and she had to give it to him—he was smart and worked damn hard. "That's great, Matthew."

"Yeah, and such interesting work. Their fingers are in everything. They've got land deals all over Canada and the US. They're bidding on a couple of highway projects in the southern states, and they've even got a contract to manage a nuclear power plant. Right now, though, that East-view headache is taking up most of our time. What's your take on that?"

"What do you mean?" she asked.

"Come on, don't be coy. You're the coroner, for God's sake."

"Well, to start, I wouldn't call the unexplained death of a young woman a headache." Matthew could be so callous at times.

He dismissed her criticism as he usually did. "Unexplained? It's clearly suicide."

Once she would have risen to his bait and argued. She was beyond that now. "Unexplained until I say otherwise. Like you said, I'm the coroner."

He persisted. "Yeah, but the prelim report said suicide. That must be the way you're leaning."

Had Baker let TDR see the preliminary autopsy report? So much for him standing up to the big corporate bully. "I'm not discussing the case with you, Matthew. So let's forget it."

Anger flashed across his face, but only someone who knew him intimately would have seen it. He spoke pleasantly. "Come on, Cate. Don't be so uptight. We're old friends."

Despite the innocuousness of his words, the anger remained. She could see it in the rigidity of his shoulders, the watchfulness of his eyes. The old feelings of helplessness and panic returned. How could she stave off his fury? For a moment she was tempted to tell him what he wanted, to protect herself. Then she remembered that she wasn't his wife anymore. She didn't owe him anything, but she did have a duty to Molly Johnson. "That's bullshit, Matthew, and you know it." She stood up. "I'm not going to discuss the case with you." Her voice cracked with anger. "Leave me alone, and do not contact me again." Several patrons turned to stare.

"Cate, I—"

She left before he could say anything more.

It was only when she turned off Laurier Street, her head finally clearing from his presence, that a thought stopped her in her tracks. Had Matthew called to console her about Jason, or to probe her about the case? The Matthew she remembered from five years ago had not been long on empathy.

There was always a hidden agenda.

CHAPTER TWENTY-THREE

CATE WENT HOME AND POURED HERSELF A SCOTCH. IT WAS 11:30. "IT'S five p.m. somewhere," she mumbled, bringing the glass to her lips. Damn it, she'd forgotten to buy cigarettes. She went upstairs and stared at herself in the mirror. Her hair might still be thick, and her legs might still be good, but Tansy was probably ten years younger and twenty pounds lighter. She pulled her hair out of her ponytail and scrubbed the mascara from her eyes. Who was she kidding? She'd made herself look pretty because some stupid part of her wanted him back. She missed the pressure of his mouth on hers, his easy charm, the way he always frowned while reading. How messed up was it that she still missed that goddamn man after what he had done to her? She took another swig of scotch and wished she'd thought to bring the whole bottle up with her.

Now Matthew was all tied up with the Johnson case. She played over their conversation, trying to see if she'd given anything away. She was sure she'd been circumspect, but then, how could she trust herself where Matthew was concerned? She sat on the edge of the tub and fought back a hysterical laugh. What a mess. She yanked off her mother's cuff, letting it bounce with a clang on the bathroom tile. It hadn't helped her. Nothing could help her. She fell apart whenever Matthew showed up, no matter how strong she tried to be.

She gulped the scotch and stood. The preliminary autopsy report was on her bedside table. She'd already read it over twice, and she leafed through it again while downing the last of her drink. The alcohol burned all the way to her stomach, and the tingling looseness spread to her limbs. She padded downstairs to get another one.

She poured a more generous glass this time, almost up to the rim, and took a big slurp so she could walk without spilling it. Some sloshed out anyway. That was OK. She sat on the couch and opened the report. She read, but the words wouldn't sink in. "Asphyxiation"; "not inconsistent." The close-up photographs of Molly's neck, bruised and swollen.

Cate took another swallow. How had her glass become empty? Back into the kitchen. More scotch. Banged her hip on the counter. Where was Molly's phone? Maybe Fabienne had it. A simple explanation.

A buzzing noise. It took her a moment to realize it was her own cell. "Yes," she answered. "Cate Spencer speaking." She could hear the thickness in her voice.

"Dr. Spencer? I'm Louisa Johnson. It's noon your time. We had an appointment to talk at eleven?"

Molly's mother. Fuck. Fuck. Shit. Could she hang up? Too late, she'd already identified herself. Cate was paralyzed. The silence stretched over the line.

"Hello, Dr. Spencer?"

"Hello, Mrs. Johnson." Cate's head was cloudy, and her stomach churned. She took a deep breath and tried to focus. "I'm the coroner responsible for Molly—I mean Miss Johnson's—case." Shit. How many scotches had she had?

The line was fuzzy, or was that her mind? Mrs. Johnson was talking. "What I don't understand is why we didn't hear from you after the detective informed us on Wednesday. I understand that is the protocol." Her voice was quick, impatient.

The tone threw Cate off; she wasn't expecting irritation. "I'm sorry. I meant to call you." Her voice sounded garbled. She tried to remember why she hadn't. She spoke more clearly. "I was waiting for the report."

"What report? What are you talking about?"

Cate stared at the phone, flummoxed. "The autopsy—preliminary autopsy."

"Detective Baker had it on Wednesday. I expected to hear from you on Thursday."

Wow, this woman really wasn't letting it go. Annoyed, Cate took another sip of scotch without thinking. "Listen, I'm doing the best I can, OK?"

There was a pause at the other end. Cate closed her eyes. She needed to pull it together. She spoke slowly, taking care to enunciate every word. "I want to inform you that the preliminary autopsy results indicate that Molly's death was a result of asphyxiation secondary to strangulation."

Another pause. She could hear quiet sniffles.

"Mrs. Johnson?"

"You're saying it's suicide?"

Cate hesitated. She didn't want to cloud this woman's grief with her suspicions. Not when she hadn't made an official judgment.

The other woman spoke before she could form a reply. "Is there something you're not telling us?"

Dimly, Cate recalled Baker saying that Molly's mother was a lawyer. That explained the questioning. "No," Cate spluttered. "No, it's just—"

"Just what? If she didn't kill herself, what happened to my daughter?" There was an edge to the woman's voice—anger or sadness, Cate couldn't tell. Probably both.

She spoke quickly. "I don't know. I can't say one way or another until I conclude my investigation."

"One way or another? What is the other option? What aren't you telling us?" Mrs. Johnson's voice was strong and accusatory. Cate was battered by her questions.

She knew she shouldn't say any more, but her mind was befuddled, and short of hanging up, she didn't know how to get out of the conversation. "It's unusual for women to hang themselves, so I have to make sure that's what really happened. There wasn't a note. Do you think she was suicidal?" She'd put that more baldly than she would have liked.

"Molly wasn't depressed. She was upset the last time I talked to her, but it didn't sound like she would kill herself."

The import of Mrs. Johnson's words penetrated Cate's confusion. "Upset? What about?"

"I don't know. Maybe she'd had another fight with Fabienne, or there was something going on at work. She wouldn't tell me, but she was unhappy."

Cate blinked and stared straight ahead, willing herself to concentrate. "How could you tell?"

"She called me out of the blue on Sunday. She never does that. When I asked her what was wrong, she changed the subject. She wanted to talk about all sorts of strange things. How her father and I met, how I knew I wanted to be a lawyer, a stuffed toy she'd had as a child—a little monkey. Silly, random things. It was like she wanted to distract herself. I think she felt better by the time we hung up."

Cate slumped back into the couch. Her head swam in confusion, and she longed to close her eyes and sleep. She spoke clearly, trying to make up for her earlier sloppiness. "As I said before, we're continuing to investigate Molly's manner of death. In the meantime, if you haven't already done so, please contact a local funeral home to make arrangements for the body."

There was a muffled sound on the other end of the line, like a sob.

Cate spoke over it. "I'm continuing my investigation, which includes discussions with . . ." her voice trailed off. She was blanking on the phrase. The silence seemed eternal as her bewildered brain trolled for the phrase. " . . . persons of interest." She grinned triumphantly at remembering. "Until that time, you're welcome to contact me at this number with any further questions." There. That sounded professional.

There was another pause, and when Mrs. Johnson spoke, it was in a clear tone. Cate admired her fortitude. "If it's not suicide, it would have to be murder, wouldn't it? Are the police investigating?"

"I'm sorry, Mrs. Johnson. You'll have to speak to the police about that." The "speak" was slurred and Cate panicked, talking in a garbled rush. "Ask Detective Baker your questions. I can't help you."

"No, you're obviously not in a fit state to help," Mrs. Johnson replied. "I'll speak to the detective myself and tell him all about this conversation." She hung up before Cate could say another word.

Cate stared at her phone. She moaned. She'd spoken to a victim's mother drunk. She pushed away her glass of scotch and curled up on the couch, hoping to pass out, for once not dreading the nightmares.

CHAPTER TWENTY-FOUR

A LOUD BUZZING NOISE DRILLED INTO CATE'S HEAD, JOLTING HER awake. She looked at her phone. It was six p.m. and she'd slept the day away, passed out on the couch. The drilling noise came again. The doorbell. Her head ached, and her mouth tasted like roadkill. The memory of her conversation with Mrs. Johnson flooded back, and she groaned aloud.

"Cate? Are you in there?" The ringing stopped, and the knocking began. It was Peter Harrison.

She pulled the blanket over her head. She didn't want him seeing her like this. She stared at the door, unsure of what to do.

The pounding continued. "I heard a groan. Are you OK?"

No use pretending she wasn't home. She stood up, smoothed her hair, straightened her shirt, and swung the door open. "What's up, Peter?"

His appearance, tall and distinguished in a tuxedo, answered her question. Shit. The TDR party.

"Cate," he said, staring at her wrinkled shirt, casual shorts, and bare feet. "Are you all right?" His wave of concern bowled her out of the way, and she stepped aside, allowing him entrance.

"Come, sit down," he said. "You look like you've had a shock. Is everything OK? Talk to me."

He walked into the living room and said nothing about the nearly empty bottle or the rumpled blanket on the couch where she had obviously been sleeping until a few seconds before.

He took her hand, his kind eyes filled with care. She swallowed a sob. Peter was a good man, and he liked her. She couldn't throw that away by letting him see who she really was. A total and irredeemable screwup.

"I'm so sorry," she blurted. "I forgot all about the party. You've caught me in full Saturday flake-out mode." She forced a laugh and gathered up her hair in a quick ponytail. He thought she was confident, capable, a winner. How would he look at her if he knew that she had talked to the victim's mother while drunk? "I'll be ready in twenty minutes. You'll be amazed at how quickly I can pull myself together. Grab a seat."

Peter tilted his head. "If you're not feeling up to it, Cate—I'm happy to skip the party. We could stay in, if you'd prefer."

"No!" The last thing she wanted was to give him the opportunity for some cozy heart-to-heart. "Twenty minutes is all I need, I promise."

The hot shower pounded her body, driving into her skin. She was scalded, but it was good. Like she was atoning for that phone call, punishing herself for her idiotic actions, and stripping her body of the alcohol that had made her behave that way. Peter's arrival shook her out of her usual pattern—drink too much, do something stupid, drink more to forget about it. This was her chance to try a different path. She would go out with this man. She'd laugh and flirt and think about normal things like a normal person.

She stepped out of the shower, shrugging into the only dress she'd kept from her time as Matthew's wife. It was a short black number that she'd figured would always be in style. She dug out her mother's jewelry, retrieving the cuff from the floor and putting on a large necklace with a ruby at its center. Serviceable black heels, not quite appropriate for the party but not quite horrible either. She grabbed a gold pashmina she'd received as a gift, back when she had friends, gave her hair a quick comb and blow-dry, and slapped on some makeup. Done. If Peter didn't exactly wolf whistle as she descended the stairs, his expressive face didn't show disappointment or disgust. She'd take what she could get.

They lapsed into silence in Peter's jeep, as though he sensed she was preoccupied and needed space. Cate struggled with thoughts of her conversation with Mrs. Johnson. She breathed in and out, trying not to remember the pain in Mrs. Johnson's voice. Her ability to compartmentalize had deserted her. Instead, she recalled every slurred syllable. She stifled a moan and forced herself to look around, to get out of her own head. They were driving through the base now, which looked even more deserted than yesterday.

Peter broke the silence. "We're boarding up the office next week. Then it will all be over."

"What a shame," she said, as he steered down the main road.

"I know," he said, and his mouth twisted. "So much history, so soon forgotten."

She glanced over at him, his ramrod posture and hands placed precisely at ten and two on the steering wheel. What would this man think of her if he knew the truth?

Peter continued. "The Avro Arrow was designed here, you know."

Cate grabbed hold of the topic like a life raft. "I should know that story, but . . ."

"Oh, it's a weird one," he said. "The Arrow was a supersonic missile-armed aircraft that we developed in the late 1950s as a response to the Soviet threat. After years of top-secret experimentation by a team of brilliant scientists and engineers, the Arrow was ready to go into production."

Peter was a born storyteller, his inflection and gestures sweeping her into the tale.

"The Avro was better than anything the Americans or Soviets had come up with at the time. Then we signed NORAD—a defense agreement with the Americans—and the plans were scuttled."

The story jogged her memory. "What happened next?"

"The entire program was disbanded, all records related to the Arrow were disposed of, and all the prototypes destroyed. They eradicated every trace of it—blueprints, models, and designs . . ."

"You mean there's nothing left at all?"

"There have always been whispers that Field Marshal Curtis, who headed the project, hid two prototypes somewhere to preserve the Arrow for posterity. It would be amazing if a museum could locate one, although it would be an antique by now."

They drove past the town, through the quiet fields. All those men who poured their hearts into the Arrow's design and production dreamed of Canadian autonomy and air superiority, only to have their life's work negated by a change in the political winds. The bleakness of the story suited her mood.

The turnoff to the party was by the gate she had come through the last time she visited the base. Three police cars, lights flashing, were parked on the base-side of the gate; on the other was a huge group of protesters, much bigger than she had ever seen. They held up signs saying "Stop the Destruction!", "Justice for MMIWG," and "Save the Cricket Frog!" She looked for Simon among the crowd. People were drumming, others singing loudly. She saw one young man in a T-shirt that said "The Resistance," holding a rock in his hand.

"They look angry," she remarked.

"They've lost," Peter said. "It makes people desperate."

THE WHITE MARQUEE SPILLED OVER WITH LIGHT AND LAUGHTER. PETER handed his car keys to a valet and then offered Cate his hand, for which she was grateful. This was her first party in five years, and walking, even in such low heels, made her nervous.

They turned toward the entrance. Suddenly his arm shook violently. "What's wrong?" she asked.

"Sorry," he said. He rubbed his arm self-consciously. "Sometimes the tremors show up."

"Tremors?"

"A souvenir from the Balkans," he said.

Cate squeezed his arm. Was this a physical wound he had sustained or the result of psychological stress? Either way, her heart ached in empathy.

Before they could discuss further, two security officers asked for their invitations and for Cate to open her purse.

Inexplicably, the party's theme was "The Roaring Twenties." At least three hundred guests packed the tent. A five-man band, complete with a sultry torch singer, played jazzy music from the era in one corner, while tuxedoed waiters moved through the crowd, passing out champagne. Cate flagged one down and drained her glass. Only Peter's startled expression prevented her from grabbing another.

Ottawa's highest society was here. She recognized many faces from the local news: tech giants, politicians, sports celebrities, even a minor pop star. She also saw the occasional person from her father's neighborhood. She'd grown up in one of the wealthiest postal codes in Canada, and while they didn't exactly throw street parties, she had come to know a few of the residents over the years.

As they wended their way through the crowds, Cate was surprised to see a familiar face. Coroners, even the Regional Supervising Coroner, weren't usually high on the list of invitees to elegant soirees. The sight of Dr. Marcoux recalled her recent conversation with Mrs. Johnson. She looked around for another waiter carrying champagne, but there were none to be seen.

Marcoux spotted Cate and waved genially. Cate gritted her teeth; she would have to say hello.

"Dr. Spencer," he said with a bow of his head. They had never reached a first-name basis, perhaps because he was almost the same age as her father. Marcoux was round, with a thick cloud of white hair encircling his bald head. His eyes usually twinkled from behind half-moon glasses.

"Good evening, sir. What brings you here?" she couldn't help asking.

"I've known Terry Wakefield for years, old college chums."

She wouldn't have pegged those two—sharp, smooth Wakefield and dreamy Marcoux—as buddies, but school ties could last decades on nothing more than shared nostalgia for cheap beer and youthful hijinks. The few friends she kept in touch with all stemmed from her boarding school days.

"And what's your connection to this shindig?" he asked.

"I'm here with Major Harrison. She gestured to Peter.

Marcoux raised an eyebrow. "From CFB Eastview?"

Shit. It was against the rules to date anyone involved in an ongoing coroner case. "Yes, but he's retiring soon," she said.

Peter didn't seem to notice any awkwardness, and the two men nodded at each other.

"I'd like to introduce my son, Toby." Marcoux turned and gently put an arm on a rail-thin man with wide-set eyes and a broad forehead.

Toby, in his early forties, stared at Cate and Peter unblinkingly. Cate noted his blank expression, a common symptom of severe schizophrenia. This flat affect was often a result of the disease itself as well as the powerful antipsychotics that could be prescribed to manage the delusions or hallucinations. Schizophrenia was a harrowing disease, and caregivers had to shoulder the brunt of the stress. Despite what Williams had implied the other day, Marcoux did not seem burdened by his son. Instead, he smiled affectionately at Toby and said, "We've been enjoying the music and decor. It's nice for us to get out of the house sometimes. We'll leave soon, though. We both get tired."

Toby agreed with a jerky nod of the head, briefly making eye contact with Cate. She caught her breath at the vulnerability she saw in his glance, and her chest tightened at the struggle he fought inside his own mind.

Cate and Peter said goodbye and moved through the crowd. An elderly woman, wearing the largest diamond earrings Cate had ever seen, stopped her. "Catherine Spencer?" she asked.

Cate nodded warily until recognition sunk in. "Of course!" she exclaimed. "Mrs. Cho, can I introduce my date? This is Major Peter Harrison. Mrs. Cho lived two houses down from us when I was growing up."

"Catherine, it is good to see you, and looking so well." The woman's sharp gaze took in Cate from head to toe, lingering oh-so-briefly on the shoes. "I was deeply saddened to hear about your brother. What a saint that boy was. Your father, I fear, is not handling his death well."

Cate didn't want to think about Jason at this party, and she didn't want to discuss her father with a neighbor. "Oh no," she said neutrally, hoping the lady would take the hint.

"He's wandering, dear," the elderly woman said. "He's out at all hours, and I'm worried one day he won't find his way home."

Cate had meant to follow up with her father and find out how he was managing but hadn't had time this week. Half-consciously, she leaned into Peter, tightening her grip on his arm.

"Lovely to meet you, Mrs. Cho," Peter broke in, "but if you'll excuse us, I see someone I need Cate to meet." Peter tugged her arm, pulling her away from the woman's presence.

"Thanks for saving me from that old gossip," she whispered, feeling especially warm toward him. Who knew competence could be so attractive?

Cate snagged another glass of champagne, taking care to sip it slowly.

They were approaching a short, chubby, bespectacled man. Peter whispered, "Don't thank me yet. Clifford can talk."

"Cate, I'd like to introduce you to Clifford Bernard." Peter clapped the man on the shoulder, and he and Cate nodded at each other. Bernard wore a suit rather than a tuxedo and instead of black tie had a beaded bolo in red, black, and yellow. "Clifford was the main negotiator for the Algonquin on the TDR purchase. He had a big say when we sold Eastview to TDR."

The shorter man smiled. "This is unceded Algonquin territory. We needed to make our voices heard."

"What exactly does 'unceded' mean?" Cate asked. The two glasses of champagne had chased away her shyness, and though she had heard the word in many land acknowledgments, no one had ever clarified it to her.

Bernard launched into an explanation as if asked that question many times. "It means that this land along the Ottawa River is traditional Omàmiwinini territory. We never sold it or gave it up, not through treaty, war, or surrender."

"I see," Cate said. "So you had a stake in the property when the Air Force sold it?"

"We should have a stake in all the land that the city of Ottawa sits on," Bernard said. "It was stolen from us by white settlers in defiance of the very property laws they claimed to uphold."

Peter interjected, "Because of ongoing land claims, the Air Force couldn't sell the land without consulting with the Algonquin. That's partly why the transfer process was so long."

"Yes," Bernard acknowledged. "We may call ourselves the Algonquin Nation, but that doesn't mean we all have the same opinion. Hammering out a deal that suited all communities was challenging." He spoke with the polished ease of a politician.

It made her want to challenge him a bit. "Did you actually reach consensus? There's still a lot of protesters."

Bernard smiled. "There are always some unhappy people, no matter how good a deal you make. There was some unsubstantiated nonsense about Lake Nigamo—Lake Mitchell—being a sacred site."

It was the first time she'd heard someone else use that name for the lake. Had Bernard known Albert Owl? Before she could pose the question, Bernard asked Peter about his plans now that the base was closing. Cate's skin prickled. She could sense someone staring at her. Matthew was moving through the crowd toward them. Of course he was here. TDR had hired the most ruthless law firm in town to protect its interests, and her ex was now at their beck and call. Matthew's gaze met hers.

She turned to Peter. "Want to dance?" she asked brightly, not caring that she was interrupting the two men.

He looked surprised but nodded. "Sure."

The band played "Someone to Watch Over Me" as she and Peter held hands and walked to the dance floor. He took her in his arms, and she breathed deeply. He smelled nice, like shaving cream and sunlight. She stepped closer and put her hand on his shoulder. He was only a few inches taller, and she fit easily into his arms. He held her firmly, his hand at the small of her back giving her the pleasant sensation of being cared for. He knew what he was doing, and despite her clumsy feet, he led her through the movements.

She found herself relaxing. He would manage the difficult bits. All she had to do was follow. She let herself float around the room. He was protecting her from another confrontation with Matthew, but maybe he could be more than that. She could be a better person with him. She was softer, less angry, and maybe even happy? The song ended, but she didn't pull away, staying in the warm comfort of his embrace.

At last he stepped back and looked at her. "That was nice," he murmured.

She could see that the dance had affected him as it had her. "Yes," she whispered.

"Come on, I'd better pay my respects to Terry Wakefield. Then we can get out of here."

She felt a thrill of anticipation. "That sounds good," she said. They grabbed more champagne as they made their way across the tent.

Wakefield was holding court at the far side of the marquee. A dozen people gathered around to congratulate him on his success. He spotted Peter approaching and said, "Major Harrison, wonderful to see you again."

Peter stepped forward. "Great to see you, Mr. Wakefield. You remember Cate Spencer, of course."

"Of course," Wakefield replied. "So good to see you, doctor."

"Likewise," she replied. "This is quite the party."

"Well, it's been a long time coming, and we wanted to celebrate."

"Congratulations. It must feel good that despite all the delays and problems, you've made it."

"Yes, I've found there are always those who protest change. It's human nature, I suppose, to be fearful of the new." He looked from Peter to Cate. "I, however, encourage people to go out and try new things. It's the only way to truly live."

"Are you starting construction soon?" Peter asked.

"Immediately," Wakefield said. "I've waited a long time to see this development happen. It's going to be the crown jewel in TDR's portfolio. I strive for excellence in all that I do, and the challenge with this project will be in meeting every one of my exacting standards."

Wakefield launched into his sales pitch. As he talked on about the luxurious homes, exclusive views, and prime location, she could feel Peter tensing. It was unfair that this development was being pushed through, despite the protesters' valid concerns. She thought of Matthew, siding with this billionaire. She drained her glass and grabbed another from a waiter.

Wakefield continued to talk. "Eastview is going to have unparalleled luxury, every amenity. We're going to combine grandeur, privacy, and convenience in one unique spot."

Wakefield began expounding on the golf course, and Cate's gaze wandered. A figure in the crowd caught her eye. Jesus, was Detective Baker here? Who hadn't got an invitation to this thing? He wasn't wearing a tuxedo but a black suit. He was ill at ease, tugging at his tie and looking around anxiously. Maybe he was here for security. She wanted to know if he'd found Molly's phone, but she also remembered Mrs. Johnson's final words to her. What if the grieving mother called the detective to complain about her behavior? Her stomach roiled.

There was no line up at the bar. She gave Peter's hand a squeeze. He looked down and she gestured toward the ladies' room. He smiled and returned to the conversation.

She went straight to the bar. "Two scotches," she ordered, "neat." The bartender served up the order, and she glanced around. Baker had disappeared, and Peter was deep in conversation with Wakefield. She shot the first scotch, grateful for its warmth. She needed to keep her edge at bay and not mess things up with Peter.

She took the other glass and wandered deeper into the crowd. When no one was looking she swallowed the second glass. That felt better. She sagged against a tall cocktail table. In a few more minutes, she and Peter would leave. She'd invite him home. Or better yet, maybe they'd go to his place. Away from her old life, into the new.

Her shoulders unknotted, and she relaxed into the scotch's force. Already the sting of her conversation with Mrs. Johnson was blurring. She heard a familiar voice and looked up. Clifford Bernard was a couple of feet away talking to Gerald MacIntyre, Rose's befuddled boss from the Archives. He was staring right at her.

She smiled and waved wanly before pushing away. Had he seen her shooting that scotch? The edges of the room had a dull haziness, and the scotch had numbed her nicely. When was the last time she had eaten something? Probably breakfast, before she'd read the article about Jason. She stumbled a bit on her heels, looking for Peter.

Sylvester Williams loomed into view. She didn't want to talk to him. She wanted Peter. Every man looked the same in their uniforms of black tie.

"Lovely party, isn't it?" he said.

He was such a douche that even this innocuous observation sounded patronizing. Much as she wanted to flee, she was going to have to make conversation. "Yup. Why are you here?" Her words were blunter than intended, and she realized that the second scotch was a mistake. She felt queasy.

Williams shrugged. "I like to keep a diversified portfolio, so I invested ten years ago when the project was first bruited about. This party is Wakefield's thank-you to some of his more, uh, substantial supporters."

Williams smiled at her, and she could tell, even through her scotch haze, that he wanted her to ask how much he had invested. She would rather be eaten by wild dogs. Instead, she tried to cut him down to size. "Lots of people have invested in TDR."

Williams chuckled. "Not to the tune of a half mil, I don't think."

Cate kept her face blank. There was no way she was going to give Williams the pleasure of seeing her surprise. "That's quite a chunk of change." She'd been going for cuttingly dismissive, but her words came out slurred. The last thing she needed was sharp-eyed Williams noticing that she was drunk. "Excuse me," she said. "I have to get some air."

Williams looked surprised as she turned and headed toward what she hoped was the door.

The tent was stifling, and Cate was sweating as she pushed her way through the crowd, which seemed to have gotten bigger and more difficult to navigate. Again, the feeling that she was going to be sick arose, this time more insistent. Faces blurred in front of her, bodies pressed against her making her feel trapped. Where was the entrance? She couldn't breathe. She looked up and caught someone's eye. A large man was looking at her. Was it the same person who had stared at her in the ByWard Market? She couldn't really tell—she hadn't got a good look at him the other day. Still, there was something about the way he was evaluating her with an icy dispatch. In a panic, she shoved the woman in front of her out of the way and stumbled herself, tripped up on her heels. They both fell, bringing a waiter's tray of empty champagne glasses with them. Everyone around them stopped and stared.

CHAPTER TWENTY-SIX

CATE'S HAIR HAD COME UNDONE AND HUNG LANKLY AROUND HER SHOUL-
ders. She sat up amid shattered glass. The woman she had pulled down
with her was already on her feet, glaring at Cate. Someone tittered,
but worse was the silence as half the party stared at her in pitying dis-
may. She felt nauseous and wasn't sure if she could manage to stand
without help, but no one came forward. She felt a sob, or perhaps it
was vomit, welling in her throat. Then a sure hand extended out to
her. She grabbed it and was pulled roughly to her feet.

It was Baker.

The crowd parted as he drew her toward a side entrance. His hand
squeezed hers. She struggled to keep up with his steps. "You're hurting
me," she said.

"You're drunk and making an idiot of yourself."

"An idiot?" Her defensiveness was automatic. They were at the
door of the tent now, the fresh air a welcome relief.

"What would you call it?"

She opened her mouth to speak but instead found herself swaying.
Baker held her up, and she put her hand on his shoulder to steady
herself. "When's the last time you ate?" he asked roughly.

"This morning?" she said.

Baker sighed and flagged a passing waiter holding a tray of can-
apés. He took a handful and waved the startled server away. "Eat
these," he ordered.

Cate looked with doubt at the smoked-salmon-smeared crackers.
"I might be sick," she said.

"You definitely will be if you don't eat," retorted Baker.

She dutifully began nibbling the edge of a cracker.

"Now, can you tell me what in the name of fuck happened back there?"

"I saw a man. I think he's been following me."

Quickly she explained about the person who had been staring at her at the ByWard Market. "I think I saw him here. Watching me."

"Do you see him now?"

She looked around the room but there was no sign of the guy. She shook her head.

Baker frowned.

"You don't believe me?" Her voice rose, and a couple of people turned to stare at them.

Baker spoke in lowered tones, drawing her closer to him. "I'm taking this seriously, Cate, but you're coming across more like a drunk paranoid than a reliable witness."

She drew back. "What the hell, Baker—"

Before she could say any more, there was a loud yell. She and Baker turned to the main entranceway. Half a dozen protesters were shoving their way into the party, shouting, "Out of the way, you fascist capitalist!" and "Stop this development."

Baker dropped her hand and headed to the commotion. Turning back to her he said, "Stay put, Cate. I want to talk to you."

She watched as he marched toward the throng, shouting orders to the guards at the door. Other men in suits and women in gowns emerged from the crowd, obviously security.

Cate wasn't going to wait for Baker to come back. She slipped out the side door the caterers were using and made her way through the food prep area. Remembering Baker's advice, she grabbed some little crustless sandwiches and hit the welcome outdoors.

She breathed deeply. It was still hot but better than the tent. That humiliating fall. Had Dr. Marcoux or Peter seen it? Oh God, what if Matthew was there? What about that man who had been watching her?

She shoved those thoughts away. The night was velvety, the stars thick in the sky. She imagined she was a million miles away from the city. Was this what Jason had sought in his far-flung missions? Peace? Starlight?

Something glittered below her, and she realized that the little path in front of her led down to Lake Mitchell. Lake Nigamo—Singing Water. Cate was overcome with a need to hear the waves lapping against its shores, to feel its cool waters on her feet.

She hesitated; the way down was dark, and she'd only have starlight to guide her. On the other hand, Peter, Baker, Dr. Marcoux, and Matthew were behind her. There was no choice. The path was well worn, probably from soldiers' frequent swimming trips. She stumbled only once. She munched the sandwiches as she walked, and her head began to clear.

It was as peaceful as she'd hoped. No one else was here. She wondered if Molly had ever been by the lake after dark. Thoughts of Molly made her remember the earlier phone call with her mother, and she suddenly wished she had grabbed a bottle of something when she left the tent. Her buzz had deserted her, and she was sad. The dim sounds of the party filtered down, a plaintive backdrop. She sat on a big boulder by the lake's edge.

The water lapped gently against the shore. Moonlight danced on the surface. Bernard had said some of his people thought the lake was sacred. She could readily believe that this spot was enchanted. Trees rustled in the breeze. A branch snapped behind her. She shifted. That sounded like a footfall. She turned and peered up the path. No one. But there was a scraggly wood on the south side of the trail. It was hard to see in the shadows. The frogs stopped singing, and the night was deeply, thickly silent.

"Hello?" she called.

Nothing.

Heart pounding, she stood. She'd taken only two steps toward the path when a figure loomed out from the dark. She screamed, but a rough hand shoved her onto the rocky ground. The air hissed from her chest. She scrambled back, but the man flipped her onto her stomach, straddling her before she could get away. His body pressed into her lower back. He clamped a gloved hand over her mouth.

"Shut the fuck up," he whispered.

She bit frantically at his hand, but the leather glove protected him.

"I'm not going to hurt you," he said. He leaned down, his breath hot and warm against her ear. She didn't recognize his voice, but he had a light accent she couldn't place. "I'm here with a message. Stop asking all the fucking questions, got it?" Cate's heart pounded in her ears, and she barely heard his words. Could she twist away and run? If she heaved herself up, could she dislodge him? The man wrapped his thick arm around her neck, and Cate grunted in panic. She was aware of precisely how much pressure he would need to apply in order to crush her windpipe. She dared not turn her head, but she moaned and tried to twist out. He was too heavy to unseat. The man leaned down. "If you don't back off, I'll fucking hurt you, understood?"

She moaned.

"Stop asking questions. Go back to your life. Understood?"

Again, Cate could do nothing but whimper.

He stood up, and she nearly sobbed with relief. She lay on the ground, her bones evaporated. "I'm going to be watching you," he said and disappeared into the wood.

A convulsive gasp gurgled up her throat. She swallowed the sweet, fresh air, her body shuddering. She scrambled to her feet, disoriented. Where had the attacker gone? Which way to safety? She found the path and ran up toward the party. She had to get out of this darkness.

CHAPTER TWENTY-SEVEN

CATE STAGGERED ONTO THE TRAIL WHEN ANOTHER LARGE FIGURE LOOMED in front of her. She screamed.

"Shh, Cate, it's me."

Matthew. She laughed, a hysterical guffaw, causing him to take a step toward her. "Are you OK? I came to find you and bring you back to the party."

She thought of the heat of the tent, the lights, everyone turning to stare at her. "I can't go back to that."

"What happened? Are you OK?" His handsome face creased in concern.

She was going to bluff her way out, insist she was fine. She didn't have to go back into the tent. She'd get an Uber. Instead, the hysterical laugh bubbled up again. "What do you think?"

"Come on," he said decisively. Matthew was always good in a crisis. He took her hand and led her down the path.

"Not to the woods." She couldn't go back in there.

They walked to the lake and found a flat dry area further along from where Cate had been. Others had obviously used the spot in the past, because it was dotted with beer bottles.

"You're upset," he observed. "Frightened." Matthew knew her better than anyone. There was comfort in that.

"I went down to the lake to get some air. Someone grabbed me. Scared me."

Matthew took her hand. "Did he hurt you, Cate?"

She wasn't injured, and she was grateful for that. A sob rose in her throat, but she concentrated on the sound of the water lapping the shore. Breathe in. Breathe out. "No, he just, just threatened me."

"Threatened you? About what?"

Cate paused again. She was feeling vulnerable, but this was Matthew. She couldn't trust him. "I don't know. It must have been some drunk asshole who likes to scare women."

"Someone from the party?"

Cate hadn't got a good look at him, but it must be the same guy. "Maybe" she said.

"Jesus, we need to inform the police. We can't have some crazy person wandering around."

Cate shook her head. Given her recent behavior, it would confirm Baker's opinion that she was a paranoid drunk. She wouldn't give him that kind of ammunition. She needed to find Peter and go home.

There was a silence. She could see that Matthew was annoyed by her refusal.

He spoke. "OK, I don't agree, but it's your call."

The adrenaline still coursed through her veins, and it made her edgy and reckless. "What, don't you want to bully me into your point of view, the way you used to?"

"I don't want to bully you, Cate. It's the opposite—I want to be your friend." He hesitated. "Maybe more."

She shook her head. "Leaving aside the fact that you're the last person I need in my life right now, what would your wife think about that statement?"

"Tansy and I aren't happy."

What was she supposed to do with that information?

Matthew broke the silence. "We haven't been happy for a long time, but neither of us was ready to admit it." He spoke in a rush, almost as if against his better judgment. "Seeing you again has changed that. Even if nothing happens between you and me, it's over with Tansy."

Cate's back stiffened, and she felt a rush of jumbled emotions. "Jesus, Matthew. Listen to yourself. The last time we spent any significant time together we were surrounded by divorce lawyers. You think the things that broke us apart are gone? We're the same goddamn people, just older."

"That's not true, Cate. At least not for me. I've changed. After our divorce, I saw someone . . ."

She cut him off. "I'm sure you dated lots of women, Matthew. You were always charming, at first."

Matthew groaned. "I've been trying to tell you, Cate, I've changed. I'm not the man you married."

"You're not the man who pounded his fist into the wall when we fought?" Her voice cracked, memories merging with what had just happened in the woods. "The man who grabbed my arm so tightly it left bruises? Who shoved me against the wall?"

Matthew closed his eyes. "Those last six months of our relationship were hell. We were so unhappy, and I didn't know how to express my anger. I'm sorry."

Cate barely heard his apology. "They were hell? You weren't the one getting screamed at. Getting shoved. You weren't the one who went down that flight of stairs."

"I didn't push you, Cate. You know that."

She paused. "Yeah, I know, but I wouldn't have fallen if you hadn't been shaking me."

"Or if you were sober." He spoke the words matter-of-factly.

She drew in her breath. Those last months of marriage—Matthew was working crazy hours, she was nursing her fledgling practice, and they were trying to get pregnant, without any success. She'd taken to having a bottle of wine while she waited for him to come home at night. He'd taken to screaming at her the moment he walked in the door.

That night she'd given up waiting for him and gone to bed. She hadn't slept, though. She lay in the dark, sipping wine, fuming at his lack of commitment, pushing on the bruises on her arm where he'd grabbed her the night before.

When he arrived home, she'd been on the attack, but so had he. He said he would sleep on the couch; she followed him to the top of the stairs. He punched the wall by the side of her head, and some wild part of her had welcomed the violence. She mocked him, told him he was like his father. He shook her and she broke free, but misjudged the space between him and the stairs. She plunged down the whole flight and lay crumpled at the bottom. An ambulance ride to the hospital and she was diagnosed with a mild concussion and a broken wrist. Along with other devastating news.

"I miscarried that night." Her voice was toneless.

"What?" Matthew's voice was bewildered.

She couldn't look at him. "I was pregnant—first trimester."

"Cate, oh my God. I didn't know."

"I didn't know myself. Some doctor." She laughed. "I've thought about it a lot since. If I had known, maybe we wouldn't have fought."

"Jesus, Cate, is that why you didn't come home? Why you ended it then and there?"

She cleared her throat. "In addition to the miscarriage, the fall caused other issues. Permanent ones. I can't have children. I'm barren." Barren, a desolate word. That's what she had felt since that night. An empty, whistling wasteland.

She made eye contact with Matthew. The color drained from his face. "Jesus."

"I didn't want to see you anymore. To be reminded of what I, what we, lost. We weren't good anymore, anyway. What was the point?"

Matthew opened his arms and pulled her to him. It felt so natural to curl up in his arms. The woods were quiet, and she leaned against his chest, hearing the steady rhythm of his heart. The scent of him. A sob welled up, and she wept into his dinner jacket. He held her and let her cry. When she was done, she sniffled, found a cocktail napkin in her purse, and blew her nose. She settled back into his arms again, all the tension gone from her body. She felt lethargic and sleepy, lacking the energy to move.

"I went to therapy, you know," he said. His voice was a low, soothing rumble against her ear. "Seeing you fall down those stairs made me realize how messed up I had become. How messed up my attitudes were. I went to anger management and spent a year paying a very nice lady a huge amount of money to listen to me talk about my lousy childhood."

Cate pushed away from him, staring into his eyes. Matthew Tomkins seeking therapy? It crossed her mind that he might be lying, but she saw the truth in his face.

"I didn't want to turn into my father, Cate. He was a violent bastard."

"Oh, Matthew." She couldn't imagine what it would have taken this proud, closed man to open up and reveal his failings.

He continued to speak, talking more to himself. "I did all the right things. I went to therapy, worked on my issues. I met a nice girl. We got married. I thought I had put us behind me. I thought I could be happy, but I haven't been."

He leaned back and looked down at Cate. "I am so sorry for what happened at the end of our marriage, Cate. For hurting you. For that lost baby."

He bent down toward her. His mouth brushed hers. It was an invitation, light, fleeting. She looked into his eyes and saw the young man she had married. The person she had laughed with and loved with for so many years.

"Cate," he whispered.

She loved the sound of her name on his lips, and she tilted her head up, returning the kiss and deepening it. She didn't want to think about the case, the man who had attacked her, or Matthew's wife. She wanted this. She needed it. It had been too long. She reached up and touched his chest, and it was all the invitation he needed.

He pulled her closer. Somehow, they found themselves on the soft grass, Matthew touching her in all the old familiar ways, but with a tenderness that was lost to them for a long while. "I've been fantasizing about this since I saw you at the police station, Cate."

"Me too," she admitted.

They made love under the stars, reconnecting, learning each other's new scars, new pleasures. They were gentle in a way that they hadn't been since they had first gotten together. By the end of their relationship, sex had become about power. It was exciting, but ferocious. This time, it was almost sweet. When it was over, they lay side by side, staring up at the stars. In front of them, the moonlight was a shimmer of silver over the inky black of the lake.

After what seemed like an eternity, Matthew spoke, his voice deep and strong. "I'll have to get going. I need to talk to Tansy."

His words jolted Cate from her dreamy state. She sat up and jerked her dress down across her thighs. "Your wife."

Matthew sat up and reached for her hand. She pulled it away and stood, adjusting her dress, looking for her shoes. He tugged on his pants.

"Yes, I need to tell her what's happened. End it."

Cate stared at him. "Don't do that." This was happening too fast.

"Why not, Cate? It's obvious we still care about each other."

"I need time to think. To sort things out." She felt pushed, cornered. "I'm not ready." She stood and took a few paces away from him, toward the path.

"Cate, we've wasted five years. I've never stopped loving you. We need to make this real. Commit to it."

She shook her head. It was as if he was stifling her, choking her. She backed further away. "No, Matthew. I'm not ready. Listen to me. Listen to what I need."

He reached for her hand. "I know you, Cate, you're self-destructive. You'll find a way to sabotage this. I won't let you."

Anger, that's what she needed. She grabbed it. "Won't let me? In case you forgot, your need for control caused our problems in the first place."

Matthew laughed. "You weren't exactly an innocent victim. I'd come home most nights, and you'd be soused." His nostrils flared. He was pissed off now. Good. "That little display you put on tonight shows that you don't have your drinking under control."

The shame of his statement fueled her anger. "Well, screw you, Matthew. I don't need you coming into my life after five years, judging me and questioning my choices." She could leave him now, divest herself of this messiness. How could she have screwed him? What was she thinking? "You're the married man, Matthew. A married man who cheated on his wife. Go have your midlife crisis with someone else. God, you're such a goddamn cliché."

"You don't mean that, Cate. You're upset because of Jason—"

"Jason?" she interrupted him. "What does he have to do with anything?"

"You're obviously grieving, angry—"

"Angry," she interrupted again. "I'm not angry that Jason died. I'm angry that you're using me to work out your own problems."

"Cate." His tone was warm and caring, and her rage grew. "Jason has died and left you all alone. Of course you're upset and angry he's gone."

Her heart pounded in her ears, and Cate's vision was blurring with fury. In her rage, she couldn't think of any response, beyond, "Fuck you, Matthew. And leave me the fuck alone." She didn't wait around, storming off through the woods. She wasn't worried about her assailant now. Matthew didn't come after her. She ordered the Uber as she walked and waited for it in the tent's shadows. The music was louder and the party more raucous. The protesters hadn't disrupted the event. Wakefield would be pleased about the successful launch of his project.

She texted Peter to apologize for ditching him. Her fall was probably hot gossip at the party, and if he hadn't witnessed it himself, Peter had undoubtedly heard about it. He would be glad she'd left without embarrassing him further. It was better this way.

HER FATHER WAS WATERING SOME FRESHLY PLANTED IMPATIENS WITH A garden hose. Cate stepped gingerly from the car. Her back ached from her assailant kneeling on her, and she had twisted her knee at some point last night. She'd awoken this morning from a fitful sleep filled with nightmares and had lain in bed paralyzed with anxiety as she remembered the attack. Only guilt about her father got her out of bed. Mrs. Cho said he was wandering.

Dr. Marcus Spencer glanced up at Cate's arrival and returned to watering. He was wearing old jeans and a stained T-shirt she'd never seen before. He was barefoot.

"A little late in the season to be planting those," she said.

"What's that?" he grunted. "What you know about gardening would fit into a flowerpot."

She held up her hands, relieved to see he was back to his usual crusty self. Maybe Mrs. Cho's concerns were overblown. "I thought I'd drop by to see how you were doing."

"I'm fine. Fine. The summer's been too dry."

"Beautiful sunny days, though," she remarked. They were like skaters, skimming across the frozen surface of their relationship, whizzing along on blades made of small talk.

Her phone beeped, but she didn't read the text, instead turning it off completely. There were six text messages and four voice mails waiting for her this morning. Mostly from Peter. She couldn't face talking to him. She owed him some sort of explanation, but what could she possibly say? On their first date, she had literally fallen down drunk, slept with someone else, and abandoned him. Instead, she had texted him again to tell him she was sorry to have left so abruptly and to confirm she was OK. She deleted the voice mail from Matthew without listening to it.

Her father turned and knelt to empty out another flat of impatiens, carefully shaking a small flower loose from the container. Its long roots had grown out of the hole in the plastic and wouldn't untangle easily. He cursed and threw it down in frustration.

Cate took a surprised step back.

"What do you want?" he snarled. "You look at me with those big, scared eyes. It makes me want to smack you."

Cate blinked. This was the closest they'd ever come to acknowledging what had gone on in her childhood. Growing up, her father's anger was constant and fearsome. While she was never severely beaten—not injured enough to draw blood or break a bone—she knew what it was like to be smacked, locked in a closet, or sent to her room without lunch or dinner. That feeling of being at the mercy of someone bigger, stronger, and more unreasonable was a constant until she was sent to the safety of boarding school.

Terror and helplessness, just like she felt last night when an attacker held her life in his hands. For a moment she was speechless. "Daddy, I—"

"Why are you here, anyway?" he asked.

He was covered in dirt, she noticed. It was smeared on his hands and his face. It was in his hair and all over his T-shirt. She looked more closely. It was an AC/DC T-shirt. One of Jason's old ones.

"Daddy," she started again, unsure what to do, what to say.

"Daddy," he mimicked. "What do you want? Where's your brother? You usually don't slink up here without him for protection. Where's Jason?" He stared behind her, as if expecting him to get out of the car. Despite herself, Cate turned and stared too, for one insane instant hoping to see him grinning in the sunshine.

Sadness pressed down on her. Sadness for Jason, sadness for her father, sadness for her own small, scared childhood self. She needed to take care of her father now, but without Jason, she wasn't sure she could.

The attacker had wanted her scared and defeated. He'd wanted her to feel small and helpless. She was sick of feeling that way. She spoke quietly. "Jason's dead, Daddy. I talked to the Canadian embassy in Kinshasa. They're working on returning his remains. We'll lay him to rest here, in Canada."

"That's good work."

Bolstered by this praise, she found herself asking, "Daddy, why were you so tough on Jason and me?"

He straightened his spine and for a moment she glimpsed the father of her youth, for good or ill. "I didn't mollycoddle you like your mother would have. In my day, children were punished for bad behavior. I raised you to know right from wrong and to learn from your mistakes."

He really had thought he was doing them a favor by being so stern and unyielding. Had his actions come from some messed-up place of love? She straightened her shoulders, mimicking his gesture. Her childhood was over, her father was a weak old man, and she wasn't going to let some maniac in the woods make her feel powerless. Screw that. Her assailant warned her off investigating the case, which meant there was a case to investigate. She was on the right track.

Her father allowed her to lead him back into the house and coax him into a change of clothes. She made him an omelet and tidied up as he ate. The house seemed secure, and her father assured her several times that he still used the alarm when he left home and at night. She called the alarm company and added her name to the alert list. It wasn't much, but at the moment, it was what she could do.

Her mind turned back to the assault, and she no longer shied away from thinking about it. If her assailant thought that he could scare her, he obviously didn't know how her childhood had honed her for this moment and how much of her own tough, strong-willed father she had in her.

CHAPTER TWENTY-NINE

SIMON THATCHER'S FAMILY HOME WAS IN THE GLEBE, A WEALTHY EN-
clave south of the downtown core. The house, a red-bricked, ivy-clad
monster, overlooked Patterson's Creek, a prime entry point for anyone interested in skating the length of the Rideau Canal. Cate rang
the doorbell. A Mercedes convertible gleamed in the driveway, the
flowerbeds were planted in rigid rows, and the front lawn was a rich,
deep green that no dandelion would dare to spoil. Her father would
approve.

A tall, slim woman in her fifties opened the door. Her brown hair
was cut in a bob and highlighted with blonde streaks. She wore a ten-
nis dress and held a racket in her hand.

"Mrs. Thatcher?" Cate asked.

The woman looked Cate up and down, taking in her messy ponytail and wrinkled linen pants. "Yes?"

Cate flipped out her badge. "I'm Dr. Cate Spencer, Ottawa coroner's office."

Her hauteur vanished, and Mrs. Thatcher gasped. "Simon—is
he . . ."

"No, nothing like that," Cate rushed to reassure her. "I need to
speak to him about an outstanding case."

Mrs. Thatcher glanced down the quiet street. "You'd better come in."

They stood in an immaculate entranceway. A crystal chandelier
overhead and hardwood floor underfoot.

"Simon isn't here?" Cate confirmed.

Mrs. Thatcher shook her head. "I don't know where he is." She
crossed her arms. "He hasn't caused an accident, has he?"

"No, no," Cate said. She shifted her weight. It was awkward standing in the hallway, but it was obvious she wouldn't be invited further into the house. "There was a suicide last Monday. I wanted to question Simon about the death."

Mrs. Thatcher's mouth pursed. "Oh, yes, we had to bail him out. He was caught trespassing. We'd been asking him to stay away from that Eastview protest for weeks. It's all fine and good when he wants to chain himself to railings in Montreal over tuition hikes, but we know the Wakefields socially." She smiled wryly. "It gets awkward when your child is marching around calling someone from your husband's investment group a Dirty Capitalist Rat Bastard. I mean, they're golf buddies!"

Cate found herself warming to the woman. "I can see how that would be embarrassing."

Mrs. Thatcher shrugged. "I can't stay angry with Simon. He's such a gentle, sweet boy."

Cate recalled the angry young man fighting against police custody.

Mrs. Thatcher continued, "His father is a different story, however. I'm afraid Malcolm doesn't understand Simon. I tell him that Simon will settle down in due course, but Malcolm doesn't have a lot of patience."

"That must be difficult."

Mrs. Thatcher wrinkled her forehead. "I'm sorry, but this has been bothering me since I answered the door. Have we met before?"

"I don't think so."

The other woman paused. "You look so familiar to me. Were you at the TDR party last night?"

Of course the Thatchers would have been there. Had they witnessed her humiliating fall? "No, I don't think so," Cate lied.

"It's strange, you look remarkably like a woman who—well, never mind." Mrs. Thatcher shook her head.

Cate's heart pounded, but she smiled wanly and returned to safer subjects. "Where do you think Simon is now?"

"I'm not sure. He and his father had a big blowup after his arrest. Simon stormed out, and we haven't seen him since."

"Has he contacted you?"

"No. Usually when he and his father argue, Simon gets in touch so I can give him the all- clear. I haven't heard a peep from him this time, though."

"Oh?"

"He probably met some girl. Women gravitate to him, you know. They sense that innate sweetness."

"Right," Cate said.

"Well, if that's everything," Mrs. Thatcher said, indicating the door.

Cate turned to go but stopped and scribbled her name and number on a piece of paper. "If you hear from Simon, can you ask him to contact me? I've left him several messages."

Mrs. Thatcher opened the door, and Cate headed to her car.

"Dr. Spencer."

Cate turned.

Mrs. Thatcher stood in the doorway and glanced up and down the street. She twisted her hands together. "If you find Simon, can you ask him to call his mother?"

"Of course," Cate said. She watched as the other woman closed the door. Mrs. Thatcher may not have wanted to admit it, but she was worried about her son. The question was, did she think something had happened to him, or did she know what he was capable of?

CHAPTER THIRTY

SINCE SIMON'S HOUSE WAS A BUST, CATE DECIDED TO CANVASS THE protesters to see if they could shed any light on his whereabouts. Only when she pulled off Turcotte Road did she realize how close she was to the scene of last night's attack. Lake Mitchell was less than a kilometer away. She took a deep breath and parked the car on the verge.

The protesters were back on their usual spot beside the road. Obviously, the official land transfer to TDR hadn't made them give up the fight. The humidity had lifted, and the sun was shining in a cloudless sky. When she stepped out of the car, she took a moment to enjoy the warm air on her skin. It was a perfect summer day, the kind that made you long for a pitcher of sangria and a patio.

If you blocked out the traffic and the disheveled group of protesters, it was a pastoral scene. The green field stretched out to a stand of trees, thrusting tall and straight. The dark evergreens contrasted nicely with the deep blue sky. Behind the trees would be more fields, then the nitrate facility leaning against the Eastview fence. From there, the ground would rise up the hill and then dip down to Lake Mitchell.

The small group of protesters held signs above their heads, and the occasional passing car honked—either in support or disdain, it was hard to say. She walked over. "Hello," she shouted above the traffic.

The group turned as one, staring at her warily. She was reminded of a herd of cattle.

"What do you want?" A tall, skinny guy with long blond dreadlocks stepped forward. Now that she was closer, she saw there were more of them than she first supposed. The ground dipped slightly from the road where the protesters were standing. Below that, another dozen people sat in lawn chairs, shaded by big beach umbrellas. Lazy reggae drifted from a laptop, and the air smelled of marijuana. Cate was struck by how young almost everyone was. They didn't bear much resemblance to the angry, mobilized group who stormed the party last night.

"I'm looking for Simon Thatcher," she said to the man.

"Are you a reporter? Last night's invasion of the TDR event was done by rogue elements. It wasn't sanctioned by our leadership."

She shook her head, pulling out her badge. "I'm the coroner investigating last Monday's death at the nitrate facility."

A woman, about twenty, put down her sign, which read "Stop TDR before our environment is DOA," and came forward. "What happened to Molly?" She had a narrow, intelligent face and cat's-eye sunglasses.

"Did you know Miss Johnson?" Cate asked her.

"We all did. She brought us coffee when she was working at the facility. She was cool."

"Was she friendly with anyone in particular?" Cate asked. "Simon Thatcher, maybe?"

The tall man spoke. "Don't tell her anything, Trinity. She's a cop."

"I'm a coroner. I don't work for the police. I'm charged with determining Miss Johnson's manner of death."

"We heard she'd killed herself," Trinity said.

The man with the dreadlocks looked interested.

Cate nodded. "It appears to be suicide."

"Why do you need to talk to Simon, then?" the man asked.

Cate wasn't really sure, but it bothered her that he had disappeared. "He was on the scene shortly after her death. He might have spoken to her beforehand, enough to have had a sense of her state of mind."

"That's bull," the dreads guy said.

"Don't be a jerk, Derek," Trinity chided him.

"Seriously, she wants to pin those bullshit vandalism and arson charges on Simon," he said. "She's in TDR's pocket."

There was something immensely irritating about Derek. Cate spoke quietly. "I couldn't give a flying fuck whether it was Big Bird or the Queen who threw that cherry bomb. All I want to do is complete my report on Molly Johnson's manner of death. I can't do that, though, until I talk to Simon."

Derek's face turned a deep red, and he stepped forward. "Listen, lady, with all the bullshit going on these days there's no way we're going to trust you. You could be setting us up, just like they did to Liam."

"Who's Liam?" Cate asked.

Derek snorted. "Liam Westin? The guy who devoted years to environmental action, only to get arrested on trumped-up kiddy porn charges. They framed him."

Cate recalled the news story she'd seen at her father's place Tuesday. "And who's 'they'?"

Derek opened his hands expansively. "Take your pick. We're talking a billion dollars on the line. People in this town are getting desperate to see a return on their investment."

"Yes, but who specifically might want to frame Mr. Westin?" she asked.

"The government, TDR, the Air Force. You should have seen the kind of bullshit the FBI and the private security firms pulled at Standing Rock for the Dakota Access Pipeline. I wouldn't be surprised if the CIA or CSIS was involved."

Cate didn't have time for conspiracy theories. Instead, she glimpsed a spot of yellow among the trees. A group of tents was pitched there. "Are you all camping here?" Cate interrupted.

"Yeah, for the last couple of weeks," Trinity said.

Derek interjected again. "We're on the site at all times, registering our condemnation of this project."

"What are you condemning, exactly?"

"The rape of the earth, the disregard of a protected marshy habitat housing two rare species of birds and the northern cricket frog. Lake Mitchell is one of the deepest lakes in Eastern Ontario, yet no one has ever cataloged its biodiversity. The federal, provincial, and municipal governments refuse to protect this land." Despite her dislike, she admired Derek's passion.

Trinity chimed in. "Yeah, and all to build homes for some of the city's richest people. We don't need another nine-hole golf course and gated community. What about putting up low-income housing? Creating a co-op garden? A women's shelter? A clean needle exchange? We could establish solar power as the primary energy source, make this a model of social equality and green energy."

Cate blinked. She could almost hear Matthew laughing at this group. He'd never had much patience for social activism, not understanding why people would put themselves out for any cause that didn't directly benefit them. When they were married, that cynicism was one more point of contention between them. Since she'd left, she realized she'd adopted his attitude.

A chubby older woman who had been listening came forward. "These lands belong to the Anishinabeg, the Algonquin. Lake Nigamo is a sacred space. The entire base is part of the land claim my people have brought against the provincial and federal governments."

Cate recalled her conversation with Clifford Bernard as the woman continued to speak. "By rights, the Ottawa and Mattawa watersheds belong to us."

Derek shifted impatiently. "Come on, Annie. That's ancient history now. I mean, what kind of guarantees of environmental stewardship would you people give? No offense, but who's to say you'd be better than TDR? The last thing we need here is a casino."

Annie shot him a withering look. "These lands hold sacred meaning to my people. Obviously, we'd build two casinos, a gas station, and a place to buy duty-free smokes."

Cate laughed, but Derek didn't seem to register the sarcasm. "It's essential that we stop any development before it begins," he said. "We've got to think of the northern cricket frog."

Trinity spoke. "No, what's essential is that we present a united front. If they see us battling each other, we'll never stop this development."

The other two nodded, and Annie stepped away, picking up her sign, which Cate noted was hung with dream catchers. "Our Land. Justice for the Algonquin," it read.

"This has been very educational," Cate said.

Derek made prayer hands. "It's important to keep dialoguing."

"I actually came to talk to Simon Thatcher," she reminded them. "Do you know where he is?"

Trinity shook her head. "We haven't seen him in a few days. He'll be back, though. His tent is still here."

Derek glared at her, but Trinity merely shrugged. "She's a doctor . . . not the cops."

"Well, thank you both," Cate said and began walking toward the tents.

"Hey," Derek called. "Where are you going? That's our space."

Cate stopped. "As far as I can tell, this isn't your land, so you've got no right to stop me." She looked him in the eye. "If you try, maybe I'll call those police you think I'm so friendly with. A squad car will be here in five minutes." She had no idea if this was true. "Something tells me you'd prefer it was just me looking at Simon's tent, as opposed to half the Ottawa PD." She held his gaze.

Eventually he dropped his eyes and muttered, "I knew you were a stooge. Just look at Thatcher's and leave our stuff alone. He's got the yellow one."

CHAPTER THIRTY-ONE

CATE PICKED HER WAY ACROSS THE FIELD TO THE SHELTER OF THE trees. Six tents were arranged in a circle around a campfire. Wood, obviously purchased from somewhere else, was stacked up beside the slightly smoking firepit. A laundry line with sloganned T-shirts, bandannas, and a worn-looking pair of army pants fluttered in the wind. A small generator, currently off, explained how the protesters could power their all-important laptops and cell phones.

The yellow tent was a good-quality four-man from Mountain Equipment Co-Op. She undid the flap and crawled in. The musty warm smell of camping took her back to the summer of third grade when she and Jason, home for two months, had pitched a tent in the backyard. They spent every day holed up in there with comic books and purloined snacks.

Trinity was right; it did seem like Simon would be coming back. The tent was filled with his things: a backpack bursting with clothes, a pack of cards on the ground beside the air mattress, his phone charger sitting in one corner next to an expensive camera. Looking at all these items intensified Cate's uneasiness. Why would Simon have left his stuff for almost a week? Surely, his disappearance and Molly's death were connected. She hesitated for a moment. She had no legal right to search this tent, but that unsettled feeling persisted. If she found a clue to Thatcher's location, she could at least find him and talk to him.

She started with the camera, but the battery was dead. Next, she dumped the contents of the backpack on the tent floor: a pair of jeans, a couple of T-shirts, a ripped pair of cargo shorts. No wallet, no secret diary, nothing of any use. She was stuffing the clothes back into the pack when she thought to check the pockets. She felt around the back pocket of his shorts and came across something. Her heart rate quickened, but it was only a lighter.

She lifted up the mattress, but there was nothing underneath. She checked the hiking boots by the tent door. Nothing in them either.

A jean jacket lay crumpled on the floor. She picked it up and shook it out. It was the same jacket he'd been wearing the day they'd found Molly's body. It was covered in pins with political slogans and one cartoon monkey. This at least proved that he had returned to the tent after being questioned by Baker. The pockets were empty.

She looked around in frustration. There must be some clue to his whereabouts, but the tent held nothing but standard camping gear, mattress, flashlight, backpack.

Something was missing. Where was Simon's sleeping bag? July days were hot, but nights could still get cool. Was it rolled up in a corner?

She didn't locate it, but she hit the jackpot when she found a small wooden box tucked under a pair of beat-up rubber boots. It was deliberately hidden away, and must contain something useful. She sat on the mattress to open it. It was filled with rolling papers and crushed green leaves. A pack of matches and one neatly rolled joint lay on top. She pinched some leaves between her fingers and took a sniff. Marijuana.

Soft footsteps fell outside, and her heart pounded in her ears. She was isolated here, too far from the protest for her cries to be heard. She shoved the box into her purse and stood, squaring her shoulders to face the entrance. A head poked through the tent flap.

An older man, perhaps sixty, looked in. "Just who the hell are you?" he asked.

"I'm Dr. Spencer, Ottawa coroner. I'm investigating the death of Molly Johnson."

The man frowned, drawing his enormous black eyebrows together. "What are you doing in my tent?"

"I thought this was Simon Thatcher's." She came forward, ducking under the entrance to stand in the clearing. She couldn't see the protesters from here.

"I'm his father," the older man barked.

She did a double take. Malcolm Thatcher did not fit her vision of a well-dressed and powerful businessman. He certainly didn't look like the husband of the immaculate Mrs. Thatcher. He was dressed in ill-fitting jeans and a loose T-shirt. His hair was messy and his eyes slightly glazed.

"Simon is your son?" she asked, with doubt.

The man drew himself up taller. "Yes, and I'd like to see some proof of identification, Dr. Spencer."

She showed him her badge.

He gave it a cursory glance. "We haven't seen the boy in a while, so I've come to collect his things."

"Of course," Cate said. "Do you know where he might be?"

Mr. Thatcher ducked into the tent. "I have no idea." He packed up the camera and the phone charger, stuffing them into the backpack.

"Aren't you concerned about him?" She peered in at him.

"I have better things to worry about. Now if you'll excuse me." He pushed past her and began walking across the field in the opposite direction from the protesters.

"Aren't you going to take his tent?" she called after him.

Mr. Thatcher didn't even bother to turn around. "Don't need it."

Cate stared after him for a moment, then walked back to the protesters.

"Did you find anything useful?" Trinity asked as she approached.

Cate shook her head. "No. You really don't have any idea where Simon might be?"

"Have you checked with his folks? We assumed he went back home."

"I just met his father. He said they hadn't seen him."

Trinity stared at her, wide-eyed. "Simon's dad is here?"

"Yeah." Cate explained about meeting Mr. Thatcher at the tent. By the time she'd finished, Derek was also listening.

"You just let him walk off with the camera?" Derek asked.

"Sure," Cate said. "Why not?"

Derek stared at her in disbelief. "Simon Thatcher's father is a fascist prick who would never set foot here. The guy you saw is the unhoused dude who lurks around spying on us. He stole Simon's stuff."

Cate stared back at the yellow tent as she recalled Terry Wakefield saying he had a spy in the protester camp—a spy who may have just stolen Simon's camera.

CHAPTER THIRTY-TWO

CATE MIGHT NOT HAVE BEEN BRIGHT-EYED AND BUSHY-TAILED FOR Albert's funeral at ten a.m. on Monday, but she wasn't hungover, and that felt good. Although Beechwood Cemetery was next to Rockcliffe Park where Cate grew up, she had never visited. Her mother's grave was in a small cemetery at the Anglican Church in nearby New Edinburgh.

She would have to ask her father about his plans for Jason's remains. They could be interred next to their mother, and there was some comfort in him being laid beside her. Cate's preference would be to scatter his ashes to the wind. Jason's life had burned fiercely and he deserved that same freedom and movement in death.

She'd talked to Brilliant this morning. He thought it was a good sign that the Canadian embassy in Kinshasa was taking an interest. They'd located the funeral home that had done the cremation on Jason's body and were making arrangements. Brilliant was continuing to prod his own contacts to expedite things. He ended the call with a somber note of warning: "I've been thinking about what you told me regarding your visit to the Congolese embassy. They have a history of being overzealous in guarding their country's reputation, so tread lightly if you deal with them in the future." Cate thanked him, but given that they'd literally thrown her out, she doubted she'd hear from them again.

As she drove up the cemetery's drive, she considered yesterday's encounters at the protester encampment. TDR had a substantial investment in the development, as had many wealthy Ottawans.

Molly could have discovered something in her work with the nitrate negatives that would slow down or stop construction. The development had taken so long and been so contentious, any further problems or claims might scuttle the whole thing, potentially bankrupting thousands. That created quite a big motive for murder.

Albert's interment was occurring at the top of the hill. She passed large shade trees and carefully mown lawns. The cemetery was obviously well cared for. Given the shabbiness of the Marier Residence, Cate was surprised that Albert's estate could afford to bury him here. The funeral was easy to spot. Cars and motorcycles were double-parked along the drive. She found a space and followed the crowd. Despite the afternoon heat, several people wore intricately beaded, brightly colored jackets. A few men had long black hair tied back into ponytails. The crowd gathered in a distinct part of the cemetery. Here all the gravestones were the same simple white, lined up in neat rows. A bagpiper, in kilt and military regalia, stood next to a large monument, his mournful wail out of place on the hot, sunny day. A large plaque explained the site: "To the Men and Women of Canada's Armed Forces Who Have Served Their Nation in War and Peace." Cate didn't even know that there was a national burial ground for veterans.

She recalled the nurse at the Marier Residence saying that Albert served in the Second World War.

The piper stopped, and the mourners shuffled toward the casket, which was draped in a Canadian flag. There was no shade in this small area, and the sun was fierce. Cate could feel the sweat pooling in the small of her back.

The Catholic priest's service was brief and impersonal. At the end, he asked if anyone wanted to say a few words.

A short, fat man stepped forward. Clifford Bernard. He dabbed a tear from his cheek with a clumsy hand but spoke with such a practiced ease it made Cate wonder if crying was just part of the act. "I am so pleased to see such a large turnout for this event. Albert Owl was an elder who worked hard for our community. As a young child, he lived on the land with his family, until the settlers took him away. Like so many of us, he was a survivor of the Indian Residential School system."

Many in the crowd nodded.

"Not too many years ago, Albert gave testimony at the Truth and Reconciliation Commission. Head shaved, forbidden to speak his language, undernourished, beaten for any infraction and sometimes just for the priest's pleasure."

Cate thought of Albert's frail elderly body lying in his bed at the Marier Residence and the small, terrified child he had once been.

"Albert survived this. He rediscovered his language. He committed to his people and his truth, and he was a fierce advocate for what he believed. He lived a good long life. We will celebrate that with a sacred fire ceremony later today. His spirit has reunited with the creator."

Bernard bowed to the assembled group and returned to the crowd.

There was a pause. The priest stepped forward. "Does anyone else want to speak?" He barely took a breath. "In that case . . ."

"I'd like to talk," came a reedy voice from the back of the crowd. Everyone turned as an elderly Black man stepped forward. He had thick curly white hair and wore a gray wool suit. He walked slowly, almost bent double over his cane.

He stopped at the front of the crowd and made an effort to stand tall. "I served with Al in the war. We were good pals. Two scrawny eighteen-year-olds trying to impress the ladies with our uniforms." The man had a raspy chuckle. "The war was over before we could get overseas. At the time we were disappointed, but looking back now, I thank the Good Lord we were spared that trip." The man dabbed the sweat from his brow and continued. "Al was damn proud of his service in the military. Damn proud. He was an unwavering soldier and friend. Thank you."

The crowd parted to let the old man pass.

A crush of people made for their cars after the ceremony; a reception was being held at the Native Friendship Center. Cate lingered with the stragglers, waiting for her chance to talk with Bernard. He was surrounded. Bernard greeted everyone warmly and appeared to know them all. He clapped people on the shoulder, laughed, his eyes crinkling with pleasure, or bent his head attentively. He said goodbye to a well-wisher, and she approached before someone else tried to speak with him. "Mr. Bernard," she said.

He turned to her with a smile. "Yes?"

"I'm Dr. Cate Spencer. We met at the TDR party." She prayed he hadn't seen her drunken fall, but if he had, he was too good a politician to mention it.

"Oh yes," he said. "I didn't know you knew Albert."

"I was the coroner called to Mr. Owl's long-term facility at his death." Blatant lie.

Was there a flicker of something behind his eyes? Recognition? Fear?

"Oh yes." He smiled.

"And yourself? Had you known him long?"

"Over thirty years. It's a real loss to our community."

"Speaking of communities . . ." That was an awkward segue. She still wasn't very good at questioning people. "Some people from your community don't seem very happy with the development, yet you were celebrating it at the TDR event."

Bernard's face flushed. "I believe I acknowledged that to you." His tone sharpened. "Exactly what are you implying?"

"I'm not implying anything," she said, holding up her hands. "I only wonder whether you have sympathy with the Algonquin people who don't think the development is cause for celebration."

Bernard leaned toward Cate, grabbing her wrist and whispering, "I promise you I always have the best interest of my people at heart. Always." His grip on her wrist was painful, and she could feel his hot breath on her cheek. She took a step back, knocked off balance by his intensity.

Bernard turned away from her, glad-handing another waiting acolyte.

Shaken by the interchange, she moved away. She had obviously hit a nerve. She shuddered, thinking of her attacker. She was getting tired of aggressive men.

CHAPTER THIRTY-THREE

CATE SCANNED THE REMAINING FUNERAL CROWD. THE OLDER GENTLEMAN who had spoken about Albert sat on a bench in the sun, fanning himself lethargically. Something about his slow movement caught her attention. Cate walked over. "Are you all right, sir?" she asked.

The man looked up, his voice faint. "I don't feel very well."

She assessed him. His breathing was rapid and shallow. His skin had a flushed undertone, no visible sweat. "I'm a doctor. May I take your pulse?"

He nodded, and she did a quick check. His pulse was rapid. "Do you have a headache or nausea?"

His voice was weak. "Both."

"I think you may have heat stroke, sir." She reached into her purse and pulled out a bottle of water. "Please, drink all of this."

He obeyed, taking a long swig.

She looked around the nearly deserted cemetery. "Are you here with anyone?"

He shook his head, still drinking. Heat symptoms could be deadly for someone his age. "You need to get out of the sun and into some place air-conditioned."

"I just want to go home," he said.

"Is your home air-conditioned?"

"Yes," he said weakly.

"Do you have a car here?"

"No," he said. "I came by bus."

The water had helped. His breathing was less shallow, although he still looked flushed. "OK," she said. "I'll drive you home."

"Oh, I couldn't let you do that," he protested.

"It's that, or an ambulance to the emergency room." She stood up and offered him her arm, which he accepted.

"I'm Cate Spencer," she said as they walked toward the car. She was careful to stick to the shade.

"Nice to meet you, doc." They paused for a moment, allowing him to catch his breath. "My name is Isaiah Turner."

They didn't talk again until they reached the car. Cate settled him into the passenger seat and hurried to blast the cool air. He let out a relieved sigh and leaned back, eyes closed.

He gave her his address in Vanier, not very far from the Marier Residence.

They drove in silence for a few minutes, Cate watching him closely for further signs of distress. His breathing was more regular and his color less flushed. Eventually he opened his eyes to remark, "The headache seems to have passed. Quite the heatwave we've been having—day after day of scorchers with not a sign of relief."

"It's true," she agreed. It had last rained the day they'd found Molly's body. "I'm glad you're feeling better. I enjoyed your words about Mr. Owl."

"We were pals. We had no choice really. There weren't a lot of brown folks serving, and it didn't matter if you were an Indian or a Negro, the Air Force just saw that we weren't white." Isaiah spoke matter-of-factly, in the mood for reminiscing.

"We stayed enlisted after the war ended, but Al eventually found work in civvy street. He left about 1947, I think. I used to see him at the Legion sometimes, but he gave up drinking thirty years ago, and after that . . ." He paused, and Cate could see that his mind had drifted back to those years of friendship. He continued, "I didn't know that he'd been to one of those schools. He never talked about it." Isaiah spoke in a musing tone. "I guess they were tough places. He told me once he'd never had a full belly until he signed up. Maybe that's why he was so loyal to the Air Force, despite everything . . .

getting three square meals a day is a powerful thing to a man who's known real hunger."

"I suppose that's true," Cate said.

Isaiah turned toward her. "I apologize for running at the mouth. That funeral just stirred up memories. Not many of us veterans left anymore."

"I like hearing these stories," Cate said. "What did you do in the war?"

"Ground crew. I was the wrong color to sit in the cockpit. Still, I had a good run of it. Served twenty years. Was even there when they worked on the Arrow. My, that was a bird."

Cate smiled as Isaiah talked on, telling stories of his exploits with the Air Force. He'd served all over the country, but he spoke about Eastview with the same fondness as Peter.

Peter. Her stomach clenched. She needed to face him to apologize. Every day that she didn't made everything worse.

At Isaiah's home, a small white house on a quiet street, Cate insisted on coming inside, to check that the air-conditioning was on and to get him settled. She poured him a glass of cold water. "Please, Mr. Turner, be sure to get some rest, and keep drinking fluids."

"Sure thing, my dear. I appreciate your concern."

"Do you have family you can call? Someone to check on you?"

"My niece comes by most nights to help with dinner and have a chat. She'll be here later."

Cate nodded, relieved. "Good."

He took her two hands in his frail brown ones and squeezed. "You're a good girl," he said warmly. "Real caring."

Cate was surprised by the tears that welled up in her eyes. "Thank you," she said. "That means a lot." She wiped them away hastily, hoping he hadn't noticed. "I think you just skirted heat stroke, and you should be fine, but remember, if you feel at all funny, you need to call your doctor right away."

"I'm in my nineties. I always feel funny."

She laughed. "Just promise you'll call."

He nodded.

She left him sitting in an easy chair, a large glass of water by his side, the air-conditioning chugging away full force.

CHAPTER THIRTY-FOUR

THE CITY'S FORENSIC PATHOLOGY UNIT WAS AT THE OTTAWA GENERAL Hospital. Five forensic pathologists worked out of the small offices in the hospital basement. Morgues were always shunted to the sub-floors. No one wanted to be reminded of what happened when life-saving efforts upstairs failed. Cate descended three steep flights. Her footsteps echoed in the deserted stairwell. What if her assailant leaped from one of the recessed doorways? She squared her shoulders. She'd deal with it.

Like coroners, forensic pathologists combined their medical knowledge with a willingness to work with law enforcement. Cate had met all of Ottawa's forensic pathologists and was always struck by their fascination with puzzles. They wanted to uncover the "why" of the sudden death. Helping the bereaved family held little interest for them, but pinpointing what precise cocktail of drugs caused a fatal overdose or exactly how a head injury re-sulted in a lethal hematoma did. Cate had also noted they had zero tolerance for bullshit.

Dr. Naomi Gold was the most junior pathologist on staff, and as a result, hers was the smallest office and the one closest to the morgue itself. It was a cramped space, the desk piled high with reports and the walls covered with photographs of her children. Images of smil-ing toddlers were incongruous with the grim work that went on next door, but perhaps that was the point: a reminder of life amid death.

Naomi was about thirty years old with straight black hair and a high forehead.

"Good to see you," Cate said.

The pathologist pointed to a seat, not bothering with social niceties. "What exactly can I do for you?" she asked. She wasn't being aggressive; Naomi simply didn't want to waste time. Cate respected that.

"I had some questions about the Johnson case."

"Yeah, I noticed that you hadn't cleared the body for release or signed off on manner of death. Didn't know if you were dragging your feet on purpose, or . . ."

Or if she was having trouble getting work done because of Jason's accident. Cate focused on the case. "Has the family requested the body?" Until the coroner cleared it for removal, it could not be released from the morgue.

"Their request came in an hour ago. O'Malley's Funeral Home is handling it. Shipment west, to Vancouver, I think."

At least Cate had managed to convey to Mrs. Johnson that she should contact a funeral home—maybe she hadn't been as drunk as she feared.

Naomi spoke again. "Why haven't you signed off on this one?"

"I don't think it's suicide. I wanted to have a look at her personal effects, maybe review the autopsy report with you." Naomi would know this was unusual behavior for a coroner. Most deaths didn't require any type of investigation, and if they did, that was a cop's job. Cate hoped the other woman wouldn't demand to know under what authority she was asking, or even worse, call Dr. Marcoux for authorization.

Fortunately Naomi didn't seem concerned about procedural niceties. She was more interested in the puzzle. "Why don't you think it was suicide?"

"No note, no signs of depression, friends and family surprised."

Naomi shrugged. "Sometimes happens like that. Depressed people mask their feelings, one event sets them off. Women don't normally kill, either, but the prisons still have plenty of female murderers."

"It's not suicide. I've got a feeling."

Naomi raised an eyebrow, and Cate knew it was the wrong thing to say. She spoke. "Can I see the personal effects?"

"Follow me." Naomi led Cate to the morgue. It looked like an ordinary operating room with a couple of metal stretchers, two sets of surgical lights in the ceiling, large sinks at opposite ends of the room, and trays of medical equipment lining the walls. The only thing setting it apart was the large bone saw occupying most of one tray. An assistant in green hospital scrubs cleaned instruments in one corner. Naomi ignored him and made her way to a line of filing cabinets at the far side of the room.

"We keep all personal effects, until they get returned to the family when the body is released." The pathologist unlocked and opened a drawer marked "J." She removed four labeled plastic bags and placed them on a table beside the cabinets. "Here you go," she said. She took out her phone and began texting.

Cate pulled on a pair of gloves and opened the first bag. Everything that was on the deceased person was sent here. That included the portion of the rope that had been wrapped around Molly's neck; its cheery yellow color bellied its sinister use.

She'd never gone through personal effects before, and it was jarring to see the clothes she remembered Molly wearing neatly folded and stuffed into a bag. She pulled out Molly's jean jacket, thinking it seemed much smaller now that it was no longer on the girl. It was dotted with pins, just like Simon Thatcher's. Pin-covered jean jackets must be the latest thing among a certain set of twenty-somethings. Unlike what she could remember of Simon's jacket, Molly's pins were not political. They were mostly animals: a cartoon owl, an elephant, and two enormous-eyed cats. One pin said, "Archivists do it for longer." There were two holes in the jacket next to the elephant button. A pin had once been there but was missing.

"Were there any loose pins found among her things?" she asked. It wasn't much to go on.

Naomi looked up from her phone. "Everything found on her person is in those bags."

Cate went through the rest of the things. Molly's jeans, her bird T-shirt, her Converse sneakers. A separate plastic bag held the contents of her pockets. Half a pack of gum, a lip gloss. Another bag contained the girl's cracked glasses. No iPhone here. Where was it? Would Baker tell her if he found it? She'd lost all credibility with him at the party.

She was loath to put Molly's things away, to break the tenuous connection she felt for the girl. Cate rubbed the shirt fabric between her fingers. It was thin and old. She wondered if it was vintage.

"Find anything useful?" Naomi interrupted her.

Cate wasn't going to mention her amorphous "feeling" about the missing pin. "I don't think so."

"That's too bad," Naomi said.

Something in the woman's tone caught Cate's attention. She spoke. "I read your prelim report. You had a funny phrasing around the cause of death. You said the bruising on Molly's neck was 'not inconsistent' with asphyxia, secondary to hanging. That's not the same thing as 'consistent.'"

"I write my reports carefully to reflect the logical conclusions of the facts I see before me. 'Not inconsistent' was more accurate than 'consistent.'"

"What do you mean?" Cate asked.

"I'll show you."

They approached a walk-in refrigerator, just like the ones found at big restaurants. Naomi punched in a code, and the door unlocked. She stepped inside, but Cate stood glued to the spot. The space was small, and the cool rush of air transported her back to the moment she'd seen Molly's body in that cold vault.

"You can do this, Kit Kat," she said to herself. Taking a deep breath, she followed Naomi. The space was packed with corpses zipped into body bags. There was hardly any room to move, and claustrophobia narrowed her vision. The cold reached out, freezing the air in her chest. She took a shallow breath, then another. The thick door closed behind her. She fought down the panic clawing at her throat, focusing on breathing evenly.

Naomi was oblivious to Cate's distress. She moved among the stretchers, reading the labels affixed to each person's bag. "Here she is," she said, pulling a gurney out. "Can you open the door?"

Cate turned and struggled with the handle of the fridge, her hand slipping on the cold metal, unable to grasp it properly. She tried again, at last getting the door open. She pushed through, gasping at the warmer air of the autopsy suite.

Naomi followed, pushing the gurney. She unzipped the thick body bag encasing Molly Johnson.

Although the cold storage had preserved the corpse, you could see unmistakable signs of change. Molly's skin was less taut, and her mouth had a bluish tinge. She was naked now, and she looked absurdly vulnerable stretched out on the table. Cate's chest tightened with anger as she stared at Molly's face. She hadn't deserved this fate.

Putting on a pair of gloves, Naomi spoke animatedly for the first time. "If you see here," she pointed to the bruising on Molly's neck, which was much more pronounced than when Cate had examined her almost a week ago, "you'll note that the marking goes directly across her throat."

"That's consistent with hanging, isn't it?" Cate asked.

"Yes of course," Naomi said. "What's more unusual, however, is this." As gently as if she was handling a piece of fine china, she tilted Molly's head to the right and pulled back her ear. The area was a mass of deep purple-y black bruises. The markings thickened around the ears. Naomi spoke. "If she was hanged from a height, we should see the ligature marks come to a point here or at the other ear. That's where the rope would have bit into the skin. We do not see that clearly. Strangulation leaves a messier pattern, without the point."

Cate could see that the pattern of the markings was unusual. The bruising thickened but was not quite the obvious point you'd expect to find. "It's hard to interpret," Cate muttered to herself, willing a pattern to emerge from the muddied discolorations on the girl's neck.

"Yes," Naomi said. "If she didn't die quickly, if she had used weak rope, or if she had struggled a great deal pre-death, then this bruising could be explained."

Cate recalled the scene. "The rope was strong. There was nothing wrong with it." She thought of the tight space of the vault, all those neat, perfectly ordered boxes lined up on the shelves, a mute testimony to the truth. "There were no signs of struggle."

Only the drip from a tap at the far end of the room punctuated the stillness. Even the assistant in the corner was quiet, as if listening to their conversation. "As I said in my report, the bruising wasn't inconsistent with asphyxiation," Naomi paused. "But neither is it inconsistent with strangulation made to look like suicide. The forensic evidence is inconclusive. This is your call, Cate."

"It was murder," she said without any doubt.

Naomi nodded. "Yes."

An enormous weight lifted from Cate. This was the call she had needed to make when she noticed the lack of disturbance at the vault. Every professional colleague was dubious, but now she had Naomi on her side. The evidence wasn't as strong as Cate would like, and another coroner might reach a different conclusion, but she knew "homicide" was the right call.

Cate left Naomi's office, deep in thought.

Her phone vibrated, and her throat tightened at the sight of Matthew's name on the call display. She ignored the call.

Someone opened the door from the stairwell ahead of her at the end of the hall. It slammed shut, echoing through the empty space. She glanced up but couldn't make out the person's features. The figure was familiar, and suddenly it felt like she was underwater or moving in slow motion. Her heart pounded in her ears, but she kept moving forward. There were no footsteps, no sounds. The person was leaning against the door as if waiting for her. She slowed. There was something menacing about his pose. He was a large man, his arms crossed in front of his chest, his face in shadow. She couldn't be sure it was the same person who attacked her. She wanted to turn around and head back to the dubious comfort of the morgue, but she was damned if she was going to act frightened.

"Hello," she called. "What do you want?" She kept walking but gripped her phone more tightly.

The figure waited one more moment, opened the door, and slipped out. She hurried to catch him, but when she wrenched open the door he was gone, his running footsteps echoing above her.

Her hands shook as she walked back to her car. She wanted a cigarette. She debated calling Baker and reporting the incident, but she'd have to tell him about the attack at the party. He'd make her account for all her movements that night, including the fact that she slept with Matthew.

The first thing she did when she got home was lock her front door. She hugged herself as she stared out at her quiet street. She took a few deep breaths, trying to settle her mind. Those breaths would have been a lot better if they'd filled her lungs with nicotine. "Be proud of yourself, Kit Kat," she said softly. "You're kicking that nasty habit. Stay strong."

She turned to her computer and completed her official report, typing "homicide" into the "Manner of Death" box and sending it off to both the Provincial Coroner's office and the Ottawa Police Department. Her role in the case was now done, but she wasn't finished with her own inquiries. She would figure out who attacked her. Punch the bully back.

Annoyingly, her phone, now buried at the bottom of her purse, was dead. When she charged it, she had three messages. The first was from Peter. She swallowed hard. She had to face him or at least listen to his message. "Cate, I think I deserve an explanation. Call me." God, she'd really messed that thing up.

The second message was from Matthew and was the call she'd ignored at the morgue. "Cate, we need to talk. Don't shut me out, please." She deleted it.

Finally, she listened to the last message. "Hi Cate, it's Naomi." Her voice was clear, no-nonsense. "I thought you'd want to know. After you left, a man came by and asked all kinds of questions about you and what we'd been talking about."

Cate's throat tightened.

Naomi continued, "He was a big guy, Black with an accent. He claimed to be police, but I know all of Ottawa's detectives. I told him to get out of my lab. Hope I did right. Watch your back."

Cate deleted the message, wishing her fear was as easily erased.

CHAPTER THIRTY-FIVE

IT WAS TUESDAY, THREE DAYS SINCE THE ATTACK. CATE STILL FELT THE kind of jittery anxiety that a nice blurry drink could ease. So far, she'd resisted the allure of a scotch just as she'd resisted a cigarette. Rather than make her feel good, her willpower made her nervous. How long could she keep it up? At least she had a distraction this morning— Rose called to say she might have found a lead.

The other woman's outfit was more subdued today, though the knee-high Doc Martens did give Cate pause as they headed for her office.

"Any word on Molly's phone?" Rose asked as they exited the elevator.

Cate shook her head. "No. I haven't heard anything."

"Well, can't you call, apply some pressure?"

Cate's mouth tightened. If she hadn't been so ashamed of her behavior at the party, never mind her phone call with Mrs. Johnson, that's exactly what she would do. "I don't need your input, thanks." Her tone was sharp, so she made a peace offering. "I submitted my official report yesterday."

They reached Rose's office.

"Oh?" She stopped and crossed her arms, as if bracing for bad news.

"I labeled Molly's death 'homicide'," Cate said.

"Oh, Dr. Spencer, thank you!" Cate couldn't avoid the hug. It was like being cuddled by a tiny, bony chicken carcass.

"Thank you so much for believing in me, for caring about Molly." Rose's eyes filled with tears, and Cate looked away, the young woman's gratitude tightening her own throat.

"It was nothing," she said. "Now let's dig into this new lead."

Rose bounded toward her office door and stopped. "Wait. If it's homicide, isn't this a police investigation?"

Cate waved that away. "I'm assisting the police." Baker would have roared at that one.

Rose raised an eyebrow but said nothing, leading her into the office. "I'll show you what I found."

Cate hesitated at the doorway. Rose's office was filled with bar-coded and labeled boxes stacked higher than Cate's head.

The looming cardboard walls made her anxious. "What's all this?"

"Crazy, eh? Gerald has been on my case since Wednesday. He wants me back doing my real job, but I don't give a rat's ass what he says. Let him fire me. I'm going to figure out what happened to Molly. I'm not actually allowed to order in so many boxes at once, but Gus, the circulation guy, is a real sweetie."

There must have been dozens and dozens of boxes. It was overwhelming. Cate couldn't move.

Rose made it to her desk and glanced back at Cate, who still stood in the hallway as she willed herself to enter the tunnel. Rose came back. "Hey, are you OK?"

Her solicitousness touched her, and for a crazy second Cate thought she might cry. Her recent emotionality was unnerving—all these tears, like part of her was leaking away. Must be an aftereffect of the attack. She nodded and stepped into the office, concentrating on the window behind Rose to ease her claustrophobia.

"What does this have to do with Molly?" she asked.

"It's what she was working on right before she died. I thought it might give us some clues to what happened to her."

"Why not review all this at the nitrate facility?"

"These? None of it is nitrate. We aren't allowed to have that here—too volatile. No, this isn't even photographs. It's paper records, government documents."

"Why would Molly be looking at them? Was that part of her job?"

Rose shook her head. "No way. We were meant to be clearing out the nitrate facility. That's been our 'number one supremo priority,' as Gerald constantly reminded us."

"How do you know this is what she was looking at?"

"I went into our tracking system and called up all the containers Molly ordered over the past few weeks. Up until the end of June it was a few boxes here and there related to the move. Totally legit. Then on June twenty-fifth she ordered in five boxes from this random collection, all military stuff. She's been ordering in boxes from the same collection ever since. When you add it all up, it comes to something like two hundred containers."

"Didn't you notice all of these boxes?"

"She was only ordering in a few at a time—I assumed they had something to do with the move."

"She was being secretive about her research?" That had big implications.

"Definitely. We talked about work all the time, but she never mentioned this."

"What's in these boxes, then?"

Rose shrugged. "They're all from the same Department of National Defense collection. We acquired them in the sixties, but as far as I can tell, most of this stuff is older. Some of it goes all the way back to the First World War."

"What does it have to do with nitrate film or Eastview?"

"Nothing, though it's hard to be sure."

"Haven't you looked at them?" Cate asked impatiently.

"I've started to, but these records are a total mess. There's no finding aid, to start with."

Seeing Cate's blank look, Rose explained. "That's a listing of the contents of an archival collection. Finding aids are like a table of contents for a book. I can't locate one for this collection."

"So you have to go through every box." Cate was deflated by how big a job this was.

"Exactly. On top of that, often the files don't even have titles, so I've had to read each file to see what it's about."

"And . . ."

"Mostly administrative stuff." Rose called up a document on her computer. "I've been keeping track. A lot of the files date from the twenties." Rose read from the list she had made herself. "There's a ton of memos and reports about disposing of military equipment, buying and selling land, building hospitals, renting facilities. Most of the collection concerns the aftermath of the First World War. The government was selling off all the stuff they'd bought to fight the Kaiser."

Cate couldn't keep an edge of irritation from her voice. "One-hundred-year-old admin files don't sound like a motive for murder."

"Tell me about it. At first, I was stoked, but after slogging through these, I'm bummed." Rose picked up a file in disgust. "This one is about decommissioning a boat shed on the British Columbia coast." She placed it back in the box. "I'm almost sorry I called you. I thought I'd get further."

Cate swallowed her annoyance, knowing Rose was disappointed too. "There has to be something about Eastview."

"I haven't seen anything yet, but I've only gone through half the boxes. I'll keep looking until we find something to catch the bastard who did this to Molly."

Her words rang an alarm bell. Unbidden memories of a hand pressing against her throat, a voice whispering in her ear. What was she doing here? Entangling Rose in a case she knew to be risky. No. "You shouldn't be involved," Cate said firmly.

Rose's lips tightened. "What do you mean? I want to catch Molly's killer."

"I know, and you've already been a help." Cate would regret not having Rose to discuss ideas with. "It's time to let the police do their job."

"That's crazy. The police don't know the records like I do. They have no idea what to look for."

"It's too dangerous. Molly was murdered over this."

Rose's voice was impatient. "I know that. It's why I have to help."

"Listen to me. There's more than Molly's murder." She told Rose about Saturday night's attack. It felt good to say the words aloud, somehow taking a bit of the horror away.

"Jesus, Dr. Spencer, I'm sorry. You must be completely freaked out."

"I'm fine. He didn't hurt me." Her words held the right note of nonchalance and bravado. She wanted to turn the conversation away from her feelings. "I've been thinking about it, and this attack might actually be a good thing."

"What?" Rose demanded.

"Well, it shows that the killer hasn't got what he wanted. If he killed Molly to prevent her from revealing something, the attack on me proves he's still feeling vulnerable."

"Yeah, I guess," Rose said slowly. She was less excited about this deduction than Cate hoped. "Coming back to the attack—"

Cate sighed. Obviously, the other woman could not be dissuaded from discussing it.

"You should report what happened," Rose said.

Cate shook her head. "I don't have a useful description or any real information. Even if Baker believed me, what could he do?"

Rose sounded bewildered. "Why wouldn't Detective Baker believe you?"

Cate didn't want to tell Rose about Baker's views on her. Her voice rose. "I'm not reporting it, Rose. That's final." Cate cleared her throat and changed the topic. "You saw Molly every day. Did she act frustrated, like maybe she hadn't found what she wanted in the records?"

Rose uncrossed her arms. "She was just the same. Relaxed, cracking goofy jokes, complaining about Fabienne. It was the usual."

That caught Cate's attention. "What about Fabienne?" Rose had never mentioned problems between Molly and her girlfriend.

Rose chewed her lip as though regretting her words. "You know, people in relationships fight. It can't be perfect all the time."

Cate stared at Rose. The other woman shifted uncomfortably.

"What was going on with Molly and Fabienne?"

Rose twisted a bracelet on her arm. "Honestly, I don't know anything."

"You suspect something, though."

Rose spoke in a rush. "Molly called me on the Sunday before she died. She left a voice mail, asking if she could crash at my place. I thought it was because she'd had a fight with Fabienne. They had a tempestuous relationship. By the time I called back, she said everything was cool and she didn't need to stay after all."

"Jesus, Rose. Why didn't you mention this sooner?"

The other woman didn't answer.

"You wanted me to find manner of death as homicide," Cate said flatly.

"I didn't want you thinking that Molly had a reason to kill herself."

Rose lied to get her way. Cate's breathing quickened, and she was hyper-aware of the boxes all around, constricting the air, narrowing her escape. "If she and Fabienne were fighting, she might have been upset, angry, depressed. Looking for a way out."

"Just because they had a fight doesn't mean Molly was suicidal. She was cheerful on Monday. She brought Timbits for the protesters."

"Donuts aren't proof of mental stability."

"You agree that something is off. What about her missing phone?"

"I think she was murdered." Cate stepped back. She needed air. "I'm taking that seriously. I thought you were too, but you can't beg me to be included and then keep secrets."

"I'm sorry, Dr. Spencer. I thought—"

"You thought you could spin the evidence to suit your conclusion. That's not how I work, Rose."

"That's not true—"

"It was a mistake to involve you." Cate was almost relieved to have discovered Rose's breach. It gave her a clean way to end their relationship and keep the other woman safe. "Stay out of this, and let the police do their job. If you don't, you might mess up the cops' case or get yourself killed."

Rose shook her head obstinately.

Cate was equal parts protective and annoyed. Her voice shook with emotion when she spoke. "Listen to me. I was attacked. These people are serious, and they are deadly. You've done more than enough. Walk away."

"So I'm supposed to listen to your safety tips, while you're not even reporting your assault?"

"I'm handling it," Cate said.

"Are you crazy?" Rose's voice became louder. "He threatened your life. He could have killed you."

Cate's throat constricted. "I know what he did, so I know how serious this is. Walk away, Rose. That's an order."

"Dr. Spencer, I'm a grown woman, and you're not my boss or mother. I get that this is dangerous, but it's not going to stop me."

Cate spoke with authority. "You withheld information from me, and you don't know what you're doing. You need to step back."

Rose seemed taller and meaner as she pointed a finger. "That's rich coming from you."

Cate blinked. "What does that mean?"

"I know all about you, Dr. Spencer. I know you used to be a GP and couldn't hack it. That's why you became a coroner. You were running away."

Cate's stomach clenched. "What the hell are you talking about?"

Rose advanced on her. "Detective Stowe sent a police sergeant by this morning with a bunch of follow-up questions. Turns out the sergeant likes to gossip. The police certainly don't think very highly of you."

Cate cringed.

Rose continued, "You can't tell me to stay out of the police investigation when you're not supposed to be in it yourself."

Cate didn't answer, and Rose's voice softened. "Look, we both have our reasons why we want to solve this case. I need to find Molly's murderer to atone for not being a better friend; you need to resolve it because of your brother's death—"

The blood roared in Cate's ears. "I don't want to talk about that with you." She took another step back. "I don't want to talk about any of this with you."

"Well, you need to talk to someone." Rose's tone was shrill. "You're completely closed off. It's not healthy. Anyone can see that you need—"

Cate's heart beat rapidly, and her mouth was dry. She was hemmed in by the boxes. Rose's face, angry and accusing, swam in front of her, and Cate practically fell as she stumbled for the door. "I'll tell you what I don't need. I don't need a break, I don't need to stop drinking, and I sure as shit don't need advice from a silly girl playing at detective."

Cate had reached the doorway; beyond it was more space, air, and an absence of Rose. She was nearly there. She turned back and Rose once again looked small and young.

The other woman spoke sadly. "Oh Dr. Spencer, I wasn't going to suggest any of that," she said. "I was going to say that anyone can see you need a friend."

CHAPTER THIRTY-SIX

BACK IN HER CAR AND UPSET FROM HER FIGHT WITH ROSE, CATE ALMOST didn't notice her phone vibrating. Matthew. She couldn't avoid him forever. She punched the hands-free button on her steering wheel. "What do you want?" she asked.

There was static on the line. "Is that how you answer the phone now, Cate?"

Was that a teasing note to his voice? It was hard to tell with the crappy connection. "Only when call display tells me it's you."

He chuckled, apparently unruffled by her rudeness. "You'll be nicer when I tell you why I'm calling."

"I doubt that." She squared her shoulders and awaited his next words.

"I wanted to tell you that you were right. Or maybe what's more important for you to hear is that I was wrong."

Her curiosity was piqued, but she wasn't going to let him know that. She paused before answering, navigating out of the Archives' parking lot and onto Wellington Street. "'I was wrong' is literally the last thing I ever expect to hear coming out of your mouth," she said.

"Like I told you, Cate, I'm a different guy from the one you knew."

She remembered what he had said at the lake—that he'd gone to therapy, that he was willing to change. Willing to blow up his life and marriage to be with her. The strength of her yearning to believe him caught her off guard. "What are you apologizing for?" she asked gruffly.

"Whoa, whoa. I didn't say I was apologizing, only acknowledging you were right." Cate rolled her eyes. The old Matthew was still there, hidden under a thin veneer of amiability. He always liked to split hairs. It made him a great lawyer and an irritating person.

He continued, "I just heard that the police are investigating Ottawa's sixth homicide: Molly Johnson's death."

His voice was rueful, not a tone Cate was used to hearing from him. She put that aside to concentrate on the import of his words. Had a press release gone out? "Where did you hear this?"

"I've got contacts."

TDR's tentacles extended into the police department. Even that thought couldn't quell her satisfaction in saying the next words: "I told you so." The stately mass of Parliament Hill was to her left, the Peace Tower bells starting their noon hour carillon.

"Yeah, you did. I should have listened to you. When will I ever learn?"

"I think you're a lost cause," she said with a grin.

She could hear the smile in his voice as he replied, "Does that work in my favor with you? From what I remember, you always liked an underdog."

"Under*dog*, Matthew. Not under-wolf-in-sheep's-clothing."

His laugh echoed in her ear, and she closed her eyes. Even during their worst fights, they could always make each other laugh. No. She couldn't go down that path. Couldn't remember the good times. Their old life was toxic and believing anything else was stupid. She shifted lanes, narrowly avoiding a green Honda in her blind spot. "What do you want, Matthew? I doubt you were only calling to acknowledge your mistake."

He took a deep breath. "That night at the lake was amazing, Cate. We're meant to be together, and I think we should try again."

Her heart banged against her chest. "You're crazy. We are poison."

"That's not true, Cate. You always dismiss my feelings."

She embraced the thread of anger in his voice—a reminder to stand firm. "You want to be with me? What did your wife say when you told her we slept together?"

There was silence on the other end. It spoke volumes.

Even Cate was shocked by the bitter edge to her laugh. "Come on, Matthew. You don't want to get back together. You don't love me. I'm some convenient focal point for your midlife crisis."

"I need to see you, Cate. To explain—"

"I'm not interested in your explanations. I'm not interested in having you in my life. Don't call me again." She hung up and turned the wheel to make a right onto Elgin, again almost hitting the damn green Honda. She regained control of the car.

She wanted a cigarette. She dug out her carrots, biting down ferociously on one. It would be a lot more satisfying if she could light it and inhale. Get back together with Matthew? Never. She chomped another carrot. Talk about self-sabotage . . . Matthew was insane if he thought she would even contemplate it.

CHAPTER THIRTY-SEVEN

CATE WAS ALMOST HOME WHEN HER PHONE RANG AGAIN. "DR. SPENCER? This is Dr. Marcoux's administrative assistant calling. The Regional Supervising Coroner wants to see you at his home office."

Cate's stomach tightened. Marcoux had never called her into his office before. "What, right now?"

"Yes. He's waiting for you."

"What's this about?" she asked, although she had a good idea.

"He said to tell you it was related to the Molly Johnson case." The secretary paused, as if embarrassed. "There has been a complaint of inappropriate conduct."

Cate hung up the phone. Damn it. Mrs. Johnson must have by-passed Baker and gone directly to her boss. She couldn't blame the woman. She hated to think of how disappointed Dr. Marcoux would be. In the past, when he'd chastised her for being late with a report, he'd been so sweet about it that she had tried to do better, if only for his sake. What she had done this time was infinitely worse. She was tempted to blow off the meeting entirely, find a bar and obliterate the memory of her screwup. The urge for a drink was so powerful she tightened her grip on the steering wheel to the point of pain. "Face the music, Kit Kat," she whispered.

While the Regional District Coroner's official office was in an industrial park in the city's south end, Dr. Marcoux conducted a lot of his business from his home on Florence Street so that he could be closer to his son. Cate had only been here twice, once to sign her initial contract and once to fill out paperwork related to her pay.

She mounted the stairs to the front door but took a surprised step back when it burst open. A slim man came out. Cate moved aside, but the man didn't even look at her, his head bent low. He shuffled past and headed down the street.

A short woman next emerged. She gave Cate a friendly smile but hurried after the man without saying a word. Cate belatedly recognized the man with the awkward, hunched gait as Toby, Dr. Marcoux's son. The woman must be his attendant. Marcoux appeared on the stoop.

"Ah, Dr. Spencer, welcome."

Dr. Marcoux stepped aside to let her in, but his gaze drifted down the street to where the attendant caught up to Toby. She put out her hand to touch him, and he jerked his arm away. Marcoux winced. "Mariela is new, and Toby is not used to her. He doesn't like to be touched."

Schizophrenia was a complex disease, and an aversion to touch was not uncommon. "Will they be all right?" she asked.

"Yes," Marcoux smiled. "I'm just an overprotective father." He stared after the pair, now walking side by side down the sidewalk. Dr. Marcoux's eyes held such a look of tenderness that Cate glanced away, embarrassed to have witnessed the display of fatherly love.

"Do you have around-the-clock care for him?"

"Oh no," Marcoux smiled. "Mariela only comes when I'm working." He turned toward the door. "Shall we go in?"

His office was a snug, book-lined room in the back of the house, featuring three large filing cabinets and framed watercolors on the walls. A human skull on the corner of the desk was the only indication that this wasn't a cozy study in someone's home.

As she entered the office, Cate's eye was drawn to a huge, ornately framed Marcoux family tree hanging in pride of place next to the window. "This is new," she blurted—not eager to discuss the reason he had called her there.

Marcoux's eyes lit up. "Yes, I recently finished it." He walked over to the wall, gesturing for her to join him.

The family tree was written in perfect, tiny calligraphy, the names and dates carefully printed out, lines extending across the paper in well-ordered generations. She glanced at the top, where the most distant relatives sat—Roland Marcoux (1697) and Emmeline Blais (1705).

"It's beautiful," she said, but she was lying. She found the family tree oppressive, the weight of all those names, all those lives, bearing down upon the people below. There at the very bottom, almost obscured by the frame, were Dr. Marcoux, his wife, Jill, and Toby. They were squashed and inconsequential. An afterthought in the great grind of history.

Marcoux did not notice her disquiet. "There is something wonderful about genealogy, Dr. Spencer. It's a bit like our job—piecing together mysteries after the fact."

Was he right? Was this what she did in her job? Boiled down all the complexity, heartbreak, and joy of a life into one line in a report? She didn't voice her thoughts. "This must have been a lot of work."

"Oh yes, painstaking. A twenty-year passion project, but you know what they say, 'Genealogy is all relative.'"

She smiled wanly.

He seemed to remember why she was there, and his tone grew serious as he headed back to his desk. "I believe my secretary told you why I wished to speak with you."

"Yes." He looked so pained that Cate felt bad for him. He couldn't be enjoying this either. He had always reminded her of her old headmaster from boarding school—a scholarly man whose greatest source of discipline was the fear of letting him down.

"Tell me, is it true? Were you inebriated when you spoke to the victim's family?" His tone was gentle.

She opened her mouth. She could go on the offensive, deny everything, or refuse to accept the blame. Instead, she nodded.

Dr. Marcoux's shoulders slumped. "I had hoped there was some type of misunderstanding. I know you've been going through a difficult time since the death of your brother."

"Jason has nothing to do with this," she protested.

Dr. Marcoux put up his hand. "Lately colleagues have mentioned that you seem inattentive, unfocused, and perhaps even erratic?"

She hadn't been expecting that. "Who's been complaining?" She thought of Williams and what had happened at the Marier Residence.

"That's not important. I'm concerned that you're burning out, Dr. Spencer."

"I've been a bit distracted lately, but I've been very diligent with Molly Johnson's death. In fact, I've been trying to assist in uncovering her murderer."

"Yes, I've been informed that you're going above and beyond your official duties."

Cate's throat constricted at the betrayal. Mrs. Johnson may have told Marcoux that she was drunk, but only Baker was in a position to object to how she was handling the case. They might not have been friendly, but she always assumed Baker would come to her with his issues rather than rat her out.

Marcoux wasn't finished. "Your questionable judgment in the Johnson case is much less worrisome than the fact that you were under the influence while talking to the victim's family. I'm not sure if grief is making you reckless, or if you have a drinking problem—"

Cate interrupted. "That's ridiculous. Mrs. Johnson called me at an unexpected hour, and it caught me off guard. Am I never supposed to have a drink on the chance that I get a call from a grieving relative?"

Marcoux looked pained. "My understanding was that you had an appointment to discuss the case, which you missed. I also understand that you spoke to Mrs. Johnson at noon, hardly the normal hour for a cocktail."

Cate had no counterargument. "I made one mistake, but I can control my drinking." She heard how desperate her voice was and how empty her words sounded. "I haven't had a drink since Saturday."

"Ah yes, the TDR shindig."

His dry tone spoke volumes. Any hopes she'd had that Marcoux might not have seen her fall were dashed.

Marcoux stared at her for a long moment, but she held his gaze. She had to work on this case.

He sighed. "I was hoping that you would be able to come to a realization about the precarious state of your own mental health. You need a break. I'm recommending that the Ontario Coroner's Office suspend you for one month, without censure or penalty. I'm hoping this time off will give you the breathing room you need to seek help."

Suspension from duty? "Dr. Marcoux, that's really not necessary. I don't want time off. My work is all I have."

"That's what I'm talking about, Dr. Spencer. You're too invested in this job, as your gross misjudgments in the Johnson case demonstrate. I'm sorry, but I'll be forwarding my recommendations immediately."

She opened her mouth to argue but found she had nothing to say. She had totally screwed up with the Johnson family. She deserved this. Self-pity washed over her. "I've got a stack of reports I haven't completed. Can I at least submit those? I won't get paid until they're filed."

"Of course," he said, his eyes softening. "Finish up your outstanding paperwork. I'm not doing this to punish you, Dr. Spencer, but in the hopes that this rest will help."

Cate's face burned. His pity was worse than any reprimand. She stood and stumbled to her car. She wanted a cigarette. She bit into a carrot.

She needed to get home and put this humiliation behind her. A drink would help nicely with that.

CHAPTER THIRTY-EIGHT

PETER HARRISON WAS SITTING ON HER FRONT STOOP WHEN SHE PULLED into her driveway. She contemplated throwing the car into reverse and peeling away. Instead, she parked. The world was intent on telling her what a raging screwup she was, and Peter had more right than anyone to be angry with her.

She got out of the car, and he stood quickly, as if coming to attention. "You didn't return my calls." His kind face radiated concern.

A choking feeling of shame rose, and she spoke coldly. "I've been busy." She crossed her arms.

"I was worried about you,"

God, what more did he have to do to highlight his innate thoughtfulness against her own innate asshole-ness? There was something about the solicitous way he looked at her that made her want to scream or shove him or kill herself. "I'm sorry I left the party so abruptly."

"Weren't you having a good time?"

There it was again, the wounded puppy look.

"I was drunk," she said bluntly. "I got sloppy and fell over and embarrassed myself, and I didn't want to embarrass you."

He took a step toward her. "I saw your fall, Cate. That's why I've been so concerned."

Jesus Christ, could nothing drive this guy away? "Peter, I'm a screwup. I drink myself to sleep most nights, get nightmares so vicious I wake up screaming, and I would literally murder someone for a cigarette right now."

He took another step closer and grabbed her hand. "We're all messed up, Cate. Don't you think I struggle? I've been battling

PTSD since the Balkans, and I'll carry that with me until the day I die."

His hand was calloused and firm, but he held hers gently, like it was something fragile and precious. He continued, "I showed up today because I like you. You're tough and honest and funny."

She looked at his face. He wasn't handsome and sarcastic like Matthew. He was ordinary-looking and kind. His tone was soft rather than commanding. She'd never heard him be mocking or rude and yet she recalled her visit to the base and the authoritative way he moved among the enlisted men and women. Peter wouldn't jeer at her better impulses . . . or shake her at the top of a stairwell.

Was this what a real relationship was? Someone you told your ugliest truths to who didn't run away? A partner who would help you with the twelve separate strands of toxic garbage that were currently running through your life? She'd have someone to sleep beside. Someone who might chase away the nightmares. All she needed was to accept what he offered.

But then what?

They would walk into her house together. He'd see the half-filled scotch bottle she'd left out on the counter as both a deliberate test of her willpower, and a comforting reminder that it was there when she needed it. Would she tell him that she'd been put on stress leave? That she'd been threatened and attacked? What about Matthew? How would she tell this principled soldier that she had slept with a married man?

She stepped back, pulling her hand away. "I'm sorry, Peter, but I can't."

His eyes flashed—pain, or was it anger?—but he turned to go. "If you change your mind, you have my number."

Inside her house, Cate didn't even bother looking for a glass, taking a long swig of scotch straight from the bottle. The fiery burn down her throat was what she craved—punishment and oblivion in one efficient swallow.

She threw herself on the couch, the bottle clutched in her hand. Her phone was dead, so she plugged it in and took another drink. She flicked on the TV. The face of Liam Westin, the protest leader arrested on child porn charges, filled the screen. He was being led into a court-house. A crowd gathered with signs, denouncing him as a child rapist.

Good, she thought vengefully. At least someone was getting the jus-tice they deserved. She drank again, feeling her limbs loosen and a kindly alcoholic fog seep into her ugly corners. It had been almost seventy-two hours since she'd had a drink, and it felt like coming home.

CATE WAS DREAMING. SHE WAS AT CFB EASTVIEW. ROSE, DR. MARCOUX, and Peter were staring at the sky, laughing and pointing. Cate knew before she looked up what she would see: Jason's plane plummeting to the earth. She couldn't save him, and her powerlessness was like a disease, draining all strength from her limbs, silencing her voice.

She woke with a start. Her doorbell was ringing. It was followed by a thumping knock. Sweating and tangled in her sheets, she rolled over and looked at the time: seven a.m. The usual headache squeezed her temples, and her mouth was thickly coated in hangover. She pulled on her dressing gown and stumbled down the stairs, too groggy to wonder who was at the door. Baker stood on her porch.

"What do you want?" she asked.

He pushed past her and walked into her foyer. "You look like hell."

"It's seven a.m."

He wasn't wearing his usual rumpled suit and tie. Instead he had on jeans and a T-shirt. He was surprisingly fit under those cheap jackets. She'd always assumed his bulk was due to donuts, not gym time. It was unnerving to have Baker in her house. It felt wrong, like finding a camel in your living room or a Coke machine growing in your backyard.

He stalked into her kitchen, his gaze taking in the nearly empty bottle of scotch, the dirty dishes.

Cate squeezed past him and put the kettle on for coffee. "What do you want?" she asked again.

"I've been calling you since yesterday."

She glanced at her phone. There were eight messages. She dimly remembered it ringing yesterday afternoon, but after the debacle with Mrs. Johnson, she'd vowed not to answer the phone drunk.

"You called the Johnson death 'homicide,'" Baker said.

She crossed her arms, wishing she wasn't wearing a fuzzy pink housecoat and was wearing a bra. "Yeah, I filed my report on Monday."

"I know," Baker snapped. "I had to pull five officers off a real homicide—one where a woman was stabbed fifteen times by her methed-out pimp—to comb over that goddamn nitrate facility. You know what we found? Mice, silverfish, and bupkes. You've sent us on a wild goose chase. There's no proof of homicide."

"I don't need to have definitive proof. I have inconclusive bruising. Finding more is your job."

"Don't get cute on this. You can't go around calling deaths 'murder' just because you've got PMS or whatever."

"PMS jokes, really, Baker? Is this 1985? I'm within my rights to call this a homicide. There was no note, Molly wasn't depressed, and the autopsy results weren't convincing for hanging."

"That's crap. I read the autopsy. Dr. Gold called it suicide."

Cate shook her head. Bad idea. She felt sick and grabbed the counter to steady herself. Baker observed her closely.

"I talked to Naomi on Monday. She has doubts about the cause. Her final autopsy report will reflect that. There's nothing to indicate suicide." Cate opened a cupboard and took out some pills. Two Tylenol and a Motrin—a sweet cocktail.

"Yeah, but there's nothing to suggest murder, either." Baker paced around her kitchen. "No handprints on the neck, no trace evidence indicating the presence of another person. The building was locked up tight. Molly would have had to let her murderer in. She had no enemies, didn't owe any money, and had no drug problems."

Baker thought he was so smart, that he had everything sewn up. "What about Molly's 4:30 p.m. appointment on the day of the murder? Did you investigate that?"

Her words annoyed Baker. "Of course we did. We can't find

anything on it. It's a dead end. My question, *doctor*"—he laid heavy emphasis on her title—"is why you know about that appointment?"

Rose had told her about it. Even though they'd had an argument, Cate wouldn't sell out the younger woman. She stared at Baker and shrugged.

Her gesture irritated Baker further. He raised his voice. "You'd better not be interfering with my goddamn case, Cate. The only thing I want to hear is you conceding it was suicide."

"It's my call. I stand by my report." Remembering her meeting with Marcoux added fuel to her anger. "Anyway, I don't appreciate you telling my boss that my investigation is out of bounds. If you've got a problem with me, tell me to my face."

"What are you talking about?" he asked.

"Someone complained to my boss that I was getting overly involved in the Johnson case. You're trying to tell me that wasn't you?"

Baker put up his hands. "Think what you want, but I follow the cop code. We don't rat each other out."

"And I'm supposed to believe that you include coroners in that?"

He shrugged. "The ones that aren't pains in the ass."

Against her better judgment, Cate was flattered that she made the cut in Baker's twisted assessment. The kettle whistled. "Want a cup?" she asked.

He glanced dubiously at the big canister of discount instant coffee. "Sure, I'll try that swill." He looked around her kitchen.

She followed his gaze as it rested again on the bottle of Laphroaig. What she did on her own time in her own house was her own damn business. She thrust his coffee at him, spilling some on his hand. Good. She handed him a cloth to wipe up the mess.

Baker spoke. "I got a call from Mrs. Johnson on Monday afternoon."

"Oh." Cate kept her voice calm. How many people had that woman complained to?

"Yeah, she was really upset. Said you'd been drunk when you talked."

Cate didn't meet his eyes.

"I told her she must have been mistaken. I told her that I had worked with you for five years, and while you weren't always on time, and you weren't always right, you cared about victims' families, and you wouldn't be that thoughtless." Cate's eyes flew to his face. He held her gaze. "I told her you couldn't have been drunk."

Cate opened her mouth, but the lie didn't come. "I was."

"Jesus Christ, Cate!" Baker put his mug down on the counter, suddenly looking tired. "That woman's only child is dead, and you can't manage to stay sober when talking to her?"

"It was a one-time thing. I'd had a very upsetting morning, and I forgot we had the appointment to talk. It snuck up on me."

Baker pointed to the bottle on the counter and raised his voice. "Bullshit addict excuses. You've got a drinking problem."

As always when men started yelling, her instinct was to apologize, to appease. Instead, she went on the attack. "Don't be ridiculous. You're pissed because I've made your job harder by calling the Johnson death 'homicide.'"

"I'm pissed off because you're royally fucking up. You were always one of the better coroners. Now you're too wrapped up in this case and hitting the goddamn bottle."

"Get out of my house."

He crossed his arms. "I'm not leaving until you change your report. Call it suicide. There was nothing at the scene to support homicide."

"You really take the cake, Baker. I suspected you were a lazy cop but didn't think you'd sink this low. Are you in TDR's pocket?"

He flushed. "Those corporate assholes don't tell me what to do."

"Did you even follow up on Molly's missing iPhone?"

He raised his voice. "Of course I did. I've talked to the girlfriend, asked her parents. Had our tech guys trying to track it down through its Sim card, but it must be powered down. That phone is missing, but I'll find it."

"Don't you think a lost phone is suspicious, or are you stupid as well as lazy?"

If he'd been her father, or even Matthew, that would have goaded him beyond reason. Baker's face turned red, but he didn't lose his temper. "Don't try to change the subject, Cate. Think about Mrs. Johnson. You're playing with her emotions. A child's suicide is gut-wrenching, and now you've confused her by calling it murder. When I find there isn't enough evidence to support that verdict, the poor woman will never recover. Haven't you done enough?"

Baker was right about that. One of the most important parts of her job was to help the living understand how their loved ones died, and she'd only complicated things. "Don't worry. I won't be bothering her again," she said. "I'm suspended from duty for a month."

"What?"

"Mrs. Johnson called my boss to complain. Dr. Marcoux thinks I'm a burnout. He's put me on stress leave."

Her revelation drained the aggression from Baker. "Jesus, Cate. I'm sorry."

She was startled by his sympathy. "Yeah," she said. His empathy brought up the pain and the shame again, and she fought back tears. She wasn't going to cry in front of him. She turned her back and began desultorily cleaning some dishes.

Baker didn't appear to notice that she was upset. Instead, he sounded thoughtful. "I wouldn't have thought she'd do that."

She was scraping at a plate crusted with three-day-old microwaved pizza, but she gave up, and turned to him. "What do you mean?"

"When I told Mrs. Johnson you weren't drunk, she believed me."

She grimaced. "Well, you weren't as convincing as you like to think."

Baker shook his head. "No, she bought it. I'm sure." His eyes fell on the bottle, but he spoke in a conciliatory tone. "Cate, I really do think you should consider getting some help—"

Her anger flared. "And I think you should mind your own business. Do your goddamn job, Baker, and leave my personal life out of it."

He put his mug down. "You're in no position to tell me what to do. In fact, you now have no connection to the case. You're just a civilian. A civilian with a brutal hangover, as far as I can tell. How much did you drink last night, Cate? Do you even know?"

She pushed past him and opened her door. "Leave, please."

He opened his mouth as if to argue further but decided against it. He walked out but stopped on her porch and turned to face her. "Cate, you need help."

"Screw you," she said and slammed the door.

CHAPTER FORTY

CATE DIDN'T WANT TO THINK ABOUT HOW BAKER WAS THE SECOND COL-
league in twelve hours to tell her she had a drinking problem. She
went back to the kitchen and picked up her cup. The Laphroaig stared
at her, but she pushed it away.

She brought the mug to the living room, curling up on the couch
and clasping the warmth in her hands. Too wired to go back to sleep,
she stared out the window. What was she going to do without work?
She should be OK for money. She had enough cases already submitted
that the checks would keep coming for a while. The real question was
whether Marcoux would allow her to return. She took a big sip of
coffee, grateful for its harsh bite.

If they determined she wasn't fit for work, they wouldn't revoke
her medical license; instead they'd just kick her off coroner duty. Undoubtedly, she could find a job somewhere as a general practitioner.
Rural communities were desperate for doctors and weren't too fussy
about work histories.

She was surprised at how bereft she felt at the thought of giving
up her coroner work. Even though she found the job satisfying, some
part of her had absorbed her father's opinion that it wasn't "real" medicine. Now she realized that though it didn't have the prestige of the
complex surgeries he had performed or the nobility of her brother's
work, it made a difference in people's lives, and she was proud of it.

The problem was that she had buggered it all up. She took another
sip of coffee and thought about Molly Johnson hanging suspended
from that rope. Baker wasn't going to investigate her death properly.
He'd put three men on it for a week or two before concluding that the

coroner's assessment of manner of death was wrong. He was within his rights to do so; her ruling had no legal authority. She needed proof. If she had that, she would show him and Dr. Marcoux that her judgment wasn't clouded, that she wasn't an alcoholic, and that she could continue as a coroner.

Cate closed her eyes and leaned her head against the couch. Thoughts swirled. The man from the market, at the party, and in the hallway. Her attacker. She shivered. Why hadn't she paid more attention to what he looked like? If she could offer Baker a description, maybe find him among some mugshots, that would go a long way to gaining credibility and putting him behind bars.

Her stomach rumbled. She was too lazy to go to the fridge, so she reached into her purse for a carrot. Damn. She wanted a cigarette. Her fingers brushed against something unfamiliar. She pulled out a small container. She had forgotten about Simon Thatcher's box of weed, with one perfect, ready-rolled joint. It wasn't tobacco, but it would have to do. She was so grateful to have something to smoke, her fingers shook as she brought it to her mouth. Simon had even helpfully supplied a pack of matches. She lit up.

The first drag sparked a coughing fit, but she managed the second more smoothly. The muscles in her neck unknotted and the zinging wire of tension she'd felt since her attack loosened.

How was everything connected? Idly, she played with the pack of matches. Why hadn't Fabienne mentioned her fight with Molly? Who had Molly made an appointment with after work? Cate looked at the matches. "Goblin Market" was emblazoned on the front with an address in Ottawa. It must be a bar or a restaurant. She had a dim memory of Jason once saying that "Goblin Market" was one of their mother's favorite poems. She took another toke and stood. Her head swam pleasantly, and she smiled. She'd forgotten how enjoyable this buzz was. She ambled over to her mother's record player, flipped through the albums neatly stacked beside it. She located the one she was looking for—*New Skin for the Old Ceremony*. Leonard Cohen's sad voice, threaded with anger, filled the room. The sound of the player, so long unused, brought her back to lying on her bed as a teen. It was darkly perfect music for a mopey, morose adolescent. There was something pure in her angst at the time—it was what she was supposed to be doing at fifteen—wallowing in perceived slights and hormonally induced moodiness.

What was her excuse these days?

She searched the bookshelf above the record player, looking for her mother's old poetry books. She flipped through *Norton's Anthology of English Poetry*, until she came to "Goblin Market." The page was smudged from repeated readings, and she thought of her mother pausing over the lines. It was written by Christina Rossetti—wasn't that the poet Peter had quoted—the "gnawings of grief"?

She skimmed the poem, a long story of two sisters who lived an idyllic life in a cottage by a river until one is seduced by the goblins and sells a lock of her hair for a piece of their fruit. It was a strange poem, lush in description and drenched in sex. The last line caught her eye.

Their fruits like honey to the throat
But poison in the blood

Poison, death—murder. Her mind drifted back to the case. Molly's jean jacket. There was something there; she knew it. She remembered the line of dancing monkeys Molly had stenciled on the bathtub; her password was "monkey" too. She'd made a scarf with monkeys. What had Mrs. Johnson said? Molly had talked about her favorite stuffed animal—some kind of monkey. All those animal pins on Molly's jean jacket, and there hadn't been one monkey. The missing pin.

Cate's eyes flew open. Regretfully, she stubbed out the joint. She knew who she had to talk to, and she had a good lead on where to find him.

CHAPTER FORTY-ONE

PINHEY WAS A CROOKED LITTLE ROAD OFF HINTONBURG'S MAIN THOR-
oughfare, Wellington Street. In the past decade, the whole neighborhood had undergone massive gentrification. Crack houses and
dilapidated buildings were now doggy spas offering poodle pedicures
and baby stores with highchairs made of reclaimed Tibetan prayer
huts, costing the price of a decent used car.

Cate hopped out of the Uber and glanced at the matchbook she'd
taken from Simon's tent. The windows of the Goblin Market reflected
the sunny morning but were otherwise dark. She hoped her hunch
was right.

The Goblin Market fit right into the new neighborhood ethos.
The sign was made of corrugated metal, painted in bright, insouciant
colors. Cate pulled on the door. Locked. A notice said they opened at
six p.m. She peered through a window. Mason jars filled with wilting
daisies sat on a few small, scattered tables. Brightly colored wooden
chairs offered a pop of color. A Victorian chaise lounge occupied one
corner, near an upright piano, a banjo, and what looked like two ac-
cordions. It was the kind of bar where you could get sixteen different
types of cocktails featuring "orange water" and a craft gin infused
with blueberries, but where the only whisky they stocked would be
blended.

There was a dim light in the hallway behind the bar. She knocked
on the window, but no response. Her phone rang. Dr. Marcoux. Her
mouth went dry. Did he somehow know she was here? Reason reas-
serted itself. Marcoux, in his kindly fashion, was probably calling to
check on her.

She ignored the call and ducked down the alley between the bar and the hairdresser's next door. Normally the tight squeeze would make her heart race, but the lingering effects of two puffs of the joint had mellowed her nicely, allowing her to accept the walls for what they were. Picking her way through beer bottles and cigarette butts, she reached the back entrance. The screen door was open, and Cate heard music from inside.

"Hello?" she called, walking through the entrance. She was in a tiny kitchen, only big enough for a double range and two refrigerators. Photographs of the Dalai Lama and Mr. T were framed on one wall. She followed the sound of the music to a dim hallway. She glimpsed the bar further down, but the music, Tom Waits, was coming from a room to her right. "Hello," she said again, knocking on the door. There was no answer. She opened it. A man sat hunched over a table, intently rolling a joint. She spoke louder. "Hello!"

The figure jumped, dropped the spliff, and looked to the door. It was Simon Thatcher. "What the hell?" he shouted. He was younger than she remembered. No more than twenty. His blond hair flopped in front of one eye, adding to his youthful appearance. He wore loose pants and a ripped white T-shirt. A hemp necklace circled his throat. His ear distenders continued to distract.

Cate's heartbeat quickened. Was she staring at Molly's murderer? She regretted not telling anyone where she was going. Too late now. "Sorry to startle you, Mr. Thatcher." She spoke in a calm voice. She didn't want to antagonize him.

The young man looked bewildered. "Who are you?"

"I'm Dr. Cate Spencer. We met ten days ago at the Nitrate Film Processing Center."

His eyes slid to the small pile of green leaves on the table next to him. "It's only half a gram. It's legal." He crossed his arms.

She put both hands up. "I'm not with the police." She eyed him. He looked more confused than aggressive. "I'm the coroner, investigating Molly Johnson's death."

He narrowed his eyes, and then recognition set in. "Oh yeah, I remember you. The doctor." He turned to the table and swept the leaves into a baggie. "It's medicinal," he said, chuckling at his own joke.

Cate's shoulders unknotted. Simon didn't appear ready to murder her. "I wanted to ask you about Molly's death."

He frowned, somehow looking younger. "You said you weren't a cop."

"I'm not, but I have to determine how Molly died." No need to say she'd already done so.

"Like I told that detective, I only talk if I've got my lawyer." He reached into his back pocket and handed her a heavily embossed business card. "Call them."

She assessed him for a moment. He sounded cocky, but his eyes projected anxiety. "Do you get into trouble so often you've got a lawyer on speed dial?" she asked, intentionally needling him. She was feeling reckless. "That must cost your daddy a lot of money." She slipped the card into her pocket.

Simon flushed. "My father can go to hell."

"Except when it comes time to pay your legal bill," Cate said. "Does your family even know where you are?"

"I'm twenty-one. I can do what I want. Besides, I've got a job here. I'm supporting myself. I don't need them."

She noticed the mop in the corner and a bucket filled with water. "You're cleaning floors? That's not going to feed and shelter you, let alone keep you in weed."

"This is only temporary," Simon said. "Why do you care?"

"I really don't."

Simon blinked. "How did you find me, anyway?"

"Your friends at the protest told me." Another lie, but Cate didn't think telling him that she'd rifled through his belongings would win his trust.

"Those assholes," Simon said, apparently exhausted by this news. His shoulders slumped further.

"They were worried about you." She sat in the other chair.

He waved a hand. "I'm fine. My dad hit the roof after the cops tried to charge me with that cherry bomb. We had a huge fight, and I split."

Simon appeared to have forgotten that he'd refused to talk to her. Absentmindedly, he returned to stuffing his half-rolled joint.

Cate wasn't sure what you were supposed to do in an interrogation but decided to keep pushing until he pushed back. "How did you end up here?" she asked.

Simon shrugged. "My friend's older sister owns the place. She's letting me crash upstairs."

"That's good," Cate said, nodding. She didn't know how to finesse the next question, so she blurted it out. "How did you know Molly Johnson?"

Simon reared back in his chair like she'd struck him. "I didn't. I never even met her."

"Come on, Simon. She stopped most days at the protest. She brought coffee and Timbits." Cate could see his thoughts progress across his face as he realized she'd caught him out.

"Oh yeah, right. I did know her from that. She'd stop and talk. She was nice. Into what we were trying to do. We all liked her."

"But you knew her better than most. You guys were friends."

"Who told you that?" Simon asked. "They're lying. I want to talk to my lawyer."

"I'm not a police officer," Cate explained again. "I simply want to determine how she died. You don't need to worry about me. I couldn't care less who threw that cherry bomb."

"There's no way I'd chuck something flammable in there. That would be crazy."

This caught Cate's attention. "Deteriorating nitrate is very volatile, isn't it?"

"Yeah, that building is a powder keg. A spark in the wrong place, and the whole thing could blow."

"Did Molly tell you about the nitrate, Simon?"

He jumped as if she had zapped him with an electrical wire, and his denial was too quick to be convincing. "What? No!"

"How did you know about it, then?"

"I had the best private school education money can buy," he said, but his eyes shifted away from hers.

"I really doubt your curriculum included the dangers of deteriorating nitrate film. Just tell me the truth. Were you and Molly friends?"

"No, I hardly knew her."

"How did you get her monkey pin, then?" she asked.

"What pin? I don't know what you're talking about."

"The one on your jean jacket. The jacket you were wearing the day of Molly's death. I know that pin was Molly's." That was a gamble, but she was confident of her odds. "Did you steal it?"

"No!" he said. "She gave it to me."

"I thought you weren't friends," Cate said.

"We weren't. We . . ." His voice trailed away.

"You what, Simon? She's dead. Her family is grief-stricken. Molly meant everything to them. What was Molly to you?"

"We slept together," he said in a small voice.

That, to put it mildly, was not the answer Cate expected.

CHAPTER FORTY-TWO

"YOU AND MOLLY SLEPT TOGETHER," CATE REPEATED TO SIMON, ABSORBING the news.

"Yeah, so?" His cheeks reddened.

"But she was gay," Cate said.

Simon shrugged. "Not all the time."

Cate hadn't requested a vaginal swab with the autopsy—you only did that if you suspected sexual assault—now it would be too late. Molly's body had been returned to Vancouver and probably already interred or cremated.

Cate recalled walking around the nitrate facility last Tuesday. There was a used condom, a soggy sleeping bag, and a broken wine bottle in the woods outside the fire exit. She remembered that there was no sleeping bag in Simon's tent. "You slept with her in the nitrate facility," Cate said. "That's why Baker caught you prowling around the woods. You wanted to get your sleeping bag back."

"How did you know that?" he asked. His mouth made a little "o" as he realized what he had just admitted. "No point in denying it, I guess. I saw the ambulance and cops go by and figured I should clear my stuff out. I didn't want trouble."

Cate almost pitied him. He had just admitted to sleeping with a woman whose case was classified as a homicide. He was about to land in more trouble than he knew what to do with. He didn't seem to realize his position, however, and Cate wasn't going to enlighten him. Not before she figured out if he'd played a role in Molly's death. "How did you two get together?"

"She drove by us every day, and I thought she was cute. She started bringing coffee, donuts, stuff like that, and we ended up talking." Simon seemed relieved to be discussing Molly. He continued, "She was pissed at the developers. She said they were railroading the Archives or something. Anyway, she showed up that Sunday afternoon."

"That must have been unusual," Cate said. Sunday was when Molly had called Rose looking for a place to stay after her fight with Fabienne. It was the same day she'd called her mother sounding upset.

Simon agreed. "Yeah, she and the other one, Rose, only ever came during the week." He continued rolling the joint between his fingers, but it was slowly falling apart. "It was quiet at the protest. Not a lot of us out there. Maybe because it was so hot. Anyway, I jogged over when I saw Molly's car. I could tell she'd been crying, and when I asked her what was wrong, she said she'd had a big fight with her girlfriend."

"What about?"

"I didn't ask. She said she didn't want to go home. She didn't have anywhere to crash, though. She was going to sleep at the facility so they could both have some breathing room. I told her I'd keep her company, if she wanted."

"That was kind of you," Cate said dryly.

Simon shrugged. "I thought she was cute, plus the facility was air-conditioned, and I needed a break from my tent. I was sweating my balls off."

"All the makings of a great romance."

"Hey, she was mad at her girlfriend, and I was looking for a comfortable place to sleep. We both got what we wanted."

"Then what happened?"

"We hung out. Sat in the clearing in the woods, drank wine, stared at the stars. She was cool."

"What did you talk about?"

"We didn't do much talking," Simon said, grinning at the memory.

"Come on," Cate said, losing patience. "You must have spoken a bit."

"We talked about our families. Her parents sound cool. They did a lot of activist work out West. Talked about school. She thought I should go back to university. She was a couple of years older than me and was really committed to her job. We argued about that. I'm not interested in being a capitalist stooge."

"She worked for the Archives. It's hardly Wall Street."

"The way I see it, you work in an office, you work for the Man."

He really was incredibly naïve. "Did you have any sense of what was troubling her?"

He looked down at his feet. "I've gone over our conversation, trying to remember if she gave me any clue about why she'd want to kill herself. I would have sworn she wasn't suicidal. She was pissed."

"At her girlfriend?"

"That was the weird thing, I don't think so. There was something else. She talked about how people were such liars and how TDR was pushing the Archives around. She thought the development was bullshit. I don't know. We drank a lot of wine, so it kind of gets blurry."

"Then what happened? Did you have sex in the woods?" That would explain the condom.

He shrugged. "Yeah, it was a beautiful night."

As far as Cate knew, the wine bottle, sleeping bag, and condom were still in that little clearing. Ten days had passed, and there had been some rain, but there might still be DNA linking him to the scene. Either Simon Thatcher was incredibly foolish in admitting all of this to her, or he was innocent.

Simon continued, apparently quite willing to recall his tryst. "We went inside to sleep, though. Like I said, I wanted the AC."

Cate thought of the freezing grimness of the area where Molly was found. "You didn't sleep in the vaults, did you?"

"Nah, that place is really creepy. Like, it gives off a mega-haunted vibe, you know?"

Cate recalled the story of the soldier who died trapped and abandoned. She was a rational scientist who didn't believe in ghosts, but if any place gave off a mega-haunted vibe, it was those vaults.

Simon continued, "We crashed in the work room with the table and all the boxes. We overslept that morning and only woke up when Rose arrived. Molly hustled me out the side door."

The same one that Cate and Rose had fled through after the cherry bomb.

"She told me that I should just come back and get my sleeping bag at lunch when Rose left for her break. She had an appointment with someone at noon, so she told me to be there at 11:30 sharp."

That must have been Molly's last meeting with Albert Owl.

"Did you make plans to see each other again?"

"No. We both knew it was a one-time thing."

"You were OK with that?" Cate watched him to see if he exhibited any signs of the jilted lover.

"I was ready to leave, honestly. She was cute but kind of nerdy. Like, she really loved talking about archives and shit. She told me all about those nitrate negatives and how flammable they are and a bunch of other stuff."

"Why didn't you go back and get the sleeping bag before Tuesday?"

"I went back to my tent on Monday morning and passed out until two p.m., so I was too late to get it back. Then I walked the protest line, and I went to my parents' for the night."

"In the Glebe?" Cate confirmed. She could see how that pleasant house with its leafy trees and air-conditioning would be preferable to a stifling tent. "Where were you late Monday afternoon?" His answer was crucial. According to Naomi's autopsy report, Molly was killed between four p.m. and seven p.m.

"At the protest. Weekday rush hour is prime visibility. I always make sure I'm there."

If that was true and others could confirm it, Simon was off the hook.

"So on Tuesday morning, when did you realize something was wrong at the facility?"

"The ambulance and cops went zooming past at about nine. Everyone was saying there must have been an accident or a break-in."

"Were you concerned about Molly?"

"Sure, I wanted to check she was OK. Also, I wanted to get my sleeping bag back."

"Why were you so worried about retrieving it?"

He flushed red.

"You'd left a stash there," Cate guessed.

"There was a baggie or two—only weed. It may be legal, but the cops will use any excuse to hassle me, and I didn't want to deal with it."

"So, that's why you threw the cherry bomb?" Cate asked.

"I didn't do that. No way."

"Come on, Simon. You came back, saw the place was crawling with cops, and freaked out. You had to get people out before they found your stash." Cate was surprised at how well this conversation was going.

"That's not true." His protest was weak.

Cate continued, seeing Tuesday's events through his eyes. "Molly had told you about the nitrate, so you were sure they'd take a fire threat seriously. You threw it into that workroom, rather than the vault, because you knew it wasn't too risky—wouldn't actually pose a threat. You chucked the cherry bomb, waited for us to evacuate, and snuck back into the facility. What I don't get is why you threw the sleeping bag into the woods. Not the best hiding place."

He looked away, not meeting her eyes, and Cate knew.

"You saw Molly, didn't you?"

He didn't acknowledge her question, but his hands trembled.

"You hid in the woods by the door. Rose and I exited, and once we were gone, you snuck in to get your sleeping bag."

He shook his head. "That door was locked. I had to go in by the front one."

"You grabbed the bag and your stash, but decided to leave via the vaults, so that you could go back through the woods. Only, you didn't know about Molly."

"That's right," he said, lifting tear-filled eyes to her. "I came down that long hall and there she was, in that last vault. She was like a puppet, hanging from a string. All limp, with these fucking eyes staring at me. It was like a horror movie. The last time I'd seen her, she'd been laughing, trying to hustle me out before Rose caught us. I was totally freaked out."

"So what did you do?"

"I bolted. I ran through that door, dropped the sleeping bag, and booted through the woods—right into the cops' arms."

"Why didn't you tell them what really happened?"

Simon stared at her. "I don't trust the pigs to hand out speeding tickets, let alone give me a fair hearing."

"How long did Baker keep you downtown?"

Simon shrugged, speaking in a monotone. "Only a couple of hours. Then my parents showed up with the lawyer."

"What did you do?"

"My father screamed at me the whole way home, so I took off. I went back to the protest, but I didn't want to talk to anyone. I turned my phone off. Turned everything off. I wanted to drop out." His face was anguished. "I keep thinking about her glasses—how they were smashed at her feet. She was practically blind, could hardly see a foot in front of her without them. I should have realized she was in a bad place. I should have stopped her from killing herself." His fingers rolled the joint back and forth until the paper burst. He stared down at the green leaves on the table in surprise, as if he didn't know how they got there.

Cate looked at this boy, shoulders hunched, replaying events over and over in his mind. She knew she should leave now, call Baker, let him make his arrest and do his investigation. She couldn't abandon Simon to such misery, however. "It wasn't suicide. Molly was murdered."

"What?" His eyes flew to her face.

"Whoever killed her tried to make it look like suicide."

"Who would want to kill Molly? Why?"

"That's what we're trying to figure out." It still hadn't occurred to

Simon that he'd be the prime suspect. "She died on Monday evening. Think back. Do you remember anyone coming or going to the facility in the late afternoon?"

Simon rubbed the back of his neck. "Rose left at the usual time, but I didn't see Molly go. I remember thinking that I must have missed her when I was taking a leak or something. I wanted to ask her if she had made up with her girlfriend, or what."

"Did you want to find out if she was still staying at the facility?"

He flushed. "Maybe."

"Is that why you left your stash? An excuse to go back?"

"She was actually pretty cool, even with all that archives stuff," he said.

Cate felt a pang for this sad boy. "This is important, Simon. Whoever killed Molly did it at the nitrate facility between four p.m. when Rose left and seven that night. If you saw anything suspicious you need to tell me now."

"Who would want to kill her?" he repeated. He met Cate's eyes. "I want to help any way that I can."

"Great, so think back to that Monday night. You say you didn't see her leave." That fit with the idea that Molly's 4:30 appointment was with her murderer. "Did you see anyone arriving?"

He looked thoughtful. "Cars go in and out on a regular basis. People going to the base, doing surveys for the development, shit like that. Plus, you can also get to the nitrate facility by going the long way, through the base."

Simon was thinking aloud, obviously determined to be helpful. "If you really wanted to be sneaky, you could park somewhere on Turcotte Road and walk across the fields to the facility."

That made sense. Turcotte was a busy thoroughfare lined with mini-malls and gas stations. No one would notice a car parked there for an hour or two. "So there's no way of knowing for sure who went there that Monday afternoon?"

"No, I'd say there's no way of knowing."

"What about your camera?" Cate asked.

He stared at her blankly.

She explained about the man who'd stolen it from his tent. "Son of a bitch," Simon said. "My mom gave me that Nikon."

"Was there anything incriminating on it? Anything that could help us catch the murderer?"

"I don't think so. I mean, mostly I was just documenting the protest, you know—like whenever the cops hassled us, I'd pull it out."

"You must have been taking pictures when the cops and ambulance went by on Tuesday morning."

Simon shook his head. "No. I'd lent it to Derek that weekend. I thought he still had it. He must have put it back in my tent at some point."

"What was he doing with it?" She kept her voice neutral. Dreadlocked Derek was now on her suspect list.

"Shit, I don't know. Probably taking photos of that cricket frog he's always talking about."

"Where would he do that?"

"The marsh down by Lake Mitchell."

"Would Derek have walked past the nitrate facility to get there?"

"Sure, that's the easiest way. Skirt the building, go over the hill, and slip through a hole in the fence by the big maple tree."

Was that how Cate's attacker had lain in wait for her at the party? Could he have gone past the nitrate facility and breached the fence separating it from the base? Maybe she hadn't seen him earlier at the party after all. If only she hadn't been so drunk.

Simon was still talking, and Cate focused. "That's how we do it when we want a swim."

"A swim?"

"That lake is awesome. Blue, clear, and really, crazy deep. Everyone swims there, everyone except Annie. She refuses. Says it's sacred Algonquin waters or something. Screw it, when it's forty-five degrees Celsius, with humidity, I'd skinny-dip in a vat of Holy Water blessed by Jesus Christ himself."

Cate didn't comment on that weird visual. Derek was near the facility, maybe at the time of Molly's murder. Had he seen something? Had he done something? Whatever Derek's involvement, she'd need to question him about Simon's story. Get some of the other protesters to confirm his alibi. She surprised herself by how much she hoped they could.

She needed to tell Baker what she had uncovered.

"Dr. Spencer?"

"Yes, Simon?"

His eyes filled with tears. "Thank you for telling me the truth about Molly's death. I feel like an asshole saying this, but it's a relief to know she didn't kill herself."

She understood what he was trying to say. Sudden death was always disorienting, but suicide left the most collateral damage. The feelings of guilt, inadequacy, and anger it evoked could be crippling. Cate had seen it happen to families of suicide victims in the past. They often never recovered, still calling her years after the death to ask if there was any further answer to the great unanswerable: "Why." She spoke softly. "Feeling relief doesn't make you an asshole. It makes you human."

He nodded jerkily, and something in that awkward movement reminded her of Toby, Dr. Marcoux's son. It was a brusque vulnerability or a thinly masked fragility that made her heart ache.

He spoke. "If I can do anything to help your investigation, anything to catch the person who did that to Molly, you tell me, OK?"

"Thanks, Simon. Your mother was right about you."

He looked startled. "My mother?"

"You should call her. She's worried about you."

He still looked confused. "What did she say about me?"

"That you're a sweet boy."

CHAPTER FORTY-THREE

CATE MET BAKER AT THE CAPITAL CITY CANTEEN, A NEARBY COFFEE shop.

He was back in his standard rumpled suit, his Fred Flintstone tie a splotch of garish orange. "If you think I'm going to apologize, forget it," he said flatly.

"Let's pretend this morning never happened."

"Cate, you need to—"

She put up her hand. "You were a douche this morning. I was a douche this morning. Let's stop and move on."

Baker shrugged. "What's up?"

"I talked to Simon Thatcher today."

"What, why?" He frowned. "You've made your ruling on the case. You shouldn't be talking to anyone involved."

"You didn't object when I told you I wanted to talk to him last week."

"I didn't?" Baker looked astonished.

"Yeah, at your office, remember? You gave me his address. Told me I could knock myself out."

"That's before I realized that you're too invested. You need to let it go. It's making you unstable."

Her face flushed. "Unstable," she repeated. "I'm fine."

"I don't give a fuck about your mental state," he replied. "You need to butt out of police work because you'll screw up this shit case even further."

"Do you want to hear what I found out?"

His face indicated his struggle—to continue to yell at her or to find out what she knew. "Well?"

She relayed everything Thatcher told her, including his tryst with Molly and throwing the cherry bomb.

"I knew that little freak was up to something," he said when Cate finished. Baker was quite cheerful now. He dialed a number on his phone and issued instructions. "This is about the Johnson case. There's a secondary scene: The clearing in the woods to the south of the nitrate facility, by the exit door. You should find a sleeping bag, wine bottle, and a condom. Make sure you bring forensics. I want that entire wood combed for evidence." He shut off the phone and spoke more to himself than to Cate. "We'll nail him for this."

"You might get him for trespassing and the cherry bomb, but you won't get him for murder."

"What do you mean?"

"He's got an alibi. He claims several people can vouch for his whereabouts."

"Those hippy dippy protesters? They were probably all stoned off their gourds. They've got no credibility."

"Nevertheless," Cate said. "Simon will have their word, and he'll have the help of his family's high-powered legal team. Anyway, I don't think he did it."

"For God's sake, you screwed up my suicide theory and now you're poking holes in the goddamn murder suspect you just handed me on a silver platter."

"You've mixed your metaphors," Cate said mildly.

"Fuck my fucking metaphors," Baker said. "Why don't you think Thatcher is our killer?"

She was touched by the "our" and by the fact that Baker wanted to know her opinion. "He was genuinely stunned when I told him about Molly's murder, and he was completely open with me. Admitting to all kinds of incriminating stuff that he wouldn't have copped to if he were guilty."

"Come on, Cate. You and I both know that most murdered women are killed by their sexual partners."

"Not this time. I think Molly was murdered because of something to do with her work."

Baker didn't appear to have heard. "We'll arrest him and see what we can shake out of him. We might get lucky and get a confession or at least trip him up."

"He has an alibi," Cate reminded him.

Baker held up a hand. "Until I check out that alibi, I'm working on the assumption that if there actually was a homicide, Simon Thatcher did it."

"You're not going to pursue that 4:30 p.m. appointment?"

"Listen, we've got limited resources. I've got to be smart about how I spend my time and my officers."

"Fine."

Baker gave her a hard stare. "Cate, I'm serious about staying out of this investigation. It's ours now. Your involvement isn't needed or wanted. Back off. Use your suspension to get your head together."

She glowered. She could respect him when he was telling her to stay out of his case but not when he was making judgments about her personal life. "I thought you didn't care about my emotional well-being."

"I don't like seeing people hurting themselves. This whole case is just one long exercise in self-sabotage for you."

"Self-sabotage—fancy concept, Baker. You learn that watching *Dr. Oz*?"

"No," he said. "At AA."

That stopped her cold. "What?"

"I've been sober for six years." He spoke matter-of-factly. "My wife left me. I wasn't sleeping. Lost most of my money in the divorce and stupid investments. I was drinking on the job. Drove drunk. Hit a tree. Thank Christ I didn't hurt anyone."

"How did you stop?" The question was out of her mouth before she knew she wanted to ask it.

"The guys at the station did an intervention. I got treatment. I go to meetings. I'm recovering. That's what you need to do."

"No. I'm not like you," she said flatly.

He spoke simply. "You've got a problem."

What did Baker, with his sanctimonious tone, know about her? "I'm not some helpless goddamn drunk." Her voice rose. "I don't drink cheap liquor out of a paper bag. I'm a doctor, for Christ's sake." She pushed back her chair and threw a five-dollar bill on the table. She didn't want Baker buying her coffee. She didn't want to owe this man anything.

She strode out of the restaurant. She was going to prove Baker wrong, and Marcoux too, for that matter. She would show them she knew what she was doing, and she was going to crack this case wide open.

CHAPTER FORTY-FOUR

ÉCOLE STE-AGATHE WAS EASY TO FIND. A PRIVATE PRIMARY SCHOOL ON the Gatineau side of the Ottawa River, the small building was tucked into a quiet suburban nest of streets. Sitting in her car, Cate crunched on a carrot from the bag in her purse. Fabienne had not admitted to any tension between herself and Molly, but thanks to Rose, Cate knew that they had argued, and Simon confirmed it was a doozy. She thought of her own fight with Rose. It would be nice to discuss the latest Simon Thatcher developments with her, but it was safer to keep her out of it.

Cate left the car and presented herself at the school office, flashing her coroner badge and asking to speak to Fabienne. The prim-looking secretary pursed her lips, speaking broken English. "Mademoiselle Aubin teaches."

Cate didn't waver. "This is important. Is there a room we can meet in?"

The secretary directed her to an empty classroom across the hall. The space was different from Cate's school memories. In place of a chalkboard, there was a whiteboard and a screen. A projector and computer sat on a table at the front. Each student's desk had an outlet, presumably for laptops. The large crucifix, with the nearly life-sized Christ figure, blood dripping from hands and feet, was the only jarringly old-fashioned note. Cate stared at the immortalized image of torture and suffering. Did the students ever get used to it, she wondered, or were they constantly jolted by its veneration of pain? Such an overt depiction of torment would never have had a place at the boarding school she had attended. WASPs didn't make their pain public;

they stuffed it down deep inside and used that repressed energy to increase investment yields and maintain the crispness of their khakis.

Fabienne entered the room. Her face was flushed. "What is this?" she asked. "I am teaching. You shouldn't be here."

Cate raised an eyebrow. She hadn't been expecting this display of aggression from ice-cold Fabienne. "I'm sorry, but I had more questions for you."

Fabienne crossed her arms and looked behind her. "You shouldn't be here," she repeated.

"Why didn't you tell me you and Molly had a fight the day before she died?"

"You can't come here asking me these questions," Fabienne hissed, closing the classroom door.

"Your girlfriend might have been murdered, Fabienne. You have to start cooperating."

"Murdered!" exclaimed Fabienne. She sank into a student's chair.

Cate regretted her bluntness. "Did you really believe she had killed herself?" she asked more gently.

Fabienne looked down. "I was devastated. I thought it might be because of our fight. I couldn't think about it. I shut myself down. That is what I do."

Even now, Cate could see the woman struggling to rein in her emotions, maintain her composure. Control was everything to Fabienne. "What happened?"

"When she first moved in, everything was wonderful. Molly was full of life, full of laughter. I loved her. But, as June progressed, she became distant. She was researching something at work, but she wouldn't discuss it with me. She was closed off—moody, no talking. We stopped sleeping together."

"What was she working on, do you know?"

Fabienne shook her head. "I confronted her last Sunday. I demanded to know what she was doing. She just said she'd found some photographs—negatives," Fabienne corrected herself. "She was always telling me that negatives weren't the same as photographs. Anyway, she said she found some negatives that were very important."

"Jesus Christ," Cate whispered, then cast an apologetic glance at the crucifix. She sat at a desk too.

"I was angry that those negatives were taking up all her time, all her attention."

Fabienne tossed her head, and Cate suddenly understood that her controlled demeanor hid a passionately jealous woman. "Did you see any of the negatives?"

"No, I threatened to burn them up. I was furious. Molly said she didn't have them with her. She said she wasn't allowed to take anything from the Archives. That was the number one rule." Fabienne's voice softened. "Molly was so proud of her profession."

"Where are the negatives?"

"They were safe in the facility," she said. "Hidden where they wouldn't get moved when everything went."

The negatives were the key to the whole case. "Did she tell you anything more about them?"

Fabienne shook her head. "No, I wasn't interested in the *stupide* negatives. I wanted Molly to pay attention to our relationship and to stop this obsession. Finally, I accused her of faking her interest in me so that she could have a place to stay. I was angry. I didn't mean it, but she left." There was a long silence.

When Fabienne spoke again, her voice sounded small and her shoulders slumped. "When that detective showed up and said she was dead, that she had hanged herself—I felt like I had broken into a thousand pieces. Shattered. I could barely function. We were angry, but I didn't think she would do that." Fabienne's voice cracked.

"She didn't do that," Cate said.

Fabienne spoke emphatically. "If that's the case, then someone killed her because of what she was working on. She told me it was big. That important people were involved."

"Did Molly seem scared? Had someone threatened her?"

"No, she was excited. She had stumbled on an important story, and she wanted to expose it."

Cate stood. "Thank you so much. This was very helpful."

Fabienne stood as well, and her straight posture returned. Cate could almost see the impassive mask sliding back into place. "If you need to talk with me again, please call or come to my home. Not my work."

"I'm sorry if I caused trouble for you."

Fabienne shrugged, a small Gallic gesture that Cate envied for its elegance. "I work for a Catholic school. I don't advertise my love life. Having Molly live with me was complicated, professionally."

"Is that why you were annoyed when you learned she had put you down as a next of kin?"

"I kept telling her we had to be discreet, but she didn't listen." Fabienne took a deep breath. "I didn't know I meant that much to her. It feels good that she considered us close enough that I could be her next of kin. I had started to doubt in the past few weeks."

Fabienne walked Cate to the school's entrance, passing a couple of girls in knee socks and tartan skirts.

She and Fabienne stood outside on the steps.

"Thank you," Cate said, turning to Fabienne. "I want to find whoever did this to Molly."

The other woman smiled sadly. "Yes. I want that too."

Cate looked across the school's lawn. A large white statue of a woman stood on the grass.

"That's Saint Agathe," Fabienne said, following her gaze. "She was a proud woman, uninterested in men. When she refused to renounce her Christian faith, the Romans sentenced her to live in a brothel for a month where she was defiled by all the patrons. At the end she continued to affirm her love of Christ. They burned her at the stake."

Cate shivered.

Fabienne noticed. "Faith is not for the faint of heart, Dr. Spencer."

CHAPTER FORTY-FIVE

THE QUICKEST WAY TO GET FROM GATINEAU TO THE EAST SIDE OF THE
city was via the Parkway. It was only as she merged off the busy road
that she noticed a green Honda exiting at the same time. It looked like
the car she noticed yesterday. She turned down a random street, and
the Honda followed. Her mouth dried out. She stared into her rearview, trying to make out the driver. It looked like a man. A big guy.

Despite the AC, sweat dripped from her forehead. She tapped
her fingers against the steering wheel. She slowed further; the Honda
slowed too. Finally, she turned into a Tim Hortons parking lot. The
Honda sped past.

She waited a moment, her heart beating fast, and pulled out into
traffic again. Sure enough, he made a U-turn at the next light and
came back toward her.

His light was red, and he was stuck behind a long line of cars. She
had at least two light cycles before he could turn again to follow her.
She squinted. There was a logo or a sticker on the car's front bumper.
She was too far to see it, but the shape and colors reminded her of
something she had seen recently.

She couldn't wait around to get a better look. Now was her chance.
She hit the gas and sped down a side street. Her heart thudded in her
ears. She looked in the rearview. He was gone.

Only as she pulled up to the protest did she realize that she'd
missed her chance to take the car's license plate number. She'd be
more alert next time. Next time. Her throat tightened. Her attacker
had told her he'd be watching her. She breathed deeply, waiting for
her anxiety to ebb.

The protesters were more energized than before. They were waving signs and shouting in unison. When she opened her car door, she realized they were singing. It took her another moment to grasp that the words weren't English. A skinny young man beat a steady drum rhythm. The song finished, but the drumming continued. She scanned the crowd for Derek or Trinity. No luck. She did see Annie, the Algonquin woman she'd met on Sunday. She walked over.

"Hi—Annie, right?" Cate said. "I'm Dr. Cate Spencer."

"Annie Wabase," the other woman said, with a friendly nod.

"Do you know where Derek is?" Cate asked.

"He and Trinity headed back to Toronto for a couple of days. They're trying to help that protest leader, Liam Westin. He's in jail."

"Damn it," she said. Was Derek really helping Westin, or had he gotten spooked by her visit on Sunday? If that was the case, what did he have to hide?

The drumming stopped, and the group dispersed.

"What were you singing before?"

"It's the AIM Song. I taught it to them."

"AIM?" Cate asked.

"American Indian Movement. You know, Wounded Knee."

"A standoff in the seventies between Indigenous people and the cops?"

"Yeah," Annie said. "We sang it in 2020 when I was protesting Wet'suwet'en. I learned it at Standing Rock."

"You went to Standing Rock?"

She shrugged. "I bunked down at the Sacred Stone Camp in those first months. Got tear-gassed by the marines, or maybe it was Big Oil—same difference, really . . . Bit by their attack dogs." She held up a hand to display a white scar, which stood out like bone protruding from her tan skin.

"You're a true believer," Cate observed. Had she ever cared about anything that much?

"There's a solidarity march next month, and I might go back down. I'm a teacher, so it's easy for me to attend events in the summer."

A teacher: that made sense. Annie projected a wearied cynicism that suited a classroom.

The other woman continued talking. "That's why I stop by here most days for a few hours. I want to show them we're mad as hell."

"Were you here last week? Specifically last Monday afternoon into the evening?"

"Is that when she died? That Molly girl?"

Cate nodded. No point in denying it.

"Yeah, I was around."

"Do you remember if Simon Thatcher was here?"

"Sure, he was always here for evening rush hour. We'd have noticed if he didn't show. We've missed him since last week. Kid has good energy."

Cate's shoulders relaxed. Her instincts about him were right. "What about Derek? Was he around?"

"I think so. I couldn't say for sure, though. Why the questions? Is this because she was murdered?"

"Yeah," Cate said.

"So, are there suspects?" Annie asked.

It was Cate's turn to shrug. "I don't know. I'm not the police."

"Why all of the questions, then?"

"I guess I care about justice."

"I can understand that," Annie said with a bitter twist of her lips. "It's in short supply these days, and you have to fight hard for it."

The intensity of Annie's tone stopped Cate. "Do you think you and the rest of the protesters can halt this development?"

Annie shook her head impatiently. "No. But I want to register how pissed off I am about our deal."

Cate recalled Clifford Bernard's strong reaction to her questions about the legitimacy of the land deal at Albert's funeral. "What do you mean?"

"The Anishinabeg never signed a treaty with the government, so in theory we own all the land in the Ottawa River watershed."

Bernard had said something similar—that this was "unceded" land.

Annie continued. "When the government was going to sell the base ten years ago, a group of us wanted to make sure that Lake Nigamo was protected. It's sacred, and we demanded clauses ensuring there would be no development around it. Anyway, we hired the best researchers we could afford and began combing the Archives, looking for proof of the lake's importance."

Maybe that's what Molly was looking for in those government records. "And did you find anything?"

Annie shook her head. "Nothing. Zilch. Zero."

Cate couldn't hide the disappointment in her voice. "That must have been frustrating."

"It was more than frustrating. It was suspicious."

"What do you mean?"

"My people have been visiting this spot for millennia. You're telling me there's not a single scrap of paper linking us to this area?"

Cate lowered her voice and took a step toward Annie. "You think someone tampered with the evidence? Stole archival records?"

"I know it." Annie's mouth twisted. "I just can't prove it."

This sounded wild. "Why are you so sure there should be specific mention of the lake in those records? I don't think the military would have paid much attention to Indigenous claims when they built this place a hundred years ago."

"That's what's weird. It's not that there's no mention of our presence. There was literally nothing about the lake, and it's a pretty big body of water. In fact, there was hardly anything about the entire base."

Cate thought about what Rose had told her: there were records about the military's purchase of boat houses in BC. It would be odd that records related to a sizable base practically in the middle of the nation's capital were missing.

Annie continued, "Without any evidence, TDR wouldn't give us any concessions to protect the lake. Now it's going to be a glorified water feature on the private golf course."

Cate had found something almost transcendentally peaceful about the lake . . . until the attack. She shivered and recalled what Simon said earlier. "Is that why you don't swim in it? Because it's sacred?"

Annie looked at her sharply. "You've been talking to people, I see. Elders say that it is a great sin to swim in that water. I never could as a kid."

"You grew up around here?"

"My grandpa was one of the only Indigenous airplane mechanics in the whole Air Force. He lived on the base until he died. Grandfather said the lake was off-limits to our people—he wouldn't let any of us native kids swim in it."

"And yet, you couldn't prove its sacredness?"

"Nope. The word of our elders means nothing in settlers' law courts. If we had the money and the time to do some archaeological investigations, we'd find proof for sure. The problem is, without any documentary evidence, we can't get funding for a dig. I tried to delay the negotiations when the government was selling."

"That seems like a reasonable request," Cate said.

Annie laughed, a bitter sound. "You'd think so, but certain factions of our people groveled for whatever pennies TDR would throw at us. We were under huge pressure to take the money and shut up. Eventually I couldn't delay any longer. Our researchers were coming up empty. I had to give in."

"That's terrible."

"Yeah, but it sure made Little Ogima happy."

"Little Ogima?"

"'Ogima' means 'chief.' Clifford Bernard is the chief who carries the most sway at the negotiating table. He's a real little big man. He's always been anxious for us to take TDR's settlement. In the end, we got a lump sum payout and two percent of any profits, but I can guarantee you that TDR's fancy accountants will make sure there are no profits, or at least none they'll share with us."

Cate couldn't help nodding in agreement. "You're completely disillusioned." Clifford Bernard had run roughshod over the people he was meant to help.

"Damn straight. The payout is great, don't get me wrong. Our communities are poor, and we need the cash, but we also need to have a sense of heritage and pride. We shouldn't be selling off our sacred spaces."

"What would you have liked to have seen happen, then?"

"Get two percent gross instead of net and guarantee that the land around Lake Nigamo remains a publicly accessible park with explanations about why it's important to our people."

"Is it too late to negotiate that?"

"Pretty much. The only way we could reopen the deal is if we could prove the importance of Lake Nigamo. We'd need archaeologists and evidence. That would halt construction dead."

Cate's mind spun with possibilities. Had Molly discovered evidence of the lake's sacredness to the Algonquin community? Something that would have put the brakes on a billion-dollar real estate investment?

Annie continued to speak. "So far, all we have is oral history, which doesn't carry much legal weight and is a dwindling resource. Every year more of our elders die, taking their memories with them. With Albert's death, we lost one of the last people who remembered the old stories."

"Wait, who?" Cate asked urgently.

"Albert Owl. He knew all the old stories, and he was adamant that Lake Nigamo was sacred. He would have died before disrespecting the lake."

CHAPTER FORTY-SIX

THE SUN WAS SETTING, AND A DOZY, COMFORTABLE HEAT, DEVOID OF humidity, settled on them. The traffic on Turcotte Road was a steady thrum. Most of the protesters flopped in camp chairs. "You knew Albert Owl?" Cate asked Annie, still absorbing this revelation.

"Sure. He was one of my granddad's closest friends. They served together in the war. I knew him all my life."

"Why weren't you at the funeral?"

Annie shrugged. "I don't attend white ceremonies. I went to the Friendship Center afterward."

"Could Albert have had evidence proving the sacredness of the lake?"

"No way." She shook her head. "If he had, he would have shared it. He was really active ten years ago, when the land was first sold. He was adamant that we had to block the development to protect the lake."

"He never mentioned any evidence, something that could have stopped TDR?"

"No, he always insisted that the lake was key. He convinced us to hire a researcher to comb the Archives. We didn't have a lot of cash, and there was a big debate. Some, like Clifford Bernard, thought it was a waste of money. Albert was furious when we didn't find anything."

"Why?"

"He said he knew the lake should be mentioned in the documents. He's the one who said that the records must have been destroyed on purpose." Annie paused, looking into space as she recalled the conversation from a decade ago. "Bernard disagreed. Said that Albert was paranoid and convinced our group to stop fighting and start negotiating. Albert was disillusioned after that; he withdrew from us and the community. I think that upset Bernard; he'd been really close to Albert—almost like a son."

That personal connection might explain Bernard's touchiness about her questions at the funeral. "Did you tell Molly Johnson any of this? The stuff about the lake being sacred?"

Annie nodded. "She stopped by the protest a couple of weeks ago. She'd brought everyone Tim Hortons. We ended up talking, and I told her about the lake and how there were no records in that Archives of hers."

Cate didn't bother hiding the eagerness from her voice. "How did she react?"

"She didn't seem too surprised. It was like I was confirming something."

A thought occurred to Cate. "Annie, did you mention Albert Owl to Molly?"

"She actually brought him up to me. She said she knew him but didn't say how. We talked about the old stories he'd tell about the lake."

There it was. A tangible connection to Molly, Albert, and the lake. Cate thought of the painting in Albert's room. What had he told Molly?

Annie and Cate chatted for a little while longer, but Annie could add no more to the information she'd already given. They exchanged numbers, and Cate headed to her car.

She let the engine run and the air-conditioning cool down the overheated interior. She closed her eyes for a moment, trying to think through the implications of Annie's revelation. Molly's interest in Albert Owl, in addition to Fabienne's news about the importance of those missing negatives, linked the two to Eastview and the development. How was she going to substantiate that link? Rose was the obvious answer. The more Cate thought about it, the more she realized she needed the other woman's help.

Baker had said they'd wrapped up their search of the nitrate facility, which meant that Rose might be back there. It was time to return to the literal scene of the crime.

Cate was surprised when she saw three police cars parked in front of the building. Of course. Baker had called his officers from the diner, telling them to expand their search to the clearing. She scanned the cars. Only cruisers. It didn't look like the detective was here.

The building appeared more desolate in the fading light than it had when she'd last seen it after the rainstorm. Squat and unkempt, there was something woeful and forgotten about the place. She rolled down her windows and turned off her engine. She could hear muffled calls from the woods as the police conducted their search. The wind rustled through the trees, and she stifled the feeling that something terrible was about to happen.

She hurried toward the main door, not really expecting to get in. Sure enough, a police officer was stationed there. "No entry, ma'am," the young officer said. "This is an active crime scene."

She flashed her coroner badge but played dumb. "What's going on? I thought this building was cleared."

The cop shook his head. "We closed it again this morning. New evidence."

While Rose couldn't be in there, the heavy police presence meant that if the killer hadn't succeeded in finding the negatives when he killed Molly, they could still be hidden in the facility.

"Have a suspect?" Cate asked casually.

The cop grinned. "Arrested some spoiled rich kid this afternoon. He's going down for a long time."

CHAPTER FORTY-SEVEN

CATE CALLED ROSE THE NEXT DAY, ASKING TO MEET UP. THE ADDRESS the other woman gave her was past Innes Road in a sort of no-man's-land between industrial usage and the farmers' fields of the Greenbelt. Low-slung warehouses and lumberyards sat next to empty lots, goldenrod waving in the breeze. She took care driving here to ensure she hadn't been followed by any suspicious cars. Cate pulled into a small parking lot next to Rose's bicycle.

A big sign indicated: "City of Ottawa Community Garden." She passed through a gate and saw green garden plots stretched out the length of a football field. Rose was easy to spot—the only person there—a small figure in a cowboy hat and a long flowy skirt, yanking up weeds. Her plot was demarcated by red and blue yarn.

Cate walked toward her, feeling surprisingly nervous.

"Did you find it OK?" Rose asked, straightening up but unsmiling.

"No problem." There was an awkward pause. Rose's back was rigid. "I didn't know you were a gardener," Cate remarked.

"I love it. Very therapeutic." Rose didn't seem relaxed.

"Oh," Cate said weakly. Should she apologize to the younger woman? She flushed remembering how Rose had thrown Jason's death in her face, as if it was a sign of weakness and failure.

"Yeah," Rose continued, yanking up what looked like a thriving tomato plant. "Gardening is super great when your boss has forced you to take a mental health day because you're 'obviously not coping well.'" Rose made air quotes around the words with her fingers.

"I'm so sorry—" Cate was about to share that she too was put on enforced leave, but Rose interrupted.

"Sure you are," the younger woman said. "I bet you're delighted that I'm forced to stop investigating. I'm the 'silly little girl playing at detective,' remember." Rose threw Cate's own words back at her.

"That's not true," Cate protested. "Or maybe I did say that," she amended when she saw Rose's face. "But only because I was worried about your safety."

"I can handle myself," Rose said.

Cate looked at her in the mellow sunshine. Rose wore no makeup, and a smattering of faded freckles were visible on the bridge of her nose, making her seem even younger. Cate suddenly remembered her mother stroking her own cheeks and telling her that freckles were the marks the sun left after kissing you. She blinked. Where had that come from? She hardly had any memories of her mother.

"Anyway," Rose said, obviously impatient, "why did you want to meet?"

"To update you on the case."

At last, she had the other woman's full attention.

"They've arrested someone in Molly's death," Cate said.

"Who?"

"Simon Thatcher."

Rose's face registered shock. "That cute dude from the protest? Why would he kill Molly?"

"They slept together in the clearing behind the facility."

Rose's mouth opened and closed. "But Molly was committed to Fabienne."

"Remember that fight you told me about?" Rose looked chagrined, and Cate had a flash of satisfaction that the other woman felt bad about withholding information. "That was the Sunday. According to Simon, Molly went out to the facility to crash for the night. They saw each other as she drove in, and one thing led to another."

"There's no motive there." Rose sounded exasperated. "Just because Simon slept with her doesn't make him the killer. It doesn't explain why Molly was ordering all those documents in, or who she had an appointment with at 4:30."

"I agree. Simon's got an alibi. He was seen at the protest. I don't think the arrest will stick."

Rose put her hands on her hips and looked at the sky for a moment. "Jesus. Molly and I were working together Monday morning, and she and Simon had screwed the night before? That's crazy. She never said anything." She sounded wounded.

A car pulled into the parking lot. Cate squinted in the sun. It was a silver SUV.

She next explained Annie's revelation about the connection between Albert Owl, Lake Mitchell, and the TDR land development.

Her words thawed the last of Rose's reserve. The younger woman spoke excitedly. "That would explain why I hardly found any reference to Eastview in those records. Someone removed proof of the sacredness of the lake so there were no barriers to the development."

Cate held up her hand. "That's a lot of work. Do you think it would have been worth the trouble?"

"It makes sense. Think about it—the government offers to sell the base ten years ago. TDR wants to buy it, and it's all straightforward until the Algonquin agitate about the lake's sacredness. Someone combs through relevant records that might have stopped or delayed the development and destroys them. The real question is how did Molly know about this in the first place?"

"Well," Cate said, "there's more." She explained what she learned from Fabienne about the nitrate negatives Molly found.

"I bet those negatives prove the sacredness of the lake. They're probably part of the military record, but whoever scrubbed the paper files forgot about the photographs. Most people wouldn't even know they existed."

"What do you mean?" Cate asked.

"We catalog and store photographs differently. Unless you were an experienced researcher, it would be easy to overlook the negatives. Molly might have found nitrate images that were missed ten years earlier. They could be the only proof remaining, so she had to be silenced."

"For the sake of argument," Cate said, "let's carry this theory through to the end. The bad guys scrub the paper records related to Eastview and the lake but forget about the negatives. Molly comes across them while cleaning out the facility and thinks they might be important. She tries to find out more in the paper records, and when she can't—"

"When she can't, she tracks down Albert Owl for confirmation," Rose interrupted excitedly. "Meanwhile all her poking around tips off the murderer."

"This theory hinges on the fact that the negatives Molly found would prove the lake was sacred. Wouldn't it be easier for the murderer to just call the negs fake and dispute them that way?"

Rose shook her head. "I told you, basically you can't forge nitrate negatives. These are the real deal—irrefutable proof. Besides, I don't think TDR or any of its investors want this thing delayed any further."

This whole line of thought was wild speculation. Every fact they laid out was circumstantial. She certainly couldn't take any of it to Baker. "It sounds like we have a theory about what we're looking for—negatives of Lake Nigamo proving its sacred value. Now it's just a question of finding them."

Rose grinned. Then her face clouded over.

"What is it?" Cate asked.

Rose bit her lip, looking indecisive.

"No more secrets," Cate said. "Remember?"

"Well, when I was getting nowhere going through those boxes, I checked the circulation history, to see who had taken them out before Molly."

Rose hesitated to say more.

"And?" Cate prompted impatiently.

"No one had ordered them in for ages. I had to go all the way back to 2014."

"That's almost ten years ago," Cate said. "That would have been when Annie's group tried to find information on Eastview."

"The Algonquin research group requested them in December of 2014. Six months before that, though, someone had ordered in all the boxes. Prior to that particular researcher, there was no big request since the early 1990s when a research team at the University of Ottawa had reviewed them."

"That timeline fits," Cate said. Whoever called in the boxes could be the murderer. "Who ordered the boxes in before the Algonquin group?" she demanded.

Rose looked sick. "It was Gerald MacIntyre."

Rose and Molly's boss from the Archives.

ROSE TWISTED HER HANDS TOGETHER. "DO YOU THINK GERALD KILLED Molly? Maybe that's why he put me on leave? Maybe he knew I was looking into the circulation records."

"Slow down. We don't need to leap to that conclusion. There must be a ton of work-related reasons he'd order the boxes."

Rose shook her head. "No, there isn't. He's only ever worked in the photography unit. Government records have never been his bag."

"That still doesn't mean—"

Rose interrupted. "If Molly found something strange or unusual, the first person she would talk to would be Gerald. We thought he was kind of a joke, but Molly followed the rules. She'd report anything unusual to Gerald straightaway."

"What's your point?" asked Cate.

"Well, she tells Gerald that she's found the negatives, he panics and kills her at the facility, making it look like suicide."

Cate recalled Gerald MacIntyre—a thin, nervous man. It was hard to imagine him killing a fly, let alone a colleague. "Why would he need to cover up the spiritual significance of the lake?"

Rose shrugged. "Maybe TDR paid him off ten years ago to destroy archival records."

"And he's been working the same low-level government job ever since?" Cate asked. "It doesn't seem like it could have been much money."

"Or they promised him a cut of the profits. Half this town has invested in the TDR development and are waiting for their payday—my parents even have a stake in it. Maybe he'd sunk his life savings into it."

"Maybe," Cate said, "but I wouldn't think he'd have that much money to invest in the first place." She squinted at the garden. "We need to find those negatives. Then we can go to Baker and hand over the evidence."

Rose bit her lip and turned away. "That's another thing. I'm sorry, Dr. Spencer, but the facility is about to be emptied."

"What?"

"We got word yesterday. TDR wants to tear down the building right away, and they must have pushed hard. As of tomorrow, they're bringing in twenty staff members, and we're packing the whole place up. It's an all-hands-on-deck situation. The negatives will go into deep storage until we build a new facility. They're going to pay us double overtime to get it done over the weekend. Rumor is that TDR's footing the bill; the Archives certainly couldn't afford that."

"Jesus." Cate took a step back. "How can they do that? It's a homicide scene."

"Gerald said that he triple-checked with Detective Baker that it would be OK. Apparently, the detective said his officers had gone through it, and they'd have everything they needed by tomorrow at noon."

Goddamn Baker was shortchanging the investigation. "OK," Cate said. "We can still salvage this. You'll have to find the negatives before they get packed up."

Rose looked even more woebegone. "There are half a million negatives in that facility, Dr. Spencer, and I have no idea which ones Molly was hiding or where she'd put them. I can keep my eyes open and scour any likely places, but I might not have much luck."

Cate searched her memory. "What about the deteriorated stuff?" she asked. "Didn't you say that it was impossible to find a contractor who could dispose of it, because it's so dangerous to move? Doesn't the Archives have to wait for that?"

"With TDR breathing down our necks, management suddenly found a contractor. Apparently, where there's a will, there's a way. Ogima Waste Management is coming next Wednesday to dispose of it in situ. Once it's gone, the wrecking balls arrive. The place will be flattened by end of next week."

The familiar name jarred Cate from her line of questioning. Annie had referred to Clifford Bernard as "Little Ogima." The word meant "chief." "What do you know about that company?"

Rose shrugged. "It's Indigenous-run, I think. Native companies sometimes get preferential deals when it comes to contracting with the feds."

Cate typed the name into her smartphone. Rose read over her shoulder. "It's a company in the west end. Clifford Bernard is the CEO."

"Jesus Christ," Cate breathed. Suddenly, a veil lifted, and she could see clearly for the first time.

"What is it?" Rose asked.

"Clifford Bernard," Cate said. It all made sense. She smiled broadly.

"Who's that?"

"He's this influential guy in the Algonquin community. He could be Molly's killer."

Rose didn't look particularly awestruck at Cate's deduction. "Why do you think that?"

"He had motive—he pushed the land sale through despite objections from his community. He tried to block research into Lake Mitchell." She remembered the bitter way Annie spoke of him. "His company is disposing of the nitrate? Come on, how much is he going to profit off that?"

Now it was Rose's turn to cast doubt. "That doesn't explain Gerald's involvement."

Cate waved away her objection. "Bernard probably paid him to get rid of the records."

"But that could be true of anyone."

"Yes, but does anyone else have such a clear history of opposing investigations into Lake Mitchell?" She was irritated with Rose's questions. Clifford Bernard was their best suspect. She recalled the way he grabbed her arm at Albert's funeral, insisting on his own point of view. He was just another in a long line of bullies, but this time Cate was going to put a stop to him. She scrolled through her phone for Baker's number.

"What are you doing?" Rose asked.

"Calling Baker, telling him our suspicions. We've got a good suspect. He's going to listen to me now."

"I don't think that's a very good idea." Rose looked at her with concern.

Cate's mouth twisted in annoyance. Didn't Rose understand? She had to bring Bernard to justice. She owed it to Molly, and somehow, to Jason.

Rose stepped toward her. "Dr. Spencer, don't do this. We haven't thought it all through. You've been telling me to slow down. Now you need to."

"No, no," Cate said. "Once the detective hears our evidence—the contract for the nitrate, Bernard's opposition to the development—he'll move on it. Baker can be reasonable."

"It's not Baker I'm worried about." Rose's voice held a sharp note of frustration. She took a breath and made a visible effort to modulate her tone. She spoke softly. "Dr. Spencer—Cate—listen to me. You need to take a beat. Think things through. You're being irrational."

Cate's head reared back. "I'm not being 'irrational,'" she spat the word. "I'm doing my job. A job I shouldn't be involving you in." How had she thought she could rely on Rose?

"This again." Rose looked angry. "I have a right to be involved. Molly was my friend."

"Some friend. She didn't even tell you about her relationship with Simon." Cate regretted the words even as she said them.

Rose flushed. "At least I have people I can call friends. I'm not a lonely, controlling asshole who won't listen to reason."

Cate turned and walked back across the field.

"Where are you going?"

She didn't bother to answer. Rose was not the ally she'd hoped for. Instead, she left Baker a message asking him to call her. They had to move quickly. The nitrate would be packed up and moved in the next few days. She was close now. She could feel it.

TURNS OUT, THURSDAY NIGHT IS NOT THE TIME TO TRACK DOWN MURDER suspects. Baker didn't return any of her calls, Gerald MacIntyre's home number was unlisted, and Clifford Bernard's office was closed.

By eight o'clock, she had given up trying to reach anyone and returned home. Arguing with Rose had been upsetting, but given the chance to sleep on it, the younger woman would realize Cate's suspicions about Bernard were warranted, and she'd be eager to apologize and help.

Cate's phone died again, and by the time it was charged she had a voice mail. It was a woman with a thick Newfoundland accent calling from the Canadian embassy in Kinshasa. She was pleased to inform Cate that significant progress had been made on her file. The embassy was in contact with Brilliant Aduba, who had facilitated things. The ashes of Dr. Jason Spencer would be returned to Ottawa within a week or so.

Cate stared at the phone in shock. Jason was coming home.

She glanced at the scotch bottle sitting on the counter's edge. No. Instead, she turned on the television and sunk into a *Real Housewives* marathon. There were other ways to numb yourself.

It was past eleven a.m. by the time daylight dragged her into alertness. She had binged on television and mindless Internet surfing until the wee hours. When she finally fell asleep, her nightmares had her tossing and turning until dawn. She checked her phone. It was dead, of course. She plugged it in and popped a couple of Tylenol.

Her phone juiced up enough for her voice mail to beep. No word from Baker about Clifford Bernard, but there was one from Simon Thatcher. Even through the recording, she could hear his excitement.

"Dr. Spencer? It's Simon. I made bail." He sounded rueful. "I know you told the cops about me and Molly. It's OK. You're trying to find the truth, and I want to help." His voice took on an angrier note. "Those assholes kept me at the station all night. My lawyer says it was a trumped-up charge, tells me we could sue for false arrest." He laughed, and Cate couldn't help smirking as well—serve Baker right. "Anyway, I got back to my parents' place this morning and finally got around to emptying out my bag. I'd left it here after my dad and I had that fight. Remember me telling you how Molly was rushing me out on Monday morning, and I was chucking everything into my bag? Well, I found an extra iPhone at the bottom. It's not mine. I think I must have Molly's phone. I know I have to turn it in, but I don't want to deal with the cops. Will you come get it?"

Cate blinked. Here was the evidence they were looking for. Calls to Bernard's phone number could be on there. Maybe images of the negatives she'd found. God only knew what else. She checked the message. He'd called an hour ago. Cate dialed his number. No answer.

Her exhaustion evaporated in a jolt of adrenaline. She kept trying his number as she dressed in her standard linen pants and T-shirt and raced downstairs.

The Thatcher home looked lovely in the noon hour sun. The red brick glowed, exuding a warm calm. There were no cars in the driveway; Mr. and Mrs. Thatcher must be out. She imagined them swinging golf clubs or sitting by a pool with tall glasses of something thirst-quenching.

She rang the doorbell. Like Simon's phone, there was no answer, but this wasn't surprising. He spent last night in jail. She'd guess he'd devote today to getting baked. She pressed longer this time, hoping to startle him out of his torpor. She could hear the noise echoing throughout the house. Was there a more abandoned sound than a doorbell ringing in an empty home? Had he become impatient and left? She called his cell. It rang and rang. Could she hear it ringing? Cate leaned closer, listening. Her stomach tightened. "Simon?" she called. She tried the door, and it opened. Her worry increased. "Simon, are you here? It's Dr. Spencer."

Just as on her last visit, the house gleamed with polish and care. "Hello!" she called. Sunlight poured through the patio doors. She looked out onto the flagstone walk. She could see someone sitting on a chair, a drink resting on the little table by their hand. Simon—too stoned to hear her calling.

"Simon," she said, walking toward him. "I've been ringing the doorbell."

He didn't move. She noticed a splash of what looked like vomit on the ground beside him.

"Simon," she shouted, rushing over. His eyes were open. She grabbed his wrist and searched for a pulse. Nothing. Simon Thatcher was dead.

CHAPTER FIFTY

SIMON'S BODY WAS STILL WARM. DEAD ONLY A FEW MINUTES. CATE could still save him. She dialed 911. She gave the address but before hanging up she saw a syringe on the ground. Simon's arm was exposed, and she could see the pinprick of an injection. "It's a possible Fentanyl overdose. Bring Narcan," she barked to the dispatcher.

She didn't have a second to waste. She lifted him from the chair, staggering under his weight, and laid him on the patio, careful not to bang his head on the flagstone. It was years since she last had CPR training, but she knew what to do the way you know how to tie your shoelaces or pedal a bike. She glanced at her watch and began. Heel of the hand to the center of the chest, steady rate of compression, adjust the neck, two breaths into that slack mouth. Begin again. She pumped away with all the force she could muster. The adrenaline thrummed through her body. She felt strong and competent. She could do this. Thirty compressions. Quick, forceful breaths. Repeat. She established a rhythm and lost herself to it. With every swift compression, she breathed out, "live," "live," "live."

Cate continued as her arms cramped. She was almost positive that the syringe had held Fentanyl. Practically every fourth call she received as a coroner was for an overdose of the drug—some poor junkie miscalculating their high or getting unlucky with their purchase. Pills were the norm, but the hard-core addict went for injection. Simon wasn't an addict, though. He'd called her to say he'd found Molly's phone, and now he was in cardiac arrest. This was no accidental overdose.

Her shoulders ached, but she was unrelenting in her compressions. "Come on, Simon!" she grunted. "Come on back."

At last, she heard the ambulance's siren and the approach of the paramedics. "He's in cardiac arrest," she said, as she continued pumping. "I've been administering CPR since I found him, about eight minutes. I'm a doctor."

A young paramedic knelt beside her, holding the defibrillator. She continued compressing, while the medic prepped the machine and cut off Simon's T-shirt with a pair of scissors. Cate's heart twisted at the sight of Simon's smooth, nearly hairless chest. He was still so young. The medic nodded to her, and she stopped her work, allowing him to apply the electro-pads. He looked at the machine, analyzing the heart rhythm. Cate wanted to scream at him to hurry, but she knew this analysis was key.

The second paramedic began working on Simon's airway, extending his neck in order to insert the LMA—a plastic tube sending air directly into Simon's lungs.

The defibrillator beeped, and Cate read the analysis at the same time as the medic. The machine indicated ventricular fibrillation. Instead of the sturdy, rhythmic contraction so necessary for the steady continuation of life, Simon's heart was twitching erratically in deadly, disorganized quivers. His hopes of recovery were not great, but goddamn it, there was still a chance. The medic charged the machine, which made a high-pitched whine.

"Clear," he said in a loud voice. Cate automatically drew back to ensure that no part of her was touching Simon's body. The shock was delivered with a "ka-chunk" sound, and Simon's body shifted with the force.

"Can you continue CPR?" the medic asked Cate.

"Yes." She returned to the compressions, pushing her hands into his chest. "Come on, Simon," she said.

While she did that, the first paramedic was getting an IV ready in order to deliver the Narcan, which would hopefully reverse the effects of the Fentanyl and wake Simon's body from its deadly sleep.

She heard loud boots behind her; the fire department had arrived. They must have been called for backup as Simon's case was VSA—

Vital Signs Absent. A large fireman knelt beside her, and she shifted her body, glad to leave the compressions to an expert who was fresh and ready to work. She stood up, backing away as a group of people swarmed Simon, all working to save his life. He was in the best hands now.

Her shoulders throbbed and she hugged her arms to ease their ache. The police arrived, and she told the sergeant this was an attempted murder. She called Baker, and by some miracle he actually answered. He was on his way.

She turned to the patio. They were loading Simon onto the stretcher. They'd take him to the emergency room and keep working to resuscitate him.

She couldn't help Simon anymore. Cate surveyed her surroundings. The large backyard was enclosed by a high wooden fence with a gate at the bottom. The killer could have easily slipped in and out from there. A few old maples provided hiding spots in the yard itself. She walked over to the gate, knowing that whoever had done this was long gone. Careful not to touch anything, she looked over the fence. It led to a small park overlooking Patterson's Creek. It was a picture of calm serenity—ducks floating on the water, a couple tossing a Frisbee, a man in the distance strolling down the path, and an older woman lying on the grass, her face upturned to the sun. All unaware of the desperate tragedy unfolding a few feet away.

She came back to the patio. An extinguished joint lay on the stones where it must have fallen from Simon's fingers. It was quick, at least. His assailant had crept in from the gate, surprised the stoned young man, and forcibly injected him before fleeing.

She looked around in a desultory fashion for Molly's phone. There was no point; she was sure the killer had taken it.

Cate was seated in the Thatchers' living room when Baker arrived. The sergeant at the door briefed him. Then Baker himself delivered the news—at 1:05 p.m. the Ottawa Civic Hospital had officially declared Simon Thatcher dead.

CHAPTER FIFTY-ONE

SIMON DEAD. THAT SKINNY, STUPID BOY GONE FOREVER. CATE WAS grateful that Mrs. Thatcher hadn't come home yet. It was one thing to tell strangers about their loved one's passing, another to break the news to someone you knew, if only slightly.

She hadn't had to tell her father about Jason, thank God. Instead the old man had called her. For the first time, she considered how difficult that must have been for him.

"So, tell me why you are at this scene?" Baker looked tired.

Cate's tone was flat. "Simon called me because he found Molly's phone. I came to pick it up, so I could give it to you."

"I looked the other way when you talked to Simon before, but you've got to drop this crap. You're in over your head."

"He called me because he didn't trust you. He found Molly's phone. Or did you not hear that part?"

"I heard you, but the problem is that my officers are searching this house top to bottom, and we haven't found it."

"Of course not," Cate said. "The killer took it. That's why he came here; why he murdered Simon."

"Thatcher was our prime suspect in Molly's death. As far as we're concerned, he was the murderer."

"Don't you see how misguided you are? How eager you are for an easy solve?"

Baker didn't rise to her bait. "If your story is true, how would the killer have known Simon had the phone?"

"Maybe I wasn't the only one that Simon told. He might have called the killer not realizing that he was Molly's murderer.

Maybe the killer was spying on him. I don't know how he knew. That's your job."

"Quite a lot of speculation. What I've got in front of me is a man accused of murdering a woman he'd recently slept with. Someone known to enjoy recreational drugs who overdosed on the most dangerous and pervasive opioid in the city."

"Now *you're* speculating, Baker. Look at the facts. This is the same MO as Molly's death. A homicide masked as something else—in this case an overdose." Baker had to see this connection. "Does Simon even have a history of opioid use? News flash: marijuana is not a gateway drug. You can't honestly believe he OD'd."

"What I believe is none of your business. You're a civilian on this case, and I'm sure as shit not sharing my theories with you."

"If you think this will be deemed an accidental overdose, then you're crazy. Simon's postmortem might reveal signs of bruising, which would indicate a struggle."

"Ah, well, we'll have to trust in your colleague's judgment and see what he says." Baker gestured to the door. "Here's the coroner now."

Sylvester Williams entered the room. "Afternoon, Cate," he said in his smooth tone. "We have to stop meeting like this." He chuckled. "You're muscling in on all my death scenes."

Baker looked at Williams with curiosity. The last thing Cate wanted was the coroner bringing up Albert Owl and their near run-in at the Marier Residence. She spoke quickly. "Dispatch sent you to the wrong location. Simon—the body—is at the Civic."

Williams turned on his heel, muttering something about incompetent administration. He was gone without asking a single question about what had happened.

Cate turned back to Baker, suddenly desperate to make him understand. "This overdose theory is bullshit. The person you want to investigate is Clifford Bernard. He's—"

Baker interrupted. "We know Bernard. He works with the force, helps us do outreach to the city's Indigenous populations."

"Well, he's more than that, which you'd know if you ever responded to my messages." She outlined Molly's research, what Fabienne had told her about the discovery of the nitrate, Annie's tale about the sacredness of the lake. Gerald MacIntyre's potential involvement in a cover-up and Bernard's shiftiness at Albert's funeral. Everything fit together. It was the only theory that made sense.

Bernard had killed Simon, and he should pay. "The Archives is emptying the nitrate facility as we speak," she said. "The negatives will be packed up, and we might never find Molly's evidence."

"And why were you at Albert Owl's funeral?" Baker asked.

Trust him to focus on the least important aspect of her story. There was no way she could tell him about her visit to the Marier Residence. "Annie told me how committed Albert was to stopping the development. I thought it might be worth going to the funeral to see what I could suss out."

Baker stroked his mustache. "So you're talking about a ten-year conspiracy resulting in two murders? That seems unlikely."

Cate could have screamed in frustration. "Don't you see? It's the only possibility. Bernard is burying proof of Lake Mitchell's importance to the Indigenous community. He skimmed a big chunk off the top of the sale for himself. It's obvious."

"A girl getting murdered by her one-night stand. That's obvious. Then the killer offs himself or overdoses out of remorse. That's obvious. Community leaders murdering people over some complicated theory—that's not so obvious."

Cate shook her head. "Simon wasn't jealous or angry. He didn't fit any domestic violence profile. He was a sweet kid." Her voice broke.

Baker paused, and his voice was gentle when he spoke. "Medics told me you were working on him before they got here."

"Yes," she said. "He was still warm. If I'd arrived sooner or tried harder, I could have—"

"You couldn't have done anything. You know that. Some come back, and some don't."

He was speaking the truth, but her frustration got the better of her. "For fuck's sake, Baker. This kid was murdered."

Baker drew back, and his face reddened.

Good, she had finally gotten to him. She continued, "Get your head out of your ass for once, and do something about this."

There was a cough behind them. They both turned. Mrs. Thatcher and a tall balding man Cate assumed was her husband stood behind them in the doorway. "Just what is going on here?" the man asked.

Cate opened her mouth to explain, but she could already see where Mrs. Thatcher's gaze lay. The woman was staring at the terrace where yellow police tape now stretched. From the fear in her eyes, Mrs. Thatcher had already guessed that something too terrible to comprehend had happened.

CHAPTER FIFTY-TWO

THE VIEW FROM THE ARCHIVES READING ROOM ENCOMPASSED VICTORIA Island—a small islet in the middle of the Ottawa River. For the first time, Cate noticed a white teepee jutting out from its eastern end. She leaned forward to get a better look and saw a sign reading "Aboriginal Experience." It must be some kind of tourist attraction.

There were less staff around than usual. Cate remembered that employees were being assigned to the nitrate facility to speed up the move. She closed her eyes and prayed that Rose would find Molly's hiding spot before the material was stowed away.

She opened her eyes to see Gerald MacIntyre arrive, his Adam's apple bobbing in his thin throat. "Dr. Spencer, I was surprised to get your call. What is the issue?"

"I'd like to speak with you concerning Molly Johnson's death."

He swallowed hard and loosened his tie. "As I told you before, you should really clear any interview request with our senior management. I've talked to colleagues. There are protocols around police investigations. My director, Oliver—"

She didn't have time for his bullshit. She flashed onto Simon's body, surrounded by a team of people trying to revive him. A surge of emotion—anger, grief, or guilt, she couldn't tell—tied her stomach into knots, and she balled her hands into fists. "I don't wish to speak to you in your official capacity."

MacIntyre's eyes bulged. "What do you mean?"

"I think it would be better if we talked in your office." He was the kind of man who responded well to authority, and she was feeling extremely authoritative.

They rode the elevator in silence, although MacIntyre could not remain still. He checked his watch, adjusted his tie, and drummed his fingers against the wall. He led her to a cramped office with a big desk and two shabby armchairs. The walls were covered in photos—mostly of two children in matching outfits. Fat-cheeked babies dressed in pumpkin costumes, little girls in identical flowery dresses.

"As you know, I'm investigating Molly Johnson's death."

"I understood that you were the coroner, not a police officer."

She gave him a sharp glance, and his brief display of defiance wilted. "We think Molly's death might be related to the development at Eastview. That she had located information that could have stopped it."

MacIntyre blanched. "I th-thought someone was arrested. S-s-some protester."

She stared at him, and he swallowed nervously. Did this mother-fucker know what had been done to Simon? She clenched her hands together. "That's not the case," she said. "Now, about Molly and East-view. Isn't it true that she uncovered something related to TDR and came to you?"

His eyes shifted, and that Adam's apple reared up so high she thought he might spit it out. "No, no, no—that's not it. She didn't do that."

His lies were so obvious that Cate almost felt sorry for him. "She came to you, and you murdered her."

"No. Absolutely not. Why would I do that?"

"Because someone was paying you to remove any obstacles to the sale of the base."

"What? No!" he said. "No," he repeated. "That's just not true."

Cate stared at him. She could wait him out. Make him uncomfortable.

He opened his mouth to speak but closed it into a firm line.

She tried a different tack. "About ten years ago you ordered in every single archives box related to a specific set of military records. Why?"

MacIntyre laughed—an awkward, nervous burst. "I order in boxes all the time. It's part of my job."

"Those boxes contained references to Eastview, didn't they? Did you call them in and remove records discussing the base?"

"No, of course not. Why would I do that?" He looked mystified.

For a moment Cate felt a thread of doubt, but now wasn't the time to pull her punches. If she went after him hard enough, Gerald would crack.

"Come on. Admit you ordered those records in."

Gerald shrugged, a weak gesture. "I have no idea what boxes I did or didn't order in 2013."

"It wasn't 2013," Cate corrected. "It was June 2014."

"2014?" Gerald asked, his shoulders relaxing. "I wasn't even in the country. I was on parental leave for the entire year. My partner and I spent it with her parents in Wisconsin."

Cate was caught off guard. "You weren't in Ottawa in 2014? You're sure?"

Gerald laughed, a more relieved sound this time. "The twins were born December 12, 2013, and I spent the entirety of 2014 on a wind-swept farm outside Madison, Wisconsin, on parental leave with colicky newborns, a wife with postpartum depression, and my in-laws. I wish I had been at work."

Cate's dumbfounded reaction to this revelation gave Gerald confidence, and he stood, speaking with surprising firmness. "If you want to talk to me again, contact my lawyer."

"Come on," she persisted. "What did Molly tell you about the—" He cut her off. "I don't have to answer you. Leave now, please."

"Mr. MacIntyre—"

He interrupted again. "Dr. Spencer, I seriously question your jurisdiction here. If you don't leave now, I will report you for harassment."

She blinked, more surprised by his show of strength than his threats. She left thoughtfully. Gerald may not have ordered those boxes, but he knew what Molly had found. She was sure of it.

CHAPTER FIFTY-THREE

IF GERALD MACINTYRE HADN'T ORDERED THE BOXES, THEN SOMEONE else had, using his identification. As far as Cate could see, the person with the strongest motive was Clifford Bernard. With no other leads, Cate decided to stake out Bernard's office. She parked across the street from Ogima Waste Management on Merivale Road, waiting.

The car was hot and her back ached, but she persisted because what other option did she have? No job to go to. No brother to confide in. No other leads and no help from Baker. Her earlier confidence that Rose would see things her way had seeped away, leaving her with the sour certainty that the younger woman thought she was a pathetic fool.

And so she waited in her car for a man who never appeared. Cars came and went, and she watched deliverymen and shoppers pull in and out of the strip mall, but no Bernard.

She gave up at seven p.m. and went home to a quiet house and that scotch bottle on the counter. This time she didn't resist. Simon was dead, and the more she thought about it, the more she realized how responsible she was for his death. He had called her at ten a.m., but she'd literally been asleep on the job. She had let him down.

What would Jason think of her actions? Jason. Her father. Molly. Albert Owl. Matthew. Her life was a shambles. The only way out now was a bloody-minded pursuit of the truth, which was helped by a few glasses of Laphroaig.

On the second day of the stakeout, she realized that the time passed more quickly with a little buzz. From then on, she'd arrive at the mini-mall opposite Bernard's office by eight a.m. She was strict with herself and wouldn't start drinking the scotch until three p.m. She only took small sips, so that she could stay alert. By seven p.m., she'd head home where she could do the serious drinking she needed in order to sleep.

It was late afternoon on the fourth day—a Monday, or maybe a Tuesday—when a car pulled up: Bernard laughing amid a group of men. Rage clouded her eyes for a moment. He'd killed Simon. Killed Molly. She thought of the heartbreak in Molly's mother's voice. Simon's parents' grief. Her own fear when she was attacked. Where was the justice in the world?

She got out of her car and weaved across busy Merivale, waving her hand at the cars swerving and honking.

Bernard and his cronies stopped to stare at her. "Dr. Spencer?" Bernard asked, startled.

"That's right," she agreed, nodding emphatically to make her point. "Doctor. I'm a doctor, and I examined Molly Johnson and Simon Thatcher. I know what you did, Bernard. I know it."

The men around them melted away, although Cate was conscious that they were within earshot. Good, Bernard deserved an audience to hear his sins.

Bernard's face went a deep shade of red, and he straightened his posture. "Dr. Spencer, I don't know what you're talking about, but I can assure you that—"

"That what?" Her voice was a loud snarl. Louder than she'd intended, but she couldn't stop now; she was too angry. "Did you do something to Albert Owl, or was it just luck that he died?"

"Albert?" Bernard repeated in astonishment.

"Maybe you were furious when you found out that they had the evidence proving the lake was sacred."

Bernard's voice rose as well. "What are you talking about? Lake Nigamo? That was an old man's fantasy. There was not a shred of evidence, not a shred."

"He wasn't an old man," Cate persisted. "He was an elder. Don't you have to listen to your elders?"

Bernard stepped toward Cate and spoke in soothing tones. "Dr. Spencer, I don't know why you're interesting yourself in this issue, but I can see that someone has been misinforming you. If our elders had a credible story about Lake Nigamo's sacredness, then I would have moved heaven and earth to prove it." He glanced at the men behind him and smiled reassuringly. "There was simply no evidence, apart from Albert's stubborn insistence. We need more than fantasy to build a case."

His patronizing tone whipped up Cate's rage anew. She shoved him in the chest, hard. His head snapped back, and he stumbled. Immediately, one of the men behind him stepped forward and pinned her arms behind her back. His tight hold bit into her skin.

"Want me to call the cops?" he asked Bernard. "That was assault."

Bernard's eyes flashed, but he spoke calmly. "No, put her in a taxi and send her home. She's obviously intoxicated. And they call us the drunks?"

Before Cate even knew what was happening, she was bundled into a car. Her anger had deserted her, and she felt numb.

The taxi passed a convenience store on the way home. "Stop," Cate shouted. "Wait here," she mumbled to the driver. She ran in and re-emerged with three packs of cigarettes. Fabienne was right; quitting was for the weak.

CHAPTER FIFTY-FOUR

CATE WAS ESPECIALLY GRATEFUL FOR THE SMOKES WHEN THE CAB
pulled up in front of her house and she saw Baker's car in her driveway.
Obviously, Bernard had changed his mind about calling the police.

She got out and paid the taxi. She searched her purse for a lighter
as Baker stomped toward her. She lit the cigarette and took a first,
blissful drag. Already she felt more in control.

Baker looked at the cigarette but didn't comment. "The head of our Indigenous community liaison program just called to say you assaulted Clifford Bernard? What in the name of everlasting fuck have you just done?"

In retrospect, she should have handled that confrontation with
Bernard differently, but she didn't regret her actions. "I'm doing your
goddamn job. Bernard is the killer. His band made millions on this
development." She couldn't keep the righteous anger from her voice.
"He has motive. He has opportunity. He has—"

"He has an alibi. An airtight one, for both Molly and Simon."

"You checked up on him?"

"Of course. I followed up on what you told me when we were at
Thatcher's."

His admission deflated some of her anger. "He could have hired
someone to carry out the murders. A hitman. Of course his alibi
would be rock-solid then."

"We're not stupid, Cate, but his motive doesn't check out."

"What do you mean? When the band settled with TDR, they
got millions. If the sacredness of the lake had come out, they'd have
nothing. Not to mention the fact that he got the contract to dispose
of that nitrate."

"I investigated all of your leads, Cate. The nitrate contract is only worth ten grand, not really enough to commit double homicide."

Her wits were slow, struggling to keep up with the information he was giving her. "Well, that's not the big news. What matters is the money the band got when they settled. You can't tell me he didn't get some kind of fat cut."

"Cate, we've been over their books. There's nothing untoward in the finances. What's more, we couldn't find any evidence of Lake Mitchell being sacred."

"That's bullshit. They stole the evidence from the Archives. The oral history..."

"We looked at the oral history angle. We talked to three different elders. No one knew anything about the sacredness of the lake. That was Albert Owl's invention."

Cate was frustrated by Baker's obtuseness. "There is evidence. Annie told me . . ."

"Would that be Annie Wabase?"

"Yeah."

"Unemployed?"

"No, she's a teacher. She . . ."

"She is on punitive leave. Her activist activities were interfering with her work. At one point, she was encouraging her students to go on a hunger strike—twelve-year-olds, Cate. Then she stopped showing up to class."

Cate blinked. Annie suspended? Why hadn't she mentioned that? "Annie doesn't matter. The truth is that the lake . . ."

"The truth is the area around the lake had an archaeological review in 1990. Did Ms. Wabase mention that? A whole team from the University of Ottawa spent three months going over every inch, looking for signs of Algonquin settlement or ritual. They found a few arrowheads, but nothing to indicate that it was ever used as a sacred site. It's just not true, Cate."

Rose had mentioned that a team from the university ordered in the records in the 1990s. "That can't be right," she whispered.

"I'm sorry, Cate, but there is nothing concrete to point away from the murder-overdose theory for Molly and Simon's deaths. All you've got is speculation."

Cate opened her mouth to argue but had nothing left to say.

Baker took a step back from her. "Bernard isn't pressing charges. He recognizes that his odds of getting a conviction against a respectable, white lady doctor are slim to nil. Next time you go apeshit, you might not be so lucky. You need to rest. Take it easy, Cate. You're coming apart at the seams . . ."

Her head swam with the tobacco and the alcohol. She held up her hand. "I can't talk to you right now, Baker. Leave me alone."

His face didn't register surprise, just disappointment. Cate nearly screamed in frustration. Instead, she stomped away from him, slamming and locking the door behind her.

She leaned against the wall. Baker was right. She had royally fucked things up with Bernard. She saw that she had grasped hold of that theory like a life raft and clung to it despite all available evidence. Why had she confronted Bernard like that? She could see herself from his eyes—wild-eyed, reeking of booze, stumbling through traffic, screaming at an innocent man. She had attacked someone. An Indigenous person who knew he couldn't even successfully prosecute her because of the color of her skin. She burned with shame.

She lit another cigarette and moved to the couch. She sat on an empty scotch bottle buried in the cushions. She let it fall to the floor with a clang. It was clear that she was having a mental breakdown. Baker, Marcoux, even Rose had spotted it. This case was wrapped up with Jason's death, with her shitty childhood, with her lousy divorce, with that miscarriage.

She should take Baker and Dr. Marcoux's advice and back away, let this case go, get some sleep, beg Bernard for forgiveness, ease back on the drinking, and maybe even start grieving for Jason. His ashes would be here soon, and they would put him to rest. She could figure out what was happening to her father and come up with a plan to care for him. She could put her life back together.

She took a deep drag of her cigarette and closed her eyes. All she had to do to return to the old life was let Molly and Simon's murderer go unpunished. She opened her eyes and exhaled. There was no choice. Despite it all, she was going to see this thing through.

She was all in.

CHAPTER FIFTY-FIVE

THE NEXT DAY CATE SAT IN BED, A NEARLY EMPTY PACK OF CIGARETTES beside her. She had barely slept, just puffing away. God it was good to smoke. She butted out a cigarette into a dirty plate. She may have smoked a pack of Du Maurier, but she hadn't had a drop of alcohol since her confrontation with Bernard. Granted that was less than twelve hours ago, but still it felt good. She lit another. She felt the smoke enter her lungs. She kept it in for a moment and exhaled. Calm. It was like yoga, but with nicotine. Another drag, hold, release.

She had gone over every clue and conversation, coming up with nothing. Molly had discovered nitrate negatives that were somehow incriminating or dangerous and that related to the East-view Base. When she realized the archival records were tampered with, she had gone to see Albert Owl. According to the nurse at the Marier Residence, they had argued at least once. Molly wanted something from Albert, something he wouldn't give her. What was it?

The obvious answer was that Molly needed Albert to confirm her evidence, whatever that was. Now Albert was gone. Baker said that other elders in the Algonquin community refuted the idea that Lake Nigamo was a sacred space. Why did Albert make those claims to Annie if they weren't true?

Cate didn't have a clear plan when she drove out to the protest site, after collecting her car from Merivale road. She simply hoped that talking to Annie might help. Her heart sank as she pulled into her usual spot. There was no sign of the protesters. Had they all gone home? It was over a week since TDR had taken ownership.

She got out of the car anyway, shielding her eyes against the strong sun. There was movement in the stand of trees where the tents stood, and she walked over. Derek and Trinity were packing up. Only Simon's yellow tent remained in the clearing. She reached for a cigarette. "Hey," Cate called out to the couple.

They both looked up, startled. "Dr. Spencer," Trinity said. Derek nodded warily.

"You heard what happened?" she asked, pointing to Simon's tent.

"It's a real bummer," Derek said.

Trinity shook her head.

"I mean a major, major bummer." His mouth quivered. Derek might not have the vocabulary to express it, but that didn't make his shock and grief less real.

"What's going to happen to his tent?" Cate asked, taking a deep drag.

"We'll bring it to his parents," Trinity said.

"We will?" Derek asked, looking startled.

"Sure," Trinity said. "It's the least we can do."

"There's no way Simon killed that girl," Derek said belligerently.

"I know," Cate said.

Derek stepped forward, his tone softening. "I mean, he was right beside me on Monday night. That's when it was supposed to be going down, right?"

"Yeah," Cate agreed. "Do me a favor and tell that to his parents, OK? They'll want to clear his name."

Derek nodded glumly.

"Hey, I had a question for you the other day, but you'd gone to Toronto."

"We tried to get in to see Liam," Trinity said. "They've got him locked up tight. No visitors."

"Fucking TDR—capitalist fascism at its best." Derek spat on the ground.

Cate wasn't going to be sidetracked. "Derek, Simon told me that you borrowed his camera to take photos of some frog?"

"Yeah, if I can prove that those warty little fuckers are in that lake, we'd stop the development for at least six months. The cricket frog is almost extinct in Canada."

"Any luck?"

"Nah. A biologist friend told me it was a long shot, but I thought I'd try."

"What about the Monday of Molly's death? Were you down by the lake? Did you pass by the Archives' building to get there?"

Derek paused, trying to remember. "I don't think so," he said. "Anyway, I don't go by the facility. There's a giant patch of poison ivy on the path. I go the long way around, on the road, and then hop the fence."

Another dead end. Cate wasn't deterred. "Do you guys know where I can find Annie Wabase?"

"The Indigenous lady?" Derek asked.

"That's the one." Cate took one final drag before stamping the butt out.

They both shrugged. Cate pulled out her phone. She had Annie's number and could give her a call. "Goddamn it," she said when she touched the screen.

"What's wrong?" Trinity asked.

"My stupid phone is dead again." Cate knew her anger was out of proportion, but she was frustrated. "The battery dies all the time, and when I turn it off to conserve power, it actually turns itself back on."

"Sounds like your phone is bugged," Derek said.

Cate barked out a surprised laugh. "What are you talking about?"

"When someone is listening to your voice mail, monitoring your calls, reading your texts, it drains the battery. Plus, they can turn that thing on at will, even listen to your conversations when you're offline. Track your movement."

Cate stared at him. "Is that true?"

"For sure. They were totally up in my business when I was out in Alberta, protesting the tar sands. Neo-liberal oligarchs. I disabled their spyware."

"Could anyone do that? Install spyware on a phone?"

"Absolutely, you just need to get your hands on the phone. It would take five minutes. Easy."

Cate's stomach churned. The day after Molly's death, her front door had been ajar. Later, she couldn't find her phone and then it had turned up under her bed. Someone could have broken in and stolen her phone to bug it, only to return it later to monitor her movements. "Can you tell if I've got it on my phone now?"

Derek laughed. "I was joking. I doubt anyone's trying to track your moves, lady doctor."

She barely heard his dismissal, because suddenly Cate realized what this meant. Simon's murderer would have heard the boy's message to her. He would have known that Simon had found Molly's phone. "Listen," she said, thrusting the phone at him. "Take this and find out if someone's put something on it. Do it now."

"Whoa," Derek stepped back. "Why should I help you?"

"Because it will help me figure out who killed Molly and who framed Simon."

Trinity stepped up. "He'll do it." She turned to Derek. "How long will it take?"

Derek shrugged truculently. "Fifteen minutes. I'll need your phone number and my laptop."

He snatched the phone from Cate and stomped over to their car, threw himself into the front seat, and plugged her phone into a laptop.

Cate felt exposed and vulnerable. Her hands twisted together. Trinity smiled, turning to the road. "Hey, were you hoping to see Annie?" she asked.

Trinity pointed behind her, and Cate turned to see an old pickup truck rattling across the field, Annie at the wheel.

CHAPTER FIFTY-SIX

turning on Trinity. "It's over then?" Her tone was aggressive.

Derek didn't look up. Trinity nodded.

"I had to see for myself." Annie's mouth twisted. "So much for fighting to the last."

Trinity stepped forward. "Liam's arrested. TDR's started construction. We lost. We've got to move on, Annie. Part of successful protest is picking your battles. We're heading north tomorrow. They're going to run gas pipelines through virgin forest. No one is paying attention. We have to make ourselves heard."

"So you leave?" Annie asked. "You give up."

Trinity looked down at her feet.

Annie threw her hands up and returned to her truck.

Cate followed her. "Hey, Annie. Can I talk to you for a second?"

The other woman turned. "Sure. It's not like I have anything else to do." She glared at Trinity.

Trinity returned to packing up their tent, and Cate moved closer to Annie, so their conversation wouldn't be overheard. "I confronted Clifford Bernard yesterday. I accused him of denying Lake Mitchell's spiritual importance, accused him of murdering Molly Johnson." Cate couldn't keep the anger from her voice.

Annie looked startled. "Hey now, I never said that Little Ogima killed anyone!"

"You told me that Bernard covered up the existence of documents proving Lake Mitchell was sacred. That gave him motive to kill Molly."

"Bernard's a scumbag, but he's not a murderer."

"You still insist that Lake Mitchell has sacred importance?"

"Of course it does," Annie said.

"It doesn't."

"Bullshit," Annie said stubbornly.

"What about the Ottawa U study, Annie? Why didn't you mention that they had already looked for signs of settlement or spiritual importance back in the 1990s?"

Annie shrugged. "One archaeological survey over a summer isn't definitive. Besides, how was I supposed to know you were going to accuse Clifford Bernard of murder?" Annie chuckled. "God, I would have liked to see Little Ogima's face when that happened."

"It was hilarious," Cate said. "I basically blew up any shreds of credibility I had left and sunk my professional career."

Annie took a step toward her. "Look, I'm sorry. I could have told you about the dig, but it was nice to have a sympathetic ear, and you were so eager to hear what I had to say."

Cate's anger drained away, replaced by the heavier burden of her own behavior. She had been an ass and jumped to stupid conclusions. "What I don't get is how you can be so unshakable in your belief in the lake's sacredness. I mean, it's not even like most Algonquin buy this story."

Annie crossed her arms. "My grandfather told me."

Cate sighed. She was barking up the wrong tree. Some murderous asshole had killed two people, and she was standing in a field talking about an old man's fantasies. "Did you ever think that maybe the whole story was a tall tale your grandfather made up?"

Annie shook her head. "It wasn't a lie. It was wisdom. This is how we learn, by being told the stories about places that have meaning."

"Didn't you think it was odd when you started talking about it ten years ago that no one else knew the story? Didn't that make you doubt?"

"It wasn't only granddad. All his buddies said the same thing—Albert Owl, Jonas Smith . . . All those elders. The old guys."

Something caught Cate's attention. All the old guys. Annie's grandfather had met Albert Owl in the Air Force. "Did all those men serve in the military with your grandfather?"

"Yeah, they were ground crew. They could never rise above the lowest ranks. They were just dirty Indians after all."

Cate recalled the painting of Lake Nigamo in Albert's residence room. The lake was central to this somehow. She remembered what Simon had said about Annie never swimming in it.

"What would happen if you swam in the lake, Annie? What did your grandfather say?"

"He said there was bad spirits in there that wanted to get us. He said we'd get sick, terribly sick."

"But people did swim in that lake. What did you make of that?"

Annie shrugged. "No native kid on the base would swim in there. Only the whites. There were always different rules for them."

What did Albert and his friends know about the lake that made them warn their children against swimming in it? Cate knew that the answer to that question would open the whole case. "Yes, but what about . . ."

Annie held up a hand. "Look, I'm sorry, Dr. Spencer, but I've got to go."

"Wait, Annie, I still want to know—"

Derek's shout interrupted her. "Holy shit, I found something."

Annie said a hasty goodbye and drove off. Cate raced over to where Derek sat in the car.

"It's a doozy," Derek said. "He's listening to your incoming and outgoing calls, tapped into your voice mail, and even reading your texts. You've got one jealous boyfriend, lady."

"Can you tell who did this?" Cate asked.

"Nah, it's a sophisticated program. The person who installed it made sure to cover their tracks. This is some quality hacking, CIA level. It's not something you can buy off the internet."

"Goddamn it," Cate exploded.

"Should I take it off?"

Cate wanted that invasion of privacy off her phone, but if she did that, then whoever installed it would know she was on to them. Plus, maybe the cops could pull some useful information from the spyware. "No," she said decisively. "Leave it."

"You sure?" Derek asked. "They can hear your messages. Listen to you. This is the whole enchilada. Whoever did this to you isn't screwing around."

"I know." Cate thought of Simon's lifeless body. "But neither am I."

CHAPTER FIFTY-SEVEN

THERE WAS ONE MAN WHO MIGHT HAVE SOME INSIGHT INTO WHAT ALBERT knew. After what Derek told her about her phone, she didn't dare make a call. Instead, it was nearly dusk when she pulled up to Isaiah Turner's house. Cate thought the odds of finding the old man at home were good.

He didn't seem startled to see her on his doorstep. Maybe that was a perk of making it to your nineties—nothing was ever that surprising.

Cate accepted the glass of apple juice he offered and grimaced at its sweetness.

"I add sugar," he said helpfully. "The doctors say I should cut back on candy and such, but one of the few pleasures I have left is satisfying my sweet tooth. It was always such a treat to get a penny candy . . . Funny how you can never get enough of the things you were denied as a child."

Cate decided not to think about what that throwaway comment meant for her own childhood. "How are you feeling?" she asked.

"Fine, fine," he said. "It was awfully decent of you to drive me home the other day."

"Good," she said. There was an awkward pause. How was she going to bring the conversation around to nebulous questions about a lake? She cast her eye around the room and spotted a photo of a tall young Black man in uniform. "Is that you?"

He glanced to where she gestured. "Yes, indeed. The day I enlisted. It was tough to get in—at first you had to be of 'pure European descent' for them to even consider you. When all those white boys started dying, they let in the 'Orientals, Indians, and Negroes.'"

"And yet you stayed on when the war ended?" Cate remarked.

Isaiah shrugged. "The Air Force was no more racist than the rest of Canada. If you think segregation, lynchings, and all that other devilishness only happened in Mississippi, you need to read your history books. I mean, look what they did to all the native folks with those residential schools."

This was Cate's opening. "Yes, like Albert Owl."

"Good old Al. I guess I'm the last of that gang left. We had some grand times together, but there were tough ones too. They made us brown folks do the dirty work."

"What kind of dirty work?" she asked eagerly.

"Why, like cleaning the latrines, scrubbing the pots, that kind of thing."

This was as much of a chance as she was going to get. "Were you ever asked to do any other stuff—maybe things you had to keep secret?"

The effect was immediate. Isaiah's face went rigid, and he spoke stiffly. "I don't know what you're getting at, Doc." He was a worse liar than Gerald MacIntyre.

Well, she might as well try to bluff it out. "I know you and Albert were involved in something on the base. Something to do with Lake Mitchell."

Isaiah's face registered surprise. "How do you know that?"

"Albert told Molly Johnson," Cate said, praying she was right.

"I don't believe it," he said flatly. "Al was a man of his word. He told me the Air Force was his first home. He wouldn't betray that oath." Isaiah's voice took on a deeper timber, and Cate had a flash of the confident man he must have been in his prime. "Albert Owl went to his grave with his lip zipped."

"You mentioned an oath. What . . ."

Isaiah's face was stony, and he stood up. "I think it's time for you to go." He walked to the door and opened it.

"Please," Cate said, rising from her seat.

"Why are you so interested in this?" he asked. "It's ancient history. Done and done. Let it rest."

"I'm a coroner, Mr. Turner. Two people have already died over this secret. Please tell me what you know."

She could see in his face he was debating whether to help her. She held her breath.

At last he shook his head. "No," he muttered. "I won't break my oath, not after all these years."

"Please, Mr. Turner."

He made a sweeping gesture with his hand, indicating she should leave. "I'm sorry, Doc. I can't help you."

Cate stared at him in frustration, but short of shaking the secret from him, she didn't know what else she could do. "Call me if you change your mind." She left, defeated.

CHAPTER FIFTY-EIGHT

ROSE LI WAS LOOKING AROUND CATE'S LIVING ROOM WITH UNABASHED curiosity. After inviting the other woman over from a newly purchased burner phone, Cate had done a frantic cleanup. She was weirdly anxious that Rose approve of her wall of books and albums, her muted gray Ikea couch, and the Danish modern coffee table she'd taken from her parents' house years ago. She realized with a start that this was the first time she'd ever invited a non-family member into this house.

"Want something to drink? I've got . . ." Cate's voice trailed off. Apart from carefully aged scotch or tap water, she had nothing to offer.

"I'm good," Rose replied, looking at a medical journal lying on a side table. Cate turned on a lamp. Evening was approaching, and the light made the room cozier.

From the coffee table, her smartphone turned itself on. After Derek's revelation, she'd been tempted to take the battery right out. Instead, she'd decided to wait and see what happened. Sure enough, every hour or so it came back to life. Someone was monitoring her calls. Checking her texts. Analyzing her voice mail. Cate shuddered, staring at the phone with loathing. Now she did turn it off, removing the battery for good measure. Tomorrow morning, first thing, she'd go to the police station and convince Baker to look into it. She wasn't going near her laptop or using her landline. Not until she had those professionally de-bugged.

She sat in an armchair opposite Rose, relieved that the other woman had agreed to come over. Cate worried that she would be angry over how they'd left things at the community garden. She flushed at the memory. She had gone off half-cocked before. This time she was determined to listen to Rose and come up with a reasonable plan.

She filled her friend in on everything that had transpired since they last saw each other. Rose knew about Simon's death and was convinced that it was connected to Molly's murder. "That must have been so intense for you," Rose said as Cate recounted her attempts at resuscitating him.

Cate shrugged. "I'm a doctor." She didn't mention that for the past five years she'd been a coroner, where emergency intervention was de facto too late, and before that her family medicine practice hadn't involved a lot of CPR.

Rose shook her head, not buying Cate's minimizing.

"Anyway," Cate said, "we've established that Clifford Bernard and Gerald MacIntyre weren't involved in these murders, leaving us with a big fat zero."

"That's not true," Rose said staunchly. "You've done a lot of good work. We know that Albert Owl and Isaiah Turner were implicated in some shady activity related to Lake Mitchell. Mr. Turner mentioned an oath?"

Cate nodded.

"Well, given that they were in the military and that it was either during the war or shortly after—"

"That's right," Cate said, remembering. "Albert left the Air Force by 1947, so it would have to be before that."

"OK," Rose said. "I would then assume that the oath Isaiah referred to would relate to the Official Secrets Act. He and Albert could have learned something that required that they swear to uphold the Act."

"There must have been a government cover-up, maybe involving Lake Mitchell." Cate paused, remembering an earlier conversation. "Simon said one of the best things about the lake was how deep it was."

Rose spoke Cate's own suspicion aloud. "What if the solution to this whole mystery is at the bottom of that lake?" Rose furrowed her brow. "I have a friend who scuba dives. He's got all the equipment. He could meet us there tomorrow morning."

Cate's heart lifted. "Fantastic, let's do this."

"Oh shit," Rose said.

"What?" Cate asked.

"Ogima Waste Management is coming first thing tomorrow to destroy the last of the nitrate—the really volatile stuff that can't be moved. The whole place will be cordoned off. We won't be able to get anywhere near the lake."

"Damn it," Cate exclaimed.

"We could do it now."

"It's eight o'clock at night," Cate pointed out.

"Yeah, but the base is deserted, and the facility is empty. This is the perfect time."

"It's almost dark, so I think the scuba would be useless. Besides"—Cate shuddered, thinking of the last time she was at the lake in the dark—"wandering around a deserted military base with a killer on the loose isn't a good idea."

They sank into a depressed silence for a moment, when something stirred in Cate's memory. "Wait, the deteriorated nitrate hasn't been moved?"

"Yeah. They'll do a controlled burn tomorrow."

Cate's mind raced. "Remember when I told you what Fabienne said about the negatives? That Molly hid them somewhere in the facility. Somewhere that was secure? As far as Molly knew, the Archives had had no luck finding a contractor to dispose of the deteriorated stuff—she probably thought it would never be moved."

"Oh my God," Rose said. "That makes sense. No one would look in those old boxes." She stood. "We've got to get over there right now, before they burn up the evidence."

"Slow down." Cate wasn't going to get Rose killed. "We can't go out there alone. It's too dangerous."

"We need to move on this. We've only got twelve hours."

"No, Rose. I'll call Baker, convince him to send out the cops. We'll do this by the book."

"There's no time," Rose said. She was already standing by the door. "Ogima will be there at nine a.m. How long will it take for you to convince the detective?"

Cate had no credibility with Baker. Besides, most of the time he didn't even return her calls. Still, she couldn't put Rose at risk. "No—"

Rose interrupted. "I've got a key, and I'm going, with or without you." She was out the door before Cate could even formulate a reply.

CHAPTER FIFTY-NINE

THE EVENING WAS DARK, CLOUDS OBSCURING THE MOON, AND CATE FRE-
quently checked her rearview to ensure that she wasn't being followed.
She had wasted half an hour trying to reach Baker from the burner
phone to let him know what they were doing. At last she gave up. Rose
wasn't answering her cell, but that could be because reception was
so bad at the facility. The track to the building was unlit. Cate tore
down the lane, heedless of the ruts and bumps her car leaped over. She
pulled up next to Rose's bike.

The building was even more ominous in the dim shadows of early
nightfall. The thick heat of day hadn't yet lifted, and a trickle of sweat
ran down Cate's back as she approached the main door. Rose had left
it unlocked.

"Hello!" Cate called. The anteroom was empty, and she glanced
into the first room where Simon had thrown the cherry bomb two
weeks ago. The negatives' acrid, chemical smell lingered, but the room
looked different. The boxes were gone. The table stood in the center,
and a lone light fixture hung from the ceiling, punctuating the room's
emptiness. She shivered and wondered why the air-conditioning was
still going full blast now that the building was nearly empty.

Cate pushed through the door to the chillier hallway lined with
vaults. "Rose," she called. Her voice echoed down the big space. A
huge pile of boxes was stacked at the far end of the hallway next to
the fire exit, facing the vault where Molly's body was found. The fluorescent lighting laid bare the starkness of the long space. Most of
the doors were open, revealing small, empty rooms. She remembered
Peter's story of the young soldier's death. She imagined his anguished

calls for help echoing off the walls, his fruitless attempts to free himself from his concrete imprisonment.

Her footsteps made a soft thump as she walked down the cement floor. "Rose," she called a second time. The air was freezing here, and the place was filled with echoes. There was a scuttling noise from one of the vaults. A mouse or a rat. Her skin prickled.

"Hey." Rose popped her head out of one of the last vaults, closest to the exit.

Cate jumped and hurried over. Rose was standing in a half-full vault. About a hundred boxes, marked "For Destruction," filled the shelves. Rose wore a mask over her mouth and nose and white cotton gloves. She handed a mask to Cate. "Glad you made it. Put this on. The deteriorating stuff gives off wicked fumes."

She peered into the box Rose had opened. Sure enough, even through the mask, Cate caught the distinctive rotten foot odor she had smelled on her first visit. The box contained a jumble of curling negatives. "Is this them?" she asked.

Rose shook her head. "No, but it's got to be one of these boxes." She gestured to the containers in front of them. "These weren't with the other deteriorating boxes, the ones by the exit or in the last few vaults, because we wanted to double-check them. Make sure they truly were too far gone. It occurred to me that if Molly hid the negs among the deteriorated stuff, she would have put them here. She knew they'd be checked again before they were destroyed."

Cate wanted to be sure she understood Rose's reasoning. "These are the images that might still be salvageable?"

"Yes, essentially. Most of the negatives were so deteriorated that they were unidentifiable. They basically turn into black goo when they're really done. Anything we thought we might be able to save, we put in these boxes. Sometimes you can at least digitize the original and get some image from it, even if you then have to throw out the negative. In the hubbub after Molly's death, I forgot about our plan."

Cate looked at the line of cardboard boxes and felt daunted. It would take hours to go through each image in every box. Still, it was their best shot. "OK, let's do this. We're looking for something no later than 1947."

Matching Rose, Cate pulled on a pair of white cotton gloves and opened a box. She sifted through the loose negatives. Most of the images were faded, some stained a weird splotchy white. Many had the eerie iridescent gasoline effect she had noticed all those days ago. When she could manage to make out an image, it was usually from much earlier than the 1940s. She closed the box and moved to the next one. Halfway through the third, her head began to ache, and her stomach felt queasy. The room's walls seemed to shrink around her, and she tried to regulate her breathing to stave off panic.

As if reading her state of mind, Rose paused. "These fumes are something else." She closed the box she was sorting and pulled off her mask. She took a deep breath of air.

Cate was thankful for the chance to do the same. Her eyes swam.

"It's the nitric acid," Rose said. "As the film degrades, it releases the gas, which further decomposes the film. When nitric acid is in gas state, it's explosive."

"Jesus," Cate said.

"Keep your gloves on too," Rose said. "I know people who have gotten rashes or blisters from handling this stuff."

They returned to the boxes and continued working, Cate fighting off the ever-increasing headache. Her skin prickled with goose bumps, and irrationally she blamed the nitrate rather than the air-conditioning. She was on her sixth box when Rose squealed, "This is it!"

CHAPTER SIXTY

CATE SLID HER BOX BACK ONTO THE SHELF AND RUSHED OVER TO ROSE.
The container she had opened appeared empty, but on closer inspection, a manila envelope lay on the bottom. Rose pulled it out. The envelope was brittle and had a code written across it in old-fashioned handwriting: C4H10FO2P. Cate stared at it. There was something familiar about that number. Beneath the code was a date, 1946.

"This must be it. I should have known Molly wouldn't put important negatives in with deteriorating ones. The off-gassing could harm them."

"Let's see," Cate urged.

The envelope wasn't sealed. Rose opened it and removed eight negatives, laying them out on a sheet of paper she placed on an empty shelf.

Cate's heart plunged. A date, 1927, was written in neat white in the bottom right-hand corner of each negative. "These can't be them," she said. "The date's wrong."

"Don't be so sure," Rose said.

Cate peered at the image; she could dimly make out some white figures. "What do you see?" she asked.

"It's not the image itself, it's the actual film."

"What do you mean?"

"These negatives are from the 1940s, maybe later. See the notching on the side of the film? Kodak added that to their sheet film to help photographers identify it through touch in their darkrooms."

"But the date on the image—" Cate protested.

"It must be wrong. Kodak only started the notching practice in the mid-nineteen-forties. There's no way these negatives are from the twenties."

"Would Molly have realized that?" Cate asked.

"Of course. Photo archivists are trained in notch coding. As soon as she saw this, she would know it was mis-dated."

"Maybe that's how the person who was looking for Eastview stuff ten years ago missed them—they had the wrong date."

"That would make sense," Rose agreed.

"So, what are the images?"

Rose was already holding a negative up to the light. "I don't know. It's hard to tell. They look like soldiers. They've got big barrels, and they're by a lake."

Cate picked up a negative as well and positioned it so she could examine the image through the fluorescent light. She squinted, taking her time, despite her headache. It was difficult to read the reversed polarity. The men looked like white ghosts against a black background. She could tell they were soldiers but not much else. "What are they doing?" she asked.

Rose had already examined several. "It's hard to be certain, but they're loading barrels into a boat."

Rose laid the negatives out on the box in front of her and took out her smartphone. "This is quick and dirty digitization, but I'll reverse the polarity, and we'll be able to read the images better."

In a minute, she had photographed each of the original negatives and reversed the images so they appeared as a regular print. Rose put the originals back in the envelope on the shelf.

Cate stared at Rose's phone. They were sharp, clear images, even on the small screen. The first photograph was of four men in uniform in a little boat on a lake. She scrolled to the next image, this one taken from further away and encompassing more landscape. "It's Lake Mitchell," she said, pleased to see her suspicions confirmed.

"Really?" Rose stepped forward and took the phone from Cate's hand.

"See, that's the oxbow in the creek. That's the big rock in the middle. That's the lake."

"Jesus," Rose said. "What were they dumping? Something tells me it wasn't candy and unicorns."

They gazed at the pictures. Cate knew that these were the images that Molly was murdered for. That Simon was killed to protect. "If they were doing something so sneaky, why would the military have photographed it?"

"It's not that weird," Rose said. "You look at any fallen regime— East Germany, Iraq, Libya—there's always a ton of documentation about the shitty stuff the government did. Hell, even in Canada. Look at all the records we have on the Indian Residential Schools. It's the nature of bureaucracy to document... Then people forget that the stuff is there, and years later researchers rediscover it in the archives and *boom*! You hold the government to account."

If nothing else, this case had taught Cate more than she'd ever expected to know about archives.

There was a noise. It sounded like the door to the anteroom opening. Had she been followed? Cate looked around for a weapon. There was little in the room but a fire extinguisher. She picked it up and aimed the nozzle at the door. It wasn't much, but they'd have the element of surprise.

They could hear muffled footsteps on the cement. There was no place to hide. Cate's heart pounded in her ears so loudly she was surprised Rose didn't comment. She held the fire extinguisher in front of her, primed to spray the intruder's face. A figure loomed in the doorway.

"PETER," CATE GASPED. "WHAT ARE YOU DOING HERE?" RELIEF FLOODED her, and she put the extinguisher down.

"I was doing one last drive-by of the base, and I saw lights down here. When I saw your car, I came in."

She smiled. His capable, kind presence comforted her. "It's great to see you."

Peter grinned ruefully. "Good. After our last conversation I wasn't sure what to expect."

Cate waved her hand away. She glanced over at Rose, who stared at Peter suspiciously. "Rose, have you met Major Peter Harrison? He's the second-in-command at the base."

"I know you. You showed up after I found Molly's body."

"That's right." He turned to Cate. "Are you OK? What are you two doing?"

She explained about Albert Owl and the negatives they'd uncovered.

"Can I see them?" Peter asked.

Rose crossed her arms. "Not so fast. Why should we trust you?"

"Rose!" Cate exclaimed. "Peter's on our side."

"Really?" Rose asked. "Even if what we've uncovered might put his beloved Air Force in a bad light?"

Peter turned to Cate. "What's she talking about?"

Cate recalled that first day when Molly's body was discovered, how Baker let Peter hang around the death scene, even though he had no jurisdiction. Cate wavered. Maybe the motive for Molly's murder wasn't about ensuring that the development happened but in burying one of the Air Force's dirty secrets. If those photos showed men dumping something illegal into the lake, there'd be a scandal and outcry. How far would Peter go to protect the RCAF?

Peter must have read the doubts in her face, because he stepped forward. "Cate, this is the first time I've heard about these negatives."

Why had Peter been so interested in her? She backed away from him, her hands fluttering. He'd been using her to get closer to her investigation. Peter ran an entire air force base; she'd seen how his men respected him. Would it be difficult to get one of them to follow her? Intimidate her at the party? He'd have access to sophisticated technology and could easily tap her phone. She felt the walls of the vault contract, and for a suffocating moment she thought they were going to collapse. Had he killed Molly? Had he murdered Simon? Anger and pain rose in her throat, nearly choking her.

She wobbled for a moment, and Peter put a hand out to steady her. His body language radiated sincerity. She stared up at him. Her instincts about people were often wrong. Matthew accused her of self-sabotaging. She searched Peter's face. He was too good for her. She didn't deserve him. Believing he was a killer would get her off the hook. Her stupid, asshole instincts told her that she wasn't worthy of kindness.

What had Rose said to her? She never let people in. She was doing it again; this time using potential murder as the excuse. She gave a shaky laugh. "Show him the negatives, Rose. He's OK."

Rose moved away, still glaring at Peter. Cate smiled at him, and he held her gaze. Did he realize how far out on a limb she had just gone? Was her trust misplaced?

She turned her attention to the photos. It was a series: about a dozen men loading barrels into a couple of boats, rowing out to the middle of the lake. The final image was of the drums being thrown overboard.

Peter held the phone up. "Those are Air Force uniforms."

"But what's in the barrels?" Rose asked.

"This is the 1940s, you said?"

"If this is connected to Albert Owl, it can't be later than 1947," Cate said.

Peter stared at the photographs again. "They're dumping chemical weapons."

"What?" Rose asked. "How do you know that?"

"Canada was a massive manufacturer of chemical weapons in the Second World War. We supplied all our allies with mustard gas and phosgene. Right after the war, they debated how to dispose of our stockpiles. The military decided to dump it at sea."

Rose interrupted. "Come on, they dumped chemical weapons into the ocean? I don't believe it."

Peter shook his head. "It's true. It was an open secret at the time. At least one Tank Landing Craft was scuttled off the coast of Nova Scotia. It contained something like ten thousand gallons of mustard gas."

"So they did the same thing here, in little Lake Mitchell? But why?" asked Rose.

"Maybe it was something worse than mustard gas. Something the government didn't want its citizens to know it was even making," Peter replied.

"Like what?" Rose asked.

Cate turned to the younger woman. "Show me the envelope again." She looked at the writing—C4H10FO2P. "That's a chemical formula," she said.

"I'll google it," Rose said, but the signal failed.

"Carbon, hydrogen, fluorine oxide, I think, and phosphorous."

Rose and Peter looked at her, impressed.

Cate shrugged. "I crammed the periodic table in pre-Med—some stuff sticks." She placed the envelope with the negatives back on the shelf.

"What is it, though?" Peter asked.

"I'm not sure, but it would be a gas, and it would likely affect the nervous system."

Rose spoke. "Jesus. What was the government doing?"

They were all silent for a moment before Rose resumed. "Molly must have discovered these photos and realized the date didn't match the notch codes. She probably studied them to figure out what they were about. She'd scan them, reverse the polarity, and really zoom in on every detail."

Cate peered at the image in her hand. "There's writing on the canisters. Can we blow it up?"

They watched as Rose enlarged the image. Sure enough the words on the canister came into view. "Handle with Care. Sarin."

"Sarin gas," Cate said. "It's one of the deadliest nerve toxins in the world."

"Yeah," Peter said. "That terrorist group in Japan who poisoned people on the subway—that was sarin."

"Was the Canadian government really manufacturing this stuff?" Rose asked.

Peter looked grim. "The Germans discovered it at the beginning of the Second World War. I knew the Americans and Russians produced it during the Cold War. I guess we must have tried our hand as well."

Rose's voice was excited. "Don't you see? We have our motive. Molly finds the images and then goes to the paper records to back up her theory but realizes everything related to Eastview has been purged. She finds Albert Owl to confirm her hypothesis."

"Albert was her expert because he was one of the soldiers who dumped the gas," Cate said.

Peter interjected. "That makes sense. I hate to say it, but the military has a long history of getting minorities to do the worst jobs. Clandestine handling of chemical weapons would definitely fall into that category."

Peter's conjecture fit with what Isaiah Turner had hinted at. He'd taken the Official Secrets Oath not because of what he knew but because of what he'd done. "Let me see that photo of all of the men together," she said.

Rose handed her the phone. There was one Black soldier. She couldn't be sure because the figures were all tiny, but she would bet her last cigarette that it was Isaiah Turner.

Rose interrupted her thoughts. "How would Molly have tracked down Albert?"

Cate picked up a negative, staring at it. "Don't soldiers have identifying information on them at all times? Dog tags or something?"

"Sure," Peter said, with doubt. "But they're usually worn under clothes."

"Look at these two guys, though." Cate pointed to two figures in white undershirts. "What if their dog tags were hanging out? What if one of them was Albert Owl?"

"Even if you zoomed in on something like that, though, it would be too tiny to read," Peter said.

"Not with nitrate," Rose broke in excitedly. "It's the most amazing film, incredibly rich in terms of what it captured. It won't work with the quick photo I took, but if you scanned it at high enough resolution, you could see every detail—right down to reading a soldier's dog tags."

Peter nodded. "Could be."

Cate spoke. "This makes sense. That's why Annie's grandfather and his Air Force buddies warned the kids to stay out of the lake. Not because it was sacred, but because they knew what was sitting at the bottom. They couldn't tell anyone about it, though, because they'd sworn an oath to uphold the Official Secrets Act."

"The documents must have shown the presence of the sarin, and someone stole them to cover it up," Peter said.

"Someone from the military?" Rose asked, staring at Peter.

He shook his head. "I don't think so. Certainly no one from CFB Eastview, or I would know about it. This wouldn't be a big scandal for us anymore because it was so long ago. I mean, we'd just clean it up."

"TDR," Cate said. "It must have been someone who wanted to ensure the development happened."

"Terry Wakefield," Rose speculated.

"Maybe," Cate said. He certainly had the strongest motive, and he would have the resources to bug her phone.

"Who else would have the motivation and the opportunity?" asked Peter.

"That would be me," a voice said behind them.

Peter, Rose, and Cate whirled around to see who stood in the door.

DR. MARCOUX'S RUFF OF WHITE HAIR LOOKED WILDER THAN NORMAL, and the large black gun in his hand belied his usual kindly expression.

Cate was too stunned to move. What was her boss doing here? The fire extinguisher languished by her side. Peter had faster instincts. He lunged toward Marcoux. A ghastly bang reverberated through the small space. Before Cate could process what happened, Peter crumpled at her feet, blood pouring from his abdomen. "Peter!" she cried. His eyelids fluttered. "Call an ambulance," she barked at Rose.

"There's no cell reception," she cried.

Cate moved toward Peter, but Marcoux aimed the gun at her.

"Don't shoot again," Cate said. "This place is filled with gas from the deteriorating negatives. A spark could blow us all up."

Marcoux was startled by her words and hesitated. She dropped to her knees to assess Peter's injuries. The bullet had entered his abdomen, and the wound was oozing blood. It was a small entry point, but the damage to the underlying structure could be significant. Cate listened to his breathing, then concentrated on stopping the bleeding. She yanked off her sweatshirt to stanch the flow. Without diagnostic testing, she couldn't be sure, but a gut wound was never a good thing. He needed urgent medical attention.

"I didn't mean to," Dr. Marcoux said. "He shouldn't have lunged at me. I didn't have a choice."

"It seems like you could have not shot him," Rose said. Her voice was hard. "Is Major Harrison OK?"

"He'll live," Cate said. "That is, if Dr. Marcoux lets him."

She and Rose stared at the older man. He seemed to have shrunk into himself.

"This all got away from me," he said feebly.

"Why?" Cate gasped. "Why are you doing this?" Her pressure on Peter's wound had stopped the external bleeding, but there could still be a lot of internal damage.

"Money." Marcoux shook his head as if bemused by his own response. He spoke slowly. "Jill died over a decade ago. I went to pieces. I was all alone, and I had to care for Toby. I was overwhelmed. I started gambling. At first it was a nice tension reliever, but it got out of control."

"You killed two people because you needed money?" Rose's tone held disgust.

The pleading note returned to his voice. "Jill and I saved for years to create a nest egg for Toby. I lost it all. Without that money, he'd have to go to a state-run facility. I couldn't send my only child. Not Toby."

Marcoux, a desperate gambling addict? It was insane, but then she recalled their Christmas lunch at the Rideau Carleton Raceway. She had attributed his enthusiasm to a novice enjoying a bit of a flutter, but she saw now he was an addict getting a hit.

She kept steady pressure on Peter's wound as she spoke. "You had invested in TDR and needed to ensure that the development went ahead so you could recoup."

Marcoux seemed relieved to talk. "I went to Terry Wakefield. He was an old college friend. He refused to loan me the money but guaranteed that if I invested what little remained in the development, I'd get it all back one hundred-fold. I did it—remortgaged the house and liquidated the last of my assets—and then the bloody development was delayed and delayed and delayed. Ten years! I'm seventy. It's too late to build another nest egg." Marcoux grimaced. "The development has to go forward."

Cate looked into his eyes and saw the anguish. Had he kept that pain hidden, or had she been too consumed with her own problems to notice? His desperation explained so much. Sometimes panic trumped all. "You killed Molly when she discovered the negatives and realized they'd further delay development."

"Yes," he agreed, swallowing hard.

Peter was losing color, his skin pale and clammy. This was not good. She needed to stabilize him. For that, she needed equipment.

Rose took a step toward Marcoux, who raised his gun. "I know you," she said.

"What?" He was clearly thrown.

She stared at him. "You're always at the Archives—at the Family History desk. You're one of our regulars."

Of course. He was an ardent genealogist. He would be intimately familiar with the Archives.

Marcoux looked surprised to be recognized. "I've spent a lot of time there, pursuing my genealogy research. As soon as I invested with Terry, I realized I should have done my due diligence. I combed through all the relevant records. When I discovered the files about the sarin gas, I nearly had a heart attack. It was an easy matter to remove them from the Reading Room and destroy them."

"You're not allowed to steal archival records," Rose protested.

"At the time, this caused me an enormous amount of stress." He laughed.

Cate cringed at the bitterness of the sound.

"Those records were ordered under Gerald's name, though, not yours," Cate said.

"How did you know that?" he asked. Then he waved his hand. "No matter. Thanks to my passion for research, I've known Gerry for years. I stole his pass when he went on paternity leave. I'm not proud of myself, but it's very handy to order in boxes of material that are restricted to the common genealogist—things like prison records or police files." The twinkle returned to Marcoux's eyes, and he winked at Cate.

The inappropriateness of the gesture and his abrupt change in temperament made her wonder if he might be mentally unbalanced.

"Is Gerald how you knew that Molly found the negatives?" Rose was edging her way down the wall, slowly approaching Marcoux. He appeared distracted by Harrison's blood, which had rapidly saturated Cate's white sweater, turning it a deep crimson.

"We have lunch occasionally. He mentioned that one of his employees had discovered something sensational that would hinder the TDR development. He was going to take it to Oliver, his director. I knew immediately what it was."

Marcoux paused, the gun lowering slightly as he recalled his next actions. "I asked Gerry to stay quiet about the discovery. He had some money invested in TDR as well, so I told him to keep a lid on the records until we could get in touch with Wakefield."

"Gerry was involved in Molly's murder?" Rose blurted.

Marcoux closed his eyes. "Her death was entirely my doing, though I think Gerry might have had his suspicions."

"What happened with Molly?" Cate asked.

"I contacted that young lady and convinced her to meet. She suggested here. I had planned to reason with her, beg her to destroy the negatives. If she hesitated, I intended to bribe her. I never meant to, to . . ." Marcoux swallowed hard and continued. "She was too stubborn, unreasonable. She knew I had stolen those records. She threatened to go to the police. What would happen to Toby if I went to jail? I begged her to give me the negatives, but she refused. I got angry, desperate, and I lunged at her . . . I wrapped my hands around her throat, and it was so fast. She was dead before I even knew what happened." Marcoux's voice shook. "It was that girl or Toby. I had no choice." He paused for a moment, his eyes staring as if he could see the scene in front of him and then resumed. "It was easy enough to make it look like suicide. I even took care to ensure that Dr. Spencer was assigned this case. With the recent death of her brother, I hoped that she'd be distracted and would quickly sign off on a suicide."

Silence filled the vault as they all absorbed Marcoux's story.

Cate remembered how she was called out a few minutes after her shift had ended. Such a late summons was unusual; normally dispatch would assign it to the incoming coroner. She'd been an-noyed at the time. She also remembered Marcoux's request for a case update—he'd called it the "TDR case" rather than the "Johnson case." God, the solution to this whole tragedy was in front of her all along.

Peter coughed, and she turned her attention to him. His pulse was weak but steady. Her thoughts spun. Marcoux was going to kill them. Their only hope was to fight back. Rose obviously had the same idea. She was closer to Marcoux now, who was so absorbed in his story he hadn't noticed her movements. Cate needed to help the other woman by distracting him. She spoke. "You killed Simon too."

Marcoux's sigh was long. "I was monitoring your calls. When he left you that message, I knew I needed to retrieve the girl's phone and dispose of the young man. It would have her calls to my number. From the sound of his voice on the message, I assumed he was quite high. It was a simple matter to walk through the back gate and ad-minister the overdose before you arrived. Then I slipped away through the park."

Cate's hands balled into fists.

He continued talking. "I didn't plan on killing a second person." His voice was thick with confusion. "I didn't want to kill anyone, but I couldn't let them find out what I'd done. They'd send me away, and Toby would be abandoned." Now Marcoux's voice held a note of an-ger. "That Thatcher boy should have left well enough alone."

How had she known Marcoux for five years and never thought of him as anything more than a benevolent figure? He was a monster.

Marcoux seemed unaware of her anger. "Even after he died, it didn't get me any further. I still didn't have the negatives. Molly had given me decoy ones. I didn't realize until I examined them at home."

Rose was closer to him now, almost within arm's reach. Cate needed to keep him concentrated on her. "So what did you do?" she asked.

"I had to find the real ones, but it was impossible. That is, until you two started putting the pieces together for me."

"You suspended me to speed up my investigation," Cate realized. "At that point, you knew I wouldn't stop looking."

"Correct," Marcoux said. "I realized you were more likely than I to locate them. I bided my time and waited for you to bring me the evidence." He swiveled toward Rose, training his gun on her. "May I have them now, please?"

Just then Peter groaned loudly, and Cate and Marcoux turned to him. Rose reached up and flipped the light switch, plunging everything into darkness.

"Hey!" blurted Marcoux and rushed to the switch. Keeping the sweater over Peter's wound, Cate stretched a leg out. Marcoux stumbled but reached the wall and flipped on the light. Rose was gone. He ran out of the room.

Cate hesitated. She couldn't leave Peter, but she needed to help Rose. She reached out with one hand and knocked over a metal trash can, which made a loud clanging noise. Marcoux reappeared, brandishing the gun. "Where do you think you're going?" Rose's departure had unsettled him.

Cate heard a door bang shut. "Rose has escaped," she said.

CHAPTER SIXTY-THREE

"IT DOESN'T MATTER," MARCOUX SAID. "SHE WON'T MAKE IT FAR. I slashed all your tires. By the time she can get a cell signal, I'll have destroyed the originals. Where are they?" Cate considered stalling him further, but he waved the gun, and she glanced at the shelf where Rose had placed them earlier. He snatched them up, flipping through the envelope, and grunted in satisfaction. "Without the negs, it will simply be my word against hers."

"What about me and Peter?" Cate asked. "Are you really going to kill us?"

"Dr. Spencer, I'm sorry, but I must. I didn't want any of this, but as they say, 'in for a penny, in for a pound.'" Marcoux gave a strange giggle, and Cate knew there could be no reasoning with him. Whatever rational thoughts had driven his decision-making were engulfed by the horror of his mounting death toll.

Peter's eyelids fluttered open, and he groaned again. If she could stall Marcoux long enough, Rose might get them help in time.

"Well, you won't get away with it. There are barrels of sarin gas at the bottom of Lake Mitchell that will back Rose's story up."

He shook his head. "I told Terry Wakefield about the chemical weapons dump as soon as I discovered it. He had those barrels quietly removed years ago."

Cate's eyes widened. Wakefield knew about the gas. What else did the billionaire know? "You bugged my cell phone with sophisticated surveillance software. Was that Wakefield? Did he help you listen to my calls?"

Marcoux grimaced. "He's absolutely devoted to this development. It will be his legacy. When I told him I needed help, he put all his resources at my disposal."

"Did he know about the murders?" she asked.

"I told him what I needed, and he didn't ask questions." Marcoux's voice held a note of pride. "He's one of the most powerful men in this country, but my calls are the highest priority for him. We're partners."

Something had been bothering Cate since they realized what was in the barrels. "Sarin would degrade. In a few months, it would have lost its potency. It's no more of a health risk now than dandruff."

"You and I know that, Dr. Spencer, because we're rational scientists. Others wouldn't react to the news the way we do. Terry's vision for the development is for the highest standard of exclusive luxury. The project would be dead if it were tainted by a toxic military dump."

"I suppose Wakefield was the one who hired that goon to attack me the night of the TDR event."

Marcoux shrugged. "Maybe. Terry wanted you kept in line, and that law firm didn't seem to have much effect."

Cate's heart plunged. "Law firm?"

"Yes, Terry told me that he selected someone from his Ottawa firm to keep an eye on you. He said there was a connection."

The air was sucked from Cate's lungs.

Marcoux continued to speak. "In the end, his insider proved useless—had no intel to provide."

Matthew hadn't sold her out. She could have laughed aloud.

"Terry's assistance in other matters was more fruitful—he has many contacts in the police force, of course. Between his connections and my access to the autopsy and coroners' reports, we were able to know precisely how the case was progressing." Marcoux looked at his watch. "All right, time is passing, and I don't like to leave Toby alone for too long. I imagine your friend will find a signal soon. I plan to be gone before the police arrive."

He placed the gun on a shelf. "If you shift a hair, I will grab this gun and kill you before you are on your feet. Is that understood?"

She nodded. From her seated position, there was no way she could move quickly enough.

He righted the metal trash can. "You're a smoker, aren't you? Is this your purse?" He opened her bag and pulled out her lighter. "Let's see how flammable this nitrate really is." He held the lighter and one of the negatives over the trash can.

"Don't!" Cate shouted.

He flicked the lighter. With a whoosh the negative was engulfed in flames and Marcoux stumbled back, startled by the intensity. Now was Cate's chance. She sprang to her feet and drove her shoulder into his chest. He stepped back, the burning negative searing his hand. He screamed in pain and dropped it into the trash can.

Before she could take advantage of the situation, he regained his balance and grabbed the gun, which he trained on her face. This was the end. She thought of Jason. She thought of her father. She thought of Matthew. She willed her eyes to stay open. She wanted to see the bullet coming.

CHAPTER SIXTY-FOUR

MARCOUX GRUNTED WITH SURPRISE, LURCHED FORWARD, AND FELL
headfirst at her feet, a long-handled fire ax jutting from his back.

Cate leaped back in shock.

Rose stood behind him, white-faced and shaking. She stumbled
forward, her hand going to her mouth.

Cate knelt down, feeling Marcoux's wrist for a pulse. "He's still
alive." She pocketed the remaining negatives. "Did you reach the
police?"

"Didn't bother," Rose said distractedly. She was staring at Marcoux's body. "He slashed your tires and my bike. I found the ax and
snuck back."

There was no time to talk. "We've got to get Peter out of here."

Rose crouched down, and together they heaved him to his feet.
He groaned and his eyes flicked open. "Come on, airman," Cate said.
"March."

They stumbled under his weight. Rose staggered backward,
knocking the trash can onto its side. It fell with a hollow clang and
Cate and Rose stared in horror.

Flames licked outward, consuming a pile of empty cardboard
boxes in an instant. They'd be dead if the fire reached the nitrate on
the shelves. The heat was already fierce. There was no time to grab the
fire extinguisher. "Let's go!" Cate yelled.

She and Rose hauled Peter through the door of the vault. "Wait,"
Cate panted. She shifted Peter's weight onto Rose. "Get him out of
here."

The other woman stumbled but inched forward.

Cate turned to Marcoux. His body lay across the doorway. She tugged him into the hallway, the flames behind him climbing toward the shelves, consuming everything in their path at an astonishing rate.

Once Marcoux was free, she slammed the door shut. There was an enormous bang. The metal door juddered but didn't budge. Her hand grazed it and she shouted in pain from the heat.

"Move." Cate stepped over Marcoux and slipped back under Peter's arm. Together she and Rose half dragged him to the exit and pushed the door open. The security alarm rang out through the building, loud, loud, loud. Cate wedged her foot in the exit door and shoved Rose and Peter through it.

She turned to Peter. "Look at me," she commanded.

He raised his head. "Keep walking, understand? Don't stop until Rose says so. She can't do this on her own. You help her."

He nodded.

"Hurry," she said to Rose. "Walk until you get a signal, and call 911."

Rose didn't move. "What are you going to do?"

Peter groaned again. "Get him to safety," Cate ordered.

She slipped back inside. Black smoke seeped out from under the vault door, filling the corridor. Eyes streaming, lungs protesting, she made her way to Marcoux. His chest heaved, struggling for breath. She glanced at the ax wound. There was no arterial bleeding. Rose's attack had missed the major organs. She pulled the ax from his back and rolled him over. His eyelids fluttered. He might survive. She grabbed his feet and began dragging him toward the exit. His head banged against the floor. He moaned and stirred weakly.

A wave of dizziness flooded her, and she dropped to her knees. The air was slightly better down here, and after a couple of deep breaths, she grabbed his ankles again, keeping low, as she hauled him across the floor. There was a loud boom, and a vault further up the hall exploded open, flames pouring out. It was only a matter of time before the whole place blew. The air was a thick, suffocating blanket. Her limbs were leaden, and it was all she could do to keep tugging the body. Sweat and smoke clouded her eyes, and her throat was raw from breathing the poisonous air.

Cate reached the exit and gasped in relief. Fresh air poured in from the open door, and she drank it in thankfully. A blast of hot wind pushed past her from behind. The exit door swung wildly open before slamming shut. She staggered forward, intent on opening the door, but dizzy from the smoke, she pitched into the stack of boxes containing the deteriorated nitrate. A box tumbled down on top of her. The sticky black negatives stuck to the sweat on her body. She brushed at them frantically, knocking over another box, which hit Marcoux.

She tried to get to the door, but her swimming head disoriented her. Her blurred vision found the exit sign. She lurched toward it and pushed the door open, but then fell, her knees barking against the cement floor. She let her head rest against it, gasping at what good air remained. Another explosion behind her. This was the end. Her vision tunneled, and she thought of Jason. Was this how he died? In a frenzy of fire and smoke?

Suddenly she felt hands grasp her arms and she was hauled forward. She looked up, as she bumped through the exit door. Rose had reappeared.

"Marcoux," Cate protested weakly.

"It's too late for him. We have to run for it."

Cate rose, feeling nauseous and dizzy, but adrenaline rescued her. Rose grasped her hand and together they turned and ran. A wall of searing heat nearly knocked them from their feet as a tremendous explosion thundered behind them.

CHAPTER SIXTY-FIVE

THE NITRATE BURNED FOR FOUR DAYS. THE FIRE DEPARTMENT WAS HELP-less in the face of its self-sustaining fury. They dug a containment trench around the building to ensure that a stray spark didn't ignite the surrounding dry summer landscape. No one was allowed on the site.

Toxic smoke billowed across the city. In the heavy mid-summer humidity, it tainted the air, filling the news with dire warnings: vulnerable people, like the elderly and infants, were urged to stay indoors.

The media's coverage of the health effects of the fire was surpassed only by its breathless interest in Dr. Marcoux's death, his involvement in the murders of two young people, and the attempted homicide of a senior RCAF officer. The police investigation of Marcoux's death was severely hampered by the complete destruction of the nitrate facility. Forensic experts were doubtful they would even be able to even recover DNA after the conflagration.

Peter was recovering well in the hospital. Cate visited him. He looked weak and pale, attached to tubes and monitors.

"Thank you," he said, grabbing her hand. It was still injured from the fire, and she eased it away from him, grimacing slightly. "You saved my life," he said.

"It was nothing."

"I won't forget what you did. You were heroic." His gaze was intense, as if trying to press his vision of her actions into her own mind.

Cate forced a laugh. "You sure you're not concussed?"

"You solved the case. Got justice for Molly. Vindicated Simon." He gestured to a newspaper lying by his bed. "It looks like you've even stopped the development."

Cate asked Isaiah Turner to corroborate what he had done back in 1946, but he refused to break his oath. Still, with the help of the original photos Cate had grabbed and the ones they'd copied to Rose's phone, the protesters had enough ammunition to demand an injunction against further development while an exhaustive search for any other chemical weapons dumps was conducted over every square inch of the site. They were estimating the investigation would take at least two years, since, thanks to Marcoux's interference at the Archives, there was hardly any historical documentation to assist in the research.

Cate shook her head emphatically. She hadn't had much time to process what happened, but she knew one thing. "I'm no hero," she said. "I didn't even know it was Marcoux." She thought of all the mistakes she'd made, all the ways she failed.

Peter straightened himself in the bed. "You were single-minded about catching Molly's murderer. That's admirable."

"When are you out of here?" she asked, changing the subject.

"Another couple of days, and I can go home. I've got to start thinking about what that means. What should I do with the rest of my life?" His voice was tentative, and his eyes sought hers. "I'm retired from the Air Force, but I'm still young. I need a fresh start."

He was about to ask for more than she could give. That moment of trust and clarity she had experienced in the vaults was gone. Cate interrupted before he could say more. "This recent excitement has made me realize I have to do some soul-searching about my own life." The thought of being with Peter, with his kindness and understanding, was almost oppressive. "I need to spend some time alone, getting straight in my own head." She avoided his eyes, made an excuse, and left.

Walking out of the hospital, she shook her head. Peter had tried to connect with her, and she had run screaming for the door. What was wrong with her?

She ran into Baker in the parking lot. His Porky Pig tie a bad joke amidst the drabness of his gray suit.

"What are you doing here?" Her voice was more aggressive than she intended, still upset about how she'd left things with Peter.

"Same as you," he said. "Visiting Major Harrison." Baker paused and straightened his tie.

She went on the attack, delighted to have a target for her own angst. "Shouldn't you be following up on what I told you about Wakefield? He helped Marcoux. He's the one who put that spyware on my phone. He hired that man to attack me. He—"

"Jesus, Cate. We have no proof."

"Check his phone records; you'll see he was talking to Marcoux."

"That is the flimsiest of circumstantial evidence."

"What about my own phone, then? Can't you trace the installation of the spyware back to Wakefield?"

Baker shook his head. "I've got my best digital team on it. They say there is no evidence of where it came from. Whoever installed it used very sophisticated techniques."

"Well, doesn't that tell you something?" Cate demanded. "Dr. Marcoux wasn't exactly a super hacker; he couldn't have done that himself. Wakefield's company is known to use surveillance. This is their MO."

"Again, it's circumstantial."

Cate's voice rose. "Have you even questioned Wakefield? Confronted him with what I told you?"

Baker raised a hand, but his voice remained calm. "We aren't going to question Wakefield unless we have something solid."

"Typical police bullshit."

"He's a powerful man—"

Cate yelled, "Exactly. You defer to Terry Wakefield because he's wealthy and powerful. He helped Marcoux cover up his crimes. He—"

Baker grasped her hurt hand, and she winced. He noticed and let go. "Keep your voice down," he hissed. "Cate, I believe you. Wakefield was at minimum an accomplice after the fact. We will get him for this, and he will serve time."

Cate blinked in surprise.

He continued in a low, urgent whisper. "We aren't questioning him because we don't want to tip him off. I'm keeping his name out of the news, and I'm drawing a tight circle around this part of the investigation. I want a rock-solid case against him, one that even his billions won't let him squirm out of."

When would she stop being surprised at Baker's commitment to the job? She was touched that he was sharing his strategy with her. "How can I help?"

"You can help by keeping out of it," Baker said. "I mean it. I don't need you scaring him off, and I don't want him to know where the accusations have come from. He's a ruthless man, and he will destroy you if he sees you as a threat. Look what his team did to Liam Westin."

"The environmentalist charged with pedophilia? Was that Wakefield?"

Baker looked grim. "I've got buddies in the RCMP. They say something is off about that whole case. They think Westin was set up."

"Jesus."

"Exactly, so keep your head down, and stay away from Wakefield."

"He hired someone to assault me the night of the party."

"Are you sure it was Wakefield?"

"I know I didn't report it right away, but it happened."

Baker held up his hands. "I'm not disputing it, but why would Wakefield be involved? An attack is outside his wheelhouse—he's more of a surveillance and evidence-plant kind of guy."

"People do unexpected things," Cate said. Just look at Marcoux. A double murderer.

Baker shook his head. "What would be the point of attacking you? As Marcoux said, he needed you to keep investigating in order to locate the negatives."

To her mortification, Cate's eyes filled with tears. It all seemed too much—memories of the assault, Wakefield's complicity, Peter's gunshot wound, the hellish inferno at the nitrate facility, Marcoux's betrayal. Baker disputing her version of events was the last straw. She needed to push everything away—obliterate the pain.

"Cate," Baker said, reading her face.

"I can't take this," she muttered and turned to go.

"What are you talking about?"

She met his gaze. "You of all people know what I mean. I can't cope with this on my own. I need to numb it out."

"Booze is the coward's way."

"Well, guess what? You're looking at a certified chicken-shit." She smiled.

"That's crap. You're a goddamn action hero—you cracked this case wide open."

His words echoed Harrison's, and she couldn't take it. "I'm not a hero. I told myself I was investigating the case for Molly's sake or some abstract notion of justice. That was lies. I grabbed this case with both hands because it distracted me from everything else—Jason, my shitty life, my father." She was unable to stop talking. "Now the case is solved, and I'm left with all that old bullshit." She took a ragged breath. "I'm alone again. It's just me and all the crappy thoughts and memories going around and around in my head. The only thing that shuts it off is alcohol."

Baker grabbed her by the arms, and for a horrifying moment she thought he was going to hug her. Instead, his fingers dug into her biceps, and he spoke fiercely. "Listen, you giant pain in the ass, what you did in unraveling this case was smart and brave, and you should be fucking proud of yourself."

She shook her head, negating his words.

"You're Cate Spencer—you're a fucking badass, and you sure as shit don't need alcohol."

She blinked. Baker thought she was a badass? Could she do it? Go to sleep every night without the booze? "I don't know," Cate said. She stepped away from him and laughed. "That was quite the impressive pep talk," she said sincerely. She turned and walked a few feet away from him when he called out.

"Cate!"

She turned.

"It's not true, you know."

"What's not true?"

"You're not alone. You've got friends."

"Oh yeah?" she asked wearily.

"Yeah," he confirmed. "I'm one of them."

He looked so embarrassed at uttering those words that she couldn't help smiling, and he grinned back at her.

"Well, shit, Baker. I didn't know you cared."

"Don't tell anyone." He took two steps toward her and spoke in a lower tone. "Listen, if you're ever ready to get help—I know a clinic. A good one. No bullshit. No hippy dippy therapy-speak."

She opened her mouth to tell him that she didn't want help. Instead she found herself nodding. "If I need it, I'll call you." In that moment she really thought she might.

EPILOGUE

IT WAS NEARLY MIDNIGHT, A LIGHT RAIN FELL, AND THE AIR OUTSIDE was cool. Cate locked up her house, the new deadbolt giving her some trouble. At last it slid into place. She turned on her porch, thinking about her upcoming task. After more calls to the Canadian embassy in Kinshasa, and some frustrating interactions with the Congolese embassy in Ottawa, Jason's ashes had come home. They waited for her at the airport now, and with them, she hoped, a sense of closure.

A car turned on the street. She looked as it slowed in front of her house, lit by a streetlight. It was the green Honda. Her heart leaped to her throat. The glare of the light against the rainy window made it impossible to see inside, but it was the same car that had followed her.

She froze, staring at the front bumper. There it was, the thing she had noticed last time she'd seen the car. An emblem. She could see it clearly as it drove past: a leopard head bordered by an elephant tusk and spear. Three words were written beneath it, too small to make out in the dim light, but Cate knew what they would read: "Justice, Paix, Travail." It was the coat of arms of the Democratic Republic of the Congo, the same one she had stared at for half an hour all those weeks ago at the embassy.

The attacker hadn't been warning her off pursuing Molly's murder investigation but telling her to stop making inquiries into Jason's death. She recalled the accident report that Brilliant Aduba had given. She'd stuffed it into a desk drawer and never read it. What was in that report?

◇◇◇◇◇◇

IT WAS OVERCAST THE NEXT AFTERNOON WHEN SHE PICKED HER FATHER up at his house.

"It's time to go now, Daddy."

"What's that?" he asked. His shirt was stained, and pots and pans littered the kitchen counter. Dust covered the furnishings in the living room. A pillow and blankets lay strewn on the couch. Was he sleeping there now?

"Remember, Jason's ashes have arrived. We're going to lay him to rest."

"What are you talking about?"

"Jason is dead."

"I know that," he said with anger, pulling his hand away. "Don't treat me like a child, Catherine. You can't talk to me like that."

"I know, Daddy, I know." He had some soup on his chin, and without thinking she reached out to wipe it away. Her hand stopped, and she met his eyes. In the old days, he would have swatted it away, and a punishment for her insolence would have followed.

"Thank you," he mumbled. For what, he didn't say.

They stood on the dock of the Rockcliffe Rowing Club. It was late afternoon, and the place was deserted. The days were starting to shorten, and although it was not yet evening, a hint of dusk was in the air. Clouds were low in the sky, and a wind was blowing strong from the east, chasing away the thick, oppressive heat that stifled the city. The nitrate fire had been out for a few days, and the air finally felt like it was clearing. Her father was small against the huge expanse of river.

The wind picked up, and she judged the time was right. She opened the container and sprinkled it out over the deep, broad river. The wind grabbed the gray ashes and swirled them into the air. As the final remains from the urn took flight, the first thick drops of rain started to fall.

Tomorrow she flew to Kinshasa.

ACKNOWLEDGMENTS

THANK YOU TO THE TEAM AT TURNER FOR THEIR ASSISTANCE AND SUPport. Stephanie Beard championed this book; Ryan Smernoff and Claire Ong guided its progress. Thanks to Ashley Stronsnider for her fabulous edit, Lisa Grimenstein for her excellent copy edit, and Emily Mahon for another great cover.

Thanks to Kaitlin Littlechild and Stephen McGregor, who read my manuscript and offered insightful and helpful feedback on my portrayal of the First Nations, characters and communities. Thanks to Beth Greenhorn for facilitating some of those introductions.

As always, I want to gratefully acknowledge my amazing critiquing group: Chris Crowder, Alette Willis, and Wayne Ng. I am the writer I am today thanks to their encouragement and support.

Thanks to Pam Ahearn, who took the time to read and consider this manuscript and offered valuable feedback that made it much stronger.

Thanks to my colleagues in the photography and preservation areas at Library and Archives Canada. Though we never discovered a dead body, we did have plenty of other surprises while moving the nitrate film from the old building out by RCAF Rockcliffe to the state-of-the-art facility at Shirleys Bay. The professionals and experts at LAC are a daily inspiration in their dedication and passion for preserving history.

Thanks as always to my friends Kathryn, Sara, Dara, Johanna, Meghan, Christa, Amy #1, Christine, Anna, Serena, Martha, Kaia, Michelle and Laura.

Thanks to my family, Tina, Emily, Mark, and mum, who are so

supportive and loving. Thanks to my extended family of Horralls, Pinders, and Siftons.

Huge thanks to my sister Susie, to whom this book is dedicated. Susie offered her time, insight, and brilliance to my understanding of the challenges and rewards of the coroner profession. I am so proud of the work that she does. She brings dignity to the dead and solace to the grieving. I also want to make it clear that the only characteristics that Susie shares with Cate are her strength and her smarts.

Finally, thanks to Andrew and Violet. You two dopes make it all worth it.

ABOUT THE AUTHOR

AMY TECTOR WAS BORN AND RAISED IN THE ROLLING HILLS OF QUEBEC'S
Eastern Townships. She has worked in archives for the past twenty
years and has found some pretty amazing things, including lost let-
ters, mysterious notes, and even a whale's ear. Amy spent many years
as an expat, living in Brussels and in The Hague, where she worked for
the International Criminal Tribunal for War Crimes in Yugoslavia.
She lives in Ottawa, Canada, with her daughter, dog, and husband.